"Come Looking for Me *is a rollicking adventure, a compelling story filled with great research and blessed with plot that has wind in its sails. Emily is a heroine for all ages.*"

ROY MacGREGOR, author of *Canadians: A Portrait of a Country and Its People*

"Come Looking for Me *is a fine offering—an unexpected romance set amid the fierce naval battles of the United States and Great Britain during the War of 1812. Cheryl Cooper succeeds in creating an intriguing cast of characters and making us care about their ultimate fate. Her extensive research and detailed descriptions of life on the sea add an unyielding realism to a story rich in action and suspense.*"

ANNE MILLYARD, co-founder and former editor of Annick Press

"*A high sea of a good read, roiling with history, cannon blasts, and storms of the heart ... I couldn't put it down.*"

KAREN HOOD-CADDY, author of *Tree Fever, Flying Lessons,* and *Wisdom of Water*

"*Cheryl Cooper has crafted a novel of epic proportions, incorporating a cast of truly memorable characters. Her meticulous research captures the conditions at sea on a British man-of-war in the early part of the 19th century, and her account of the challenges facing a naval surgeon is particularly engrossing. Written in a flowing, graceful style,* Come Looking for Me *is a satisfying book that is difficult to put down. A wonderful read!*"

DR. WALTER HANNAH, physician, former midshipman with the Royal Canadian Navy

Come Looking for Me

A NOVEL

CHERYL COOPER

For Jean,

All The Best,

Cheryl Cooper

Blue Butterfly Books

THINK FREE, BE FREE

Sept. 10, 2013

Blue Butterfly Book Publishing Inc.
2583 Lakeshore Boulevard West, Toronto, Ontario, Canada M8V 1G3
Tel 416-255-3930 Fax 416-252-8291 www.bluebutterflybooks.ca

For complete ordering information for Blue Butterfly titles, go to:
www.bluebutterflybooks.ca

First edition, soft cover: 2010

LIBRARY AND ARCHIVES CANADA CATALOGUING IN PUBLICATION

Cooper, Cheryl, 1958–
Come looking for me : a novel / Cheryl Cooper.

ISBN 978-1-926577-07-4

I. Title.

PS8605.O655C66 2010 C813'.6 C2010-904615-3

Design and typesetting by Gary Long / Fox Meadow Creations
Text typeface is Dante
Cover photo © Bigstock Photo / Bas Meelker (background) / Corey Ford (ship)
Printed in Canada by Transcontinental-Métrolitho

Text paper, Enviro 100 from Cascades, contains 100 per cent post-consumer recycled fibre, is processed chlorine free, and is manufactured using energy from bio-gas recovered from a municipal landfill site and piped to the mill.

Blue Butterfly Books thanks book buyers for their support in the marketplace.

To my mother, Marie Isabelle Evans,

and my grandmother, Isabelle Fleda McCubbin Moreland (1904–1985),

who listened and selflessly gave of their time.

War of 1812

Admiralty Orders to
Captain James Moreland of HMS *Isabelle*:

Seek and destroy all enemy frigates along the coast of North America.
Search the crew for deserters.
Sink the ship or re-flag her for England.

Tuesday, June 1, 1813

Early Afternoon

Aboard the USS *Serendipity*

"Sail, ho!"

Emily awoke with a start. Loud voices sounded overhead on the weather decks and a drum rolled in the distance. Rubbing her eyes, she looked around at the sumptuous furniture and large galleried windows of the cabin, and, with a fresh pang of fear, remembered Captain Trevelyan. She was a prisoner on his ship, the USS *Serendipity*. For how long she had been in captivity, she was not quite certain. Still vivid in her mind was that dark morning when Trevelyan had seemingly come looking for her, taken her from her ship at gunpoint, then forced her to watch as its groaning timbers were set afire. But had that been three weeks ago, or four? And did time really matter anyway? It had done little to lessen her guilt and grief. Her days were all the same. The views beyond the windows were all the same. There was no sight of land out there ... only sea.

The voices grew louder. The crew moved swiftly on their decks, shouting orders to one another. Beyond the thin walls of the cabin Emily could hear Trevelyan speaking to one of his young servants.

She climbed out of her cot and crept to the door, opening it a crack to listen.

"Captain Trevelyan, sir, they're sayin' there's a man-o'-war two points off the larboard."

"My spyglass please, Mr. Clive."

"Is it one of ours, sir?"

Trevelyan squinted through his spyglass for some time. "Take a look for yourself."

"She's British, sir."

"British, yes, but she's not just any ship, Mr. Clive. That's the *Isabelle.*"

"The *Isabelle*, sir?"

"She has seventy-four guns and two decks, the lower one equipped with a full battery of thirty-two-pounders. Been in service for over thirty years ..." Trevelyan lowered his voice. "And I've been waiting for her for almost nine."

"A seventy-four, sir? She'll have a large crew, then."

"I doubt it, Mr. Clive. Britain has been warring far too many years now. My guess is she is horribly undermanned and what crew she possesses will be poorly trained, made up of thieves and lunatics from the emptying of English prisons."

"Did ya once serve on the *Isabelle*, sir?"

Trevelyan was slow to reply. "I know her well, Mr. Clive. Now get to your station. And if you see Lind, ask him to come to my cabin straightaway."

Thinking Trevelyan would sweep into his cabin at any moment, Emily hurried back to her cot. But no one came, not even a crew of sailors to take down the cabin's surrounding bulkheads in order to utilize the cannon housed inside. For what seemed like hours, she lay still, trying to shut out the noises of the *Serendipity*'s men readying themselves for battle, fixing her attention on the ship's gentle rise and fall on the waves. Finally, just as she felt herself drifting back to sleep, the sound of heavy footsteps jolted her upright. Trevelyan came through the door, pulling off his bicorne hat. He scratched his straw-coloured hair and stared long and hard at her.

"Out of your cot, madam. There will be no laying about this afternoon. In a matter of minutes the cannons will be sounding."

Emily climbed out and stood, looking away from his cadaverous face.

"At this moment, the crew is lighting our guns against the enemy," Trevelyan continued. "Therefore, as it won't be convenient for you to wash my shirts or polish my silver today, I shall give you a pistol so you can help shoot a few of King George's men."

"I will not take up arms against my countrymen."

"You may have no choice."

"I doubt you would trust me with a pistol in my hand. Our definition of enemy differs ... sir."

Trevelyan smirked and turned to reach for his sword, which hung on the wall by his own cot. Emily searched the water beyond the windows for a glimpse of the *Isabelle.*

"If you're figuring this will be your escape, you can forget it. The *Serendipity* may be a smaller ship, but she's faster and more easily manoeuvred. Of course, you have already seen evidence of her capabilities against larger ships with more guns." He sheathed his sword with a violent thrust.

Emily looked at him with dead eyes.

There was a swift knock at the door.

"Enter!" said Trevelyan. Lind lumbered into the cabin, a coil of thin rope in his hands. He stank like a barnyard. Emily grimaced as he approached her.

"Tie her up, Lind." Trevelyan eyed Emily's tattered clothes, then added, "In my latrine." He moved towards her, gripped her face in his scarred hands, and forced her to look up into his dark eyes. "I'll see you afterwards, once we have our prize." Releasing her with a shove, he added, "Perhaps then we could order you *a bath*."

Emily's eyes widened. There was a sick sensation in the pit of her stomach. Whatever did he mean by such an odd remark?

Replacing his hat, Trevelyan gave a low laugh and left the cabin.

Almost immediately, the first round of guns fired from the *Serendipity*. The blasts shook the ship's walls and floorboards. Through the rattling windows, the *Isabelle* came into view, close enough for Emily to see her open gunports and her gun crews huddled around the short-barrelled carronades on the weather decks. The sight of the British colours flying from her mainmast and stern caused Emily's chest to tighten.

Boom, boom, boom! The *Isabelle* fired back. The *Serendipity*'s hull shuddered with each blow. Emily had to steady herself against Trevelyan's desk. All the while, Lind slowly unwound his rope and laughed, showing her his collection of mossy teeth, then with one sudden motion he lunged forward and grabbed her around the waist.

"No use in fightin' me, lass. Old Lind will win," he cackled, leering at her. "I'm gonna tie ya in thee toilet and then I'll go searchin' out thee captain's private store o' rum. We might as well enjoy ourselves while thee lead flies."

Emily rammed an elbow into his soft belly. As he keeled over, she made a dash for the door.

"If ya figure on goin' out there," he snarled, clutching his middle, "ya'll be meetin' up with thee captain's marines. And I don't 'spect they'll be as gentle with ya as old Lind will be." Beads of sweat rolled down his florid face as he straightened himself and brandished the rope.

The two warships were in full battle now. The crack of the cannons and carronades was deafening, and the smoke from their barrels poured into the cabin. There was a confusion of orders and men's frantic replies. Emily could hear the screams of dying men, and she prayed that British grapeshot would find its way straight through Trevelyan's torso. Coughing, she watched Lind starting towards her again. He was grinning.

"Be a good girl and let old Lind tie ya up nice and tight." Licking his lips, he leaped at her, grabbed her wrists, and jerked her towards him. Emily kicked him in the knee as hard as she could. The exertion propelled her backwards onto the floor of the latrine just as the windows behind Lind exploded, blowing him onto the cabin floor with a terrible thud. A hail of glass shards ripped into him. He lay there stunned, his eyes bulging from his torn face, his outstretched arms slippery with blood.

Emily bolted from the latrine and struggled to push Trevelyan's desk against the door, hoping it would hold against any marines lying in wait. Lifting her skirt to avoid the spreading pool of Lind's blood, she hurried to the windows and seized a large fragment of wood to smash out the bits of jagged glass still lodged in the frames. The *Isabelle* was so close …

Between the ships, which were lying broadside to each other, floated a swirling mass of debris: barrels, bits of mast and rigging, segments of timber, a legless goat, and dead seamen. Emily surveyed the scene for a moment, then peeled off her silk slippers, stuffed them into her spencer-jacket, and tucked her skirt up into her drawers.

Behind her, Lind exhaled a long moan. She swung around to find him sitting up, wiping blood from his face. His head resembled a chunk of slaughtered meat. Despite his wounds, he seemed in no mood to give up. Spying Emily, he began crawling towards her, his right arm reaching, his torn fingers opening and closing crab-like before him. Emily clambered into the window frame and was almost away when Lind managed to grasp her foot. She held onto the frame, oblivious to the glass that cut into the palms of her hands, and kicked until her foot struck his mangled face.

"Damnable woman!" he rasped, collapsing on the floor.

Over the gunfire and Lind's howling complaints, there came a clattering racket near the door. Looking up, Emily realized the cabin's bulkheads were at last being taken down. In a matter of seconds the room would be swarming with men and marines. She braced herself for the jump, hesitating a moment to give Lind one last thought. "Perhaps, Mr. Lind, when Trevelyan is done battling, he can order a bath for *you*."

With that, she plummeted over the ship's stern. As she hit the water, she struck a length of broken mast. Her right ankle erupted in pain, snatching her breath away. The sea that engulfed her was cold, and red with blood spilled from the sailors who bobbed on the waves next to her, their faces burned or maimed, their sightless eyes turned towards the warring ships. Emily felt a clutch in her stomach; her heart raced uncomfortably. Shutting her eyes to the horrors, she tried swimming, but her escape had left her exhausted and the chilly saltwater that washed over her torn hands forced her into submission. She held on tightly to the broken mast and allowed the waves to carry her.

Over her head flew cannon balls and whirring chain and bar shot that punched devastating holes in the ships' hulls and sliced through their sails and rigging. Sprays of wooden splinters fell like dangerous rain. Emily quickly ducked beneath a section of fallen sail, hoping to protect herself. Amidst the screams of war, she could hear the distinctive voice of Captain Trevelyan, and peering through a hole in the sail, up through clouds of cannon smoke, she saw him, his face obscured in shadow, standing over her like Goliath on the side of his ship.

"Shoot her, Mr. Clive."

Forgetting her pain, Emily frantically began pushing aside bodies and debris from her path. *Oh, God, swim, swim,* she urged her poor limbs. The *Isabelle* loomed large, the long barrels of the lower guns seemed almost within reach. She could see the barnacles that clung to the waterlogged timbers and the bits of oakum wedged into the cracks, and while she kicked her way towards safety, she was aware that *he* still hovered over her.

Swim, swim.

Several minutes had passed now since Trevelyan ordered her execution, and hope began to burn in Emily's young breast, but as she raised her hand from the water to touch the side of the *Isabelle*, a ball of lead struck her from behind. This new pain was unimaginable. Gasping, she flailed about, striving to concentrate on the solid timbers that shuddered before her. Once again, she tried reaching out to them, but her vision blurred and her strength evaporated. With a cry of frustration, she felt herself, and the fragment of mast to which she clung, drifting slowly away into a blackened void.

Early Evening
Aboard HMS *Isabelle*

TWELVE-YEAR-OLD MIDSHIPMAN Augustus Walby, or Gus, as he was known in shipboard circles, stood by the starboard rail of the *Isabelle*'s quarterdeck, surveying through his spyglass the battle carnage that lay in the water. Sensing someone standing next to him, he turned to find Captain James Moreland, a tall, thick man with yellow-white hair, faded blue eyes, and a sad face. The captain laid a hand on Gus's shoulder and silently peered into the settling smoke.

"You have the keenest eyes of anyone on this ship, Mr. Walby. Please keep a lookout for any of our men who have fallen overboard and may still have life in them."

"Aye, aye, sir. Can you tell me, sir, has the *Serendipity* retreated or do you think that she is simply going to turn around for another go at us?"

Captain Moreland grunted. "My guess is they are running away, Mr. Walby. We managed to shoot away a good deal of their yards and rigging. If they continue fighting they'll have nothing left with which to sail."

"Should we not go after them?"

"We've troubles of our own. It might be wiser to repair ourselves before fighting them again."

"Sir, one thing I don't understand... the *Serendipity*'s a frigate, is she not?"

"She is."

"Why, then, would she take a shot at us when she is smaller and has far fewer guns. We did nothing to provoke her, did we, sir?"

"We did not," the captain replied, watching her retreat. "However, Mr. Walby, we are in American waters and we are the enemy. Most likely their captain is a brazen young fellow."

"Thank you, sir." Gus touched his hat in a salute.

Overhearing the captain, First Lieutenant Lord Octavius Lindsay, a bad-complexioned youth with greasy hair, stepped forward. "Will it be necessary to return to Bermuda then, sir?" he asked.

"I must consult with our carpenters first to learn the extent of our damages." Captain Moreland paused to shout an order to the men working high up on the yardarms. "Sails up, men. Slow her down. And remember, one hand for the ship, one for yourself."

"But we would lose much time if we had to return to the island," said Octavius.

"In a hurry to take an American prize, are we, Mr. Lindsay? Or is it the prospect of shore leave in Halifax that has you impatient? I am hoping we can make our repairs at sea; however, we cannot fight this war with a crippled ship." Captain Moreland ran his large blue-veined hands along the rail, then continued on down the quarterdeck with Octavius following on his heels.

Gus Walby lifted his spyglass to his eyes once again and slowly moved it along the sea's surface, searching for survivors. There were plenty of dead men bouncing lifelessly on the waves like grotesque channel markers. Gus was relieved that he could not identify their remains. Already, some of the hands had set out in the ship's small boats and cutters to retrieve the bodies of their mates so that they could be given a proper burial at sea. The lucky ones who had survived their first fight unscathed rushed to clear the slippery decks of the dead and wounded. There was a terrible sound of moaning and sobbing as those still living were lifted and carried down to the hospital on the upper deck.

Suddenly Gus cried out. Through his glass he could see someone moving about on the waves, one arm gripping the remains of a mast, the other extended, as if beckoning to the *Isabelle*. He called out to Captain Moreland.

"Sir! You might find this of interest."

Retracing his steps, the captain took Gus's glass from him.

"At three points, sir," said Gus, "floating on a piece of masting. I—I believe it's a woman."

Captain Moreland gazed through the glass for a long while before chuckling and calling out, "Mr. Evans, Mr. Beck, if you please, gentlemen. Have the skiff lowered into the water. It seems a *lady* escaped our enemy ship."

"With all respect, sir," interjected Lord Octavius Lindsay, "our repairs are minimal. We can still sail. Shouldn't we at least try to make a run after that American frigate rather than stopping to pick up some *laundress*?"

Captain Moreland's eyes hardened. "You surprise me, Mr. Lindsay—in more ways than one." He brushed past his first lieutenant to oversee the lowering of the skiff. "At three points, men, holding onto our fallen mizzenmast, no doubt."

"Should I get Dr. Braden, sir?" asked Gus, running behind the captain, his eyes gleaming with excitement.

"Not just yet, Mr. Walby. My guess is our poor doctor already has far too many patients in his hospital at the present time. However, you could run down to the orlop deck and tell Mrs. Kettle I would like a word with her."

Gus saluted and ran off.

"Mr. Evans," said Captain Moreland, "once you have rescued the lady, take her immediately to my cabin. I'll have Commander Austen meet you there and stay with her until Dr. Braden has a chance to see her. Now then, off you go."

He turned back to Octavius. "Mr. Lindsay, go down to the hold and check on the amount of water in the bilge."

With a scowl on his face, Octavius set off to the bottom of the ship.

THE CARPENTER'S MATE, Morgan Evans, and his buddy, Able Seaman Bailey Beck, were lowered into the darkening waters. In the distance, on a pink-and-purple horizon, the tall sails of the *Serendipity* were gradually disappearing. Although the wind had been in the woman's favour, nudging her bit of debris in the direction of the *Isabelle*, the men still had to row out a long way. Bailey held the oars while Morgan leaned over the side to pull her from the sea. She whimpered as he lifted her from her mast.

"Careful now, Morgan," said Bailey. "She may have grievous wounds."

With the woman safely in his arms, Morgan inched backwards until he felt the skiff's wooden seat, then slowly sat down. All the while his eyes never left the woman's face

"She's lovely!" he gasped.

"She ain't no cookin' woman."

"Look at her finery: blue velvet and silk. I've never met a woman who wore such clothes."

"Aye! Though she's a bit ragged, she's a lady, all right. And I bet ya ain't never been in the company of a *lady* before."

"Oh, we're in a jokey mood, are we?" Morgan kicked at the water sloshing about in the boat's ribbed bottom.

"Hey, yer gettin' me clean pants all wet."

"Just row, Bailey. Yours may be wet, but mine are all bloody. I'll have a fight on my hands with Mrs. Kettle to get her to launder them again for me."

Bailey winked as he picked up the oars. "Might as well enjoy the feel o' that woman in yer arms. May be a while 'fore ya has another one."

By the time their boat was hoisted up to the *Isabelle*'s stern, word had spread that a woman had been found in the sea. Those men not on duty below deck, or in the hospital having their wounds tended by Dr. Braden, poured onto the deck to watch the spectacle. Gus was also there, having delivered his message to a grumbling Mrs. Kettle and returned in a flash.

Octavius Lindsay stood alongside the starboard rail, watching the proceedings. He sniffed and swung around to address Commander Austen. "The Admiralty, with few exceptions, does not allow women on our war ships."

Commander Francis "Fly" Austen was an imposing man of nearly forty years who had been present at many of the celebrated navy battles, although, to his disappointment, not Trafalgar. He stared at the woman Morgan Evans cradled in his arms. "You forget, Mr. Lindsay, we have Mrs. Kettle on *our* ship."

"Is Mrs. Kettle a woman? I hadn't noticed, sir."

"It appears this woman is not as wide in the beam as our Mrs. Kettle. It might be rather pleasant having her on board."

"With—with all respect, sir, we are *fighting* a war."

"Aye ... that we are."

Octavius sniffed again. "Well, I will make sure she is put off at the first port."

Mr. Austen raised one eyebrow. "I don't believe that will be *your* decision to make, Mr. Lindsay."

The moment Morgan Evans stepped out of the skiff and onto the poop deck, Emily opened her eyes to find hundreds of seamen lining the rails, craning their necks in her direction. In her weakened state, she could not discern individual faces; everything seemed a blur of blue frock coats, red uniforms, checked shirts and scarves, legs in white trousers, heads in bicornes and felt hats. She gazed skywards to find that even those perched on the rigging platforms and yardarms had paused in their tasks. It was so quiet on the ship that Emily heard nothing but the wind beating the sails. No one spoke. No orders were shouted. Each man seemed latched to his allotted space on the deck. And when her rescuer spoke, his voice was disembodied and distant, as if it came to her in a dream.

"You're on the *Isabelle* now, ma'am," he whispered. "You should be safe here."

Emily looked up at him. He was a young man of nineteen, perhaps twenty years, with dark shaggy hair and a pleasant smile. He wore a funny woollen hat that resembled a large sock. With a nod of her head she thanked him, then she shivered and sank back against his chest.

7:30 p.m.
(Second Dog Watch, Three Bells)

CAPTAIN MORELAND took a deep breath and plunged into the depths of the hospital. It stank of medicines, vomit, and coagulating blood. Every hammock held a wounded seaman, and crowded on the floor were a dozen more waiting to be seen by the doctor. The younger ones were snivelling, the older ones swearing, and some of those in between recited verses from the Bible.

In the middle of the mess, Dr. Leander Braden, dressed in a soiled shirt that had been clean that morning at breakfast, quietly worked on those with the worst wounds. James Moreland hated entering this part of the ship after a battle. The wounded reminded him of his own seafaring sons, now grown up and sailing on separate, distant ships, on distant seas, and he could not bear witnessing the removal of the sailors' shattered limbs or knowing that hideous scars would disfigure their youthful faces.

Noticing James's grave countenance, Dr. Braden wearily gave instruction to his assistant. "Brockley, continue stitching the man's wounds—and for God's sake, be gentle." He left the operating table, stooping to avoid hitting his head on the ceiling beams, and made his way over to where James stood.

"How many did we lose, Doctor?"

Leander wiped his hands on his black apron, then raised his arms to steady himself on the low ceiling. "Eighteen, including young Patrick and George."

James groaned. "And how many wounded?"

"Seriously? Maybe twenty-five. I haven't had a chance to count."

James fell silent awhile. "I have great admiration for you, Lee. You handle this bloody business so calmly. I'm afraid it makes me quite insane. I suppose when I was younger I could bear it better. I'm just..."

Leander looked at him over his round spectacles. "You have me all wrong. I don't handle it well at all. I do know that given more skilled assistants and a decent supply of medicine we could save a lot more lives. Grog and a few instruments for amputating limbs are simply not enough."

James shook his head sadly. "Our men are fortunate to have you. Most of our ships are plying the seas without any kind of surgeon. We are overburdened. These wars have gone on far too long." He glanced over at Leander's inept assistant, Osmund Brockley. "I must let you get back at it, for I am guessing Brockley is quite lost without your guidance."

"The man has no skill whatsoever."

"Yes, I am sorry about that. Now, I'm off. I must discuss repairs with the carpenters." James had just turned to leave when he remembered the main reason he had come to the hospital in the first place. "We pulled a young woman from the water. Young Walby spotted her. She must have jumped from the Yankee frigate. Well, Lee, when you have time ... she requires medical attention."

"James, I can hardly tend to a woman in this space. She would have no privacy here."

"Morgan Evans has taken her to my quarters and Fly Austen is attending her there. She can come down here when your hospital has cleared."

"Any idea who she might be?"

"No, but I can assure you she's not a common prostitute," James said, mounting the ladder that would take him to the fo'c'sle deck.

Intrigued, Leander returned to his gruesome tasks. Several able seamen had lead in their legs, and the sailing master would have to have his foot amputated. As always, it would be arduous extracting lead and lopping off limbs with the ship tossing from side to side.

8:00 p.m
(Second Dog Watch, Four Bells)

IN THE GATHERING GLOOM James Moreland, accompanied by the ship's carpenters, Mr. Alexander and Morgan Evans, combed every square inch of the vessel to assess the damage. The mizzenmast was a broken stump, its top half lost at sea, the weather decks were littered with piles of splinters, and the figurehead below the bowsprit had been completely blasted away. The hull had suffered a few minor blows and the bilge had taken on a good deal of seawater.

"Can we refit at sea, gentlemen, or should we return to Bermuda?"

"I think it best we return to port, sir," said Mr. Alexander. He was a man of fifty years, balding, with a gentle face. "We'll need a few days to fix her up, and with these waters swarming with enemy ships, if one were to surprise us now..."

"We're only a day and a half from Bermuda, sir," added Morgan, clasping his woollen hat in both hands.

"Your call, gentlemen." James called out to the coxswain at the helm. "Set a course, Mr. McGilp—south by southeast. Back to Bermuda it is."

Lewis McGilp nodded and began cranking the ship's wheel about. "Aye, sir, south by sou'east."

"Thank you, Mr. Alexander, Mr. Evans. That'll be all." The carpenters saluted and disappeared into the darkness. Left alone, James wandered to the ship's bow where he rubbed his eyes, unbuttoned his blue frock coat, and dreamed of the green meadows around his Yorkshire home. Eight years ago he had officially retired from the Royal Navy. At that time, having had enough of the seas to last his lifetime, he chose to move away from the coastal regions of England. Now he longed for those expanses of green in the north of his homeland.

England had been at war with Napoleon and France on and off

since 1793, and now they had become embroiled in yet another military conflict, this one with the United States. The American president, Mr. Madison, had declared war on Britain in June of 1812, citing grievances that included the British navy's habit of seizing American seamen and forcing them into service on their ships. But as James saw it, his navy was guilty of nothing more than searching out British deserters who had taken employment on American vessels, or fellow countrymen who had actually been pressed into the American navy. Regardless of the reasons for the animosity between the two countries, it remained that the British navy was so seriously short of officers, seamen, ships, and supplies that it could not effectively fight this new, distant war. As a result, James, at the age of sixty, when he asked for nothing more than a few years to enjoy his family, his farm, and his books, had been ordered by the Admiralty to take command once again of his old ship, the *Isabelle*, and to sail the western Atlantic waters, halting all enemy ships to seek out deserters and fellow countrymen alike, and to prove to the world that the mighty British navy still ruled the seas.

James stayed near the bowsprit for some time, staring out at the black waves, listening to the *Isabelle* crashing through the heavy waters. The intensifying winds slapped the fore topsail above him. He looked up to the men on the foreyard and called out to them in a booming voice that rivalled that of his bosun's mate waking the crew in the morning. "Careful, lads. We don't want anyone falling now. The doctor has his hands quite full at the moment."

He was greeted with laughter and salutes.

The quartermaster turned over the sand glass and the bell was rung four times. In the shadowy darkness, James watched his men climb down the thin ratlines from their high posts while others climbed up to begin their four-hour watch. He took a deep breath of the briny air and slowly made his way to the wardroom.

8:00 p.m.
(Second Dog Watch, Four Bells)

MEG KETTLE STOMPED into the captain's quarters in a huff. She had seen the woman pulled from the water, seen the way the crew looked at her, and heard what they were saying about her. Meg was not happy.

Fly Austen was waiting for her in a red-velvet wing chair. Behind a sheet of sailing canvas, the woman was asleep in the captain's cot.

"Ah, Mrs. Kettle. Thank you for coming."

"I see she rates thee captain's bed," Meg hissed.

"There was no other place to put her. The hospital is overflowing."

"If 'twere me, I doubt ya'd be puttin' me to bed in thee captain's cot. In thee hold with thee shingle and barrels of grog would be more like it."

Fly glanced over the woman's form. She had a massive bosom and hips as wide as the ship. Her greying hair was pulled severely from her meaty face and there wasn't an ounce of charm in her thick features.

His reply was not immediate. "Well now, Mrs. Kettle, the captain has ordered that a bath be prepared for our guest."

"A bath? We ain't in a fancy London hotel."

"We can spare her a bit of our fresh water," Fly said firmly.

"Thee lads on this ship 'ave to wash in saltwater."

Feeling impatient with the woman, Fly stood up. "We replenished some of our stores of freshwater recently in Bermuda, Mrs. Kettle. Freshwater will do."

Mrs. Kettle grunted as she folded her arms over her breasts.

"And then there's the matter of clothes," Fly continued, unable to meet her cold eyes. "She'll need a nightdress. Could you find something for her?"

"I only 'ave one and I ain't givin' it to her just 'cause she's some fancy lady."

"Could you maybe sew something together for her?"

"I cleans thee clothes, I don't make 'em."

"Very well then. I'll ask Magpie to take on the job."

"Magpie? He sews sails!"

"Aye, and he's very good with a needle. I'm sure he could sew together a bit of flannel for her."

Mrs. Kettle snorted like a hog.

"Well, see to the bath, please."

"And will ya be hangin' 'round while she bathes?"

"The bath, if you please, Mrs. Kettle."

There was a knock at the door.

Fly opened it, putting his finger to his lips.

The officers' cook tiptoed in with a tray. He had a shock of orange hair, and one eye that was askew as a result of a fall from a yardarm years ago. Although he did possess a proper Scottish name, no one could remember it, or ever bothered to ask; instead, he was simply addressed as Biscuit by officers and seamen alike.

Upon seeing the tray, Mrs. Kettle rolled her eyes. "Oh, nice, and we're served supper in bed as well."

"That will be all, Mrs. Kettle," said Fly, showing her the door.

She waddled out, muttering to herself.

"I have a bit o' porridge for thee dear lass, sir," said Biscuit, setting down his tray and trying to steal a peek through the canvas. "And some of me best biscuits."

"They're not full of maggots, are they?"

"Not at all, sir. These are some of me finest… reserved only for thee captain and his officers, and for lovely lassies pulled from thee rollin' waves."

Fly laughed. "I must admit, when they're not full of maggots and weevils, your sea biscuits are very good, very good indeed."

"It's thee pinch o' sugar and shot o' rum I puts in 'em, but don't tell no one." Biscuit tried for another look at their guest. "And I brought her a cup o' grog. Should bring her round."

"That's very kind of you, Biscuit."

"Oh, and sir, there won't be no milk in thee coffee tonight."

"And why not?"

"We lost our goat today. Poor Lizzie. Her legs were clean shorn away by Yankee grapeshot and I had to pitch her into thee drink." Biscuit lingered, hoping Commander Austen was in a talkative mood.

"She's not going anywhere, Biscuit. You'll see her soon enough."

"Right then, sir, let me know if she needs anythin' else."

"Some of your best wine wouldn't go amiss."

Biscuit saluted and slipped through the door.

AN HOUR LATER, Dr. Braden came to the captain's cabin carrying his black medical chest. Fly, with a glass of wine in his hand, greeted him at the door with a bow.

"Is that allowed when you're on active duty, Mr. Austen?"

"Probably not, but there's been no sign of James for hours. It seems he's turned his quarters over to our lady."

Leander Braden angled his head towards the washtub in the corner of the room. It contained a few inches of green, brackish water. "Is the tub for her or you?"

"Her, of course, although Mrs. Kettle did make a fuss about having to lug it up here."

"I am sure she would have."

"You've changed your shirt, Doctor," said Fly. "The last time I saw you ... you were covered in gore from head to toe."

Leander reddened and moved in through the canvas to stare down at the lady's pale, sleeping face. "Do you know the extent of her injuries, Fly?"

"James gave me strict orders not to touch her. However, it appears she's broken her ankle and has a ball of lead in her shoulder."

"I cannot examine her in the cot. Help me move the desk in here."

Swiftly the two men cleared James's desk of his maps and papers, and then pushed it behind the canvas. As they eased their guest out of the cot and onto the desk's hard surface, Emily opened her eyes with a start.

"Fly, if I'm to operate, I'll need some sand on the floor—the sea's a bit rough."

"Right away, Doctor."

"And if you could send word to Mrs. Kettle telling her I require her assistance here."

With a grin, Fly saluted his friend and set out on his mission.

Emily's dark brown eyes watched the doctor. Despite her condition, she noted that his auburn hair was thick and wavy, and that he wore his sideburns long on his handsome face. Behind his round spectacles, his eyes were intelligent and as blue as the sea.

"Do you have a name?" he asked.

"Emily," she answered weakly. "And you?"

"Leander Braden, ma'am. I'm the ship's physician. We have only one other woman on board… Meg Kettle is her name. I'll need her to help you undress. I'm afraid you've taken some lead in your shoulder and I must get it out as quickly as I can. While we wait for her, may I begin cleaning your wounds?"

Emily nodded and watched as he dipped a cloth into the cold water of her bathtub and wrung it out.

"It looks like you scratched yourself badly on some glass."

She didn't answer him. Instead, she winced and looked away while he cleaned and dressed the cuts on her hands.

Fly soon returned with sand for the floor. His eyes immediately fell upon Emily.

"This is Commander Francis Austen, Emily," said Dr. Braden. "However, we all call him Fly, being he's as annoying as the common housefly."

Emily was too exhausted to return their cheerful smiles.

Mrs. Kettle came huffing and puffing into the room. "Let's get this over, Doctor. I 'ave me chores to do."

The men exchanged knowing glances.

"Mrs. Kettle, I must examine Emily's ankle and shoulder. Her jacket must be removed as well as her stockings."

Mrs. Kettle rolled her eyes and planted her puffy hands on her wide hips. "It ain't in me duties to be undressin' young ladies for yer examination."

"Since you are the only other woman on this ship, I have no other alternative."

Mrs. Kettle yanked the canvas shut behind her. "Off with yer clothes. The doctor needs to be lookin' at ya." She pulled at Emily's blue velvet spencer-jacket, causing her to cry out in pain.

"Careful, Mrs. Kettle, please. She is grievously injured," Leander called out, wishing he had given more thought to the wisdom in summoning the laundress in the first place.

"I wonder if she's that gentle with the men in her cot," whispered Fly.

Leander looked disapprovingly at his friend over his spectacles.

"Right then, Doctor, she's ready fer ya," said Mrs. Kettle, coming from behind the canvas curtain.

"Thank you for sharing your invaluable time."

"S'pose I didn't 'ave a choice now, did I?" She opened the door. "Make sure ya check her female parts."

Dr. Braden raised his eyebrows.

"If she's been roamin' thee seas with Yankee sailors she's likely with child. And if she hurled herself overboard, she likely didn't fancy thee father."

9:30 p.m.
(First Watch, Three Bells)

OCTAVIUS LINDSAY took his place at the mess table in the wardroom. "Biscuit, it's terribly late and I'm starving. What have you cooked up for us tonight?"

"Lobscouse, sir." Biscuit plunked down a pot of unsavoury-looking stew in the middle of the table. "Ya'll be lucky to get anythin' tonight,

Lord Lindsay. Think of yer buddies we gave up to thee sea this afternoon."

"It's all part of the service," Octavius retorted. "I wouldn't be surprised we throw your old bones overboard before this war ends."

"And what would ya do without yer old cook to boil yer porridge for ya and serve up yer rations of grog, eh?"

"Aye, you have a good point there, Biscuit," said Fly Austen. His eyes were bright and his cheeks flushed as a result of his previous partaking of spirits in the captain's cabin. "Do try to stay clear of enemy fire."

"If they come after old Biscuit, I'll cut 'em up with me cutlass."

"That's if you can see them coming," snorted Mr. Spooner, the stout purser.

"I'll have me one eye lookin' at 'im and me other lookin' for 'im," said Biscuit, dishing up the mixture of salted meat, potatoes, biscuit bits, onions, and pepper.

The men laughed, then rushed to guzzle a glass of wine before having to taste Biscuit's supper.

James mentally counted his dinner guests. There were only six seated around the mess table; normally there were eight who dined together. "I know our sailing master, Mr. Harding, having lost his foot, is recuperating in the hospital, but where is our doctor? Still at work?"

"Operating on our lady's shoulder in your cabin, sir," said Fly, passing the wine to Mr. Spooner.

"You gentlemen begin without me." James pushed back his chair and stood up. "Biscuit, while I'm gone, replenish the decanters."

He walked up one deck to his quarters, now a makeshift operating room, and quietly stepped inside. Osmund Brockley, whose large tongue hung out of his mouth as he beheld Emily's bare shoulders, was pinning her arms to her sides. Leander swabbed the gaping hole in her right shoulder and picked up a large prong-like instrument.

"James, would you mind giving Emily the rope?"

"Have you given her anything to dull the pain, Lee?" James whispered, feeling very warm all of a sudden.

"Laudanum and rum."

Emily readily accepted the piece of rope from James and bit down on it as hard as she could. Tears of agony streamed from her dark eyes as the doctor entered her wound in search of the lead. Her body tensed as she endured the pain. Osmund grunted as he tightened his hold on her.

"There now, I've got it," Leander said, triumphantly holding up the offending ball. "We'll just clean and bandage you up and let you get back to sleep."

Emily smiled wanly before closing her eyes.

James waited until Leander was done before motioning him into a corner of the room.

"Now that you've looked her over, what's the word?"

"She has a broken left ankle, and severe cuts on both hands. She's dehydrated and half starved. Her bullet wound, however, should heal up nicely."

James pursed his lips as he listened. "Well, dinner is on the table in the wardroom. It looks quite unpalatable, but you should take time for some refreshment."

"I don't dare leave her alone with Osmund. He's been making very strange sounds. There's no telling what that man might do."

"Yes, quite. I don't like the look of him." James scratched his head. "Should we ask Mrs. Kettle to sit with her?

"Heavens, no," said Leander. "Given the chance, she'd toss our guest overboard."

"In that case, would you allow me to call up Gus Walby?"

"By all means! Young Walby's a most trustworthy fellow."

James hesitated a moment, then gave Leander a sheepish grin. "But first, let us have her removed at once to your hospital. I'm afraid I would not be setting a good example to the men if she were to stay alone with me in my cabin."

10:15 p.m.
(First Watch)

ON THE LOWER DECK, Bailey Beck and the two cook's mates, the Jamaican brothers Maggot and Weevil, gathered the few belongings of the sailors who had lost their lives earlier in the day. Their clothing and possessions would be sold off at the mast on the following day to the highest bidder, and the raised money sent home to England to benefit their dependents. The men worked by lantern-light, humming sea shanties, and fortifying themselves with the extra ration of grog Captain Moreland had ordered for them to ease the burden of their unpleasant task.

Above deck, despite the sadness of the day and the repair work that had to be done, James allowed those hands who hadn't rushed to their beds in exhaustion to gather as usual for a bit of entertainment. Biscuit played his fiddle and the young sail maker, Magpie, his flute. The men clapped and cheered as Morgan Evans hopped up on an overturned crate to lead them in singing an ode to grog:

While up the shrouds the sailor goes,
Or ventures on the yard,
The landsman, who no better knows
Believes his lot is hard,
But Jack with smiles each danger meets,
Casts anchor, heaves the log,
Trims all the sails, belays the sheets,
And drinks his can of grog.

THE DIN ON THE WEATHER DECKS awakened Emily. For a few bewildering moments, she glanced about her tiny room—illumined by a lantern, which swung gently on a wooden peg by her feet—trying to remember how she came to be in this new place ... on this new ship. Someone had placed her in a cot next to a sealed gunport, and closed off her corner with the aid of two lengths of canvas suspended over a rope affixed to the ceiling timbers. Despite the noise overhead, she could hear moaning and weeping beyond the canvas. One or two people were moving quietly about, speaking words of reassurance to those who wept. A foul stench assaulted Emily's nose and made her stomach queasy, but she had no desire to investigate its source; she was too preoccupied with her own sorrows and discomforts. Her mouth was dry, her left ankle throbbed, and there was a vicious pain in her right shoulder. How she longed for a cool drink of water, and the luxury of a real bed and a fat pillow. How she longed to forget everything that had happened to her in the past few weeks. Unable to tolerate the pervading smells of her surroundings, she buried her nose in her blanket and prayed that sleep would soon return.

To her surprise, a little yellow-haired fellow suddenly appeared between the canvas curtains. He wore tight white pantaloons, a dark-blue frock coat, and a big grin.

"Are you feeling better, ma'am?" he asked cheerfully.

"No, actually ... my whole body hurts. And I feel ill, but perhaps that is a result of the horrendous smell about this place."

"I am sorry about that. Dr. Braden has opened all the gunports for you, with the exception of the one by your head, but I'm afraid, whether the ports are opened or not, most of the ship carries with it an awful odour."

"Could I ask you to open this port as well? It may alleviate some of my suffering."

Emily watched the boy closely as he worked to lift the heavy port into place. When he was done, the bracing air that instantly found her corner did much to improve her temperament.

"Dr. Braden says you broke your ankle and that you were shot in the shoulder. I hope it wasn't one of our men that shot you."

"It was definitely not one of yours." She smiled up at him. "And what is your name?"

"Augustus Walby, but everyone calls me Gus. May I ask yours?"

"It's Emily, but I should like it if you called me Em."

"Should I not address you as Miss ... something?" he asked, looking uneasy.

"No, please, just plain Em. Now tell me what it is you have in your hands."

"A novel. Mr. Austen gave it to me. Have you been introduced to Commander Austen yet?"

"I may have been. Does he go by the name of Fly?"

"He does. Dr. Braden calls him that. I understand they have been friends for a long time; grew up in the same town in England. It was Mr. Austen that suggested you might like it if I read to you."

"And what is the title of your novel, Gus?"

"*Sense and Sensibility*. It was written by Mr. Austen's younger sister, Jane."

Emily's eyes brightened. "I know it! I would be happy to have you read it to me."

"It would be my honour, ma'am."

"Remember, Mr. Walby, it is *Em*."

"I fear the captain would send me to the flogging post should he overhear me addressing you by your first name."

Emily narrowed her eyes. "He wouldn't dare while there's still breath in me."

Gus laughed, showing a line of perfect white teeth, a rare thing in the navy.

"Who taught you to read?" she asked.

"My mother did when I lived in England. Mr. Lindsay and Mr. Austen help me now when they have some free time. They help all we young midshipmen with our letter writing, too. Mr. Austen is a particularly good teacher, although this war keeps him awfully busy. I don't really care for Mr. Lindsay. He has no patience when we make mistakes."

"Where in England does your family live?"

"They lived in London."

"Lived?"

"My parents are both dead."

Emily's face softened. He was so young.

"I live with my uncle. He's a sea captain and expected me to enter the navy."

All at once, Emily felt fiercely tired. "I would love to have you read Jane Austen to me, Gus, as long as you're not offended if I should drop off to sleep. But before you begin ... could I trouble you for a cup of water?"

"Right away ... Em."

"May I inquire, sir, who this woman is?" asked Octavius after Captain Moreland had rejoined his men in the wardroom.

"She's a mystery, Mr. Lindsay," said James, cutting into his meat. "From her speech, we have deduced that she is an Englishwoman, and from her manner of clothing, a gentlewoman. Whether she really was a prisoner of war on the *Serendipity* is yet to be confirmed. Regardless, it confounds me why any woman would be fool enough to be on the Atlantic with war raging all round."

"Might it seem likely her father has a large plantation in Jamaica, or Antigua, perhaps, and she was travelling there to meet him?" asked Leander.

"Or, perhaps she was en route to Canada to be with relatives who have already settled there," suggested Fly. "War and politics are driving many away from the United States as well as from our England."

James gave Leander and Fly a thoughtful nod.

"Whatever the case may be, you *will* leave her in Bermuda, will you not, sir?" asked Octavius.

"I have not yet made that decision," said James.

"But having a woman like her on board, sir ..."

Leander looked up quizzically from his supper. "Yes, Mr. Lindsay? The problem with that is ... ?"

"Why, the men will become unruly. They will fight over her."

Leander frowned. "But I understand they have Mrs. Kettle to look after their needs."

"Doctor, you may be older than thirty, but surely you can see through those spectacles of yours."

"Mr. Lindsay … the woman is injured. Removing her to shore would be unwise."

"Ah, our doctor does have eyes. More wine please, Biscuit." Octavius waited until his goblet had been refilled. "And would she not receive better medical attention in a proper hospital?"

"In Halifax, yes," said Leander. "The conditions in Bermuda do not impress me."

"But we're fighting a war, Doctor. She can only get in the way. Why not leave her in Bermuda and allow a merchant ship to carry her home to England?"

Running a finger around the edge of his wine glass, James piped up. "She's an attractive woman, Mr. Lindsay—that is evident to us all—but no man shall harm her or neglect his duties as a result of her presence on this ship; otherwise, they'll be duly punished. No. She'll remain with us until such time as we reach Halifax. In the meantime, we must find out who she is."

"What if she's a spy?" Octavius ventured unhappily.

There was a roar of laughter that rivalled the thunder of the sea beyond the windows, and the men unanimously agreed that the wine had gone to Octavius's head.

"Perhaps you'll be fortunate enough to discover if our *guest* has appetites to rival those of Mrs. Kettle's," quipped Fly. "And, should this be true, I daresay you'll be parting with a good portion of your pay."

While his messmates snickered, Octavius rolled his eyes and muttered, "You're quite a boor, Mr. Austen."

"Tell me, Doctor, when might I be able to speak with her?" asked James. "She may have valuable information regarding the *Serendipity*."

"Ah, so my spy theory holds weight, does it?" cried Octavius, lifting his chin.

"Perhaps, Mr. Lindsay," James said patiently. "Either way, she may be able to tell us whether or not there were any Royal Navy deserters on board that American ship." He looked over at Leander and repeated his question.

Leander clasped his hands and regarded him over his spectacles. "The young woman is exhausted, James. I would suggest, at the very least, we give her a few days of rest."

"I will wait twenty-four hours, Doctor. No more." James drained his wine goblet, then twisted his neck to face Biscuit, who stood behind his chair, awaiting orders. "I am wondering, Biscuit, if you could put more thought and effort into our supper tomorrow evening."

"Ah-hah, war rations and we're complainin', sir! I could pilfer all o' yer rum rations and boil up sauces to hide thee poor quality o' thee meat then, heh?"

James smiled as he poured himself more wine and raised his glass. "Gentlemen! To our native land, to the health of our King George and to our indispensable cook."

"Our native land."

"King George's health."

"Our cook."

The men lifted their goblets in toast and broke into mirthful laughter.

Wednesday, June 2

7:00 a.m.
(Morning Watch, Six Bells)

AT SIX BELLS the next morning, Leander Braden rose from his hammock to resume his duties in the small hospital in the forepeak of the *Isabelle*'s upper deck. He and his assistant, Osmund Brockley, had completed their operations on the battle-wounded the night before, having had to amputate three legs, two hands, and one foot, in addition to closing forever the eyes of many young men. But at this early hour, there were still six seamen with a multitude of injuries, in various states of consciousness, groaning and twitching in their troubled sleep, who required Leander's care and attention.

The hospital air was heavy with the putrid smell of medicines, blood, excrement, and festering wounds, despite Osmund having thrown open all of the nearby gunports. It aggravated Leander's crushing exhaustion and the creeping stiffness he felt in his shoulders. With a sigh, he settled at his desk to begin making notes in his medical journal, but he could not concentrate. He gazed over at the old sails that Morgan Evans had rigged up at one end of the hospital for the comfort of Emily, his newest patient, and for several minutes he allowed himself to wonder who she was, and why it was she had jumped from the *Serendipity*.

Leander had just managed to return his attention to his journal when Biscuit and his assistants, Maggot and Weevil (so named for their weekly task of drawing the maggots and weevils out of the biscuit barrel), entered the hospital ward from the galley next door, bearing bowls of porridge and plates of sea biscuits.

"Biscuit," Leander called out sternly as the cook tiptoed towards Emily's corner, "you may leave the food here with me and I'll make certain she gets it when she wakes up."

"Ah, but Doc, I got up real early to make fresh biscuits for thee lass. I'd likes to present 'em to her. There ain't no weevils burrowin' in 'em."

Leander held his gaze.

"Ah, but Doc, I was below deck cookin' up yer supper when Morgan brought her on board."

"We're dyin' for a wee peek," said Maggot. Behind him, his brother, Weevil, nodded eagerly.

"All in good time, men. Now I insist you all leave."

But the three interlopers stood rooted to the floor.

Leander frowned. "You wouldn't want to catch a *contagious* fever now, would you?"

The possibility of catching something did the trick. Biscuit and the brothers, suddenly remembering urgent duties elsewhere, dropped Emily's breakfast feast on top of Leander's journal—spilling his inkwell—and shoved at one another as each tried to be the first to exit the hospital. No sooner had they fled, however, than Lewis McGilp, the coxswain, sauntered in from the galley.

"Yes, Mr. McGilp?" asked Leander, still frowning at the annoyance of his spilled ink.

"It's my throat, sir. It's mighty sore," he said, looking sheepish.

"Come in then and I'll examine you."

Lewis hopped up on the operating table, opened his mouth, and said, "Ahhhh" just as Octavius Lindsay climbed through the hatch from the fo'c'sle deck, straightened his frock coat, and took off his bicorne hat.

Looking over his round spectacles, Leander addressed him. "Let me guess, Mr. Lindsay: you are suffering from a stomach ailment, most likely caused by the poor quality of last night's fare."

Octavius shuffled his feet in his Hessian boots, striking his greasy head on a hanging lantern. "That's it, Doctor, and I'm feeling so poorly I cannot attend to my duties."

"I've a tonic that should help if you'll just wait until I've seen to Mr. McGilp."

Octavius dropped down on a stool and fixed his black eyes on the canvas curtain.

Morgan Evans was the next to appear. He stood beside Octavius and tugged the woollen sock from his head.

"What afflicts you, Morgan?" asked Osmund Brockley, coming towards him with a reeking chamber pot that required dumping into the ocean.

"I missed the mark doing my repairs and smashed my left hand with my hammer," he responded in a muted tone, studying the cracks in the floorboards.

"Mr. Evans," said Leander without turning around, "I have never known you to injure yourself with your hammer before. Is this nonsense?"

"No, sir," said Morgan quickly, holding up the swollen fingers of his left hand.

"Fine. I will attend to you after Mr. Lindsay. Take a seat where you can find one."

Morgan sank to the floor while Leander completed his examination of the coxswain. "Mr. McGilp, there is no evidence of swollen glands. May I suggest you wear a jacket and extra scarf while standing at the helm, especially during the night when there is much dew on deck."

Lewis jumped down from the table. "Aye, sir, thank you, sir."

Leander cleaned away the pool of ink on his desk then made a brief note in his journal. When at last he wheeled about to signal to Mr. Lindsay to come forward, he discovered a crowd of sailors standing in the hospital doorway, all waiting their turn, their wide eyes fixed on the private corner where Emily lay.

Osmund rolled his oversized tongue about. "They say they've either taken in some bad water or ingested too many weevils, sir."

Leander folded his arms across his slender frame. "Gentlemen, unless you have fallen from the shrouds, broken your neck, or are bleeding profusely, I would ask that you come back later when there is sufficient air in here for us all to breathe."

The men, excluding Octavius Lindsay and Morgan Evans, all shuffled out grumbling to themselves. Osmund broke into a succession of guffaws that sounded like the brays of a donkey, while Mr. Harding, the sailing master, keenly watched their departure from his hammock, his footless leg propped up at a forty-five-degree angle.

"Doctor," he said with a grin, "I fear it's not *your* services that brought them down here."

"That is abundantly obvious," replied Leander, uncrossing his arms. "Now, Mr. Lindsay, about that tonic ..."

AT EIGHT BELLS, when his morning watch had ended, Gus Walby wandered into the hospital holding the first volume of *Sense and Sensibility*.

"May I read to Miss Emily, Doctor?"

Leander laid a long finger to his lips. "I just scared a dozen men away. If they learn you have been allowed to stay, I'll be walking the plank at midnight. She's only now awakened, Mr. Walby, and hasn't yet taken breakfast." He reached for the bowl and plate on his desk. "Her porridge is cold, but she may like some biscuits."

Gus tucked his book under one arm and took the food from Leander. He walked carefully to Emily's canvas corner, cleared his throat, and awaited her invitation to enter.

A landsman named Mr. Crump, who had just lost a leg to Leander's blade the previous day, looked up from his nearby cot.

"Doctor, why would ya be turnin' away all those sailors and allowin' the likes of Mr. Walby a chance ta see her?"

"For the simple reason that Mr. Walby has only good intentions and I fear the other men do not."

Leander, who was now moving from cot to cot, re-dressing wounds and checking for signs of infection, listened with great interest to the conversation behind the canvas.

"Good morning," Gus chirped, setting Emily's breakfast down on a shelf near the gunport.

"Good morning, Gus." Emily tried raising herself in her cot, an action that sent a shot of pain down her arm. She gritted her teeth. "Better stay where I am," she admitted finally. She lay back on her pillows and looked up at Gus. The sight of his youthful, innocent face warmed her heart.

"Did you have a good rest, Em?"

"I did, but only once the doctor gave me some laudanum. I recall hearing your mates above deck singing tunes about reckless sailors and cans of grog. And I suspect the doctor gave me some of *that* as well." Emily noticed she was wearing a nightshirt and quietly wondered when and how she had been placed in it.

"The men dance and sing on deck every night they can unless the weather is poor."

"Even when they've lost friends in battle?"

"That's when they need it most, Em. Takes their minds off sad things."

"I see."

"Are you hungry?"

"I'll take breakfast later, thanks." She did not want to tell him that the hospital smells had quite put her off eating.

Gus stepped closer to her cot. "May I ask how you broke your ankle?"

"I was fleeing a monster who stank like a manure patch."

Gus's eyes widened. "Was it the captain of the *Serendipity*?"

"No. It was his toady, Lind."

"And did you jump overboard?"

"I did."

"You were very brave to do so," said Gus, looking quite impressed.

Emily lowered her voice. "Thanks to your gunners' accuracy, an explosion of grapeshot tore through the stern windows, striking Lind down just as he was about to tie me up in the captain's privy. I jumped out the broken windows and landed on something... a fallen mast, I believe."

"Why was that man, Lind, going to tie you up in the privy?"

From within the dark hospital came the doctor's insistent voice. "Mr. Walby, I understood you came by to *read* to Miss Emily."

Gus's face registered a look of guilt. "Oh! Would you like me to begin reading now?"

"Please." Emily relaxed in the cot, a small smile on her lips, and listened to Gus's sweet voice as he read Jane Austen's book. She turned her head towards the opened gunport. The ocean waves of green, blue, and turquoise were strangely calming this morning. She watched them rise and fall, thankful for the light and a view to the outside world.

When she turned back to Gus, she found Dr. Braden's sea-blue eyes gazing upon her through the crack in the canvas.

7:00 p.m.
(Second Dog Watch, Two Bells)

BEFORE NIGHTFALL, as those members of the *Isabelle*'s crew not on watch began making their way to the weather decks with their flutes and fiddles for a bit of entertainment, James Moreland and Fly Austen entered the hospital with the purpose of speaking to Emily. With the help of Osmund Brockley, Leander had moved his remaining patients so that their hammocks hung as far from the canvas curtain as possible, affording the captain and his commander some privacy during their interview. Fly came bearing a can of grog and handed it to Emily, saying, "Compliments of our cook, who, I might add, was crestfallen he couldn't deliver it to you personally."

Sitting up in her cot with several extra pillows at her back, Emily quipped, "Is this to loosen my tongue before the interrogation?"

"Aye, we had thought it might help," Fly confessed.

James stepped towards her cot, his arm extended. "James Moreland, ma'am. We did meet last night, but it was ... well, you were ..."

"A bit disoriented?" said Emily, shaking his hand. "I am sorry for that. How do you do, sir?"

Leander slipped through the curtain and stood quietly next to Fly just as James asked, "And how are your injuries tonight?"

"Much as they were last night, sir."

"Leander assures me you will make a full recovery."

"I am very thankful to Dr. Braden," she said, keeping her eyes on the captain, who pulled up a nearby stool and dropped down heavily upon it.

"You were on the American frigate, the *Serendipity*."

"I was."

"How long were you their ... guest?"

Emily gave a wry smile. "I was their prisoner, sir."

James cleared his throat. "Their prisoner, then."

"I cannot say for certain ... three weeks, maybe four."

"Were you mistreated?"

Emily's voice went icy. "Yes. Every day."

Avoiding her eyes, James pressed on. "How was it you managed to escape?"

"I jumped out the stern windows, which you conveniently blew out with your cannon fire."

Emily saw a flicker of amusement cross Fly's face. Her eyes drifted to Leander, who stood watching her, one fist held to his lips. For a moment his blue eyes locked with hers.

"Were you shot before or after you jumped?"

"After, sir."

"Any idea who was it that pulled the trigger?"

"I believe his name was Mr. Clive."

James s140

hifted on his stool. "You are a British subject?"

"I am."

"And your home?"

"Dorset, sir."

"Your father's name?"

"My father died three years ago."

"His name?"

Emily was slow in answering. "Henry … Henry George, sir."

James paused in his questioning, his eyes narrowing as if he were running the name *Henry George* through his mind. Finally, he asked, "His occupation?"

"He was a farmer."

"A farmer," echoed James flatly. He took a deep breath. "And your mother?"

Emily's lips disappeared into a thin line. "She died when I was very young. I do not remember her at all."

"But you *do* remember her name?"

"Yes, of course. It was Louisa."

"Do you have any other family?"

"No … sir."

James studied her, a small frown playing between his brows. "How old are you, young lady?"

"Eighteen, sir."

"Did you ever hear tell of any Englishmen on the *Serendipity*?"

"I was locked in the captain's quarters and never once allowed beyond their confines. I was neither acquainted with the crew, nor those that Captain Trevelyan kept in his gaol."

James glanced up sharply. "Trevelyan?"

"Yes, sir."

The colour drained from James's face and there was a slight waver in his voice. "Captain *Thomas* Trevelyan?"

"That was his name."

"Did you ... did you ... at any time overhear the extent and nature of *his* war orders?"

"No, but I suspect they were comparable to yours, Captain Moreland: to sink or take a prize all enemy ships along the Atlantic coast."

The men exchanged glances, then regarded Emily with expressions of curiosity.

James's left leg bounced up and down as he resumed his questioning. "How was it you came to be Trevelyan's prisoner?"

Emily hesitated. She lowered her glance, and stared at the bandages on her hands.

"I would appreciate your answer before sunrise."

"Sir ... please ... I do not want ... I do not wish to speak of that morning."

"Very well, then," James said unhappily. "Was there anyone else, besides yourself, taken prisoner?"

Emily's lips quivered, her eyes still on her hands.

James inhaled in exasperation.

"May I, sir?" asked Fly. James settled back on his stool and gave Fly his assent with a wave of his hand. Quietly, Fly tried a different tack. "I assume it was Trevelyan who attacked your ship, Emily."

She nodded.

"What kind of ship were you on?"

"I'm not certain."

"A large ship-of-the-line? A frigate? A merchant vessel, perhaps?"

"I am guessing ... it was most likely a merchant ship, Mr. Austen."

"Bound for ... ?"

Emily looked up suddenly, and tossed her head, as if trying to recapture her previous confidence. "Upper Canada."

"What was this merchantman carrying?"

"Besides human beings? I do not know."

"Guns ... soldiers ... food supplies?"

Emily shrugged helplessly.

"With whom were you travelling?"

"Companions."

"Companions? And did your companions have names?"

"Does it *really* matter, Mr. Austen?" challenged Emily. "Surely their names are of no consequence to you."

Angered, James rose from his stool. "That is for *me* to decide." He studied her a moment. "Was this merchantman of yours conducting some sort of reconnaissance mission?"

"How would I know?" Emily snapped, adding with sarcasm, "Perhaps her hold was crammed with crates of gold."

James's voice rose in response to her impertinence. "There must have been *some* reason why Trevelyan attacked your ship?"

"My guess is ... he attacked it for no other reason than the British colours flew from her topgallants."

"What was the name of your ship?"

Emily turned towards the darkening sea beyond the open gunport. "I—I don't remember."

"*That* I find hard to believe," muttered James harshly.

"Sir, as passage was booked for me, I did not concern myself with the ship's name."

James drew nearer to her cot. "Would you perhaps remember the name of this unknown ship's captain? Surely you were acquainted with him. If you could provide me with *this* detail, I may then be able to deduce—"

At that moment, Leander placed his hand gently on James's shoulder and said, "Sir, I think we best allow Emily more rest."

James rubbed his eyes, causing the baggy bits to redden. "For God's sake, might we at least know who you *really* are and why you were on a British merchant vessel?"

"Sir, I have told you," Emily said in a tone that pushed the boundaries of civility. "I am from Dorset. My parents' names were Henry and Louisa George. They are now both deceased. My father was once a farmer. I was on—what I believe was—a merchant ship. We were bound for Upper Canada. If I have displeased you, I am sorry, but I do *not* know Trevelyan's reasons for attacking my ship, *or* why I was taken prisoner."

James gave Emily a cold stare. "I find it hard to believe, young lady, that *you* are the daughter of a Dorset farmer." He threw aside the curtain and stalked out.

With frustration etched on his face, Fly followed, shooting a glance at Leander and mumbling, "We have learned *nothing* at all of importance."

From their hammocks, the sailors—those who were conscious—followed with interest the captain and the commander as the two of them marched across the hospital room and stomped up the ladder.

"Doctor," Mr. Crump called out, "I swear this be more excitin' than doin' battle with thee French. It does wonders to ease thee pain of losin' me leg."

"Aye," said the sailor swinging next to him, "a bit o' melodrama makes me not mind missin' out on me can o' grog, bein' in here."

The wounded sailors craned their necks in an effort to see the patient lying in the cot beyond the canvas. Leander studied the two of them over his spectacles with consternation and heard them grumble their disappointment when he yanked shut the crack in the curtain.

EMILY SENSED LEANDER standing next to her cot long before he spoke. "I would like to re-dress your wound when you're feeling up to it."

"Now is as good a time as any," she said despondently, turning over so he could reach her bandages. Slowly, his skilled hands removed her soiled dressings and cleaned away the blood and ooze. She closed her eyes to the warmth of his freckled hands on her skin and listened to the *Isabelle* as she cut through the roiling waves, almost forgetting the searing pain where the ball had entered her body.

"If I'd been left in the sea yesterday, Doctor, I would not have minded."

Leander gazed at her long hair, the golden waves spread across the white blankets of her bed reminding him of a field of wheat.

"Well, perhaps you have a great deal more living to do."

She said nothing more until he had finished applying fresh bandages.

"May I speak plainly ... as patient to doctor?" She rolled over to look up at him. Leander peeled off his spectacles and placed them in the top pocket of his black apron. "Is there any reason ... any reason at all why I must tell you every last detail about myself?"

Surprise registered on his handsome face. He lowered himself upon the stool that the captain had earlier occupied and pulled it closer to her cot.

"Not unless you're a spy for President Madison or you're working for Napoleon himself."

"I assure you I am neither, Doctor."

"And your presence on the *Isabelle* will, in no way, harm the crew."

"I cannot think how it could."

"If you could recall the name of your ship or its captain, it would certainly assist Captain Moreland."

She met his gaze steadily.

"Otherwise, you may keep your history to yourself." He rose to leave, then paused by the curtain. "But you should know this: Captain Moreland plans to put you ashore the moment we arrive in Halifax harbour. And if that is not agreeable to you, you must decide how you will answer him."

Thursday, June 3

11:00 a.m.
(Forenoon Watch, Six Bells)

ALMOST TWO DAYS after her encounter with the USS *Serendipity*, the *Isabelle* dropped anchor in the deep waters off Ireland Island, Bermuda, alongside a privateer with a blood-red hull, three merchant ships, and one British ship-of-the-line called the *Amethyst*. The winds and tides had been in Captain Moreland's favour, and his crew had easily steered clear of the dangerous reefs that surrounded the Bermuda Islands. In the past, many ships had not been as lucky; they had been ripped open on the shoals and sunk in the turquoise waters. Under the sunny Bermudian sky, their wooden skeletons could be seen rotting in the sand, constant reminders to passing sailors of their fate should their course not be accurate.

Once the *Isabelle*'s crew had been fed their breakfast, they fell to work on the repairs that could not be achieved at sea. For a few hours now, the sounds of hammering and good cheer had reverberated around the ship as it bobbed gently on the clear waters.

"Sir, what about a new figurehead?" asked Mr. Alexander as Captain Moreland, in the company of Octavius Lindsay, surveyed the ongoing repairs to the ship's waist. "Shall I ask Morgan Evans to carve you a new one?"

"I think not, Mr. Alexander. There isn't time for fixing a new one, and besides, I find them rather ostentatious and outdated. Just smooth out the sides where our figurehead once rested."

"What about painting, sir? The ship needs painting," insisted Octavius.

"I thought you were in a hurry to see Halifax, Mr. Lindsay. Painting will only further delay us."

"But, sir, we don't want the Americans to think our navy is old and inferior."

"But, Mr. Lindsay, we are old and rapidly becoming inferior."

"With all respect, I never expected to hear you say such a thing."

"Mr. Lindsay, we've lost more sea battles and men in this new war than I care to count. Too many years of war are taking their toll. If we're not quick and attentive, the *Serendipity* will come upon us again and this time there will be *no* retreating."

"What would Lord Nelson have said, sir, if he'd heard you utter such defeatist words?"

"Young man," said James, inspecting his new mizzenmast, "Nelson has been gone for eight years."

Octavius's face fell as the older man brushed by him to look over the rails. A pinnace from the *Amethyst*, which was anchored nearby, was approaching the *Isabelle* carrying four officers.

"Now come with me, Mr. Lindsay, to greet our guests," shouted James. "Let us find out what news is about in the few days since we were last here. Prepare for their landing, lads. Down with the ladders."

AT THE END of the forenoon watch, the bell sounded eight times. Leander and Fly sat on the poop deck bench by the stern and taffrail, drinking cups of black coffee as they observed the sailors climbing down from their four-hour watch on the new mizzenmast and topgallant. As the winds blowing from the south were warm and humid, both men had shed their jackets.

"I much prefer my coffee with milk," said Fly, grimacing before he gulped his hot drink.

"I overheard Biscuit threatening to hang himself if he cannot find a goat in Bermuda."

Fly chuckled. "Let us hope he meets with success."

Leander set down his coffee cup to untie his cravat. "Is James in his cabin with his visitors from the *Amethyst*?"

"He is. I am anxious to hear what news they bring."

"I hope it's good news and will improve James's humour. I fear he is wearying of war."

"We're all weary," said Fly, growing pensive. "I miss the days when we battled for the prize and sailed it back triumphantly into Portsmouth Harbour. I miss the pleasure of opening the enemy's hold of riches and thrilling the crew with fistfuls of shillings at the end of their tour. This war's a hard one and there've been precious few rewards. These American ships are smaller, they carry fewer guns, and there's seldom any treasure to be gotten from them—when we do get them, that is. They're very good, these Americans. Their crews are fresher and their ships have been built with the best timber from these new American forests. They fight differently, too. Not like the French. Of course, as so many of them hail from England, they understand our tactics and our motivations. We've been softened by our numerous victories over the French." Fly held out his cup to be refilled by Weevil, who stood silently by with a silver coffee pot.

"Last night, when you questioned Emily, the name Thomas Trevelyan seemed to startle James," said Leander. "Am I right?"

Fly nodded. "I too caught his reaction, but he's a private person, our captain, and he's not spoken of it since."

"Are you acquainted with the name Trevelyan?"

Fly sipped on his second cup. "I am not, but our navy's a large one, with thousands of men, thousands of officers. I did question Mr. Harding, as he has sailed with James before. He felt 'Trevelyan' had a familiar ring to it. In fact, Harding thought he might have had something to do with a bit of objectionable business—back in '04—involving James and the *Isabelle*."

"What sort of business? What do you mean by that?"

"Why, the very torment of every last one of our sea captains—a mutiny."

Leander leaned back to regard Fly. "Captain Moreland? A mutiny? I cannot imagine his men rising up against him."

"My sentiments exactly. Unfortunately, Mr. Harding could provide me with few details of the affair. He said he'd once heard a rumour about it, but nothing more."

"But, a mutiny ... would the details not have been made public?"

"In this case ... apparently not; otherwise, I am sure *I* would have heard tell of it."

"So, it is possible that there is some connection between Trevelyan and this affair of '04?"

"Aye, and if there is, I am certain we shall find out in time."

Fly handed his cup and saucer to Weevil, thanked him, and lifted his face to receive the warmth of the sun. Leander followed suit. For a few minutes they were silent, enjoying the working seamen's chatter and the squawks of the seagulls circling the harbour.

"Your lady patient ... how does she fare?"

"She still lies in my cot, sleeps a great deal, and is greatly troubled, I fear."

"During your examination ..." Fly hesitated. "Did you find if she is carrying a child?"

Leander grinned. "Although it was unnecessary to examine her that fully, I can tell you she is not."

"If she stays on this ship much longer that may change."

"Have you been away from your wife too long, Mr. Austen?"

"I believe we've all been away from attractive women far too long, including you, Doctor." Fly clapped him on the back.

"We haven't been *that* long away from England."

"Yes, but you, my friend, have been far too long without a wife."

Leander looked out to sea.

"My sister, Jane, is still without a husband," continued Fly. "Brother Charles and I think you would make her a splendid husband. I know she's older and may not be able to provide you with ten children, which is what I intend to have, but you won't find a more amiable, intelligent companion anywhere."

"I don't believe Jane would be contented with a ship's physician who earns a few shillings a day and prefers the sea to setting up shop in an English parish."

"Perhaps you'll not always feel that way. Of course you know the Austen family would embrace you wholeheartedly."

"Maybe it's time you look elsewhere for dear Jane." Then, more cheerfully, Leander added, "But I am enjoying her *Sense and Sensibility* immensely. Although I do not possess his purse, I find myself sympathizing with her character Colonel Brandon. I must write to tell her so."

Fly's brown eyes narrowed. "You're reading a woman's novel? Such a great departure from the poetry of Robbie Burns and the stories of Walter Scott you claim to enjoy! And here I thought I had loaned the volumes to Gus Walby for Emily."

"You did, but I often listen in when he is reading aloud to her. It is my hope your sister's book will draw Emily out."

"You were saying she is troubled."

"Not being able to trust Osmund Brockley alone with her, I have spent my nights in the hospital. I have hung a cot near hers ..."

"Outside or inside the canvas?"

Leander pulled a face. "For the past two nights she's had nightmares and awakened with a cry." He did not tell Fly he'd given her laudanum to return to sleep.

"The ship she was on when the *Serendipity* attacked ..."

"She claims she cannot remember. I simply do not know."

"How is it Mr. Walby's gained access to our guest?"

"The boy is twelve and missing his mother. I'm hoping it will help him to be around such a woman, even if she is a troubled one. A bond is forming between them already. She's freely told him how she jumped from the *Serendipity*'s broken windows to make her escape.

Perhaps, between Mr. Walby and your sister's book, we'll gradually learn more about the mysterious Emily."

A sudden breeze tugged at Leander's black felt hat, compelling him to push it down further onto his forehead. "Tell me, Fly, how is it your bicorne stays on your head in these winds? I've yet to witness an officer losing his hat to the sea."

Fly slapped his knees. "That's my secret, my friend... Mr. Weevil, we're done with coffee. Some red wine now, if you please."

12:30 p.m.
(Afternoon Watch, One Bell)

CAPTAIN PRICKETT of HMS *Amethyst* drank heartily of the wine Biscuit set before him upon the rectangular oak table in Captain Moreland's private quarters. He was a heavy-set man of fifty, with three chins and a belly that could no longer be contained within his uniform coat. His first lieutenant, Lord Bridlington, was a fair-skinned, effeminate fellow with a long crooked nose, who preferred Biscuit's beef and potatoes to the red wine. The two men had been escorted to the *Isabelle* by two of their marine officers, who now waited outside the closed door conversing with the *Isabelle*'s purser, Mr. Spooner. Once pleasantries had been dispensed with and the men were well into their dinner, Captain Moreland leaned back in his red-velvet wing chair with a glass of wine.

"You say you have little news of the war, gentlemen?"

"There is not much to report, I'm afraid," said Mr. Prickett, eyeing the iced spice cake that Biscuit had baked from fresh provisions sent in from shore early that morning. "We've not been long from England."

"Aye, and we've yet to meet an enemy ship," said Mr. Bridlington, addressing the ceiling of the cabin as he spoke, "which makes the sailors very restless indeed for some action."

"What brings you to Bermuda?"

"We're to escort those three East India merchant vessels you saw anchored in the harbour on a round trip from Portsmouth to Bermuda to Halifax and finally on to Quebec." Captain Prickett snapped his fingers at a young servant boy standing quietly behind the first lieutenant's chair. "You there ... a piece of that cake wouldn't go amiss."

The servant boy jumped to do his bidding.

"What do the merchant vessels carry?" asked James.

As Captain Prickett's mouth was soon full of cake, Mr. Bridlington answered for him, his eyes, once again, turned to the ceiling. "Supplies of all kinds: livestock, tools, munitions, troops ... they even carry passengers bound for Upper and Lower Canada. Hardy fools, I say, leaving England at a time like this." He made a sucking sound with his red lips.

"So you've seen no one on your travels?"

"Aye, we did stop for a visit with the captain of the *Expedition* a few days out from Portsmouth. Captain Uptergrove was his name ..."

"William Uptergrove!" James's tired features sprang to life. "I served with him at St. Vincent. And he's still commanding the *Expedition*? Why, he's as old a relic as I am! And where had old Uptergrove been?"

"On a re-supplying mission to our interests in the Caribbean. He was able to provide us with the only war information gathered thus far." Captain Prickett shovelled another bite of cake into his mouth. "According to Uptergrove, we're not making much of an impact over here. Why, we've only eleven ships-of-the-line and thirty-four frigates trying to accomplish a variety of tasks: protecting the St. Lawrence, blockading American ports, escorting British merchant ships, hunting down enemy frigates—to name a few.

"Furthermore," said Captain Prickett, spraying bits of cake onto the oak table, "it is believed that up to ten per cent of the United States Navy consists of men of British origin. The question is: are they deserters or were they pressed into the service by the Americans?"

Mr. Bridlington clasped his delicate hands under his chin. "We're not faring much better on land. The number of our regulars is very low indeed. We are forced to fight alongside Indians. Quite frightening, really!"

Captain Prickett wiped his whiskered mouth with a napkin and examined the plates of unfinished food set before him. "We must soon finish our business with Old Boney; otherwise, this Yankee campaign will be our undoing."

Biscuit came into the cabin with the silver coffee pot.

"Ah, coffee would be nice. And I'll have more beef and potatoes. Your beans are quite good too, Moreland. We won't be seeing fresh vegetables again for a time."

Amusement registered in James's faded blue eyes.

"The day before we met with Captain Uptergrove, his *Expedition* had come upon a most mournful scene," said Mr. Bridlington. He dropped four teaspoonfuls of sugar into his coffee cup before casting his gaze upwards. "A British merchant ship robbed and its hull beaten to a pulp most dreadfully before being burned about fifty miles southeast of Halifax. It was sinking when the *Expedition* first spotted it in a telescope and Uptergrove said there was a terrible carnage drifting on the water."

James straightened in his chair. "And its crew? Were there any survivors?"

"By the time Uptergrove arrived on the scene, a good number were floating lifelessly on the water," said Prickett, his face now flushed with good food and wine. "He was, however, able to rescue a babbling old woman, a wounded young man whose injuries had rendered him unconscious, and a child."

"That's *all*?" asked Captain Moreland. "Could the old woman provide Mr. Uptergrove with any information?"

"Apparently she had quite lost her wits. Uptergrove could only glean that they'd been bound for Upper Canada and that it'd been an American ship that had struck them before dawn."

James became irate. "If she was a merchant ship, why the devil was she destroyed by an American warship? Stealing her crew and cargo I can understand, but such barbaric destruction I cannot."

"Quite a mystery, isn't it?" said Mr. Bridlington, shaking his thin face.

"How many weeks back did this occur, gentlemen?"

"Four perhaps," said Captain Prickett, just then discharging a tremendous fart. "Good Heavens, excuse me, gentlemen. It must have been that exquisite cut of beef."

Mr. Bridlington giggled. But James took no notice. He leaned back thoughtfully in his red-velvet chair and studied the rich colour of his wine.

4

Sunday, June 6

9:00 a.m.
(Forenoon Watch, Two Bells)

"'*... She played over every favourite song that she had been used to play with Willoughby, every air in which their voices had been oftenest joined, and sat at the instrument gazing on every line of music that he had written for her, till her heart was so heavy that no farther sadness could be gained ...*'"

"Gus, could I ask you to stop your reading for now?" Emily pleaded from her bed.

Beyond the canvas curtain, Leander paused in his letter writing.

"Are you tired?" asked Gus.

"Tired? How could I be? I've done nothing but sleep for the past several days. No, I am not tired, but this part in the novel is so sad."

"Shall I come back this evening before my watch?"

"Please do. You read so well. I am sure I could not read that well when I was your age."

Gus reluctantly closed the book. "Who taught you to read, Em?"

Emily thought a moment before answering. Crooking her finger, she invited Gus to come closer and whispered, "Am I correct in believing—nay, in hoping—that our conversations are just between you and me?"

Gus was taken aback. "Of course they are!"

"Well, then, I shall tell you. Would you believe a string of tutors and governesses taught me to read?"

"Why so many? Were you a naughty child?"

"No, it was my father. He had a cruel streak in him, and being a man of great wealth figured he could exercise it upon my poor teachers. They were all wonderful, but that didn't stop him from dismissing them at will."

Gus angled his head. "Perhaps your father, being a man of great wealth, knew Lord Lindsay's father, as he is the Duke of Belmont."

"I am sure he must have. My father travelled in many circles, Gus." Suspicious that Leander would be straining to lend an ear to their quiet conversation, Emily called out to him. "Doctor? May I trouble you a moment?"

She smiled at the scrape of his chair.

His auburn head peeked around the canvas. Even behind his round spectacles, the doctor had striking eyes, Emily thought.

"Doctor, I've been deteriorating in your cot far too long... not that I don't appreciate you giving up your cot... but I wondered if I might walk above deck to air my lungs... and exercise my one good leg. It would be nice to see Bermuda before we leave."

"I'm afraid I'd have to consult with Captain Moreland." Leander stepped farther into her little corner. "Women are not usually allowed to move freely above deck at sea."

"He may give his consent, Doctor, as we are anchored," said Gus. He looked back at Emily and added, "Although the sight of you on the weather decks might cause the men to fall from their yardarms."

Emily laughed, but Gus was quite serious.

"If I were fitted out with a walking stick and maybe a pair of Biscuit's old trousers? A straw hat would hide my hair... then again, I do recall seeing men with hair longer than mine when first I came on board. Surely, if appropriately outfitted, no one would guess my identity."

While Gus regarded him anxiously, Leander tried to hide his amusement with one freckled hand.

"As your doctor, I would strongly recommend fresh air and exercise; still, I must seek permission from the captain."

Emily was disheartened. "I recall being allowed to wander freely on the weather decks of ships when I was a child—" She caught herself, and for a moment stared at Leander, praying he had taken no notice of her incautious words. Seeing him raise an inquisitive eyebrow, she looked away and said no more on the subject.

At length, he replied, "I am sure *much* has changed since then."

Gus's eyes shone. "I will go see the captain straightaway." He dashed off before Leander could stop him.

"Doctor," said Emily, hoping to steer the conversation in a new direction, "might it be possible for someone, other than Mrs. Kettle, to lend me some clothes?"

Leander smiled broadly as he took off his spectacles. "I believe Mr. Austen has asked Magpie to sew something together for you."

"Magpie?"

"Our sail maker. He's brilliant with a needle and thread."

"You are all very kind."

"I would advise you against taking exercise in my nightshirt."

Emily smoothed the muslin shirt she wore. "I thought this might belong to you."

Unable to hold her gaze, Leander examined the ceiling boards above his head.

"I could see you writing a letter at your desk," said Emily.

"Could you?"

"Were you writing to someone back home?"

"I was, as a matter of fact."

Emily tried to urge him onward with her eyes, but she did not meet with success.

"Is there someone to whom you would like to send a letter?" he asked. "I could arrange for you to be given parchment and ink."

Emily shook her head. "No."

"Right, then, I'd better return to it while we await the captain's word." He left her abruptly.

No sooner had Leander reinstated himself at his desk than Gus, breathless from his errand, rushed into the hospital shouting, "Dr. Braden, sir!"

"Mr. Walby," Leander scolded, "please remember my patients here require peace and quiet."

Mr. Harding piped up. "You kidding? We haven't had a moment's peace since that woman moved into your hammock."

"You're not complaining now, are you, Mr. Harding?" asked Leander. From his pillow the sailing master gave him a wink and a cluck. Leander turned back to Gus.

"Captain Moreland said it was fine, sir."

"Did he now?"

"On one condition," Gus added.

"And that condition is . . . ?"

"He said that if one man falls from the rigging and breaks his neck, Emily's to be sent packing below deck for all time."

In her corner, Emily laughed out loud.

9:30 a.m.
(Forenoon Watch, Three Bells)

GUS'S NEXT ERRAND was a visit to the sail room on the orlop deck to see whether Magpie had completed his task. He found the young sail maker sitting cross-legged on the floor amongst his tools and yards of canvas. His tiny room, crammed with rolls of fresh sails, was poorly ventilated and illuminated with only one lantern. It amazed Gus that Magpie could do such wonderful work in such small quarters.

Magpie set aside the sail he was stitching and looked up hopefully. "Have ya come fer the clothes, sir?"

"Captain Moreland said she could go for a walk on the weather decks, but not in Dr. Braden's nightshirt."

"I bin waitin' fer someone to come fetch 'em. I had 'em all done yesterday, sir." Magpie sprang to his feet and carefully picked up the neatly folded bundle on his stool. "Did the cap'n say I could meet her, sir?"

"I didn't ask him, but I don't see why not."

"Should I wash up first, sir?"

"You're quite presentable as you are."

Magpie plucked his flute from the jumble of blankets on his bed and held it up. "Do ya suppose I could play her a tune? She might like knowin' I 'ave a bit o' refinement."

Gus shook his head. "Music is forbidden in Dr. Braden's hospital. Come along then."

Tingling with excitement, Magpie followed Gus up two decks, through the animals' stable, the grog room, the sailors' galley, and the mess before reaching the hospital ward. As there were still some sections of the *Isabelle* he had never seen before, his eyes were open to everything around him. When Gus and Magpie entered the hospital, Mr. Harding called out, "Magpie, I hope illness is not forcing you to join us."

"No, sir. I'm quite well. I do hope yer foot's feelin' better."

Mr. Harding breathed in and exhaled sadly. "As my foot is swimming in the sea, I'm certain it is feeling better than it ever has before, unless, of course, it's been chewed upon by a hungry shark."

"Won't be no shark chewin' on yer foot," called out the sailor in the neighbouring hammock, "so long as it spotted Mr. Crump's tasty leg first."

Mr. Crump grumbled his displeasure at the lot of them making jokes at the expense of his lost leg, shut his eyes, and pretended to be asleep.

Leander folded up his letter and rose from his desk to greet the little sail maker. "She's just beyond that curtain, Magpie."

In the dimness of the hospital, Magpie's eyes sparkled as he followed Gus.

Emily was sitting up in her cot. The moment she saw Magpie, surprise transformed her features.

"Mornin', ma'am," he said, thrusting out his small right hand.

"They call me Magpie on account o' me black hair, and 'cause I talk all the time and get into trouble a lot."

"What is your real name?" Emily asked, taking his hand in hers. There was a half-moon of grime under each of his fingernails.

"Haven't a clue, ma'am. I never had no family to give me a proper name. Only name I ever bin called is Magpie."

"How old are you?"

"When they measure me against Mr. Walby here, they figure I'm about ten."

"And you're a sail maker?"

"Aye, ma'am ... learned the trade from old Beck Bailey, who was hankerin' fer a promotion. He wanted to be a bo's'n, but he don't read none. The cap'n—not Cap'n Moreland mind—promised him work above deck if he'd teach me the sail makin'. First learned it when I was seven."

"Seven? That young? And you can make clothes too?"

"Aye, ma'am. I make 'em and I repair 'em. I hope ya like 'em." He proudly held out his little bundle.

As she accepted them, Emily thought her heart would burst. "I'm sure I will."

"We'll wait outside, Em," Gus said, jabbing Magpie with his elbow.

"And if ya be needin' any alt'rations, ma'am, I'll be standin' by."

Emily took a deep breath when they had closed up the curtain. For a time she fingered the workmanship of the jacket and trousers, her dark brown eyes fixed upon the sea beyond the open gunport, then with a determined shake of her head, she called out, "Dr. Braden? Are you still out there?"

"I am."

"May I ask you something?"

He poked his head round, catching her brushing away a tear.

"I have no interest in seeing Mrs. Kettle again, but I do require some assistance. Would you help me?"

Fully aware that an audience of men and boys stood eavesdropping a few yards away, Leander gave her a quick nod. He took a step towards her then stopped, not certain where to begin.

She looked up at him questioningly, and quietly said, "Should we take off the nightshirt while I'm still in the cot?"

"Of course." He smiled uneasily as he came closer.

Trying her best not to cry out in pain, Emily eased the shirt up around her legs. She took another deep breath. "Can you take it from here, Doctor?"

"Do you feel up to this, Emily?"

She attempted to smile. "Up to what, Doctor—taking exercise on the weather decks or having you take off my nightshirt?"

The hospital walls thundered with the mirthful howling of its occupants. Leander turned scarlet.

"If there is any more laughter out there," he yelled over his shoulder, "I'll give you all a shot of laudanum that will put you out for days."

Instantaneously, a hush descended upon the hospital.

"Well done, Doctor," Emily whispered.

Knowing her shoulder was still raw, Leander slid the nightdress over Emily's head as carefully as he could. Underneath, she wore her chemise and his eyes passed over her breasts. His hands shook slightly. The feel of her soft hair, those dark expressive eyes of hers, the interesting curves of her face ... she was beautiful. He picked up the blue jacket that Magpie had sewn for her and helped her into the sleeves one at a time, certain he could hear the men's laboured breathing in the distance. Once Emily had done up her jacket's brass buttons, he leaned over her cot and murmured, "Now, I'll pull the trousers on over that ankle of yours." She shuddered as he touched her feet.

He turned his head towards her. "Did I hurt you?"

"No, I'm ... quite fine." Emily held her breath while he gently hiked the trousers up her legs.

"Now, I hope you can finish the last bit."

He walked over to the open gunport, his back to her as she struggled with the trousers. Pulling them over her hips and up to her waist, Emily had to stifle the urge to laugh when she noticed the flap front. Then, kicking off her blankets, she hooked her legs over the side of her hammock. "Ready for step two, Doctor."

Leander spun around, knowing his face was still flushed, and observed her figure in the sailor's clothing as discreetly as possible.

"Ah, you'll be needing shoes!" He dashed to a cupboard in the wall and opened its door to reveal three shelves on which he had neatly arranged his own hats, shirts, and cravats. He pulled out a straw hat and her blue silk slippers. "Before you went for your swim the other day," he said, holding up the slippers, "you smartly tucked these into your jacket." Kneeling down, he placed them onto her feet.

"I don't know how well they'll wear climbing the ship's rigging and spars," said Emily, "but they do match my new jacket."

Leander looked at her thoughtfully. "I have never known a *farmer's daughter* who was able to climb the rigging and spars of a ship."

"In another lifetime, Doctor, I—" She forced a smile rather than finishing her sentence.

Leander held out his straw hat to her. "Maybe we could save spar climbing for another day."

Emily gathered up the long waves of her hair with the stronger of her two arms. When she was done, Leander popped the hat on her head.

"Right, now, lean forward a bit," he whispered.

As she did so, he moved in so close to her face that she could smell the pleasant muskiness of his shirt. He placed one of his slender arms around her back and eased her out of the hammock and onto the floor.

"Mr. Walby," he called out, "we're ready for you now."

Gus burst through the curtains as if on cue, waving a walking cane. Reaching across the hammock, Leander took the cane, handed it to Emily, and stood back to watch as she hobbled like a happy child towards the curtain. Gus held it open for her. In the hospital room, the men looked on from their hammocks with a curiosity to rival a group of elderly women observing couples at a ball.

"Emily," said Leander, avoiding his patients' stares, "the winds are strong on deck. Mind the hat."

11:00 a.m.
(Forenoon Watch, Six Bells)

"SIR, THE DOCTOR has allowed that *woman* to wander freely above deck."

Octavius, whose pimply face was red and puffy from the hot Bermudian sun, interrupted James as he conferred next to the capstan with Mr. Harding, who, following Emily's example, had obtained from Dr. Braden a crutch and an admonition against over-exerting himself, and left his hospital cot to resume his duties. There was much to discuss, as the *Isabelle* would be leaving Bermuda later that day.

Jerking his head up, James squinted into the sun to search the decks within his sight. "I cannot see her anywhere, Mr. Lindsay."

"She's standing with Gus Walby and Magpie—of all people—by the fore ladders."

James looked again. "I see Mr. Walby and young Magpie, but by the stars, I see no woman dressed in a corselet and chemise."

Octavius compressed his lips in annoyance. "Sir, the Admiralty clearly states that no woman, be she an officer's wife or a cook, appear above deck while at sea."

"I'm well versed in navy rules, thank you. Need I remind you we are anchored in port?"

The first lieutenant pointed towards the mainmast's yardarm. "See how the men pause in their chores to watch her."

James and Mr. Harding both looked up, shading their eyes from the bright sun.

"They are doing a fine job keeping their eyes in their heads and on their tasks," Mr. Harding said, shifting his weight about.

"Which is more than I can say for *you*, Mr. Lindsay." James stared at him long and hard until Octavius looked away.

"Sir! The men don't have to look at Meg Kettle in the darkness of their cots. We are not all true gentlemen here."

Aware of the men toiling nearby, James dropped his voice. "We may have beggars and thieves from Newgate prison on board, but as far as I know there are only honourable men among us."

"Captain Moreland, I fear ... I fear you are growing soft." No sooner had he uttered the words than Octavius regretted them, as he watched James's face change colour.

"Mr. Lindsay," James hissed through his teeth, "I will not make a scene here. Meet me in the wardroom at two bells."

Octavius opened his mouth, but said no more. He saluted and swiftly strode off.

Mr. Harding waited until James's complexion had regained its normal pallor. "Forgive me, sir ... that young man ... I know you're well acquainted with his father, but that bold tongue of his deserves a flogging."

"Like his father, Mr. Lindsay is hotheaded and impulsive." James's glance locked on the young sailor who limped alongside Magpie and Gus Walby. "But he is right."

"How so, sir?"

"I *am* growing soft."

ONCE GUS HAD HELPED Emily negotiate the ladder to the fo'c'sle deck, he apologized to her. "My lesson with Mr. Austen begins shortly. I must leave you here. But you'll be quite safe with Magpie." His eyes brightened. "Today we're studying the signal flags and communications at sea. It's my most favourite subject of all."

"Then you must go. I'm not concerned for my safety, although I had my doubts trying to get out of the doctor's hammock." She gave a satisfied glance around the ship. "Just tell me, is there a quiet place where I may sit with Magpie and enjoy this fresh air?"

"Aye, on the poop deck. You'll find it quiet there this time of day. Unfortunately, it's at the very back of the ship and it will mean more ladders to climb. The quarterdeck is closer, but if you're caught loitering there, you'll most likely be ordered to 'shove off,' as only officers and midshipmen may stroll there during their leisure hours. Shall I escort you to the poop deck before I go to class?"

"Thank you, I'll manage with Mr. Magpie."

Hobbling along the fo'c'sle deck with her walking cane, Emily drew no stares. The doctor's straw hat hid her long, fair hair, and the baggy trousers and waist-length jacket Magpie had fashioned for her disguised her female form. She had supposed her blue silk shoes would be a dead giveaway, but no one seemed interested in her feet. Moreover, Gus had assured her that several of the men were new to the *Isabelle*, and thus many faces were still foreign to one another.

As if reading her thoughts, Magpie piped up, "Ya'll get away with it today, ma'am, but tonight at supper they'll be askin' me the name of the sailor I was walkin' with at noon."

"Do you not get leisure time?"

"Aye, but they don't usually see the likes of Magpie up on the poop deck."

"In that case, let's just sit here."

Emily and Magpie perched themselves upon two overturned barrels alongside the starboard railing of the ship's waist, and there fell quiet to appreciate the scenes around them. The decks were teeming with sailors—toiling, talking, taking leisure—reminding Emily of a busy street in London minus the coiffed ladies in their bonnets and redingotes. High on the yardarms, the men stood precariously on their footropes, letting down the sails in preparation for their return to the sea. Those on the mast platforms watched the empty horizons for enemy sails. They were like birds in a mountain nest, isolated and free. She longed to be up there with them and determined she would be once her ankle and shoulder had healed.

Following Magpie's gaze out over the square, stone buildings in the dockyard and the low, mossy-green hills of Ireland Island, Emily noticed there was only one other ship in port beyond the *Isabelle*, a small two-masted vessel with an unusually bright red hull. HMS *Amethyst* and the three East India merchantmen, of which she'd overheard Dr. Braden speaking to Mr. Harding in the hospital earlier, must have departed, she thought. Emily had hoped to catch a glimpse of the

Amethyst's Captain Prickett and First Lieutenant Bridlington, as their manners and fondness for the *Isabelle*'s food had apparently provided Captain Moreland with a good amount of entertainment.

Pulling her eyes away from the thickets of mangrove and hedges of oleander that lay beyond the naval buildings, Emily was surprised to find Magpie studying her face with interest, much as Captain Moreland and Fly Austen had the night of their interrogation. Quickly he looked away, furtively slipping a gilded object into his trousers pocket, and turning his attention to the stretch of new canvas that whispered above his head.

"What is that you have there?" Emily asked, referring to her tantalizing glimpse of gold.

"Aw, it ain't nothing," said Magpie, still looking at the sail. He pointed upwards. "Ain't she a beauty, ma'am? I sewed her meself."

"Yes," Emily said absently. It was her turn to study him. His eyes were almond-shaped, fringed with long black lashes, and his dark curls blew with abandon in the warm breeze. His little fingers were stained black and his leather shoes had lost their heels, but his trousers, shirt, and red necktie were all clean, and the stitches around the patches were neat and even. There was a catch in her throat as she asked, "Where did you live before joining the navy, Magpie?"

"In London, ma'am. I was a chummy, a climbin' boy."

"A climbing boy? Do you mean you cleaned chimneys?"

"That I did. Still can't get the soot out o' me nails."

"What a horrible time you must have had."

"Oh, aye, and I had a mean boss—Mr. Hardy was his name. He stood around eatin' meat pasties while I climbed the dark flues. And if I didn't wanna go up, he'd prick me feet with a pin. I've burns on me legs and arms, and me lungs don't take kindly to colds."

"How did you ever escape Mr. Hardy?"

"I didn't jump out o' no windows, ma'am," he said with an impish grin. "Nay, I was climbin' at a big house one day and I had a fall. Bruised meself badly. The man o' the house was kind enough to give me water and let me rest awhile on his couch. He gave Mr. Hardy a terrible tongue lashin' on account o' me bad treatment, and ordered

Mr. Hardy to leave his house at once, sayin' I would be stayin' with him. Imagine me surprise! His wife was kind too. She give me the best dinner I've ever eaten and told me to eat up 'til me sides busted. I remember it still: roast o' pork an' potatoes, a kind o' mint sauce, biscuits, cheese, and a baked bread puddin'." He sighed at the memory. "It was grand. After dinner the man asked me if I wanted a postin' on a sailin' ship. Said he was a big gun in the Royal Navy and could get me a post if I was keen. Course I didn't wanna go back climbin' so I jumped at the chance."

"Who was this saviour of yours?"

There was mischievous glint in Magpie's eyes and his thin chest swelled as he proudly said, "He was called the Duke o' Clarence."

Emily's mouth fell open. "The—the Duke of Clarence? Our King George's son?"

"One 'n' the same, ma'am."

"That is astounding!" Her dark eyes danced as she clapped together her bandaged hands in merriment. "Imagine you making the acquaintance of the Duke of Clarence."

Magpie's smile vanished. "Why? 'Cause I ain't nobody?"

"Oh, I didn't mean it in that vein, Magpie. I just think the poor duke has long been criticized for his lifestyle and politics and here he's shown true kindness to the *Isabelle*'s sail maker."

"D'ya know him too, ma'am?"

Emily shrank back on her barrel. "No. I've just read about him in the newspapers. That is all."

For a moment Magpie's almond eyes watched her, as if expecting her to say more, but when she did not, his expression changed and he peeked up shyly at her. "Do ya like the clothes I made fer ya, ma'am?"

"Your handiwork is truly exquisite! I look every inch a sailor now, do I not?" Emily leaned closer to him. "Everything is perfect and yet … I cannot guess how it fits me so well."

"Dr. Braden helped me guess yer … yer proportions, ma'am."

"Did he now?" Emily grinned pensively.

"*Magpie!* Why aren't you below sewing our sails?"

The low voice startled Magpie, who sprang off his barrel to salute the young man with the bandaged left hand who stood before them.

"You don't have to salute me," the man said.

"Aye, but I do, sir. Yer a carpenter's mate and higher on the scale than me."

"Nonsense," the carpenter's mate replied. His hair was long and shaggy, and beneath his knitted hat, which resembled a long sock, his tanned face was familiar. He jerked his paint-splattered thumb towards Emily.

"Who's your pal, Magpie?"

The boy faltered, his eyes darting nervously between Emily and the carpenter's mate.

"Mr. George, midshipman, at your service, sir," Emily said loudly, raising a fist to the brim of her straw hat in salute.

The young man looked wary as he returned the salute. "How do you do? Morgan Evans is my name ... sir." His stare flickered beneath her face and settled on her silk slippers. "You must be one of the new ones on the *Isabelle*. Welcome aboard, Mr. George."

"Thank you, sir."

There was the faintest hint of a smile on his lips as he nodded and sauntered on down the deck.

"Ya didn't fool Mr. Evans, ma'am."

"Apparently not." Emily watched after him until she could no longer discern his funny hat amongst the throng of sailors.

"He's the one what plucked ya from the sea."

"I thought he looked familiar."

"Beg yer pardon, ma'am, but if ya wanna pretend you're a midshipman, ya don't hafta salute a carpenter's mate like Mr. Evans."

"I have much to learn ..." Emily's voice trailed off as she caught sight of a young officer standing against the quarterdeck railing, his chin raised in challenge, glaring down upon her with his dark, penetrating eyes.

"Who's that, Magpie?" she whispered, nodding in the direction of the insolent observer.

"That's Lord Lindsay, ma'am." Magpie shivered. "I ... I don't like him much."

1:00 p.m.
(Afternoon Watch, Two Bells)

When the air resounded with two bells, Magpie had to resume his duties, even though, unbeknownst to Emily, he had missed his dinner to sit with her. Emily couldn't help feeling sad. Her taste of freedom had been all too brief and she had enjoyed their discussions on naval regulations, the fine art of sail sewing, and Biscuit's culinary repertoire. Unable to wander the decks alone, she reluctantly began her trek back to the hospital, telling her little companion he didn't need to assist her. "I'll have to make my own way around the *Isabelle* sooner or later."

Having successfully managed the first ladder down to the upper deck, she found herself outside the officers' wardroom. Behind the closed door came two voices raised in anger. She recognized one as the captain's, but was not certain of the other. Emily slowed her pace in an attempt to hear their words.

"It's one thing giving that woman freedom to exercise above deck; it's quite another allowing her to trifle with the likes of Magpie and Morgan Evans on the main deck."

"Magpie is a boy of ten."

"Mr. Evans, however, is not."

There was a crash as if someone's fist had found a tabletop. "Enlighten me here. I fail to understand your concerns, brought on by an abundance of grog no doubt..."

Emily's heart stopped when the floorboards creaked behind her. A stench of perspiration and rotting teeth struck her nose with the force of a club. A growling voice breathed down her neck.

"Lost yer way, sailor?"

"Aye, sir. If you please, which way to the hospital?"

It was Biscuit, the cook, carrying a tray of wine, sweets, and goblets. He resembled a flame with his shock of orange hair standing straight up on his forehead. One of his eyes widened in delight, while the other—horribly out of alignment—searched about for her. His long grey sideburns were sprinkled with food crumbs, as were his chest hairs, which sprang from his open-necked checked shirt like a stowed animal struggling to escape.

"Yer arse backwards, sailor. Thee hospital's in thee front o' thee ship and yer in thee back." He lowered his peculiar eyes to her right foot. "Seein' as yer crippled, would ya like me to carry ya there after I take thee wine in to Captain Moreland?"

"I can manage."

"Yer an awfully *pretty* young sailor. I'd be watchin' meself wand'rin' thee decks alone, especially in yer condition."

"I appreciate the warning, sir."

Unable to endure Biscuit's odour, Emily stumbled away from him and made for the nearest passageway. She found herself in the sailors' mess and, uncertain of the path back to the hospital, stood there awkwardly, the room stretching dauntingly before her like a bridgeless gorge. The dinner hour was over, but several men lingered, swilling their mugs of beer, enjoying their leisure time with their mates. They sat in groups, reclining on benches, barrels, and sea chests, and at the tables sandwiched between the menacing carronades lying silent in their open gunports. Hanging on a hook above each table was a swinging bucket of steaming food, and nailed to the walls were racks of wooden spoons and bowls.

Emily beheld the boisterous scene before her, relieved that the sailors were preoccupied with a variety of pursuits: gambling, arguing, singing, arm wrestling, and blowing tunes on flutes. In all her eighteen years, she had never been in a room with so many men. She could hear the thump of her heart and was shocked to admit it was not anxiety that caused its rapid beating.

It was not long before she was noticed. One by one, the men slapped one another and gestured in her direction. They ceased their flute playing, paused in their wrestling, and quit arguing long enough to take a good long look at the newcomer with the walking cane. A strange hush permeated the mess where only moments before there had been hilarity and din. Emily could hear a whistle blowing above deck, and beyond the gunports the squawk of the seagulls. A flush crept up her neck.

An enormous shirtless fellow with a squashed-in nose and peg leg spun around on his bucket to look her up and down. "Nice shoes, sailor," he shouted, causing his mates to erupt into laughter. From behind the heckler, Morgan Evans's face appeared.

"You're speaking to a midshipman, Jacko. I didn't see ya salute."

"A mid?" Jacko's thick features displayed shock. "I ain't never seen a mid wearin' blue silk shoes."

"It's Mr. George." Morgan gave Emily a respectful nod. "Sir."

"Ah, Mr. George, come 'ave a drink with us." Jacko raised a hammy arm to her.

There was more laughter and muttered remarks. It was impossible for Emily to respond as her throat had gone dry. She stood there like a gaping idiot, uncertain of what to do. Then behind her came a familiar reek, and a clap on the back that would have sent her sprawling across the floor had Jacko not caught her with one of his huge hands.

"Come sit a while, Mr. George, sir," said Biscuit, steering her towards Morgan's table. "These lads here—thee ones admirin' yer shoes—just happen to be me messmates. Shove over lads so our friend can join us." Biscuit pushed Emily down hard on the bench, compressing her between Morgan and Jacko, then, finding a space for himself across the table from them, he snapped his fingers at the nearest servant lad. "You there, boyo, fetch me two mugs o' beer."

Gradually the noise in the mess resumed as the men returned to their various amusements. Emily sat frozen between Jacko's sweaty bare flesh and Morgan, who had quietly pulled his woollen sock off his head, while eight pairs of inquisitive eyes fixed themselves on her reddened face.

"Mr. George's been in thee hospital these past days and hasn't had a drop to drink 'cause—as we all know—Doc Braden don't allow spirits in his domain." Biscuit took the mugs from the hovering servant boy and handed one to Emily. "Now, drink up, young lad. This stuff is sure to put hair on yer chest." He winked his good eye at her.

Emily sipped the horrid, watery stuff, forcing herself to swallow it rather than spit it all over Jacko, as she would have liked to do. Morgan leaned his right arm on the table and cradled his head on his upturned hand to look at her. "There's no fear of you getting drunk if you're going to drink your beer that way."

"Mr. George," said Jacko, showing her two rows of green teeth, "ya look like a regular fop in them shoes. Don't want the other lads thinkin' yer a bit of a Beau Brummel now, do ya? They may get the wrong idea about ya. Now, seein' as I'm the shoemaker here on the *Isabelle*, how be I knock ya up a pair o' sensible black leathers? And if yer agreeable to partin' with a couple o' pounds, I can arrange to put silver buckles on 'em."

Finally Emily found her voice, though it was a good deal softer than she would have liked. "I'm afraid I have no money." She took another sip of beer, this time a larger one, and grimaced as it went down. It tasted as if it had been brewed with Biscuit's bath water.

The men roared."You! A mid! Wearing silk shoes, and ya say ya 'ave no money?"

"Young fella like you must 'ave a rich family."

"Don't tell me they sent ya to sea without a shillin' to yer name?"

Emily gulped down more beer and confirmed the sailors' remarks with a nod of her head.

"But lads, ain't Mr. George a pretty boy?" said Biscuit, raising his beer mug. "Maybe he could earn his silver buckles. Ha, ha, ha!"

"Jacko here's fond o' pretty boys such as yerself," said a sailor with a swarthy complexion and bloodshot eyes.

"Mind ya'd have to keep it quiet from thee cap'n," said Biscuit. "Cap'n Moreland don't stand fer no mischief. If he catches ya, he'll have ya strung up on thee yardarm."

Morgan watched the colour drain from Emily's face. "Pay them no heed, Mr. George." He smacked her playfully on her right shoulder. An agony of pain tore through her body and she doubled over, but rather than cry out she hid in her beer mug and choked down the contents.

"You there, boyo." Biscuit snapped his fingers again at the servant boy who stood nearby. "More beer fer our friend here."

When Emily's pain subsided and she'd caught her breath, she set down her drink and glanced up to find Dr. Braden standing over the mess table.

"Doc, what brings ya to this part o' thee world?" asked Biscuit, his bad eye rolling in his orange head.

Dr. Braden slid his spectacles down his nose and gazed upon Emily with a look of incredulity. All eight of the sailors stared at her as she sank lower on the bench, trying to disappear behind Jacko's mountain of flesh. "I've come to fetch an errant patient of mine," he said coolly.

"Ah, but as Mr. George here's off duty, he was gonna have another beer with us," said Biscuit.

Dr. Braden frowned and looked around the table at each of the men. "Mr. George?"

Jacko put his slippery arm around Emily. "I'm gonna make 'im a new pair o' black leathers so he won't look such a fop in them silk shoes."

Leander's face relaxed. "Oh, I see. Mr. George. You threw me off, gentlemen, since I know Mr. George by another name."

Emily opened her mouth to explain herself and instead emitted a magnificent burp. The men crowded around her rocked with convulsive laughter.

Morgan grinned. "We'll have him toughened up in no time, Doc." In disgrace, Emily pulled the rim of her straw hat down over her eyes.

Above deck, the bell rang out and a shout was issued. "All hands, sails aloft."

The men swilled their drinks, gathered their cards, quit their benches, buckets, and sea chests, and hurried towards the nearest hatches. While Emily watched in remorse as they scattered, she noticed Mr. Lindsay, the young officer with the challenging stare, standing rigidly to one side of the door through which she had entered the mess, his beady black eyes locked on her. She shuddered.

"We'll be leaving Bermuda, sir," said Morgan to Dr. Braden. Then to Emily, "Come have a beer with us lads again tomorrow, Mr. George, sir." He put a fist to his woollen hat in salute. Emily sat there, red-faced, and said nothing.

When the mess had almost cleared, Biscuit turned to Dr. Braden. "Seein' as his ankle's troublesome, shall I carry him back to thee hospital fer ya, Doc?"

From under her hat Emily ventured a peek up at Leander and saw his jaw working. In her woozy state, she could not be sure whether it was a flash of anger or twinkle of enjoyment she detected in his sea-blue eyes. Pushing herself up from the bench with the aid of her walking stick, she answered for herself. "Certainly not, Biscuit. Just . . . just lead the way, if you please."

7:30 p.m.
(Second Dog Watch, Three Bells)

"ARE YA AWAKE, MISS?"

Against the dim light of the hospital lanterns, Emily could see the silhouette of Osmund Brockley, standing outside her curtain, holding her supper in his hands.

"I am, Mr. Brockley. Come in."

He stooped low as he passed through the canvas, carefully cradling her bowl of jellied green soup. "Biscuit sends the pea soup with his compliments and wants ya to know he made a special pudding fer yer dessert."

"How kind of him," Emily said, inching her body up against her pillow. "I didn't hear the supper bell."

Osmund pulled a wooden spoon from his pocket, wiped it off on his apron, and dropped it into the bowl before handing it off to Emily. "Supper was over long ago, Miss. Ya been sleeping awhile."

"Where is Dr. Braden?"

"Dining with Captain Moreland and his officers in the wardroom," he said, rolling his thick tongue around his cracked lips.

No doubt the men's supper conversation was colourful, thought Emily. What she wouldn't give to have been a fly on those walls! She suddenly became aware of the rise and fall of the ship. "We're at sea, Mr. Brockley?"

"Aye, we pulled anchor hours ago, Miss." He pulled in his tongue to give her a grin. "Yer exercise above deck must have tuckered ya out."

"It did indeed," she said, avoiding his bright eyes. "Thank you for the soup."

"Holler when ya want yer pudding."

Osmund gawked at her a moment, then left. Emily dipped the spoon into the thick green muck and slowly brought it to her mouth, banishing all thoughts of its cook and his crumby whiskers.

Later on, as she finished the last of her pudding and contemplated a dull, restless evening, she heard tentative steps approaching. Gus Walby cleared his throat.

"Come in. Please."

Gus slipped through the curtain into her corner and stood by her hammock holding *Sense and Sensibility*. Emily could see that his blue eyes were full of excitement.

"Have you come to rescue me from my boredom?"

"I promised to come and read to you before my watch."

"But the First Watch has already begun, has it not?"

"*My* watch begins at midnight. I've never done the Middle Watch before. Captain Moreland must have confidence in me for we'll soon be entering enemy waters again."

"May I watch with you? I'd give anything to be away from this bed."

Gus's cheeks reddened. "You'd better not, Em. You caused quite a stir this afternoon." He reached for the stool at the foot of her hammock and sat down upon it. "When you didn't return to the hospital, Dr. Braden asked me to look for you, as he had his hands full stitching up the head of a sailor that'd fallen from the shrouds. But I couldn't find you anywhere. I was mad at myself for leaving you, but I never thought Magpie would have led you to the mess."

"Magpie did no such thing! When it was time for him to return to his duties, I told him I was quite capable of finding my own way back to the hospital. I soon discovered I was quite lost and not capable at all."

"Is it true, Em? Were you really drinking beer with Biscuit and his mates?"

"Did Dr. Braden tell you that?"

"Oh, no." Gus lowered his voice to a whisper. "I was invited to dine with the officers this evening and it was there that Mr. Lindsay announced he'd been informed you were drinking beer with a group of men that were saying lewd things to you. All Dr. Braden said was it was obvious the men had no idea they were in the presence of a lady; otherwise, they wouldn't have been so vulgar."

Emily leaned closer to Gus. "Is this Mr. Lindsay the same man that teaches you writing?"

"Aye, he's a first lieutenant."

"Fascinating!" Emily said, more to herself than to Gus.

"Were you quite offended by the men's remarks?"

"Not at all. I've had occasion to hear far worse. It's not just men on the sea who misbehave."

Gus looked embarrassed. "I shouldn't have said anything at all..." His voice trailed off when Dr. Braden entered the hospital. In one brisk action, Gus opened Jane Austen's novel and randomly began to read.

In the lamplight, Emily could see Leander's shadow stop next to his desk, where he raised his head and stood unmoving as if listening to Gus's reading. For a full chapter, he stayed in that position, and when it was complete, he called out, "It's late, Mr. Walby."

"Good night, Em. Sleep well. I hope we can continue tomorrow."

Emily replied with a silent nod.

When Gus was gone, she lay swinging in her hammock, listening to the wind howling through the tiny cracks in the ship's timbers and the sea crashing as the *Isabelle* battled her way through the waves. Periodically, a bell sounded, an order was shouted, a whistle was blown in the distance, but the rest of the ship was eerily silent. There was no entertainment above deck this night. Near Emily's head, the gunport was closed up, and her little corner was dark and lonely. She hoped Leander might check in on her, might be in the mood for some conversation, but the only sounds outside her canvas curtain were the moans and snores of the wounded men in their cots, and the scratch of a pen. Emily closed her eyes and waited for sleep to come.

The first crash of cannons sounded in the early morning before light. Emily sat upright in her hammock and blinked in the blackness of the lower deck. As yet, no lanterns had been lit in the room where they all slept. Through the cracks in the ship's timbers, she could see flashes of light that were followed by thunderous outbursts of guns. The hits to the hull of their merchant ship rattled Emily's teeth and landed her on her back as she scrambled out of her cot. There was confusion and chaos above her head as the crew raced to defend themselves with their guns. In the darkness of the large cabin the women started screaming and the children began to wail. Emily could not see a thing as she groped her way to the next hammock and, with trembling hands, felt around for the terrified child who lay there. She scooped up the youngster and shouted to the other women to grab their children and take them to the corners of the room. But no one answered her. No one seemed to hear her. All around the ship the explosions and ensuing battle cries were deafening.

Before long, the American captain ordered his men to lash the ships together for boarding. As she crouched down in a gloomy corner, Emily could smell the stale stink of the enemy seamen as they crept through the decks with their pistols cocked and cutlasses in the ready position. She held her breath, hoping somehow they would not find her, and calmed herself by rocking the unknown child in her arms, feeling its soft hair against her cheek, wiping away its tears, but it was impossible, as the women and children sitting in the darkness next to her were hysterical. Voices—frantic voices—called out her name, over and over again. Suddenly, the silhouettes of three men came upon her and lifted a lantern to her face. The tallest one wore a cocked hat. He tore the child from her arms and held his pistol to her breast ...

Emily awoke and cried out. Her heart pumped madly in her tightened chest and she gasped for air, her dark thoughts dragging her into an abyss where there was only oppressive sadness. Feeling icy cold, she began to shudder.

Within seconds a hospital lantern was lit and Leander stood next to her bed. "It was a dream ... just a dream," he said gently, pulling the blankets she had cast off in her fitful sleep up around her shoulders. "Breathe in deeply and exhale slowly through your mouth."

Emily closed her eyes and tried concentrating on her breathing. "It was so black," she mumbled on her pillow.

"Keep breathing—slowly and deeply. I'll be right back."

Fighting the temptation to revisit her nightmare, Emily lay there alone, trying to restore her breathing and heart rate with pleasant memories of her childhood home in England. It had been such a lovely house: three storeys high, stucco and beam, full of cosy corners, secret cupboards, and happy people. And the surrounding gardens had been so fragrant, all riotous colour, humming with tiny creatures. Father was there, smiling and waving to her as she played near the pond under the willow trees ...

But it was no use. The haunting sounds of sobbing women and children, and the delirious voices of her unseen companions as they ran about, calling out to her in the shadows, kept interrupting her images of England ... kept echoing through the corridors of her mind. Where were they now? Caught in the ship's remains, their scattered bones lost in the ocean's dark depths? Try as she might, Emily could not flee from her fear and her guilt that somehow ... she had been responsible for their fate.

Leander returned quietly with a lantern and cup of water for her. "There's a tincture of laudanum in it. It will help you sleep."

Longing for nothingness, Emily greedily drank the contents.

Leander hung the lantern on a hook by the head of her bed, then pulled up the footstool and sank down upon it, watching her as he did so. She wore his muslin nightshirt, which hid the curves of her breasts. Her pale hair was damp with sweat, and bits of it curled around her face. Her cheeks were flushed and tears clung to her lashes, making her look more like a frightened young child than the self-assured woman of eighteen years he had been used to seeing. A wave of intense feeling swept through him and he longed to hold her in his arms.

When Emily's heart had slowed, she opened her brown eyes and looked at Leander as if seeing him for the first time. He was dressed in a blue-striped, open-necked nightshirt; his rumpled hair stood up in small tufts on the crown of his head, and a shadow of auburn stubble was visible around his lips.

"Would it help to talk about it?" he asked, resting his elbows on his thighs.

Emily exhaled through her open lips. "Thank you, but no ... not yet."

He nodded and gave her a half smile. "The sea is calmer now. Shall I open the gunport? A bit of fresh air might help."

"Please."

Emily's eyes followed him as he stood up and walked around the foot of her bed—his head and shoulders sloped forward to avoid hitting the ceiling—then slowly they dropped below the hem of his nightshirt as he worked to unlatch the gunport. His calves and ankles were well turned out and she took pleasure in the bone structure of his feet. A breeze, making its way through the open gunport into Emily's corner, ruffled his nightshirt, outlining his slim form. Her eyelids grew heavy as a surge of warmth spread throughout her body.

Leander retraced his steps to the stool and sat patiently in the event she needed anything. For several minutes, with his head leaning on an upturned fist, he looked upon her quiet face and closed eyelids, and was therefore startled when her lips suddenly twisted into a grin and one of her eyes popped open.

"Doctor Braden," she whispered, "you have a lovely, fine nose."

Leander lifted his head and raised his eyebrows, uncertain that he had heard her correctly. He opened his mouth to question her remark, but her breathing had steadied and her features had relaxed. He knew she was sound asleep.

Monday, June 7

11:30 a.m.
(Forenoon Watch, Seven Bells)

Before noon the next morning, Meg Kettle waddled through Emily's curtains, balancing a washbasin on one hip. Her thick face was scarlet and there were enormous sweat stains in the armpits of her beige calico dress. "Git up, git up. It's Monday. Wash day fer ya." She dropped the basin next to Emily's hammock and stood, hands on her hammy hips, huffing and puffing.

Emily sat up in her bed and wiped the sleep from her eyes, unable to decipher Mrs. Kettle's ensuing mumbled irritation as the woman headed towards the gunport, her backside swaying like a prodigious pendulum.

"We'll 'ave to close this up," she said gruffly. "We're hove to, so Captain Moreland and his men kin 'ave their wash in thee sea, and it wouldn't do fer ya to have a peek at their bare behinds. Mind ya, Mr. Austen looks fine without his britches. What I wouldn't give ta ..."

Emily's hands shot up in surrender. "Thank you, Mrs. Kettle. I'm up then."

With a bang, Mrs. Kettle shut the gunport. She wheeled about and with her squinty eyes sized up Emily in her crumpled nightshirt.

"Well then, it's wash day fer yer clothes as well. Gimme yer shirt and whatever's underneath and that what Magpie made ya. I'll 'ave 'em all back 'fore thee supper bell."

"The supper bell? And what shall I wear in the meantime?"

Mrs. Kettle snorted. "A pair of thee doctor's boots fer all I care." She grabbed Emily's jacket and trousers, which were hanging from a hook, ignoring Emily's protests that her new clothes hardly needed cleaning at all, then trudged through the curtain, shouting over her plump shoulder, "Toss me what yer wearin' now onto thee floor and ye can hide yerself under thee blankets for thee day."

Out in the hospital room Emily heard Leander's warm voice. "Being your usual solicitous self, are you, Mrs. Kettle?"

"I'm washin' that woman's clothes only on yer account, Doctor. If ya want me opinion, I would 'ave—"

"As a matter of fact," said Leander, elevating his tone, "I do not."

With hands on her hips and a scowl between her eyes, Mrs. Kettle pounced upon Dr. Braden's patients with a loud warning. "Ye lads keep yer trousers on whilst that woman's walkin' naked amongst ya." Their heads bobbed obediently on their pillows. She waved a fat finger at Leander. "And you, Doctor—be sure to tie thee lads down in their beds while she's 'avin' her wash."

"I assure you I have rope ready for just such a purpose."

With a grunt, Mrs. Kettle bent over to scoop up Emily's discarded clothes lying on the floor by the curtain. When she was done, she growled, "Fer all thee trouble that woman's bin causin', woulda bin plenty easier if we'd just pitched 'er overboard in Bermuda."

Leander laid his slim, freckled hands on her shoulders and steered her gently towards the exit. "Mrs. Kettle, with bated breath we shall await your return at suppertime with our clean clothes."

Sitting in her hammock with the blankets pulled up to her neck, Emily could hear not only the older woman's cursing as she passed from the hospital into the galley, but the subsequent snickers from the men as well. Of them all, Osmund Brockley possessed the noisiest laughter, braying like a possessed animal, and when finally he had laughed himself dry, he asked of Leander, "May I take in her breakfast now, Doctor?"

"No," came the terse reply.

Leander was soon standing before her curtain. "May I come through, Emily?"

"By all means, Doctor."

Leander sidled in, his back to her, carrying a bundle of clothes.

"Good morning," he said, holding the clothes up for her to see. "I managed to get these for you from the ship's purser, Mr. Spooner. I'm afraid they won't fit well, but they'll do for Mondays."

"I am quite decent, Doctor."

There was a shy look of uncertainty on Leander's face as he laid the new clothes by her feet and turned towards her.

"I was beginning to worry you would not speak to me again after finding me with Biscuit and his messmates."

Leander quickly cleared his throat. "Yes, well." He looked at her over his spectacles, his blue eyes meeting hers, and drew in breath. "But—do you not remember anything of last night?"

"Last night?" Emily angled her head. "What happened last night?"

Leander hesitated, uncertain how to proceed. "You—you had a nightmare."

His words hung in the humid air of her little corner. Emily's eyes shifted past him to stare absently at the closed gunport.

"Perhaps I—should not have reminded you …"

"No, I remember. And you gave me some water and laudanum." She looked back at him. "If you are not careful, Doctor, you will surely waste your entire supply of laudanum on me. And here Mrs. Kettle thinks I am nothing more than an idler. Perhaps we should tell her that you perpetually have me in a drug-induced slumber."

Leander moved closer still to the head of her hammock. "We will tell no one of it."

The ship rolled and he raised his slender arms to steady himself on the boards above his head. He grew suddenly sombre. "After breakfast, Captain Moreland would like to have a word with you in his cabin."

"Am I in trouble for yesterday?"

"I cannot be sure. He said little to me, only that he wished to see you."

Emily sighed. "Do you suppose he will banish me to his gaol cell in the bowels of this ship with the ever-affable Mrs. Kettle as my protector?"

"If the captain seeks my counsel, I will recommend you stay where you are."

"Comforting words; however, do not forget I *am* only a woman."

Leander studied the floor.

Seeing his lips move silently, Emily asked, "What is that you say, Doctor?"

He dropped his arms at his sides. "Oh, I… I wondered whether you would be able to make the trip to Captain Moreland's cabin with that ankle of yours."

Emily smiled at him. "I cannot leave it here."

He smiled back. "I will ask Gus to escort you there… and back." Reaching out to pull the curtain aside, he whispered, "Will you require assistance with your new clothes?"

"As I have lost my underclothing to Mrs. Kettle's laundry pile," she whispered back, "I had better try this one on my own."

2:00 p.m.
(Afternoon Watch, Four Bells)

THE CAPTAIN'S CABIN DOOR swung open, revealing Biscuit's flaming orange head. Gus took off his hat. "Miss Emily is here. The captain is expecting her."

Biscuit's good eye gave Emily a thorough going over, moving from the top of Dr. Braden's borrowed straw hat down to her bandage-wrapped ankle. She had on a pair of loose-fitting brown trousers, a checked shirt, and a polka-dotted red scarf tied at her neck. On her feet were her blue silk shoes. Biscuit chortled, and then muttered, "New slops, Mr. *George*?"

Gus peered up at Emily, a puzzled expression on his small face. With her eyes, she entreated that he ask no questions. From within the cabin came Captain Moreland's insistent voice. "Thank you, Mr. Walby. I will call for you again later. Please come in, Emily. You may keep your hat on."

While Biscuit stepped aside, Emily passed into the room, holding her breath against his sour stench. With an outstretched arm, the captain motioned her towards a red-velvet wing chair at the opposite end of the oak table from him. Fly Austen leaped up to help her settle in, placed her walking cane across her knees, and returned to his own chair on the captain's left.

Glancing around the table, Emily found four pairs of keen eyes staring at her as if she were a curiosity at a local market. With the exception of the young officer with the bad complexion, the men all had warm smiles for her.

"You have already met Mr. Austen," said the captain, "and I gather you made the acquaintance of our sailing master, Mr. Harding, in the hospital."

"Yes, sir," said Emily with a brief nod.

"But I do not believe you know our first lieutenant, Octavius Lindsay."

Emily looked his way, feeling his dark eyes attaching themselves to her body like two black leeches. He had thin lips and greasy coal-coloured hair, and the aspect of a person who would not age well. She watched as his lips curled.

"I understand, ma'am, that you lived in Dorset. Perhaps you have made the acquaintance of my family. We have one of many properties in Dorset, my father being the Duke of Belmont."

As Emily had already developed a distaste for the man, she replied, "How wonderful for you, Mr. Lindsay."

Octavius raised his black eyebrows in surprise, then looked askance at Captain Moreland. With a nonchalance that irritated the younger man, James held up the decanter Biscuit had brought in for their interview.

"Would you care for some wine, Emily?"

"No, thank you, sir."

Fly Austen addressed her amiably. "Have Dr. Braden and Mr. Brockley taken good care of you in the hospital?"

"They have both been very kind. You have all been kind to me." Emily excluded Octavius in her glance.

"And your injuries?" asked James. "You are on the mend?"

"I am much improved these past seven days."

"Good, good. It is our hope that you are comfortable while you are here on the *Isabelle*; however, Emily, your safety too is important, and you have given us some anxiety of late. As a result, we have felt it necessary to lay out certain restrictions for the duration of your stay." James leaned back in his chair, resting his thick, intertwined fingers on the belly of his buttoned-up coat, trying to harden his facial features and inject a note of harshness into his voice. "Henceforth, you will be forbidden to set foot above deck during the day. Should you require exercise, you may take it, but only after the evening eight bells, and only with an escort of my choosing. Secondly, there will be no more mixing with the sailors. The areas on the gun decks where the men take their meals and where they hang their hammocks at night will be off limits to you." Seeing Emily's face fall, James felt a twinge of frustration. "You have proven yourself to be an affable young woman, but the men on my ship ..." he stopped to choose his words. "I fear they will misinterpret your gregariousness."

While James poured more wine for himself, and Mr. Harding and Fly gazed at the view beyond the cabin's mullioned windows, Mr. Lindsay fixed a hostile stare upon Emily.

"But, sir, it was not my intention to end up in the mess yesterday," she said. "I'm afraid I was hopelessly lost."

"Ah, but while there," said James, "you were imprudent enough to sit among Biscuit's messmates and accept their offerings of beer."

"It did not happen that way, sir."

"Are you telling me you were forced then?"

"I was not, sir."

James threw up his hands. "Then I'm afraid I am quite confused."

"*I* understood you to be a woman of impeccable breeding," Octavius eagerly interjected. "Obviously I was mistaken."

Emily lifted her chin to him. "You know nothing of me."

"Nonetheless, my good opinion of you has dropped a notch."

"I do not care—or need—to be held in your high esteem, Mr. Lindsay."

Octavius's face flushed a deep red. "My father could ruin your family."

Emily threw him a direct look. "Are you quite certain of that?"

James slammed his hand down on the table. "Enough! Mr. Lindsay, you forget yourself. You are not exempted from civility on *my* ship."

With a dramatic flourish of his shoulders, Octavius jerked his face away and fumed like a schoolboy. James set his weary gaze upon Emily. "And you, young lady ... unless King George himself sits on a branch of your family tree, I suggest you hold that arrogant tongue of yours."

Emily tightened her grip on her walking cane.

Mr. Harding pursed his lips, his eyes shifting expectantly between Emily and James. Fly fingered the crystal stem of his wine goblet and gave her a small smile which she did not dare return.

"Do we understand one another, Emily?" asked James.

She was slow to respond. "Yes, sir."

He pressed his fingertips to his temples and rubbed in circles. "The men involved yesterday," he continued, "including young Magpie, have all heard their punishment for failing to return you safely to the hospital. They will lose their grog ration for three days, and it will be their sole responsibility to holystone the upper decks for the next four. Furthermore, unless under extenuating circumstances, they are not to keep company with you again."

Emily's mouth fell open in disbelief. "But that is unjust! The men did nothing wrong. They ... they thought I was a man."

"Ho, ho, ho," said Mr. Harding, peeking up at her. "Did they now?"

Octavius threw back his dark head to laugh. "They knew exactly with whom they were toying, you foolish child."

Emily's eyes flashed as they fell on Mr. Lindsay. "You call me a child, yet I am astounded that someone such as yourself—with so obvious a belligerent and *puerile* disposition—is an officer of the Royal Navy."

Shocked by Emily's insult, Mr. Harding choked and dribbled his mouthful of wine down the front of his dark-blue uniform. James looked annoyed, but made no comment; instead, he simply handed the sailing master a handkerchief. Not accustomed to being spoken to in such a manner—especially by a woman—Octavius shot forward in his chair and grasped the edge of the oak table, an expression of contempt on his homely face.

But Emily did not care. She gave Captain Moreland a beseeching look. "Sir, please, I am not a leper. And Magpie, of all people, I should like to see and speak with again."

"Magpie must learn to stay and sew his sails in his dark hole on the orlop," said Octavius, in a low, threatening voice.

Emily stood up quickly, swaying in pain as her injured foot hit the floor. "Perhaps we wouldn't be having this conversation at all, Mr. Lindsay, if *you* had minded your own business in the first place, and kept your eyes and thoughts on your sea watches and not on *me*."

"*Sit down*, Emily," ordered James. He turned on Octavius. "And you, Mr. Lindsay, not another word."

"I will not, sir," cried Emily. "Do you not see? You will have every man on this ship despise me for this ... this madness. Why, you might as well just string them all up on the *Isabelle*'s yardarms until their necks have broken."

The weary lines on James's face dissolved in red anger. A deathly silence descended as if an unseen force had dropped a suffocating shroud upon the oak table. When James next opened his mouth his voice was frighteningly chilly. "We are currently fighting a war, and I have spent more of my time on your *damned* affairs than I have on fulfilling my orders from the Admiralty. Mr. Austen, summon Mr.

Walby and have her taken back to her hospital cot. Madam—you are dismissed."

The moment James finished speaking, the *Isabelle* resounded with raised voices.

"Sail ho!"

"Four points off the larboard."

"What does she look like?"

"A large vessel, standing towards us!"

"Clear the ship for action."

The drums sounded to beat to quarters. Emily's head hurt so much it seemed to her that every drumbeat was a blow to her skull. Almost instantaneously, there came a knock at the door. Fly moved swiftly to answer it.

"There's been a sighting, sir."

"British or Yankee?" asked Fly.

"Too soon to say, sir."

"Thank you, Mr. McGilp. Have the men lower the boats. If lead is about to fly, we don't need their scattering splinters killing us."

"Gentlemen," said James, trying to regain his composure. "To your stations, then. This cabin must be cleared for action." He watched the three officers make their hasty departure, Octavius's fiery gaze once again falling upon Emily when he rose from his chair. As they were leaving the room, James spoke again, this time, very calmly. "Under the circumstances, Emily, I will ask that you find your own way back to the hospital. Go to the hatch on the fo'c'sle. The ladder down will bring you to your destination."

EMILY WAS ABOUT TO MAKE her painful way down the ladder when she spotted Gus on his way up. Clutching his bicorne hat and cutlass, he beamed up at her, his eyes swimming with excitement. "There's been a ship sighting, Em. Dr. Braden asked me to find you. He wants you to get back below."

"Do we know yet? Is it an American warship?"

"We can't be sure. Please! Just get below. The worst place to be is above deck." He scurried off, securing his hat upon his blond head.

Emily stepped back as dozens of men now began pouring up the ladder, tripping over one another in their haste and articulating a variety of emotions:

"Our Father, who art in heaven, hallowed be thy name ..."

"Goddamned Yankees."

"We'll slice 'em up nicely."

"Thy Kingdom come, thy will be done ..."

"Move along. Git yer arse out of me face."

"England expects every man to do his duty. England expects every man ..."

"Now let ev'ry man drink off his full bumper, and let ev'ry man drink off his full glass; we'll drink, be jolly and drown melancholy ..."

"On earth as it is in Heaven ..."

"And here's to the health of each true-hearted lass ..."

Once safely returned to the hospital, Emily found Leander and Osmund clearing away the clutter on the desk. Osmund, his thick tongue hanging out of his mouth, grabbed a roll of bloodstained cloth and plunked it down hard on what would now become the operating table. Leander opened it and began arranging his surgical equipment. He glanced up when Emily entered.

"What can I do?" she asked quietly.

Leander spoke rapidly. "Sit down on the floor in the corner. Make certain the gunport is closed up and stay clear of it."

Emily slid the straw hat off her head, her wheat-coloured hair tumbling down around the shoulders of her checked shirt. Feeling faint and headachy, she limped towards the canvas curtain.

"Doctor Braden," pleaded Crump from his hammock, "please let me get up, sir. I'm willin' to fight."

"Mr. Crump, you have just lost your leg. You must wait until Mr. Evans has time to fit you up with a new one."

Mr. Crump grumbled like an active volcano, cursing saints Peter and Paul.

"Emily ..."

She whirled about to find Leander holding out a pistol to her. "Take this. If it's an American warship, you may need it." Catching her expression of anxiety, he softened his tone. "I suspect you know how to use it."

6:30 p.m.
(Second Dog Watch, One Bell)

CROUCHED ON THE FLOOR of her small corner, as far away as was possible from the gunport, Emily heard the echo of one bell. It had been some time since Fly Austen climbed down the ladder to the hospital to inform Leander that it was indeed a Yankee frigate and to make ready for the wounded.

"Fly, as there are only two of us here," Leander had said, peering over his spectacles at his friend, "please try to make short work of it."

"Shall I send in Biscuit? He claims to know something of medicine."

"I forbid it. His smell alone will surely do me in."

Fly had laughed as he ascended the ladder to the fo'c'sle deck.

Emily was surprised they could joke at a time like this, especially when her own heart had been thumping uncomfortably for the past two hours. Her legs were already cramped from crouching, and her ankle throbbed. The waiting was agony. Why weren't the guns firing?

Leander suddenly pulled aside the curtain and held up a lantern. "Are you all right?"

"I'm terrified."

"I have a shot of rum here for you. It might help." He bent his long frame to hand her a small cup.

Emily downed it, ignoring the burning sensation as it passed to her stomach. Leander shook his head as he looked down upon her. "I'm afraid by the time we reach Halifax, you will not only be a laudanum addict, you will also have developed a fondness for grog."

"And I will entirely have you to blame." Emily handed him back the cup with a sigh. "Then, of course, if Captain Moreland is obeyed, I shall have nothing to look forward to, with the exception of my cot, grog, and laudanum."

"Your interview did not go well?"

"It was horrendous. Captain Moreland is being quite unfair, particularly to the men with whom I was sitting yesterday—suspending their grog rations amongst other things. He has even gone so far as to punish poor Magpie for not escorting me back here before returning to his duties. I will soon have many enemies on the *Isabelle*, the worst of them that vile Mr. Lindsay, although where that man is concerned, I do not give a fig."

"I can assure you that for every one enemy you may have on the *Isabelle*, you have two hundred friends."

Emily lifted her face to him.

"You surely know," continued Leander hesitantly, "it wasn't me who informed Captain Moreland of your whereabouts yesterday."

"I know."

The guns began thundering at last. The ship's timbers shuddered and shook, knocking Emily up against the clothes cupboard beside her. Leander was hurled backwards, but was saved from a fall by the wooden post supporting the bottom end of her hammock. Steadying himself, he seized the blanket from her bed and tossed it to her.

"Here, place it over you. If the hospital is hit, you may escape the inevitable flying splinters. Stay down and stay safe." He soon vanished, taking the lantern light with him.

Alone in the dark she whispered, "And you too."

CLOAKED IN THE SMOKY CLOUDS of gunfire, the *Isabelle*'s crew seized the battle respite to regroup and clear the decks of their fallen comrades. The heart-wrenching wails of the wounded and their pleas for help were everywhere—on the damaged decks, high up in the twisted ropes, and in the agitated waters between the two ships. Amidst the butchery and blood waddled Mrs. Kettle, lifting her skirts to the gore underfoot, cussing in a clamourous voice that surely could be heard on board the enemy frigate.

"It's brutes they are, them Yankees!" She inspected the freshly cleaned shirts and trousers not yet collected from the drying lines that crisscrossed the fo'c'sle, now all sooty, blood-splattered, and full of holes. "And they would 'ave to pick me laundry day to shoot their cannons at us."

"Next time, Mrs. Kettle, you will take down *all* the laundry the moment we see a sail on the horizon ... as you were instructed to do," admonished Fly, slipping along the starboard railing. He was heading towards Gus Walby, who had his spyglass focused on the enemy ship's stern. "Mr. Walby," he hollered above the roar of the wind, "can you tell me the name of the ship?"

"It's the *Liberty*, sir. The *Isabelle* did a fine job of raking her. Why, her stern windows have been completely blown away."

"If we were lucky, President Madison himself would have been standing in front of those windows."

"We had the advantage of the weather gauge, didn't we, sir?"

"We did, but she still managed to inflict plenty of damage. Look! Look up at our sails."

"Slices of Swiss cheese, sir!" cried Gus.

"Quite so!" Fly cupped his hands around his mouth to yell to the men who had the unenviable task of dodging grapeshot and cannonballs high up on the yardarms. "Topsails only, men!"

"Aye, sir. Topsails."

"Quickly now, Mr. Walby, get yourself below. The moment we come up broadside to her, the guns will be firing again." Fly laid one hand on Gus's shoulder. "And please do us all a favour and take Mrs. Kettle with you."

"I will try, sir."

* * *

On the gun deck, the air was stifling and rank with the smell of fear. The half-naked gunners were black with gunpowder. Tiny rivers of sweat carved lines upon their blackened torsos as if the men had been scratched with giant fingernails. Clustered around each of the heavy guns was a crew of six, each member with his assigned duty. One man sponged out the gun barrel to remove traces of burning powder so others could insert the new powder charge, wads, and shot, and prepare all for the gun captain, whose task it was to aim and fire the gun. The young lads called "powder monkeys" scurried about, having carried up fresh charges from the magazine deep in the *Isabelle*'s hold.

Striding amongst the men and the guns was James, the polished brass buttons of his dark blue jacket glinting like cats' eyes in the gathering gloom. Already his Hessian boots were scuffed and his cream-coloured breeches covered in filth and blood. His face was red with exertion and he kept one hand glued to the silver hilt of his sword.

"Deep breaths, men. Do not shoot again until we are broadside-to-broadside. We cannot afford to lose a single shot. Aim for her hull, but remember, our goal is to cripple her, not to sink her." He stopped his pacing to stand behind Octavius. "This time we will have our chance to board her and search for deserters. I will leave you to it, Mr. Lindsay, as I must learn what damage has been done to our *Isabelle*."

7:30 p.m.
(Second Dog Watch, Three Bells)

Emily could stand the noise and suffering no longer. Streams of blood had now found their way into her dark corner. She could not see it, but she could smell it and feel its stickiness. On all fours, she crawled out through her canvas curtain into the hellish scene in the hospital. The room was clogged with bleeding, dying men whose eerie shadows were cast upon the wooden walls by the swaying light of the lanterns. Those who could stand leaned against one another, but most were huddled or lying on the floor. Every one of the hammocks was full, including the extra dozen that Osmund had hung up before the battle began. Young boys sobbed, calling out for their mothers; others groaned mournfully; most said nothing at all, presumably having already died or passed from consciousness.

"Please, Dr. Braden, please see me next. I can't breathe, sir."

"I'll be with you soon, Mr. Smith. Hold on." Leander's voice was as calm as if he were tending to patients on a routine day.

"A drink of water ... just a drink of water."

"I want me ma ..."

"I can't see! Oh, God, I can't see!" shrieked a hysterical boy, rocking back and forth on the floor, his face red and mutilated.

Emily's eyes filled with tears. She had seen it all before, though it was no easier to bear this second time round. Here again was the reality of battle beyond the politicians' rousing rhetoric and the reckless bravado of common men. Here again it lay before her—in all its dreadful glory—and she had no recourse but to face it head on. She yanked the red scarf from her neck and used it to tie back her hair. Then, crawling to the bucket of water Leander kept next to his operating table, she unhooked a cup from the bucket's side and filled it. Balancing the cup in one hand she weaved her way through the throng of suffering sailors to the man who had pleaded for water.

She put the cup to his swollen lips and said softly, "Here, drink this." He coughed and spit, but managed to get some down. There were no shoes on his feet, his pants had been half torn away, and a spreading bloodstain on his soiled shirt showed he had been struck in the chest. With laboured breathing, he looked up at her and said, "Thankee, Miss." A moment later his bruised head slumped forward and he slowly slid down against her breast, his blood seeping into her clothes. Emily heard him utter a long moan and knew that he was gone.

A teenaged lad crouching nearby said, "He's dead, ma'am."

Emily suppressed a whimper and put her hand on the lad's arm. "Could you help me carry him out to the galley?"

"Aye, ma'am. Only got a bit 'o lead in me leg, but I don't feel it none."

The lad hooked his strong, bare arms under the dead sailor's limp ones and lifted him up while Emily held onto his legs. Blinking back tears, she fought to keep her stomach down as they carried him through the stifling, stinking hospital and out into the galley where they lay him carefully on a grey blanket near Bailey Beck, who was already at work there sewing the dead men—with an eighteen-pounder at their feet—into their hammocks for burial at sea. Emily thanked the young lad and searched out others who needed aid, this time walking rather than crawling through the sea of misery, mindless of her own cares and annoying ankle. Struggling to contain her emotions, she gave water and a comforting word to those she knew would die before Leander was able to see them.

Before long the guns boomed again. Above deck, the bellowing grew louder and fiercer so that Dr. Braden had to raise his voice in order to be heard by Osmund, who was darting nervously about the room like a fox with a pack of hounds on its heels. Emily could hear the whirr of chain and bar shot intended for the *Isabelle*'s rigging, and could feel the large cannonballs pounding her walls. She reached up for the ceiling boards to balance herself as she waded through the room, catching a word or two spoken by the men.

"Sounds like we be broadside to 'er now."

"Lord, help thee lads."

"Dr. Braden, I only got a couple 'o cut-up fingers. If ya could just bandage me real fast, I could git back to fightin'."

"I'm sorry, Mr. Morris, you will have to wait your turn," Leander said, focusing on a lead extraction from the arm of a shrieking, thrashing, red-haired midshipman. "Mr. Stewart, if you could stay still I might have an opportunity to remove the lead ball. If not, I will be forced to send you to the back of the line, and when I see you again in about three days, I will most likely have to remove your entire arm."

Not heeding the doctor's words, the midshipman continued to thrash about on the table.

"A good punch to the face will settle 'im down, Doc."

"Thank you for that, Mr. Crump, but I don't normally adhere to those methods."

"Ohhhh!" moaned the midshipman. "Please send for my mother. She'll hold my hand and smooth my hair."

Those of the less wounded sailors within earshot chuckled. "If thee lad lives he'll 'ave trouble livin' them words down."

"I'm afraid, Mr. Stewart, your mother is not here with us." When the boy did not cease his flailing, Leander finally lost his patience. "Osmund, you'll have to sit on him."

"Right, then." Rolling his thick tongue around his cracked lips, Osmund hopped up onto the operating table and plunked his full weight down onto the boy's buttocks, gripping his skinny wrists with his enormous hands. The midshipman howled and cried out for mercy, but Osmund held him fast and firmly enough for Leander to do his work.

Emily pulled her attention away from the midshipman's plight and snatched some clean rags from the chair at Leander's back. She then refilled the water cup and went to kneel next to the boy with the mutilated face.

"I can't see!" he cried. "I can't see."

Dipping a rag in the cold water, Emily wrung it out a bit and gently began dabbing his bleeding face. His hair was matted with blood, and on his head and left cheek were oozing gashes. In the shadowy light, with some of the blood washed away, she realized, with dismay, that his left eye had been shattered.

"Is that you, m'am?"

Emily paused to study the small, torn face in her hands. "Magpie?"

"One 'n' the same, ma'am, but not bein' very brave, I'm afraid." He began to sob. Emily wrapped one arm around his thin shoulders, whispering, "Hush, now. I'll stay with you." She then searched the room for the teenaged lad, only to find that he was sitting nearby, watching her with interest.

"Could you manage to help me again?" she asked. "I know where there's an empty hammock."

"Aye, ma'am."

With his strong arms, the lad scooped up Magpie and, limping, followed Emily to her private corner. As they weaved and bobbed through the huddled throng, she felt Leander's eyes on her. Turning her head to him, she found that he had paused in his work to send a grateful smile her way.

Tuesday, June 8

2:00 a.m.
(Middle Watch, Four Bells)

GUS WALBY HURRIED UP THE LADDER to the poop deck. Captain Moreland stood in the dark and pouring rain, drinking cold coffee and watching the progress of his boarding party as they organized a group of about fifty presumed British deserters on the quarterdeck of the *Liberty* for transportation onto the *Isabelle*.

"Sir, Mr. Austen asked me to tell you we are ready to bring the men aboard," said Gus, shivering in his sodden muslin shirt. "He says there are forty-six of them. They all speak like Englishmen but, except for one man, all claim to be American citizens."

James, wearing his knee-length Carrick coat to shut out the wind and dampness, droplets of rain falling from his bicorne hat, closed his eyes to think. "Thank you, Mr. Walby. Tell Mr. Austen to take them down to the gaol for the balance of the night, then tell Biscuit to make certain they receive food and water. We will begin questioning them one by one in the morning."

"And what about their captain, sir?"

"A pompous, cantankerous young fellow named Butterfield, I believe." James gave Gus a sardonic smile. "As he is no longer a threat to us, let him stay with his diminished crew."

"Did he surrender his sword to you, sir?"

"I did not ask for it, Mr. Walby."

Gus shivered again. "And the ship, sir? Mr. Austen would like to know what your orders are regarding it?"

"Unlash her, let her go," said Captain Moreland with surprising calmness. "She's in no shape to sail far, and I'm afraid we're in for a spell of bad weather. I cannot trust this night to spare skilled men to take her a prize."

Gus tried to hide his disappointment. "Anything else, sir?"

"Aye, take what weapons you can, then let them all take their chances in the storm. I can do no more for them."

Gus made a hesitant salute, then spun around and began retracing his steps to the ladder leading to the quarterdeck. James called him back.

"Mr. Walby?"

"Sir?"

"Here, take my coat," he said, unbuttoning his Carrick. "It will be long on you, but I believe you will wear it well."

"What about you, sir?" Gus said, coming forward eagerly to accept the heavy coat.

"I need to rest awhile. I'll be in the wardroom. Tell Mr. Austen to meet me there at six bells before breakfast, and ask him to bring with him that one fellow who admitted to being an Englishman."

Gus slid proudly into the captain's Carrick, fingering its large brass buttons.

"Now, Mr. Walby, tell me ... can you remember all that?"

"Aye, sir!" Gus grinned. With a second, more serious salute, he negotiated the slippery ladder, careful not to trip on the long coat's hem, and soon vanished into the shadowy confusion on the main deck. For several minutes James watched the activity below him. The scarlet-jacketed marines had positioned themselves at intervals along the larboard railing, their muskets still pointing at the enemy ship in case there was any further resistance. Mr. Harding hobbled about, pressing his hat to his head, shouting through his speaking trumpet so the men on their lofty footropes could hear his orders.

"Main staysail only. Reef all others."

The men's replies to the sailing master were lost to the wind and the snapping sails.

Already the carpenters were at work on repairs. Mr. Alexander was carving a new crossjack yard while Morgan Evans was rebuilding the belfry. Others would be occupied below deck caulking holes with oakum and pitch. James watched as Morgan moved his tools to allow the quartermaster to strike the unharmed bell five times.

Scurrying about with a large basket under one arm was Meg Kettle, visibly muttering as she tried to gather up the last of the men's laundry.

Infernal woman, thought James. Never does she follow orders. Pity a blast of Yankee grapeshot—or British for that matter—didn't find her backside when the guns were firing.

His eyes shifted to two midshipmen perched on the capstan, watching the progression of the American seamen onto the decks of the *Isabelle.* If he'd had the energy, James would have yelled out to them to "stand tall on the deck," but at this late hour he could only feel relief that the boys had survived the encounter with the enemy.

In the faint illumination cast by the dozens of lanterns hung from the rigging, James could see the slant of the rain. He was thankful for the darkness, thankful that it hid the bloodstains on the decks and the faces of the men who had fallen during the engagement. He averted his eyes from the place on the fo'c'sle, near the small boats, where a silent, still row of sailors lay, and instead looked upwards to view the tangle of ropes and ruined sails. The *Liberty* had forty-four guns on board, no real match for his seventy-four-gun ship, even though he did not possess enough gun crews to man them all. Still, she had inflicted plenty of damage to the *Isabelle*. He shook his head in frustration. Yet again they would have to refit, but where could they go? Bermuda was out of the question this time. Draining the last of his coffee, he leaned into the wind and crossed the poop deck to the railing opposite the side where the two ships were lashed together. There he stared into the foamy waves that beat against the *Isabelle*'s hull. It was late. A storm was approaching from the east and there was still so much work to be done. James tightened his grip on the railing and stared into the cold wet blackness.

5:00 a.m.
(Morning Watch, Two Bells)

EMILY STIRRED AS THE ECHOES of two bells entered her sleep. She opened her eyes and felt the *Isabelle* being tossed about on a rough sea. Having slept on the damp floorboards of her little corner, she awoke in some pain: her back was stiff and her ankle and shoulder ached. In the darkness, she raised herself slowly, stretched, and, steadying herself against Leander's clothing cupboard, tiptoed over to open the gunport, only to close it up again when a heavy spray of saltwater poured in, soaking her shirt. She stopped to listen to the sounds on the ship. It was hauntingly silent after the explosions and screams and pandemonium of a few hours ago. She could hear the wind howling and the crash of the waves and Magpie's steady breathing as he slept in her hammock.

It had been near midnight when Leander had finally been able to examine the lad. He had removed the ruined remains of his left eye and bandaged his small head, and as Magpie slipped into a laudanum-induced sleep, he had turned to Emily saying, "It is always infection that I fear …"

Now, at this early morning hour, aside from the occasional snore or whimper from the wounded sailors swinging in hammocks or curled up on thin blankets on the hospital floor, all was quiet beyond her canvas curtain. There was one lantern still burning. Its dim light revealed Leander writing at his reclaimed desk, the surgical instruments having been rolled up and stowed away. Making notes in his medical journal again, Emily guessed. He looked up and pulled off his spectacles when she emerged from her corner.

"Doctor," she said in whispers, picking her way towards his desk, "it's five in the morning. Have you had no sleep at all?"

"A brief nap." He suppressed a yawn. "How is Magpie?"

"Sleeping soundly, poor fellow." Emily glanced down at Leander's journal to find that he was not writing medical notes at all, but a letter. Gently she reached out to take the pen from Leander's right hand. "There is a blanket on the floor by his hammock. It is yours. Go and get some sleep. Your … letter can wait."

Willingly, he folded it up, tucked it into the pocket of his breeches, and smiled up at her. "Strangely, I am not tired. Later it will hit me." He leaned back in his chair. "I could use some fresh air, though."

"I'm guessing we're in the midst of a storm."

"This is nothing. I have known far worse," he said, rising to stretch his back. "No, Emily, that blanket is yours. You of all people deserve more sleep. I won't be gone long." Leander detected an expression he could not discern in her dark eyes. "Perhaps I should not leave you here alone with so many wounded?"

"No, Doctor, that doesn't concern me." She took a step closer to him, looking up at his handsome face. "I should like to come with you."

"It might be too dangerous."

Emily's face brightened at the innuendo. "Would Captain Moreland disapprove of you as my escort?"

His face reddened in the half-light. "You are quite safe with me, madam," he said, looking everywhere but at her.

"Am I?"

Leander dropped his arms at his side and his eyes widened.

"Right, then," Emily whispered with a jaunty smile. "I will take my chances." She limped past his desk and headed towards the ladder up.

"What about your walking stick?" Leander asked when he had recovered.

"Perhaps you will lend me your arm instead," she said, disappearing through the hatch.

A slow grin took hold of his features as he hurried to his clothing cupboard, next to the sleeping Magpie, to retrieve his two reliable raincoats. As he headed towards the ladder with the coats draped over his arm, Mr. Crump lifted his head from his pillow.

"No mischief now, Doc."

5:30 a.m.
(Morning Watch, Three Bells)

BISCUIT HANDED OCTAVIUS LINDSAY and Gus Walby each a steaming mug of coffee as they stood shivering by the bowsprit on morning watch. "Drink up, Mr. Lindsay. Drink up, Mr. Walby," he said cheerfully, trying to shield the remaining mugs on his tray from the driving rain."Here's thee only warm sustenance ya'll be gettin' fer a while. Can't fire up me galley stove in this storm. And thee Doc says he ain't got no time nor hospital room for anyone comin' down with thee fever."

"Well, he would if he rid himself of that woman," said Octavius, wrapping his lips around his coffee cup.

Biscuit sneered, his bad eye rotating in his orange head. "And he ain't about to do that now, is he, Mr. Lindsay?" He continued on his way, struggling against the ship's pitching to keep his tray and himself aloft as he sought out other waterlogged seamen in need of some warmth.

Octavius grunted out a garbled reply and rounded on Gus who was still clad in Captain Moreland's coat. "Mr. Walby, your watch ended long ago. Why is it you are still above deck?"

Gus squinted up at the first lieutenant through the rain. "You don't mind, do you, sir? I can't sleep."

"Suit yourself."

"Might I ask, sir ... why you don't like Em?"

Octavius gave a throaty laugh. "*Em*? You're on a first-name basis with her?"

Gus nodded. "I read to her."

"Can she not read herself?"

"Of course! Mr. Austen gave me the volumes of his sister's book, *Sense and Sensibility,* to read to her to pass the time while she lay recovering in her cot."

"Such rubbish! Your time and hers would be better spent, Mr. Walby, reading books on navigation and signalling, and teaching her how to use a sextant."

Gus said no more, turning his eyes away to peer into the fierce blackness before him. He shivered in his coat, thankful he wasn't one of those phantom figures who worked the sails, some of them at more than one hundred feet above sea level, standing in their bare toes on nothing more than an inch of rope. Yet another large wave leapt onto the fo'c'sle deck, soaking Mr. Lindsay, who scowled beside him.

"Damn and hell," Octavius cursed, his coffee mug overflowing with saltwater. He tossed the mug and its contents over the side of the ship, and in a voice suddenly stripped of its earlier sarcasm said, "Two battles and I haven't received a scratch. If I am so lucky to survive this war, Mr. Walby, I shall leave the navy. I detest being ruled by the Articles of War. Surely I deserve far better than cold, diluted coffee and weather such as this."

Gus, shocked to hear such words from a senior officer, set down his mug to seize hold of a lifeline. "What would you do, sir?"

Octavius studied the young boy for a moment. "Beg my father to pay my way through law school."

"With respect, sir, why didn't you choose law in the first place?"

"Because, Mr. Walby, I am my father's eighth son. He chose my career for me. I did not have a say in it."

"Did your mother have no sympathy for you, sir?"

Octavius's eyes grew distant. "My mother is a senseless, self-absorbed woman who cares nothing for me. She certainly did not come to my defence when I pleaded for a career in law. Why, she did not even bother to come out of the house to see me off when I left for sea. I was told she was having her hair dressed at the time." He shook his head and took a deep breath. "Such foolish talk, Mr. Walby. Pay me no heed. I must do my rounds."

As Octavius fought his way through the gusty winds, he brushed the saltwater from his face. Looking after him, Gus whispered, "At least you have a mother."

"THIS IS NOT AT ALL SAFE," cried Leander into the wind, gripping Emily's arm as they made their way to a sheltered spot near the small boats and cutters that had once again been secured to the *Isabelle*'s waist.

"It's exhilarating," she shouted back happily, clutching the collar of her borrowed coat.

"Most of the men become seasick in this weather. You, on the other hand, seem to delight in it."

"I loved being on a ship when I was a young girl. I was never seasick a day, Doctor."

"Hmm! Yes, you have already mentioned something about being on ships when you were a girl, and wandering freely about on weather decks."

Emily gave him a mysterious smile and hobbled ahead of him to sit upon a low wooden bench that was nailed to the deck beneath the protective shelter of the smaller boats. Leander sat down beside her and quietly watched her as she looked out upon the frothy waves. The wind had loosened strands of her pale hair, which she'd tied back with her red scarf. Her cheeks were rosy and her eyes shone in the duskiness of early morning. She had thrust her hands into the large pockets of his borrowed coat, her small frame all but disappearing in the folds of the sturdy material, save for her blue silk shoes. Again he wondered who she was.

"Why, Doctor, if the winds would stop blowing so wildly, I'd race you up to the main topgallant."

Leander stared at her. "Are you trifling with me? Could you ... I mean ... have you actually ever climbed to the main topgallant?"

Emily relaxed her shoulders, and gave him an admissive nod.

Leander could only gaze upon her in wonder. He wanted to tell her that Captain Moreland would be most interested in this bit of information, but, fearing she would cease speaking so freely, he merely said, "That's incredible!"

"The truth is, Doctor, I was a climber almost from the time I left the womb."

"A climber? How so?"

"As a child, I would climb anything that stood before me: a fence, a tree, a balustrade, a barn roof, even though—in doing so—I caused my poor nurses such alarm."

"I am certain you must have," said Leander. "But I suppose ... there is something in you that does not leave me in complete surprise by this knowledge."

"If anything, my father encouraged this kind of behaviour," Emily went on, a wistful smile on her lips. "He was proud of my climbing feats ... most likely because I was his only child, and he had wished—as all men do—for a son."

"A son that would enter the Royal Navy rather than ... than taking up farming?"

Emily avoided Leander's inquisitive glance. "Do not worry yourself, Doctor, I shall not encourage a competition to the topgallant."

"If you did, I would have to decline. I'm afraid I am a physician, not a sailor."

"Perhaps not a sailor, but there must be some of the adventurer in you?"

Leander paused to consider that one. "I believe there is more of the adventurer in *you* than in me."

She smiled, and a faraway look crept into her eyes.

"Now if you were to run up the main topgallant this minute," he continued, "you might shock the sensibilities out of a few men. I understand many of them hate being up there themselves."

"But wouldn't it be great fun, Doctor? Captain Moreland and Mr.

Lindsay would be quick to consult their Articles of War to decide just how they could punish me. Should they withhold my grog rations? Give me a cobbing or a flogging? Seize me up to the shrouds for a night or have me court-martialled?"

"Perhaps they could give you all five punishments!"

They both laughed, then fell silent, listening to the men on their watch, shouting at intervals to one another above the howling tempest.

"Heave the lead, if you please."

"Winds from the northeast."

"Compass reading."

"No sounding yet, sir."

"What is our speed?"

"We're scudding at a rate of seven knots."

Leander was the first to speak again. "There is a hood to the coat. It might help to keep you dry. I wouldn't want you to catch a chill."

"Thank you, Doctor, but I welcome the rain. It is so hot and smelly below deck. I wonder that you can work in such conditions."

"I have done it such a long time now, I hardly notice. Then again, the quality of the air is not a priority when a man is dying on the table before you."

Emily turned to look at him and smoothed back her hair. "Why are you a ship's physician? You are not like other navy surgeons and physicians that I have known or heard about."

Leander frowned at her question. "How is that?"

"You're clever and well-educated and don't seem to have a problem with drunkenness."

"I thank you for the compliment, but I must confess to enjoying spirits upon occasion."

"When you are lopping off limbs?"

"No, never upon those occasions."

"That's what sets you apart." She continued to look at him, making him uncomfortable. "So ... why are you on a ship, Doctor?"

For the longest time he did not reply and Emily wondered if he would prefer to follow her example and evade her question. She was about to apologize for her impertinent curiosity when he opened his lips in answer.

"I left England eight years ago, when my old friend Fly encouraged me to join the *Isabelle*'s crew—they being in need of a doctor as their last one had died of typhus. With Nelson and his Trafalgar victory, everyone at that time seemed caught up with navy fever, myself included. I found I quite enjoyed life at sea, despite the fact the food is often revolting and I've banged my head a few too many times on the deck beams."

Emily searched his face. "Do you have no family left in England?"

"My mother and father still live in Steventon, near Winchester."

"And you have no other family?"

Leander looked down at her young face, damp with sea spray, and the dancing tendrils of her wheat-coloured hair. "I was married once. My wife died delivering me of a son. Two months after burying her, my little boy died. I was their attending doctor, but I could not save their lives." He watched her dark eyes grow sad and quickly added, "It was a long time ago, Emily."

She shifted her gaze away towards the swollen waves that rose up like shapeless beasts to challenge the *Isabelle*. For several minutes, as if mesmerized by the harsh scene, she said nothing, but when she turned again towards Leander there was a sympathetic smile on her face.

"The woman you write to—who is she?"

"How do you know I write to a woman?"

"I—I am only guessing."

He leaned back to stare at her in surprise. "You are an intriguing woman—one who is content to ask questions of others, but avoids answering them about herself."

She angled her head. "Are you interested in learning something of me?"

"Every man on this ship is interested in learning something of you."

"Good answer, Doctor! But now we are talking about you. And you were about to tell me the woman's name."

He raised one auburn eyebrow and met her questioning eyes straight on. "Jane. Her name is Jane."

"Jane?"

Leander was certain there was a hint of disappointment in her voice. He could see the next question forming on her lips when Fly Austen blew past their sheltered corner.

"Leander!" he cried upon discovering his friend. "I would have thought you were snoring soundly in your hammock at this hour." Then realizing it was Emily sitting with him, he added, "Oh! Good morning, ma'am."

"I might have said the same about you, Mr. Austen," Leander said.

His dark, wavy hair blowing wildly about, Fly laughed into the wind and reached out to steady himself on the nearest cutter. "I should like nothing better; however, at six bells, James wants to begin questioning the men who were brought on board. I'm on my way below to see how well our *guests* fared the night." He looked from one to the other with a wide grin. "And you two are—?"

"Out for a breath of fresh air, Mr. Austen," Emily said quickly. "The hospital, as you can well imagine, is oppressively hot and crowded."

Fly still grinned. "And your many patients, Doctor? Who's attending them?"

"The ever-capable Mr. Brockley, of course."

"Well, then, they're in very good hands."

A furore of voices suddenly pierced the howling wind. Those on watch, having stood silent and hidden at their posts, hastened to the larboard rail to investigate the hubbub at the front of the ship near the bowsprit.

"Man overboard!"

"Nay, *men* overboard!"

"Heave-to, lads; slow her down."

"Throw 'em a barrel, a spar—anything that'll float."

"Can we lower a cutter fer 'em?"

"Nay, too dangerous in this weather. Heave-to."

"It's Morgan ... one of 'em's Morgan Evans."

Emily's right hand flew to her mouth and her stomach began churning in horror.

"They must have fallen from the yards," hollered Fly. "Leander, your services may be needed. You will excuse us, Emily?"

"Certainly," she said faintly.

Fly hurried off, pulling his way into the gale by grasping onto the larboard rail. Leander stood up slowly, as if he loathed the thought of leaving her. "I'll first take you back to the hospital."

"No. Please. I'm coming with you."

6:30 a.m.
(Morning Watch, Five Bells)

IN THE DREARY MORNING LIGHT, Emily could see the two men bobbing on the raging sea—so small and helpless, like young birds fallen far from their mother's nest. She stood well back and out of the way of the sailors as they hurled buckets, benches, broken spars, and barrels into the slate-grey waves, in the hopes that the men might reach one of them.

"Who else, besides Morgan, fell in?" she asked Gus, who stood next to her alongside the larboard rail, squinting through his spyglass.

"Mr. Alexander. They were both trying to fix a broken yardarm on the foremast."

"Can they swim?"

Gus shook his head. "Most of us cannot."

Emily's gaze fell upon Gus's little blond head; a mixture of excitement and worry animated his young face as he watched the carpenters through his spyglass. She thought of poor Magpie asleep in her hammock.

"I'm glad you're safe, Gus," she said.

He beamed up at her. "I'm glad you are safe as well, Em."

"The men—they will need blankets when they are pulled in. Dr. Braden has a few in the hospital. Would you mind fetching them?"

Gus handed her his spyglass. "Right away!"

When he was gone, Emily shrank back from the rail and pulled up the hood on Leander's coat, knowing the sight of her above deck was liable to cause Captain Moreland or Mr. Lindsay to have a stroke, in the event they should happen by. She said a silent prayer for Morgan and Mr. Alexander, and turned her back to the east wind to fix her eyes upon Leander, who had joined the chorus of sailors leaning over the rail shouting encouragement to the carpenters as they laboured to reach one of the floating objects.

"Morgan—the barrel—grab onto it! Swim harder, man! You're almost there," Leander cried. Folds of his long forest-green coat furled around his tall frame like an untethered canvas on its yard, revealing the slim curves of his legs in his brown stockings and knee breeches. And when he turned his eyes towards her, as if reassuring himself she was still close at hand, Emily felt a wonderful surge of warmth flow through her.

Still pulling on his uniform coat and looking as if he had just roused himself from his hammock, James swiftly arrived on the fo'c'sle deck and joined Leander at the rail. "Can we save them?"

"Morgan's got a hold of a barrel," said Leander. "Looks like he's going back for Mr. Alexander."

James spun around to seek the whereabouts of the sailing master. "Mr. Harding, a word, if you please."

Mr. Harding quit his station next to Lewis McGilp at the wheel and limped over to the rail.

"Do we have any idea where we are, Mr. Harding?"

"The gale has blown us off course. We won't have an exact location until we see the sun again and can make an accurate measurement, sir."

"We may never see the sun again. What is your guess?"

"Dangerously close to Cape Hatteras, I'd say. Definitely off the North Carolina coast."

"Did you try sailing into the wind?"

"We did, but the rudder received a hit during the fight, and the unfurled sails are so full of holes they are next to useless. We need to repair her, sir. It is almost impossible to steer her in her present condition."

"Why wasn't I awakened earlier?"

"We—you were up half the night."

"And so was every other man on this ship." James frowned. "If we're smashed upon the shoals of Hatteras, we'll all soon be sleeping."

"With respect, sir, what more could have been done?"

"We could have prayed, Mr. Harding."

Teetering a hundred feet above them, one arm pointing towards the western horizon, the lookout bellowed, "Land, ho! Land, ho!"

Peering into the gloom, James was certain he could see the dim outline of land in the distance. His heart quickened. "Mr. Tucker? What is our depth?"

"No soundings as of yet, sir."

"Heave the lead lines again," James ordered, taking a deep breath before returning his attention to his carpenters' pitiful predicament. Morgan now had one arm locked around the barrel and another trying to hold onto Mr. Alexander, who sputtered and croaked in fear. The shouts of the men on the *Isabelle* became desperate and louder than before.

"They're closer now. Throw 'em lifelines."

"C'mon, Morgan. C'mon, now."

"You can do it."

"You're almost home."

Seeing the lifelines hit the water, Morgan released the barrel and battled his way through the waves towards them, one hand still gripping the collar of Mr. Alexander's shirt.

Suddenly a massive, merciless wave rose up like the foot of a giant and crashed down upon the carpenters' heads, shoving them beneath the sea's white surface. "Good God!" gasped James, scrambling farther down the rail to watch in horror. There was an outpouring of despair on the *Isabelle*. Two young midshipmen standing against the rail wheeled away from the disturbing scene and wept openly. Gus reappeared, quietly gave Emily two blankets, and went off to console his distraught friends.

"Pull in the lifeline!"

Old Bailey Beck had tied a cord of rope around his belly and was being hoisted up onto the side of the ship by a couple of sailors when James guessed his intentions. Sensing his disapproval, Bailey calmly stated, "I'm goin' in after me buddy, Cap'n, even if I die tryin'," and with his long, white hair and dungaree shirt blowing around him, sprang from the *Isabelle* like a mythical druid in self-sacrifice. Feet first, he splashed into the swirling waters. When he surfaced he began paddling like a dog towards the place where the men had gone under.

"Cap'n, sir—Old Beck—he canna swim."

"Damn fool! I don't need the loss of another man on my conscience."

The moment James demanded Bailey be pulled in, Morgan reappeared, crying out, gasping for air, both of his hands clenching the lifeline. Emily clutched her chest in fervid relief while yelps of delight and applause erupted amongst the onlookers—if only for a brief time. It was soon apparent to them all that Morgan was alone. The waves continued to rise and fall, but Mr. Alexander was no longer there. The celebration ceased and all became eerily silent, save for the wind's moans and the unceasing crash of the waves that knocked about the *Isabelle*.

Emily inched nearer to the circle of seamen toiling to retrieve both Bailey Beck and Morgan from the water. No words were spoken, only grunts of effort heard, and when the rescued men's feet finally touched the *Isabelle*'s firm deck, Bailey grabbed his buddy and held him close. "Thanks to thee Lord for sparin' ye."

While Morgan rested his head on Bailey's bony shoulder, Emily could see the anguish on the young man's white face, and his slim body shuddering from head to toe. Even with pain and misery filling his eyes, he noticed her hooded figure amongst the sailors, coming towards him with the offering of grey blankets. With trembling hands, he took them from her, glancing at her feet, and in a strangled voice said, "Mr. George. Sir." Emily placed a sympathetic hand on his shivering arm before he and Bailey Beck were whisked away to the hospital, Morgan twisting his head around for a last look at her.

Beside her, Leander cleared his throat. This time his eyes did not meet hers. "I must return below. It would be unwise for you to linger much longer. Stay with Mr. Walby—please."

He left before Emily could reply. She watched him lean down to exchange a few words with the young midshipman, and then he disappeared down the main hatchway. Gus stretched his neck around to seek her out, and once he had spotted her in Dr. Braden's oversized coat, sent a warm smile her way.

"Back to work. Back to work, men," Fly Austen ordered as he stomped through the crowd of loafers still lining the rail, all of them staring forlornly into the brightening sea as if hoping that somehow Mr. Alexander would appear in the water within rescuing distance of the *Isabelle*. Fly waved his arms madly about to break them up, but there was no harshness in his voice.

Six sombre bells sounded around the suffering ship and from some unseen location a ghostly voice cried out, "Fifty fathoms! Grey mud." Nearby a sailor repeated the words.

Emily sidled up to Gus, whose fair hair was dark with dampness, and whispered, "Mr. Walby, I heard Captain Moreland speaking of shoals near Cape Hatteras. Are we in danger?"

"Aye, it's a worry. It's not just any shoals, though, Em. It's the Diamond Shoals. The sands in these parts are constantly shifting and extend more than ten miles from the Cape. I've only heard tell of them, but I do know plenty of ships have foundered here. There're no natural landmarks on shore, except for the lighthouse, and its light is rarely burning. As well, there are strong currents here, and the currents, along with this northeast wind, are forcing the *Isabelle* towards those shoals." Seeing a look of alarm cross her pretty face, he added, "Don't worry, Em. You're sailing with a good lot."

Trying to oust the ruined rudder and the useless sails from her mind, Emily swallowed her fear and put on a brave face. "For so young a man, your nautical knowledge is impressive."

"Ma'am!" Gus was so happy to hear praise, he did not dare tell her that Mr. Harding had only yesterday taught him all this. He hung his head backwards to inspect the sails that still cracked liked whips above him. "I think the winds have started to die down a bit. In fact—" His voice rose an octave. "In fact, I'm sure of it."

Hearing his words, James and Mr. Harding both gazed upwards. "You're quite right, Mr. Walby." James stared out upon the lonely spot where Mr. Alexander had been swallowed by the sea. "But what a price we've paid for this bit of luck." Sighing, he turned to Mr. Harding. "Should God spare us on this day and we're lucky enough to avoid the shoals, drop the anchors the moment the lead comes up with sand and begin making those repairs. I'll be in my cabin with Mr. Austen and the first of our prisoners." James leaned closer to the sailing master and lowered his voice. "In the meantime, tell the officers on watch to keep a sharp lookout. The wind has cruelly tossed us into unknown waters. Let's hope no one's waiting for us."

The captain's ominous words caused Emily's knees to grow weak. An image of a shadowy uniformed figure filled her thoughts, leaving her despairing as she began making her way back to the hospital. She held the hood of Leander's coat close to her face as she jostled her way through the sailors hurrying back to their stations, unaware that Octavius Lindsay, who stood in conversation with three sailors in her path, had seen through her disguise; his penetrating eyes singled her out as she headed towards the ship's stern and crawled along the starboard rail to the ladder down.

Thankful that the northeast winds had subsided and she could get her footing, Emily soon discovered she was following on the heels of Fly Austen, who was leading a shirt-clad prisoner from the *Liberty* towards Captain Moreland's cabin. The prisoner was a giant of a man with impressive arm muscles and a dishevelled copper-coloured pigtail that hung down his stooped back.

"I will ask our cook to bring you a mug of hot coffee for your interview," said Fly to the man, "although I daresay you'd prefer wine."

"A can o' grog wouldn't go amiss, Mr. Austen, sir. It soothes all that ails a man," replied the prisoner in a low gravelly voice as distinctive as the British colours that flew from the *Isabelle*'s stern and mainmast. Emily stopped suddenly in her tracks to stare after them. Her heart quickened and her mouth went dry.

She was acquainted with this prisoner.

7:30 a.m.
(Morning Watch, Seven Bells)

BISCUIT SET DOWN A TRAY laden with hot coffee, sea biscuits, and strawberry jam upon the Captain's rectangular table. "I'll have thee stove warmed up in no time, sir, now that thee wind's abatin'. Will ya be wantin' a proper breakfast?"

"Thank you, Biscuit. A bowl of oatmeal would be most welcome." James shifted in his chair to look at the prisoner. "What about you, Mr. Brodie?"

"I'll gladly accept whatever's put in front o' me," he said, eyeing the biscuits hungrily.

"Well, I'll be!" exclaimed Biscuit. "Yer a Scotsman!"

"That I be, frae bonny Scotland."

"It's obvious ya ain't no Yankee."

"Thank you for pointing that out," said James with some humour.

"Maybe later, after they're done interrogatin' ya," Biscuit went on merrily, "we can raid thee grog barrels together and speak of thee auld country."

Mr. Brodie gave his countryman a toothless grin.

"Biscuit! See to your cooked breakfast."

"Sir." Biscuit bowed and reluctantly left the cabin.

Fly poured James and Mr. Brodie a mug of coffee, then one for himself. He downed it as quickly as a shot of whiskey. In the grey morning light that filtered in through his cabin's windows, James could see that Fly's face had aged overnight. The whites of his eyes were red, and his complexion was pale and puffy.

Leaning back in his chair with his mug of coffee, James stifled a yawn and tried to assume a more serious attitude. "Tell us, Mr. Brodie, where were you born?"

"In Girvan, Scotland, sir, in thee year of our Lord, 1789."

"And how long have you been a seaman?"

"I joined thee Royal Navy when I was ten. Worked me way up to captain o' thee maintop. Sailed on thee *Victory* with Lord Nelson himself. I was there when he was shot at Trafalgar in '05."

Fly could not help the wave of envy that swept over him. "You are lucky, Mr. Brodie. That is an honour of which few men can boast."

"We all admired Lord Nelson, but..." He turned his copper-haired head to look at Captain Moreland. "I admired you more, sir."

James straightened in his chair and set his mug down on the table. "You once sailed with me?"

"That I did. Before thee *Victory*, I was thee sail maker on thee *Isabelle*."

James's face twitched. "I thought my memory was still sound... I do not recall a man such as yourself."

"I was still a young lad. Early '04 it was. We was on blockade duty at Brest, off thee coast of France."

Fly watched James's face drain of its colour, much the way it had when Emily had first mentioned the name of Thomas Trevelyan.

"I believe it was your last voyage, sir, before ya—well, before ya retired," continued Brodie. "Ya'll remember... ya was commandin' thee *Isabelle* at Brest along with King George's son, thee Duke o' Wessex. As I recall it, sir, Wessex scared thee lot o' us."

"I've heard tell that Wessex was a harsh disciplinarian and notorious for swearing like a tinker," said Fly, glancing at James. "Am I right, sir?"

James picked up his mug and sipped his coffee thoughtfully. He gave a slight nod, but made no comment. Instead, he switched the subject. "Mr. Brodie, you were brought on board last night with forty-five other men. Do you know or recognize any of the others?"

"Not a one, sir. But I can tell ya they'll all swear to bein' Yankee. Hard to tell when I heard plenty o' English tongues among 'em."

"We'll deal with them in our own way later," said Fly, rubbing his face.

"How long then were you a crew member on the *Liberty*?" asked James.

"Two days, sir."

"Why only two days?"

"Before that I was a prisoner on a Yankee frigate, thee *Serendipity* it was."

Fly saw a slight quivering of James's hands around his mug. When his captain said nothing in reply, he asked, "Under the command of Thomas Trevelyan?"

"Aye, Trevelyan was his name. I was lyin' in his gaol, keepin' company with rats whilst he did battle with yas a week back. Ya did enough damage he had to flee to Norfolk, Virginia, to make repairs, but me, I was sent straightaway to thee *Liberty*, 'cause their own Cap'n Butterfield had been ordered to go after ya, to give ya chase, even though ya was a bigger ship, possessin' more guns."

Fly and James exchanged glances.

"You said you were a prisoner on the *Serendipity*." James's voice was hoarse.

"Aye, sir." Mr. Brodie looked again at the biscuits. Fly slid the plate under his nose and gestured for him to help himself. "Much obliged, Mr. Austen."

"When and how were you taken Trevelyan's prisoner?"

Mr. Brodie gobbled a biscuit before answering. "I was on an East India merchant vessel called thee *Amelia*, bound for Upper Canada."

"Were you being escorted by a man-of-war?"

"Nay, thee *Amelia* was a large vessel with plenty o' eighteen-pounder guns of her own." He reached for a second biscuit and rapidly disposed of it. "We was carryin' supplies of all kinds: farm equipment and seeds, wine, materials, linens, guns, gunpowder, you name it. As well, we had a number o' families, mostly women and children, travellin' to meet their military husbands posted at York, Kingston, and Quebec."

"Go on."

"We was nearin' Halifax when we was attacked. About four in thee mornin' it was. Trevelyan—he caught us by surprise—subjugated us with his guns and grapeshot, then lashed his ship to ours and boarded us. Straight off, his men killed a good number of our crew. But others, includin' me, was tied up and hurled like sacks o' taters onto thee main deck of thee *Serendipity*. We could hear thee women and children screamin' and cryin' below on thee *Amelia*. But we—we couldna do a thing." Mr. Brodie lowered his head. "Lord, it was awful hearin' those babies cry." After a moment he raised his eyes to James and Fly. "Me and thee others was taken below to Trevelyan's gaol, and later on it was, I overheard a couple o' his men say they'd burned thee *Amelia*."

James suddenly looked more alert. "How long ago was this, Mr. Brodie?"

"Can't rightly say, sir, on account I was knocked about thee head badly. Maybe four weeks back."

"Sir?" Fly looked at James questioningly.

"Mr. Austen, do you recall in Bermuda we were visited by a Captain Prickett and Lord Bridlington from the *Amethyst*? You were not present at our meeting, but they told me that about four weeks back my old friend William Uptergrove had come upon the debris of a burned merchant vessel, sitting fifty miles southeast of Halifax." He turned back to Mr. Brodie with a furrowed brow. "Can you offer any explanation as to why your ship was destroyed and not just taken a prize?"

"I canna, sir."

"Didn't you say you had plenty of guns?" Fly asked in an agitated manner. "Where were your gunners? How could Trevelyan have taken you by surprise?"

"I'm afraid I dunno, sir. I was off duty at thee time and, well, thee night before I'd had a wee bit too much grog and had been makin' rather merry. I can tell ya this—our captain was as weak as a woman, sir. He had trouble keepin' thee men in line."

"You said that Trevelyan took others from the *Amelia* besides yourself … How many?" asked James, his fingers clasped beneath his nose. Fly, cognizant of what James was getting at, looked eagerly at Mr. Brodie.

"Don't rightly know, sir. There was twenty men in thee gaol. Maybe there was others." Mr. Brodie quickly swallowed his third biscuit. "But this much I can tell ya. Trevelyan took a woman from thee *Amelia* before he burned her."

James regarded Mr. Brodie with interest as the Scotman drained his coffee mug.

"I saw him holdin' Mrs. Seaton roughly like and she screamin' like a banshee."

"Mrs. Seaton?"

"Who is she?"

"Thee lovely lass who always spoke to me whenever she took exercise above deck."

"What do you know of this Mrs. Seaton?"

Mr. Brodie shrugged. "Not a lot. *She* was always askin' thee questions o' me. She always wore such pretty dresses and hats. Oh … I do recall this one time, when thee weather was fine, she put on men's trousers and climbed a wee way up thee shrouds just ta say hello. Shocked thee lot o' us."

"Was she travelling alone?"

"Nay. There was a woman with 'er, a servin' woman, she was."

"Anyone else?"

"Aye, Mr. Seaton—her husband. Never spoke ta him. He had an aloof, arrogant kind o' look to 'im."

Fly pressed his lips together and went quiet while Mr. Brodie happily polished off the plate of sea biscuits. Through the galleried windows at their backs, the sun began to peek through the clouds, sending warm light shadows to dance upon James's oak table.

"What became of Mr. Seaton and this serving woman?" asked James.

"Don't rightly know, sir."

"You said there were many women on the *Amelia*. Why then would Trevelyan have taken only Mrs. Seaton?"

"Not certain of that either, sir, but I can tell ya this—Trevelyan's servant, a mongrel named Lind, came down below ta give we Amelias food. When I asked him about Mrs. Seaton, he smiled and said she was ironin' thee cap'n's shirts."

A spasm of irritation crossed Fly's face. James's voice stayed even. "Anything else?"

"Aye. Lind said Trevelyan holds an ancient grudge against Mrs. Seaton's father."

James's jaw worked as he stirred his coffee with a silver teaspoon. "And where is she now? Still on the *Serendipity*?"

"I've asked, sir ... no one can say."

James stood up suddenly, the legs of his chair scratching the worn floorboards. He stepped over to the windows to gaze out upon a calmer sea, then abruptly marched to the door of his cabin, yanked it open, and bellowed, "Call for Mr. Spooner." At last, he wheeled about to face the big Scotsman, who quickly rose from his chair.

"You have been most helpful, Mr. Brodie. Our purser, Mr. Spooner, will see to your provisioning—clothes, a hammock, and whatever else you may need. As we're quite short of men and our young sail maker was injured in yesterday's skirmish, we'll need you to begin working in the sail room. And should you possess any carpentry skills, we would surely welcome them." He extended his right hand to Mr. Brodie who gripped it fervently.

"'Tis a pleasure to be back on thee *Isabelle*, sir."

Once the door had closed behind Mr. Brodie and Mr. Spooner, James shot a glance at Fly, who was trying to snooze with one eye closed.

"Before we question the other men from the *Liberty*, I'd like to drop anchor and start in on our repairs." He unbuttoned his jacket as he plunked down wearily into his wing chair. "But first—we have men to bury." He folded his arms across his belly and closed his eyes. "So stay where you are and sleep well."

"You too, sir." Fly shuttered his other eye.

"I was thinking," mumbled James, half asleep already, "perhaps it is time to interview Emily again."

"My sentiments exactly, sir."

9:00 a.m.
(Forenoon Watch, Two Bells)

MAGPIE'S MOANS AWOKE EMILY, who had been sleeping on the stool next to his hammock, her cheek resting against the post closest to his head. She stood up to stretch the knotted muscles in her back, wincing as her swollen foot touched the cold, wet floor, but when Magpie's remaining eye popped open to find her standing watch over him, her smile was warm.

"How're you feeling?" she asked, reaching out to touch the bit of his forehead not covered in bandages to check for signs of a fever.

Magpie moved his lips, but was unable to give Emily more than a whimper of pain.

"Is there anything you need?"

His ghostly face brightened a bit.

"What is it? A cup of water, perhaps?"

Magpie lifted a corner of the blanket currently covering his body, and whispered, "Me special blanket."

"Is it in the sail room down on the orlop deck?"

He nodded.

"Right, then. I will go fetch it as soon as I am able."

A look of alarm suddenly crossed Magpie's features, and he tried raising himself up on one elbow.

"Lie still," Emily gently admonished him. "I know. You are worried I'll be severely punished if Captain Moreland should catch me down on the orlop."

"Aye," he said, gritting his teeth as he lay back down upon his pillow.

Emily's lips curled into a mischievous grin. "The men will soon be summoned to the burial service on the main deck. I will go then."

He gave her a feeble smile and closed his eye.

The minute Magpie slipped into sleep, Emily parted the canvas curtains to survey a scene of bedlam in the hospital. Four more men had died that morning, and their bodies were being carried from the hospital by Maggot and Weevil, whose linen shirts were soaked in sweat. One of the dead men was the teenaged lad who had helped Emily carry Magpie to her bed yesterday, the one who had claimed, "Only got lead in me leg, but I don't feel it none." Emily's chest knotted in emotion as she said a prayer for the poor young man.

The groans and wails of the injured resonated around the cramped quarters. Some of the men hollered profanities while others mumbled senseless remarks in their stuporous sleep. The air was rank with body odour, bitter medicines, and festering wounds. Moving amongst the chaos and the cots, administering food, medicine, and words of comfort were Leander, Osmund, and two loblolly boys whom Emily had never seen before. Leander was pale, moving slowly, his cream-coloured shirt once again splattered with blood. Behind his round spectacles, his blue eyes were red-rimmed.

Seeing her, he said, "I'm afraid, Emily, this is not the most pleasant place at the moment."

"Your gaol is full, Doctor, and as I refuse to bunk in with Mrs. Kettle, you're stuck with me."

Mr. Crump, ever ready with his quick wit, piped up. "Ya wouldn't be gittin' any peace at all if ya was bunked in with dear Meggie Kettle."

Emily, far from being affronted, smiled at Mr. Crump. "I'll take my chances here in the hospital, thank you."

"Safest place fer ya, Miss Emily. The men here, even if they had a hank'ring to jump ya, are incapable of doin' so." He patted the stump of his amputated leg.

Leander frowned at the saucy landsman. "Mr. Crump, your tongue is liable to get you tossed from my hospital."

Mr. Crump's hand flew to his mouth and his eyes widened. "I'll hold it then, Doctor."

Emily turned to Leander. "If you don't soon get some sleep, you'll end up a patient yourself."

He smiled wanly. "And if I do, would you give me rum and laudanum and an occasional cup of water?"

"No. As punishment for allowing yourself to get sick, I would bestow that honour upon Mr. Brockley."

Leander threw up his slim arms. "In that case, I am going. I'm going to get some sleep."

"You're welcome to my corner, although the floor in there is wet, so you'll have to sleep on the stool next to Magpie."

He dipped his hands into a basin of pink water and dried them on a square of cloth. "Thank you, but I have a cabin down on the orlop deck. Unless we do battle again in the next few hours, Osmund should be fine with his charges. And Mr. Evans, as he still possesses all of his limbs and faculties, has promised to watch out for you while I'm gone."

Morgan saluted Emily from his cot, but his eyes did not meet the compassionate light that shone from hers. She turned away from Morgan and lowered her voice. "How is he, Doctor?"

"Very low. He has said nothing since his coming here." Leander fumbled in his pockets for his cabin key, unaware that the letter he had been writing in the night to the enigmatic "Jane" had slipped out and onto the damp hospital floor. Emily was about to pick it up when Osmund, carrying a bucket of body wastes, crushed it with his large foot.

"What about Miss Emily, Doctor? Whose bed is she gonna sleep in now Magpie's in her cot?" Osmund stood there with his fetid bucket, licking his thick lips, awaiting the doctor's reply.

A flush of colour crept into Leander's white face. "That, Mr. Brockley, is not your concern. Keep your thoughts focused on your tasks or I'll send you packing along with Mr. Crump." Having said that, he meandered slowly through the maze of hammocks towards the galley door.

With Leander gone, a hush fell upon the hospital. Emily could hear her footsteps on the floorboards as she squeezed her way through the hammocks, offering a drink of water to those with parched lips, aware that several pairs of curious eyes had locked onto her every move. She was frantic to rescue Leander's letter from the floor, but didn't dare, in case any of the men had witnessed it falling from the doctor's pocket. Like a hovering hawk about to go in for the kill, Osmund stood awkwardly by, still holding his bucket, his tongue hanging out of his mouth as he watched her.

"Mr. Brockley," came a firm voice from one of the hammocks behind Emily, "we could all breathe a bit easier if you would please take that which you are holding and dump it over the side of the ship."

Osmund awakened from his reverie and sprang into action. Grunting an apology, he tripped his way up the ladder, sloshing some of the bucket's contents upon the rungs. It was Morgan Evans who had spoken. Smiling, Emily refilled the water cup and went to stand next to his head. He looked up at her like a shy schoolboy and took the cup from her hands.

"You are very kind to me, Mr. George," he said quietly.

"And you have been nothing but kind to me, Mr. Evans," she whispered. Seeing a shadow of a smile pass over his face, she pulled the nearest stool up to his bed. "I have been told that you were the one who rescued me from the sea."

"It was my pleasure, Mr. Geo ... ma'am! But I can't take all the credit. It was Mr. Walby who first spied you through his glass."

"Perhaps it was, but Mr. Walby might have laboured in vain to pull me from the fallen mizzenmast and into the cutter, now wouldn't he?"

A shot of red rushed into Morgan's unshaven cheeks, which set Mr. Crump howling in mirth.

"Oh ho, Miss, ya made Morgan blush like a maiden," he laughed, scratching the stump of his leg. "Be careful what ya be sayin' to him; otherwise, he'll think ya fancy him."

Morgan pulled the pillow from beneath his head and hurled it at Crump, hitting him in his raised stump.

"Oooh, me leg, me leg," he cried in pain.

"At least, Crump, Morgan's still got thee necessary parts for a woman," said a rheumy-eyed sailor whose head was bound in bandages. "Can't rightly tell how much thee doc had to cut away from ye."

A storm of laughter arose from those who had been eavesdropping.

"Aye, I heard Morgan complainin' he hadn't had a woman in a long time," quipped a young powder monkey with a badly burned face. "And he thinks he's too good for the likes o' Meggie Kettle."

Morgan turned purple with humiliation and gripped the sides of his hammock.

"And what would a young lad like yerself be knowin' of our Meggie Kettle?" the rheumy-eyed sailor asked the powder monkey.

"I seen what she does with the men in her cot when she ain't at her laundry," the little boy said, sitting up in his hammock, thrilled to be included in the men's discussion.

As the hospital vibrated with merriment, Emily noticed Biscuit standing behind her, holding up a pitcher of grog, his old face rosy with drink and hilarity. He cleared his throat and bellowed, "Here, here, now! I bring yas all a bit o' refreshment and what does I find? Ya've all takin' leave o' yer senses, forgettin' yerselves in front o' our lady guest. So yer mothers never taught ya any manners? Well, old Biscuit will have to teach yas all a bit o' thee etiquette."

"But I saw ya laughin' with the others, Biscuit," sneered the powder monkey.

"Shut up there or I'll be fryin' the other side o' yer face on me galley stove."

The banter ceased the moment Osmund returned with his empty bucket. Spying Biscuit's grog pitcher, his eyes lit up. "Hurry up. Pour it round. One never knows how long Dr. Braden will be gone to his bed."

Biscuit happily set about doing Osmund's bidding, and once the attention had shifted from Morgan, the young carpenter collected the courage to look up at Emily again.

"I am truly sorry for all that."

It was on her lips to tell Mr. Evans she had quite enjoyed the conversation—it being such a departure from the idle chit-chat that women of her class were wont to indulge in when left to their own devices in their richly-decorated drawing rooms—but she thought better of it and encouraged him instead to get some sleep.

Four bells soon sounded around the *Isabelle*, summoning the men from their beds and mess tables, their below-deck stations, and down from their lofty posts on the masts, to the burial service. While Emily moved among the hospital hammocks, offering a bit of solace to the injured wherever she could, she imagined the scene as the seamen—officers, marines, sailors, idlers, landsmen alike—silently assembled above deck under a mournful sky that refused admittance to the sun. There they would pray and sing hymns, and Captain Moreland, whose many duties included that of ship's chaplain, would read out the names of the thirty-seven men killed in yesterday's conflict. And when the sermon was over, the bodies—sewn into their hammocks with a heavy ball of lead at their feet—would be poured into the now-purring sea, there to join Mr. Alexander in his watery grave.

The moment Osmund became engaged in changing soiled dressings and Morgan's eyes finally closed in sleep, Emily filched a felt hat from an oak hook and set out to fetch Magpie's blanket from the sail room on the orlop deck. She paused only once, to pick up the remains of Leander's crumpled letter from the damp floor, concealing it in the pocket of her trousers as she passed from the room.

10:20 a.m.
(Forenoon Watch)

WITH THE FELT HAT sitting low on her forehead, Emily wandered the empty decks of the *Isabelle* as invigorated as a child in a cave of treasures; so distracted, she was able to forget her ankle, which caused her such grief climbing down the ladders. In the distance, she could hear men's muted voices, but no one crossed paths with her, leaving her alone to delight in exploring every shadowy storeroom, corner, and compartment. She marvelled at the cramped living conditions of the sailors, touched the chests, ditty, and duffel bags containing their meagre possessions, and stopped to pet the poor animals in their lonely stables.

"I know how you feel," she commiserated with the female goat brought aboard in Bermuda, stroking her narrow fuzzy face. "I have a mind to take you exploring with me." Worrying she might cause a livestock stampede were she to open the stable gate, Emily reconsidered her proposal, kissed the goat's head, and pushed on.

The orlop deck was below water level, and had neither gunports nor windows to let in daylight. It was dark and the air was musty, heavy with mildew and brine. Little scurrying sounds on the floor around her silk shoes reminded her that she was not completely alone, and caused her some repulsion. The timbered walls beneath her steadying hands were wet and slippery, like the perspiration of a labouring sailor. She shivered, wondering if the walls were full of shipworm. In the carpenter's storeroom, she stole a lighted lantern—comforted by the thought that neither Mr. Alexander nor Morgan Evans would report it missing—and raised its dim illumination to each closed door, searching for Magpie's sail room. After several moments of wandering in circles, she finally found it, tucked away in the deck's narrowing bow, between the bosun's storeroom and the sturdy base of the foremast.

Inside Magpie's confined quarters, she hung the lantern by the door and stood back to survey its scanty contents. Lined against the longest wall were several rolls of sail canvas, each tied up with a neat knot of rope and identified with either a wooden tally or a small square of card paper on which was written the name of the sail in black ink: *sprit topsail, fore topgallant royal, mizzensail, lower main studdingsail, flying jib, main staysail.* In the centre of the room was a slim wooden post with a tackle looped around its base, and beside it on the floor a clean length of square canvas. Emily could see Magpie's needle still stuck in the fabric where he had been cross-stitching near a clew on the lower corner of the sail. Near the wooden post was a small, low bench with a series of holes in it to house Magpie's few sail-making tools: a mallet and awl, and a thick spool of twine. In the darkest corner sat a pile of torn, tattered sails, and above that hung Magpie's hammock.

The only personal item in the room, besides the bed, was Magpie's chest, half-hidden in the old sails. Emily crept over to it and crouched down to read the name carved into its oaken lid: *Mr. Magpie, Esq*. She couldn't help smiling as she lifted the lid. Inside was his *special* blanket, a pond-green square of downy quilting, neatly folded upon his hairbrushes and few articles of clothing. As she gently pulled the blanket from the chest, something fell from its folds, striking the floor and spinning away out of sight. Emily swept the sweating floorboards with her hands, over and over again, searching for the wayward object. She was about to abandon all hope of finding it when the lantern's weak light gleamed upon a shiny something next to a roll of jib sails. She reached out for it, seized it, and brought it up to her eyes.

"Good Lord!" she gasped, staring in astonishment at the gold-framed miniature she held in her hands. It was a portrait of a young woman with dark eyes, her hair swept up on her head in a tumble of pale yellow curls adorned with pearls. Beneath her smiling lips was a collar and braided jacket of sapphire-blue velvet, and across her white throat, a single strand of pearls to match those in her hair. On the back of the tiny portrait, written in calligraphic script, were the words *Princess Emeline Louisa Georgina Marie, daughter to Henry, Duke of Wessex, 1810.*

Emily sank to her knees upon Magpie's quilt, still beholding the miniature, and started to laugh, a few chuckles at first, then bursting forth into a gleeful convulsion that seized her for such a long time the muscles in her chest ached and her lungs screamed for air.

"Why our little sail maker has a good amount of explaining to do!" she cried out to the shadows that quivered about her like small nautical sprites in the lantern-light.

Emily threw herself down upon the softness of the quilt to gaze around the dank room as she caught her breath. Near her outstretched arm, two cockroaches twitched with curiosity before vanishing within the layers of tattered sails beneath Magpie's hanging bed. Beside the door she spied a rope-tailed vermin hastening through a hole in the wall, and from the low oaken-timbered ceiling above, droplets of water splattered down upon Magpie's chest and workbench. Without warning, a feeling as dark as the room engulfed her and tears began spilling from her brown eyes. Clutching the miniature to her breast, she buried her face in the quilt and wept bitterly for the happy young woman she once had been. She wept for the walls and willow trees of her childhood home, for her lost girlhood of yesteryear, and for those she loved, now lying lonely and forgotten in churchyards and unmarked graves. Emily lay there, twisted into a fetal position, choking up suppressed emotions until she heard the distant, disturbing sound of splashing water as the dead bodies of the seamen were entrusted to the sea.

Realizing there was little time left before the service ended and the men returned to their stations below deck, Emily bolted upright to dry her tears on the sleeves of her checked shirt. She shoved the miniature into her trousers pocket alongside Leander's untouched letter, scrambled to close up Magpie's chest, and slipped the quilt under one arm. Just as she was about to rise to her feet, there came a whooshing noise behind her and the sail room went black.

She heard him before she could see him, his breathing heavy, his breath laced with rum and the essence of unwashed teeth. He let out a low laugh that stopped her heart, and then he started towards her, the heel of his boots scraping the floorboards. It was a minute before her swollen eyes could adjust to the gloom, but without the lantern light she could only make out a grey, sinister shape. She dropped Magpie's blanket and froze, remembering another murky figure that had once come towards her in the dimness of the lower decks, intent on harming her. A rat crawled about on her as if she were a heap of trash. Shuddering in revulsion, she opened her mouth to scream, but no sound came out. The boots came closer and another menacing laugh pierced the silence.

"There's nowhere to hide," whispered a thick voice.

In her numbed horror, Emily shrank back upon the pile of tattered sails, unable to think clearly. The sail room was far too narrow to avoid the looming shape before her, and she had nothing on her with which to fight. No pistol, no cutlass, not even a hairpin. He jerked at the buttons on his coat, one tearing from the fabric and clattering to the floor, much as the gold-framed miniature had done earlier, then he stepped closer to her to fumble with the flap on his trousers.

"There'll be no snivelling," he said, breathing rum down her neck. He shoved her backwards upon the sails and jumped on her, his sudden weight snapping her head back against Magpie's oak chest. She cried out in pain as he tore at her shirt and trousers.

"Shut up, shut up," he hissed, forcing her to roll over onto her stomach. His guttural sounds and unwashed stench caused bile to rise in Emily's throat and anger to burn in her breast. An image of Magpie's workbench with its awl and mallet rose in her tortured mind. If she could just reach it. Her right arm was pinned under his knee, but with her left she thrashed out, frantically grabbing at the blackness around her, praying her hand would soon find the bench. Her movements angered him, and she felt a draft of air as his fist rose and crashed down upon her face. This time she screamed, with such fierce volume it hurt her own ears.

"Damn you to hell!" He tensed up, as if listening for approaching footsteps, and as he did so, Emily's fingers closed around the awl. She swung the pointed instrument about wildly before bringing it down hard upon her assailant. He growled like a cur, throwing her against the wooden pole, her back striking the metal tackle. Before she could recover, his heavy hands were on her neck, crushing the life from her. Her small hands had not a chance of prying his hellish ones from her throat. Helplessly she lay there, fighting to stay conscious by focusing on a pinpoint of light that shone like a beacon behind the grotesque creature crouched over her. She heard the shuffle of feet and voices rising in pandemonium, and soon several more lanterns swayed in the sail room. Cursing and sputtering, her assailant was pulled from her and dragged into the shadows. Released, Emily turned away from the men who crowded into the room, holding their lanterns high and gaping down at her as if she were a wonder from the ocean's bottom. She curled up into a ball next to Magpie's workbench, gasping for air.

Above the sailors' nervous mutterings, Emily heard a terse, wrathful command. "All of you—get out. Get out! Now!" There was a scurry of footsteps as the room emptied. Then the same voice, firm, but gentler this time, said, "Mr. Evans, take *that man* to the master-at-arms."

"May I carry her to the hospital first, sir?" came Morgan's voice.

"No! I shall carry her myself."

"Aye, sir."

With the sailors gone, peacefulness permeated the sail room, though Emily, her face hidden in her arms, sensed there were those who remained behind. She heard the subdued words, "Mr. Walby, close your mouth and avert your eyes," and felt a pair of slender arms about her, lifting her bleeding head from the floor, covering her bruised, quaking body with the pond-green quilt that lay forgotten nearby. Into her ear the reassuring voice whispered, "It's all right now. He's gone."

Opening her eyes, she saw Gus Walby standing over her, his chin trembling, his eyes shining with tears. The man who held her said, "Run ahead, Mr. Walby, and ask Osmund to move Magpie from her cot. Then alert Captain Moreland of what has taken place here."

Gus bolted from the sail room like a whirring ball of lead. A second glance upwards revealed what Emily already knew. It was Leander who watched over her, his arms that comforted her. A wave of relief passed through her and she relaxed her head against the warmth of his body.

11:30 a.m.
(Forenoon Watch, Seven Bells)

WITH THE COMPLETION of the burial service, Captain Moreland and Fly Austen trudged to the wardroom in search of a glass of wine before the other officers came in for their noon dinner. They stood, goblets in hand, by the galleried stern windows while Biscuit, who was supposed to be laying silverware on the table, buzzed around them like a horsefly, delighting in describing the meal he had prepared for them.

"Mutton chops—just thee way ya likes 'em, soused herring from me secret store o' pickled delicacies, cheese I bin hoardin' since we set out from Portsmouth, butter and toast, and I'll serve up a big pot o' tea fer ya. And then I'll bring in some cold pie and more wine to round things off."

James cast his cook a look of incredulity. "You're draining our stores of victuals at an alarming rate, Biscuit. Do you suppose there'll be anything left to eat when—and if—we ever arrive in Halifax?"

"Without a doubt there will be," said Fly, hiding a yawn, "for Biscuit either sets a feast before us or he sets out to starve us."

Biscuit scratched his crusty beard. "Ah, it's to cheer yas up, Cap'n. Ya bin down o' late."

James stared out the windows at the grey monotony of crested waves that rolled past the *Isabelle* and was reminded of the dead young men he had given to the sea an hour earlier. He would have to write to their families and break their mothers' hearts; grapple with himself to find the words to describe their brave sons' last heroic moments on earth. It was a task he abhorred. The truth was, their sons were victims of a senseless war, killed by guns manned by men who were in all likelihood English compatriots. The bulk of his letters would be sent to England, but some would be postmarked Ireland, Denmark, and Prussia, and one would have to find its way to Brazil.

In the end, they would find their way to all of the mothers on different continents, connected by grief, weeping for their common loss. James's chest felt heavy and his head ached. He felt an overwhelming desire to sleep. Finally he spoke again. "I should like to have a few days of blessed monotony. No battles, no punishments, and dear God, no more deaths."

Knowing their captain and his state of mind, Fly and Biscuit said not a word. Fly sipped his wine pensively while the room grew quiet, with only the occasional tinkling sound as Biscuit finished laying the silverware. Not five minutes later, young Walby appeared breathless outside the wardroom and snatched his navy-blue cocked hat from his blond head.

"What's yer business here?" demanded Biscuit, going to the door. "The cap'n and Mr. Austen is busy."

Gus looked watery-eyed past Biscuit to the men standing by the windows. "Captain, sir, Dr. Braden asked me to come for you. There's been a … a commotion in the sail room, sir."

James came towards Gus. "What sort of commotion?"

"A fight, I mean … an assault. Emily's hurt."

"Emily?" James's eyes grew large. "What the devil was she doing in the sail room?"

"I don't know, sir, but Magpie's crying, saying it's all his fault. And … and *he's* been taken to the master-at-arms."

"Magpie?" cried James. "With the master-at-arms? You're telling me Magpie assaulted Emily?"

"No, not Magpie, sir. *Him*. He hurt her badly."

"Speak plainly, Mr. Walby. We cannot follow your ramble," said Fly kindly, extending an arm towards a chair. "Here, sit a while and begin again."

"I'll stand, thank you, Mr. Austen," said Gus, trying to gather himself together. "The thing is, sir, that while we were on deck for the burial, Emily was attacked in the sail room."

James's faded blue eyes hardened and he took a step closer to the small midshipman. "And who was it that attacked her?"

Gus took a deep breath. "Mr. Lindsay. Octavius Lindsay, sir."

12:30 p.m.
(Afternoon Watch, One Bell)

Aft on the lower deck near the gunroom, Octavius Lindsay languished on the floor, his feet bound in shackles that were fitted to the deck and to an iron bar. Behind him stood a scarlet-jacketed marine sentry, concentrating on the nothingness in front of him. As most of the crew were still at their dinner, there was no one else about, except Meg Kettle, who sat curiously in the shadows, mending shirts. Hearing determined approaching footsteps, Octavius looked up, his eyes swollen and watery, to find Captain Moreland, Mr. Austen, and Gus Walby standing over him, wearing stern expressions.

"Kindly wait by the fish room hatch, Mr. Walby," said Mr. Austen. The young midshipman nodded and chirped "sir" but did not move as far along the deck as he'd been instructed.

James hardly recognized the miserable heap of humanity on the floor before him as his haughty first lieutenant. There was a bleeding gash on the side of Octavius's head, and his features were twisted in anguish and fear. He resembled a young boy who'd been tormenting his younger sister and was about to face a severe reprimand from his intimidating father. James felt a muscle twitching in his cheek as he said sharply, "I am truly disillusioned, Mr. Lindsay. I can find nothing of the senior officer in you."

"Captain, please, show mercy, sir. Please don't send me to my death." Octavius dropped his head between his knees and began blubbering incoherently.

"I don't know whether to despise you or to pity you."

Octavius began rocking back and forth on the floor, and in a voice choked with terror sobbed, "Please, sir, don't hang me. Give … give me fifty lashes, flog me around the fleet when we return to England, just please … I don't want to hang."

James's blue-veined hands flew to his mouth and he shut his eyes as if in pain. A moment later he cried out, "For God's sake, man, *what* were you thinking? What could you possibly have been thinking?"

"You are a friend of my father's," Octavius beseeched him. "He can make you a rich man when this war is done. I'll see to it. I'll personally see to it. Just don't put me to death."

"Mr. Lindsay, you are familiar with the Articles of War by now," James said, reaching out to steady himself against the nearest post. "I may have no choice."

"I didn't know it was her. I swear I didn't know it was her."

James straightened himself. "What nonsense! You've despised that woman from the moment she came on board."

"I wouldn't have harmed her. I thought ... I thought—"

"You thought what?" snapped Fly.

Octavius hid his humiliation with his hands. A wrenching silence followed, broken only by the prisoner's guttural sobs. Captain and commander turned their backs to him and moved away while Gus Walby braved a few steps towards them, still keeping a respectable distance.

"What will you do with him, sir?" Fly asked in a steely voice.

"I don't know," said James wearily. "Given the seriousness of his offence and the fact that he is an officer, his punishment will have to be decided by a court-martial. We have no choice but to wait until we reach Halifax. Only there will we find enough captains and perhaps a few admirals willing to sit and determine his fate."

"Shall we leave him here in the bilboes with the marine?"

"Aye, for now. It'll be sufficient punishment keeping him here for all to see and taunt. Would you go ask Osmund Brockley to see to his head wound? I need time to think." James placed his right hand on Fly's shoulder.

"Are you well, sir?" asked Fly, alarmed by the ashen colour of James's face.

"I am in desperate need of some fresh air." Together they left the gun deck, leaving behind the forgotten Mr. Walby.

Meg Kettle, who had been silently mending her shirts in the shadows, waited until the captain and Mr. Austen were long gone. She then perked up and laughed at the young midshipman, who stood gaping down at the prisoner as if he were a spectacle at St. Bartholomew's Fair.

"'Ave ya bin able ta figure it all out, Mr. Walby?"

Gus looked surprised, as if he'd only then just noticed her sitting there. His lips parted, indicating to Meg that he might speak. Instead, he clamped his mouth shut, turned suddenly on his heels, and hurried away. Meg stood up to address the pathetic prisoner on the floor and made a sucking sound with her tongue. "Tsk, tsk, tsk. Thee men, if they didna despise ya before, will be despisin' ya now. Why ya just put a nail inta yer own coffin."

1:30 p.m.
(Afternoon Watch, Three Bells)

ACCOMPANIED BY A MARINE SENTRY, Fly climbed down the ladder from the foc's'le deck and into the hospital. The room was as quiet as a crypt. Osmund tiptoed around with his chamber pots and bandages. Mr. Crump had nothing amusing to say. Along with Biscuit and several seamen who were crowded round the galley entrance, he kept a silent watch on the thin sheet of canvas that separated them from Emily, as faithfully as if he were above deck combing the seas for an enemy sighting. On a stool next to a slumbering Magpie, who was now in his new hammock, Gus Walby sat clutching Fly's sister's novel, *Sense and Sensibility*, evidently hopeful that he would soon be invited to enter Emily's sacred corner. Near Gus sat Morgan Evans, who respectfully pulled his knitted hat from his shaggy-haired head and saluted the moment Fly glanced in his direction. The wounded sailors—those who could—sat upright in their beds and saluted him in turn, though immediately afterwards their focus darted back to the canvas.

"Where's Dr. Braden?" Fly asked the cook when his boot-clad feet were firmly planted on the hospital floor.

"In with thee wee lass, sir."

"You are rather subdued, Biscuit."

Biscuit hung his orange head. "Outta respect for thee lass, sir."

Fly waved his arms in a dismissive gesture at the men lingering round the galley entrance, and in a muted voice ordered them away. "Back to work, back to work, all of you vagabonds. The last thing the doctor needs is to have you all underfoot."

"Mr. Austen, you'll let us all know how she fares?" pleaded an old sailor.

"I will. Now out you go."

Fly waited for the "vagabonds" to clear out before making his way to the canvas curtain where Leander, having heard him come in, stood ready to greet him. It did not escape Fly's notice that his friend appeared haggard and uncharacteristically dishevelled, that his brow was furrowed in worry, and that his lips were set in a grim line. "Come in," said Leander quietly. "It's all right. She's in a deep sleep."

Fly stared down at the quiet form in the cot. There was a hideous blue-black bruise on her face and the reddened imprint of fingers on her neck. "Does she have similar injuries elsewhere on her body?" he asked, finding himself unable to cease blinking.

Leander, his fist held to his mouth, turned his gaze from Emily and glanced up at Fly over his spectacles and nodded. Neither man spoke for a while. Beyond the open gunport, the wind had picked up and a low rumble of thunder could be heard in the distance. Above their heads, the bell sounded three times. Fly stepped closer to Leander and spoke as softly as he could so that the vigilant sailors lying in the hospital could not hear his words.

"You must know, my friend…she was *not* Lindsay's intended victim."

"What?" Leander gave Fly a bewildered stare.

"Evidently, *he* had not been informed that our little sail maker was wounded and lying here ... in the protection of your hospital. He all but made an outright confession. Perhaps it was his distraught mind speaking ... perhaps he figured his punishment would be more lenient if James and I knew the truth."

Leander seethed with revulsion. "I'll kill him! I swear I'll kill him!"

"Most every man on this ship will harbour the same sentiments once they have heard of Mr. Lindsay's exploits. But I believe it best we tell no one else of this sordid intelligence, leastwise Emily. For now, I need you to put down your fighting scabbard and come with me to the captain's cabin."

"Can it not wait until later? I cannot leave here just now."

"I have brought with me a marine sentry to guard Emily in your absence."

Detecting Fly's concerned expression, Leander asked, "Has something else happened?"

"James has come down with a fever."

4:00 p.m.
(Afternoon Watch, Eight Bells)

WITH AN AIR OF IMPORTANCE, Biscuit dished up bowls of mutton stew for his mates seated around his mess table on the upper deck.

"I tell ya, it was Octavius Lindsay that done it. I was there in thee wardroom when Gus told thee cap'n, and I heared it from Morgan, him havin' seen thee mischief with his own eyes."

"And what did the cap'n 'ave to say?" asked Bailey Beck.

"Not a word," replied Biscuit. "Went pale as a white whale and stormed from thee wardroom with Mr. Austen in tow."

"They'll be stringin' Mr. Lindsay up on the yard for his crime. That I'll be wantin' to see," said Jacko, rubbing his mountainous naked belly in anticipation of his meal.

Bailey let out a snort. "No way the cap'n will give 'im death what with his aristocratic connections."

"A floggin' with a cat o' nine tails would be too lenient," Biscuit growled.

"It'll come to court-martial," said another of their mates.

"Nay! No time for court-martiallin' out here," said Jacko. "Stranded in enemy waters, in a broken-down ship? And where would we be findin' enough British captains and admirals to do the court-martiallin'? Nay, we'll be days fixin' up the *Isabelle* just to git her sailin' agin."

"Morgan says Lord Lindsay didna succeed in his intentions, if ya catch me meanin'," snickered Biscuit, handing Jacko his bowl. "And here I thought he fancied thee lads."

"Oh, aye!" laughed his mates.

"Our Emily," Biscuit continued, "she fought him off like a true seasoned sailor, though he knocked her about somethin' fierce. Word is her head was bleedin' all over thee sails and her face has an awful mean wound on it."

Jacko punched his right fist into his left palm. "I'd like to git me hands on the bastard. I'd kill 'im with one snap o' the neck."

"Not before I would roast him in me galley stove," said Biscuit, his bad eye rolling about in excitement.

"If justice ain't dished up, why we'll dish it up ourselves," said Bailey. "We'll wait til Mr. Lindsay's on the night watch and we'll give 'im a Jonah's lift into the sea."

"Or a ball o' lead durin' the next battle with them Yankees."

The men raised their mugs of grog and said, "Hear, hear."

"Who's Emily?" asked their newest messmate. The men all turned to gape at him—a giant of a man with muscular arms and a long copper-coloured ponytail that fell a long way down his back. Biscuit cackled and placed his puny arm around the man's thick neck. "Lads, meet Bun Brodie. Off thee Yankee *Liberty*, but don't ya be holdin' it against 'im, 'cause he's a Scotsman. And with young Magpie losin' half his face, he's gonna fill in fer maker o' thee sails."

The men nodded politely in Bun Brodie's direction. "Pleased to meet all o' yas," he said before asking again about Emily.

"She's thee fair lass we plucked from thee sea a week or so ago," Biscuit explained. "She'd jumped off a Yankee frigate that went by thee name o' *Serendipity* whilst we was doin' battle with her."

"Thee *Serendipity*, ya say? Ya mean Captain Trevelyan's frigate?" asked Bun before shovelling a hunk of stew into his mouth.

"One 'n' thee same."

Jacko smiled. "Our Emily, she's a right spirited girl. Why, two days ago she joined us at this very table for a cup o' beer."

Biscuit laughed suddenly, spewing bits of stew about. "And you, Jacko, thought she was a man. Mr. George, hah!"

Red colour flooded Jacko's squashed-nosed face. "Aye! I did think it a bit queer him wearin' them blue silk shoes."

"She fooled the lot o' us," said the sailor with the swarthy complexion and bloodshot eyes.

"Well, not me, and I don't s'pose she fooled young Morgan either," said Biscuit gleefully.

"Where is Morgan?" Bailey asked Biscuit. "It was him that was s'posed ta be on mess duty."

"Probably back in Dr. Braden's hospital, still pretendin' to be needin' medical attention so's he can keep an eye on Emily."

Bun Brodie spoke up while the men laughed. "And would ya be knowin' this Emily's last name?"

Jacko angled his big head and squinted at his new mate. "How come yer so curious 'bout Emily? Ya won't get far with her, man. Mr. Lindsay already tried." The table of men broke into grog-laced peals of laughter. "But... but we do 'ave Meggie Kettle fer ya. She'll look after ya real nice-like in yer cot."

"I was on thee *Serendipity*," said Bun solemnly. The men quit chuckling and lowered their mugs to stare at him. "I was on thee *Serendipity* whilst ya was battlin' it out."

"Oh, nice," said Biscuit. "So ya was takin' shots at we Isabelles, killin' thee lads, was ya now?"

"Ach, no, I was chained up in her hold doin' some prayin'."

Biscuit glanced around at his mates before settling his good eye upon Bun Brodie. "So, what d'ya know 'bout our Emily?"

"I was told there was only one lass on thee *Serendipity*. Her name was Mrs. Seaton. She was Trevelyan's prisoner on account he didna fancy her father."

"Who might her father be?"

"And what was his crime?"

Bun looked around placidly at his attentive messmates as he chewed away on his mutton stew. "I 'aven't a goddamn clue."

Friday, June 11

1:00 a.m.
(Middle Watch, Two Bells)

IT WAS SOME TIME LATER that Leander found an opportunity to speak to Emily alone. He had attended to her injuries and periodically given her tinctures of laudanum to ease her pain and help her to sleep, but few private words had passed between them. On the day of her attack in the sail room, Captain Moreland had fallen ill with a fever and much of Leander's time had been spent making sure he was comfortable, as well as assuring the men that their leader had not contracted typhus or yellow fever or some such sickness that would most likely result in half the ship coming down with it. Many of Leander's patients still required plenty of attention, being in grave danger as a result of their wounds. Moreover, with the crew working around the watch to repair the *Isabelle* while her anchor was dropped off the coast of Cape Hatteras, several minor injuries—from cuts to falls to hernias—required his professional services.

At two bells in the middle watch, Leander was writing notes in his medical journal when an ensemble of stentorian snores finally resounded around his hospital. Long before midnight, he had sent

Osmund and the loblolly boys to their beds on the orlop, and the marine who had been ordered to stand watch by Emily's bit of canvas whenever the doctor was not present in the hospital was not due back until Leander left again for his breakfast in the wardroom in roughly six hours' time. As he peeled off his spectacles to rub his tired eyes, a familiar voice called out softly to him.

He found Emily in distress, sitting up in her hammock with one hand clutched to her chest. Her long hair fell forward in damp waves upon her muslin nightshirt, and her troubled face was flushed, partially concealing the purple wound on her cheek.

"You've had another dream, Emily?"

She closed her eyes and nodded. "May I trouble you for a cup of water, Doctor?"

"By all means. Shall I put something in it to improve its taste?"

"Aye! Plenty of rum, if you please."

Emily drew in deep breaths to calm herself while Leander quietly went to work preparing her a concoction from the small glass vials in his medical chest.

"Here, drink this, then lie back," he said upon returning.

"I am in less discomfort when I sit up," she said with a forced smile, taking the cup and draining its contents.

Leander stood awkwardly by the canvas opening. "Is there anything else I can do for you?"

"You are leaving?"

"It's 1:00 a.m. I thought it wise to retire so I will be of some use to you and the others in the morning."

Emily stared down at the empty cup in her hands. "Would you stay awhile?" She looked up at him. "Please?"

Leander sank down upon the stool without hesitation, his eyes never leaving her face as he waited for her to speak again. She gave him a small, grateful smile. "Where did you put Magpie?"

"On the other side of the hospital, as close as was possible to the galley entrance, so he may benefit from the warmth of Biscuit's stove."

"And he is doing well?"

"As well as can be expected. His own injuries are healing nicely, but the little fellow blames himself for *your* injuries. He confessed to us all that he was the one who asked you to go to the sail room for him."

"No! He only asked for his special blanket ... *I* offered to fetch it for him." Emily pressed her lips together. "Does he have his blanket with him now?"

"He does, and sleeps all the better for it."

"I am most anxious to see the dear boy. Does anyone keep him company?"

"Gus has come twice each day to read to him, and Morgan Evans visits him whenever he can to give him the ship news, and bring him his soup. And each time they come, they make a point of asking after *you*. Morgan feels tremendous remorse for your misfortune. It was him I put in charge that morning." To himself, Leander added, *But then I am the one to blame as I never should have left your side that day*, and was about to give voice to his thoughts when Emily let out a great sigh.

"Poor Morgan. He has hardly had time to heal from the loss of Mr. Alexander. I cannot imagine the guilt he must feel. But what happened to me, Doctor, is no one's fault. The truth is, I was elated to have escaped from this corner, if only for a brief time. I am not accustomed to wasting away in a hospital bed, being dependent upon men to dress me and bring me food and help me cope with my nightmares." She lay back against her pillow and studied him a minute. "Not a one of you has told me outright the identity of my assailant."

"Let us not speak of him tonight."

"I do know, Doctor. I have heard the men in their hammocks whispering his name."

Leander averted his gaze momentarily and when he looked back at her, her eyes glistened with tears. "My bruises will heal. I know I will be fine; however, I—I long to see Magpie. Is that possible, Doctor?"

"I will arrange it for you in the morning."

"What will become of Mr. Lindsay?"

Leander's reply was cold. "His punishment will be decided when Captain Moreland has fully recovered. I expect it will be a harsh one.

In time, he may hang or be shot. At the present, he sits clapped in irons on the gun deck, with no more regular company than a single marine sentry—and Mrs. Kettle, who delights in provoking him as she sits with her mending."

Feeling sick upon hearing this, Emily rolled her head around on her pillow to look out upon the gusty night through the open gun-port and listen to the calming murmur of the waves breaking upon the *Isabelle*'s anchored hull. Unencumbered by curious onlookers and jealous quips from the other men, Leander gave her a lingering look. But Emily took no notice. A long time passed, and when there was no further conversation, Leander wondered if his concoction of water, rum, and laudanum had taken effect. Overhead, he heard the haunting peal of three bells, and beyond the canvas curtain came snores and soft groans as the men slept on. He was about to leave when she looked back at him, an impish expression tugging the ends of her mouth. "If I thought I could get away with it, I should like to climb to the top of the *Isabelle*'s mainmast to seek out the stars and stay there until the sun rises."

Leander leaned in closer to her, amusement playing upon his handsome features. "Does that mean your head and back injury, to say nothing of your broken ankle and shoulder wound, are all much improved?"

"If I tell you I am much improved, will you come climbing with me?"

Leander smiled. "I would surely fall. And if I were spared immediate death, I would find myself without anyone to take care of my injuries."

"Then you have no faith at all in Osmund and the loblolly boys?"

"Sadly, no. If left to them, it would be better for all if I broke my neck and was simply slipped over the ship's side."

"A tragic end for the fine physician, Leander Braden." She angled her head in a jaunty manner. "Do not speak of your death when I believe ... you have a good deal more living to do."

Recalling his own words to her when she had admitted a desire to be left to die in the sea, Leander grew wistful. "Should I be fortunate enough to have you hand me the occasional cup of water, I *would* desire to live."

Ignoring the intensity of his eyes, Emily laughed. "Oh, I would do more than give you water. I'd give you plenty of rum and laudanum to ease your suffering, and when you wanted recreation, I'd read Miss Austen's novel to you, especially the chapters that include Colonel Brandon and Miss Marianne. I could chase away from the hospital those that annoyed you, and I'd re-dress your bandages if you would allow me to—" All vestiges of her merriment suddenly vanished and in the softest voice she added, "dearest Doctor."

Leander could not be certain of the true meaning of her words; he could only be certain of the effect they had on him. He started from his stool, heartened and overwhelmed with thoughts of covering her mouth and darling bruised face with his lips. He shifted closer still to her bed, conscious that his pulse had quickened, and his desirous thoughts had caused his face to grow warm. Rather than reaching out for her as he longed to do, his trembling hands gripped the side of her cot and he hovered there, staring down at her as she lay quietly on her pillow, looking back at him, waiting. He felt the ship rise and fall under his feet, and heard her sigh, and, inexplicably, he felt paralyzed. Forcing his hopeful gaze to the floor, he dropped his arms to his sides and mumbled, "Good night" before leaving her to return, with reluctance, to his routine existence outside the canvas curtain.

4:00 p.m.
(Afternoon Watch, Eight Bells)

OCTAVIUS LINDSAY BEGRUDGINGLY dropped his trousers and lowered his half-numb backside onto the seat of the heads in the farthest forward part of the *Isabelle*, behind the remains of her once-proud figurehead. "I don't see why I cannot use the officers' private toilets," he shouted to the master-at-arms, who stood arms akimbo next to Octavius's stone-faced marine sentry on the foredeck.

"There'll be no special treatment fer condemned prisoners on this ship," the master-at-arms bellowed back, following up his words with a great guffaw that was so loud it pierced the ubiquitous din of banging hammers.

"I'll remind you that at the present I am not a condemned prisoner. I am an officer and therefore shall be deserving of a just hearing," said Octavius in a voice rife with indignation. He settled his eyes on the swirling water that slapped the sides of the *Isabelle* far below his bare feet and muttered, "And I have been treated most abominably."

Hoots and jeers dropped down upon Octavius's ears like an icy rain from the shrouds, sails, and yardarms far above his head.

"I don't see no officer. I kin only see some poor lubber with his breeches down round his ankles."

"What d'ya know! His Lordship's arse ain't all spotted like his mug is."

"Well, I vum. It looks much like mine."

"And I bet a month's worth o' pay Mr. Lindsay is cravin' a look at yer fleshy backend."

"Ha, ha, ha, ha."

With hunched shoulders, Octavius bit his lip and silently put to memory the faces of the seamen hurling insults at him. If he were fortunate enough to get an opportunity, he would dispatch each and every one of them. He gleaned tremendous enjoyment from imagining his bloody revenge with sword and pistol and bare hands. Gone was the blubbering idiot he had succumbed to in front of Captain Moreland and Commander Austen. It had been foolish of him to fall apart that way and run off at the mouth. Well, there would be no more of that. Octavius squared his shoulders in his torn, ruffled shirt and sat up higher on the heads. He felt no remorse whatsoever for his actions against that woman. In fact, she deserved a good roughing up. "I bet her ladyship won't be quite as high and mighty the next time she lays eyes on me."

"Hurry up with yer business, Lord Lindsay. The sooner yer done, the sooner we kin string ya up."

Octavius smirked while the sailors enjoyed a hearty laugh. *I'll deal with the devil before any of your kind get the pleasure of seeing me dangling from the yard,* he swore to himself, scanning the blue-green seas for the sails of a Yankee warship.

Sooner or later, one was bound to find them.

10:00 p.m.
(First Watch, Four Bells)

FLY QUIT THE WARDROOM TABLE, where he had arranged for two senior officers to remain in his stead and continue the interrogation of the last few men taken from the *Liberty* while he went above deck for some air. But as he made his way to the nearest ladder, he slowed his step to listen in on the conversation between the captain of the marines and a man who had given his name as Silas Pegget, a man whose cheeks had a curious network of deep scars upon them.

"Your papers, please, Mr. Pegget."

"I haven't any, sir."

"Tell me then ... what is your place of birth?"

"New Bedford, Massachusetts, sir."

"And that of your parents?"

"Wolverhampton ... England."

"How long have you been employed with the American navy?"

"Just over two years."

"You look to be over thirty."

"Aye, sir. I'm thirty-three."

"New Bedford has for some time been an important trade port. Were you a whaler at any time?"

"No, sir."

"Perhaps you were in the merchant trade?"

"No, sir."

"Then what did you do before joining the navy?"

"I worked in the post office," said Silas Pegget, adding, after a fit of sneezing and wiping his craggy face with a ragged bit of cloth, "from the time I was ... fifteen, sir."

While the captain of the marines continued his questioning, Fly shook his head in frustration. At times, it was an exercise in futility, trying to determine those who were legitimate citizens of America and those who most likely had—at some point in their career—sailed with the British Navy, regardless of whether or not the individual in question possessed papers.

Fly slowly ascended the ladder to the weather decks, which he found deserted at this late hour, save for the men who silently stood watch on the fo'c'sle deck and high in the masthead lookouts, keeping their eyes peeled for movement on the vast horizons, and Morgan Evans's carpenters, who had forfeited sleep to continue toiling and mending wherever they could, using as little lantern light as possible. Spying Gus Walby crossing the quarterdeck, Fly asked him to check below for any lights left burning by the exhausted crew members who now slept, but who, only an hour before, had been entertaining themselves with song and dance and other forms of revelry. He then considered himself officially off duty, and made his way to the poop deck. There he stripped off his uniform coat and sat down next to Leander on the bench that was carved beneath the taffrail, in the fluttering presence of the British ensign.

"Imagine finding you here, old fellow," Fly remarked. Noticing the mug in Leander's right hand, he added, "Drinking grog no less. Are you drunk yet?"

Leander gave his friend a half-smile. "No, but I intend to be before long."

"Let me join you then. Who is filling your mug?"

"Biscuit. He's somewhere in the shadows, no doubt hiding a mug of his own."

"Biscuit!" Fly called out.

Like a red squirrel peeking out of his tree hole to sniff about for predators, Biscuit's flaming orange head appeared on the ladder between the poop and the quarterdeck. "Aye, Mr. Austen?"

"Come here with your grog can. I insist you fill up Dr. Braden's mug and one for me as well."

There was a slight sway in Biscuit's stride as he crossed with his tray of refreshments to the back of the deck where the two men sat. His checkered shirt was unbuttoned lower than usual, exposing thick tufts of red chest hair, and in his reddish whiskers were bits of pastry, leftovers from the piece of pie he had just devoured.

"Your breath is foul," said Fly while the cook poured their drinks.

"Ach, I kin explain, sir. Ya see, I was bakin' some o' me sea biscuits down below and as ya know, they taste well on account o' thee rum I puts in 'em."

"Ahh!" said Fly. "So then it was one shot in your bowl, one shot in your hole, was that it? And here I understood Captain Moreland was withholding your rum rations for your display in the mess with our lady guest a few days back."

"He threatened to, Mr. Austen," said Biscuit, balancing his tray with one hand and scratching his hairy chest with the other, "but luckily for we nefarious perpetrators, he didna follow through with it. Ya see, Morgan almost drowned and Magpie lost his eye, and since I'm thee indispensable cook, Jacko and thee boys did thee holystonin' part o' thee punishment. But not a one o' us lost our grog."

"You are most fortunate our captain lies low in his cabin. If it were up to me, I'd have you on your knees this instant, swabbing the decks. Now get to your hammock, man," said Fly, wresting the pitcher of grog from Biscuit's grasp, "for I'll not tolerate a grumpy cook at the breakfast table."

Detecting a twinkle in Mr. Austen's eyes, Biscuit quipped, "And fer yer kindness, sir, I'll be servin' ya up some marmeelade with yer fresh sea biscuits in thee mornin'."

Fly stared after Biscuit's comical wavering shape until the night's blackness had swallowed him whole. He then turned back to Leander.

"Did you check in on James this evening?"

"I did. His fever is gone, but he's not recovering as fast as I would have hoped."

"*Will* he recover?"

"If he could rest for a week without interruption, his health may be restored."

Fly looked out upon the faint purpling shadow of low-lying land and the glimmer of light coming from the Cape Hatteras lighthouse a few miles south from where the *Isabelle* lay anchored. "Our lives on this ship are as uncertain as that beacon on Hatteras—never knowing from one day to the next when we may be shining or flickering or extinguished altogether." His dark eyes flashed in the night as he glanced about to seek out any eavesdroppers. "We've been sitting here for five days now, adrift in enemy waters, as helpless as a wounded whale while we patch up our ship to make her seaworthy once more. Our captain is ill and our men tired. Moreover, we have forty-odd prisoners of questionable origins along for the ride, who, despite the fact that we feed them from our pitiable rations and have given a few of them some form of occupation, may rise up against us when next we meet a belligerent Yankee frigate."

Leander searched the night sky until he had located the moon—a slice of pale orange drifting through silvery clouds—at his back. He set down his mug and sighed. "And you're wondering, in all this, where our enemies are hiding?"

Fly nodded. "My guess is that when we cut the *Liberty* loose during the storm, she ran aground south of us, on these flat Carolina islands, or was dashed upon these shoals, and all hands were lost at sea. I expected someone to come looking for them and ... for us."

"Are you certain of our position?"

"I know of no other lighthouse in this vicinity, although one can hardly call it a lighthouse. Its light is so dim and unreliable, it does little good for those of us on the sea."

"Then we are not far from Norfolk, Virginia."

"Correct."

"Is there not a large base there?"

"There is. We've spotted sloops and schooners, and, strangely enough, that odd privateer with its ostentatious red hull—the one that was anchored beside us in Bermuda—but, so far, no warring frigates." Fly took a long draught from his mug. "I have an uneasy feeling."

Leander slouched down on the bench and allowed his head to fall back against the railing. Fly followed suit, past caring for the officer-like behaviour necessary in front of those dark figures who stood dreaming on duty far above him on the gusty yards. As the bell tolled the late hour and the *Isabelle* rose and fell rhythmically, lulling Fly and Leander into a stupor, they grew melancholy, listening to the mysterious mutterings of the velvety sea.

"You know, old fellow, you are as easy to read as one of my sister's stories."

Leander roused himself. "How's that?"

"I can see a change has come over you." As Fly's alert eyes bore into his blue ones, Leander felt the dreaded red creeping up his neck. "Why, back in my days on the *Canopus*, our doctor was a veritable cussing idler who left most of his work to his mates and loblolly boys. He never kept any notes on his treatments, and if anyone dared come down with a suspicious fever, he avoided the sick bay altogether."

"Your point?" asked Leander, avoiding Fly's bright stare.

"You, on the other hand, are always on duty, always at your desk, always in the hospital. When did you last lie about above deck wearing a sun hat to protect your fair, freckled face, reading your beloved Burns and Scott? Or join the officers in the wardroom for a drunken singsong after supper?"

"I am doing that very thing now."

"No, tell me, when?"

"Between battles and lopping off arms and legs, there's been little time for that kind of leisure."

Fly craned his neck up into Leander's face. "Mind you, the audacious Dr. Willen of the *Canopus* did not have a woman lying in one of his hospital hammocks, wearing his nightshirt, and depending on him for rehabilitation and amusements. If he had, he might have found reason to spend longer hours there."

As Leander was at a loss for words, Fly's voice softened. "I see it in your eyes, friend. I hear it in your words, and detect it in your actions and occupations. You are besotted with our gentlewoman."

Under the controlling powers of grog, Leander could not hide the sheepish grin that took hold of his mouth. "I fear she has awakened emotions in me I never thought I would feel again."

Fly's features fell. "Ahhh! So there is no hope left for my sister Jane? You would have her remain a spinster in Chawton cottage and leave her with no other company than my other sister, Cassandra, and my poor old mother?"

"Must I humble myself to remind you, Fly, that I am no worthy suitor for any woman?"

"Pshaw! Hogwash!"

"I'm a lowly physician floating in the Atlantic on a wounded ship."

"It's well known you're a common butcher, but a good one at that."

Leander paid no attention to Fly's remark and went on sullenly. "I have very little money to my name, and my permanent address is a dark corner on the *Isabelle*'s orlop deck."

"Does your desperation spring from the fact that in your heart you know it's me Emily desires and not you?"

Leander pulled a face and gave Fly an emphatic, "No."

"And why not? She doesn't know I'm happily married to my Mary, and have a daughter and three sons waiting for me on the Isle of Wight."

"No, perhaps not, but if your marital status was otherwise, Emily would surely consider Mrs. Kettle the better companion for you."

"Ha, ha. You can be very humorous when you are half-seas over, old fellow."

"Old fellow? The last time we checked you were older than me by a good five years, Mr. Austen."

"Maybe so, but one would never know it the way you're conducting yourself, as mournful and out of sorts as if you already stand knee-high in the grave."

Leander stared into his empty mug. "I—I know so little of her. She has dropped tantalizing hints here and there, but despite this, I find myself no closer to knowing whether she is actually a wealthy man's daughter, destined to marry one of King George's silly, aging sons, or a beautiful, intelligent dairy maiden who chooses to remain secretive so she would have us all believing she is well-born."

Leander's words jolted Fly into recollection, as if someone had just struck a match to a candle in his brain. He frowned, trying to remember something Bun Brodie had said in his interview in James's cabin, three long days ago, after the battle with the *Liberty*—something about a woman named Mrs. Seaton who had been travelling with him on board the *Amelia*, bound for Upper Canada in the company of a serving woman and the arrogant Mr. Seaton, and who had suffered the misfortune of falling into the hands of Thomas Trevelyan. Was it possible—? Could she be—? Fly considered sharing this information with his friend, but upon studying his distraught countenance, decided against it. It could wait. He smiled and tried to be jovial.

"Would it matter to you where she came from? Shakespeare's Juliet discovered her Romeo was from an opposing house, the son of her father's sworn enemy. It made no difference to her."

Leander regarded his friend sadly. "I should like it if my life were to turn out somewhat differently than Shakespeare's young lovers."

"It's been too many years since you loved and were loved. Why, you've forgotten all joy in life. Come, now, you have much to offer." Fly gave him a good looking-over. "You're young, strong enough—perhaps a bit too thin—occasionally funny, and despite your aged mannerisms and bookishness, you have been labelled as being 'well formed.'"

"Well formed? By whom?"

"None other than Mrs. Kettle, who is known to take up a spyglass to us while we bathe in the sea."

Leander shrugged and raised his grog mug. "Well then, here's to Mrs. Kettle."

"Furthermore," said Fly, "you have something most men do not: an education, and a brilliant one at that. You could make a decent living anywhere. Make a move, before you become weak and infirm, or are altogether extinguished. Go and live. I could offer you my cabin, or, better still, post a marine sentry outside your berth on the orlop deck."

"You are truly filthy minded."

"Aye. That I am."

Just then Gus Walby came flying up the ladder to the poop deck, swinging a lighted lantern before him. "Mr. Austen, sir."

"Mr. Walby?"

"No lights burning down below, sir."

"Fine, thank you. Now extinguish your own. We don't want any enemy frigates learning our position."

"Sir," Gus said, dousing his flame.

"And you can check again in an hour. Old Bailey Beck's been known to leave his hammock late in the evening to strike a match and play cards with Morgan and Jacko."

"I will, sir. Until then, may I seek your permission to go to the hospital and read with Emily for a bit?"

Fly angled his cheery countenance towards his drinking companion. "That is up to our doctor."

"Yes, yes, of course you can, Mr. Walby." Leander felt a twinge of envy.

"Sir!" Gus broke into a tremendous smile and hurried off.

Leander looked after him wistfully. Fly laughed and clapped him on the back. "Come, now, mask your devotion and let us drink to life." Seeing Weevil standing near the *Isabelle*'s waist, Fly called out to him. "You there!" The cook's assistant came running. "Fetch a bottle of your best French wine and take it ... take it to my cabin."

"Right away, sir," said Weevil before dashing off.

Fly lowered his voice to Leander. "Let us continue our refreshments below in privacy. Otherwise, the men will lose any respect they may hold for me when I break into a drunken song."

Reluctantly Leander left the comfort of the bench to follow Fly, and as the two carefully negotiated the steps down to the quarterdeck, the beacon that shone from the lighthouse on Cape Hatteras vanished from view.

8

Monday, June 14

7:00 a.m.
(Morning Watch, Six Bells)

THE CRY OF THE BOSUN'S MATE was loud and penetrating. "All hands ahoy! Up all hammocks ahoy!"

Emily opened her eyes to find a light patter of rain falling outside her open gunport and her ocean views obscured by a dense fog. She could hear the men dropping down from their hammocks on the decks below, and outside her curtain, Osmund Brockley fidgeting and clearing his throat. Barely had she time to pull her blanket around her and utter an invitation to enter when he burst through the canvas carrying her breakfast tray, babbling like an undisciplined child in need of attention.

"Mornin', Miss. Dr. Braden ordered breakfast early fer ya as he thought ya might like to meet with young Magpie in the galley before the men are piped into breakfast. Ya'll find Biscuit cursing by his stove in there; otherwise, it'll be quiet and ya can have a private word or two. Mind ya, not for long. The duty cooks usually come in around seven bells."

"Thank you, Osmund. You can set the tray down on the stool. I'll eat later."

Osmund unloaded the tray and stood back to regard her with his peculiar round eyes and blank expression, reminding Emily of a sailor who had taken a few too many knocks to the head. It never ceased to astonish her that he actually possessed *some* abilities in the hospital.

"We're busting to know, Miss, why ya've asked fer a private interview with young Magpie," he said.

Emily's eyes rounded in surprise. "Are there are no secrets to be had on this ship?"

"Oh, no, Miss. We all know one another's business on the *Isabelle*."

"Well, I'm sorry to disappoint you, Mr. Brockley, but I shan't be divulging all mine this morning." Seeing him squirm with curiosity, Emily hid her amused expression and looked about for her clothes. She'd last seen them hanging from the wooden peg on the post by her feet.

"My clothes! They're gone."

"Aye, Miss, but ya see it's Monday—Mrs. Kettle's laundry day—and on account of Dr. Braden disliking the way Meggie blows in here and causes a rumpus with the men, he asked her to fetch yer clothes late last night whilst ya were sleeping."

"Why, I didn't even receive certain articles of clothing back from last week's washing."

"Oh, they were probably ruined or lost during the exchange of gunfire with the *Liberty*," Osmund said, licking spittle from his thick lips.

Emily neglected to tell him that it was her chemise that had never been returned, for fear of being told that a sailor or, worse still, Mrs. Kettle herself, had filched it as a souvenir.

"I cannot very well sit in the galley with Dr. Braden's nightshirt on."

Osmund broke into his characteristic donkey-braying laughter. "Aye, Miss, although it would provide a fine spectacle for all the men first thing in the morning." Seeing her glower, he quit laughing and smartened himself up. "Ah! And it's a bit damp today with the mists and everything. It wouldn't do fer ya to catch a cold."

"My blue jacket and white trousers, the ones Magpie made for me... would you know of their whereabouts?"

Osmund nodded. "The doctor told me where I'd find them." He

lumbered over to the cupboard and with a grunt of satisfaction pulled out the neatly folded clothing, tossed them upon Emily's cot, then banged the cupboard door shut.

"And where is Dr. Braden this morning?" Emily felt her face grow hot, for no other reason than having spoken aloud his name.

"With the captain."

"Is Captain Moreland still unwell?"

"The doctor's not saying much, but none of us have seen him since he first took with fever. All's I know is Mr. Austen is worrying hisself sick that we'll be attacked again whilst the captain's ailing. Mr. Austen's ordered extra men on every watch, especially with the *Isabelle* sitting idle in these fogs."

Emily began pulling her blue jacket on over Leander's nightshirt and tried to ignore the anxious feeling that sent her heart beating out of control and twisted her stomach into reef knots. "Will we be able to sail again soon?"

"I hear there're more repairs to be made, Miss, and then we'll have to wait fer the right winds to carry us away."

"Surely no one would fire upon us when we do not pose a threat?"

"We'll know soon enough now, won't we, Miss?"

"Please tell Magpie I'll meet him in a few minutes," she said, her voice cracking.

"Right, Miss, but if it's secrets ya have to tell the lad, speak 'em quietly."

"Why is that, Mr. Brockley?"

"'Cause we'll all be listening in."

Emily and Magpie sat upon two overturned buckets in the galley, as far away as was possible from Biscuit, who, in the company of Maggot and Weevil, was preparing the officers' hot morning rations in true Biscuit style—with plenty of confusion and bad language. Dominating the room was Biscuit's pride and joy, his Brodie's Patent galley stove, a huge black hulk of a thing that hissed and shrieked like a monster and was capable of roasting, boiling, and baking simultaneously. Biscuit cheerfully buzzed around it, toasting bread, flipping eggs, stirring oatmeal, and barking at his mates to "clear me way, lads, excellent cookin' in progress."

Standing in the entranceway between the galley and the hospital stood the ever-present marine sentry. He kept watch over Emily and Magpie, glaring at those who dared to pause a moment in their chores to show interest in their quiet conversation. Emily sat with her back turned to them all and focused her attention on the little sail maker. He sat stoically before her, the right side of his face frighteningly bandaged and bruised. Leander had worried about infection setting into his wound, but surely enough time had passed and he was safely beyond that point. Neatly folded upon Magpie's lap was his special pond-green blanket, and he told her he wasn't afraid to carry it with him as none of the men had once teased him about it.

"Of course they wouldn't tease you," Emily said kindly.

Magpie's cheeks glowed pink. "The Duke o' Clarence's wife gave it to me. Mrs. Jordan was her name. And she said to me, 'This is to keep you safe and warm at sea.' I—I sleep better when I 'ave it with me." He peeked up into Emily's face. "Dr. Braden says in a week or so he'll take away the bandages and be fittin' me up with an eye patch. Will I scare ya? Will ya be lookin' at me and thinkin' of Thomas Trevelyan?"

"Thomas Trevelyan?"

"He's a pirate, ain't he?"

"The worst kind! But how is it you know of Trevelyan?"

"He's the captain of the *Serendipity*, that first ship we done battle with, ain't he? The ship ya was on. Ya told Captain Moreland it was Trevelyan."

"I suppose I must have done." Emily tried to remember back to her first interview with James Moreland and Fly Austen. Evidently, there were big ears listening beyond the curtain that day. "And was I also overheard saying that Trevelyan was a pirate?"

"No, but why else would ya've jumped his ship and risked drownin' yerself in the sea?"

Emily reflected on that one a moment. "When I look upon

you, Magpie, I will be reminded, not of Trevelyan, but of the most courageous of men."

The young lad beamed at her for a brief second before his smile faded. Emily could see his eye examining the bruises on her face. "You're so kind to me, ma'am, and I…I don't deserve it. I don't deserve it at all."

Emily reached for one of his hands, so small and brown the little soot-stained fingers, and squeezed it gently. Liking the feel of his hand in her warm one, Magpie left it there as long as he could, until Biscuit's wandering eye fell on the two of them and he pulled it away to deal with a few tears that had somehow dropped to his cheek.

"A few days ago," he said quickly, "Morgan told me that the new sail maker—what's replaced me—is a big man named Bun Brodie and he was sailin' on the *Liberty*. Mr. Brodie was tellin' the men one suppertime there was only one lady that he knew of travellin' on the *Serendipity* and her name was Mrs. Seaton."

Emily struggled to disguise her dismay. "And what did this Mr. Brodie say happened to this Mrs. Seaton?"

"He never knew. He don't know what happened to her, but…" Magpie looked timid and hesitated to say more.

"Go on."

"The men think—maybe yer Mrs. Seaton."

Emily didn't reply. She raised her pretty head and a distant look crept into her brown eyes as she sat there, stiff and erect, on the overturned bucket. She stayed silent such a long while that Magpie worried his remarks had been impertinent.

"Magpie," she said in a whisper, "the day you asked for your blanket, I found something in your chest."

Magpie grew excited and began squirming about on his bucket like a young kitten. "Ya found me miniature, then, didn't ya?"

"I did!"

"It's you, ain't it?"

Emily nodded slowly.

"I knew it was ya the day Morgan pulled ya in. I just knew ya was the lady in me picture, that first time I seen ya smile. Ya looked just like her, even with yer hair all wet. And ya was wearin' the very same blue velvet clothes! I just knew I was lookin' at a princess."

Emily placed a finger to her lips, grateful for the great racket Biscuit and his mates were making behind her. "I may be a princess, but I am not a very important one. I'm not heir to the English throne or anything." There was a twinkle in her eye.

"Imagine me, Magpie, sail maker on the *Isabelle*, knowin' a princess, even if she ain't important. Why, you should be livin' in the captain's cabin, drinkin' tea from his fine china, and havin' Biscuit cook ya up ten-course suppers on silver plate."

Emily laughed. "Hush, now! That is exactly what I do *not* want." Leaning in closer to the lad, she dropped her voice. "The day we were left alone above deck... why didn't you tell me of your suspicions then?"

"Oh, I was wantin' to, somethin' fierce, but I was too scared of ya, and I was bein' respectful, ya bein' royalty and all, and 'cause I was wondrin' to meself what ya was doin' jumpin' out o' ships. I was thinkin' maybe ya was runnin' away and didn't wanna be found out. I—I did ask ya then, ma'am, if ya knew the Duke o' Clarence, and right off ya said no."

"I am sorry for that. I had my reasons for giving you that reply. The truth is, Magpie, I do know your Duke and Mrs. Jordan very well indeed, although to me they are Uncle Clarence and Aunt Dora. Three years ago, when my father died, I lived with them for a short while. Uncle Clarence has always treated me like one of his own daughters."

Magpie puffed up his small chest, so proud he was, as if they were speaking of his own parents. "And the duke, he's the admiral of the fleet! I didn't even know 'til yesterday. Heard the men talkin' about that too. Did ya know he was the admiral, ma'am?"

She nodded again. "He was given the appointment in December of 1811, if I remember correctly, by his brother, the prince regent."

Magpie's little face suddenly clouded. "Won't yer Uncle Clarence be worryin' about ya, gettin' shot at and attacked in sail rooms and all, ma'am?"

Emily's eyes glazed over. "He knows nothing of my getting shot at and attacked in sail rooms, but I am certain ... he is quite frantic to know of my whereabouts." She blinked and returned her attention to Magpie. "So tell me, was it my uncle who gave you the miniature?"

Magpie bobbed his curly head. "The day I was cleanin' their chimney, I was admirin' it and says out loud, 'That's the loveliest lady I've ever set me eyes on.' The Duke told me ya was his niece. And Mrs. Jordan kindly gives it to me along with the sea chest and me blanket here. Ya won't be takin' it back from me, will ya?"

"No, it is yours to keep." Emily grew sombre. "Magpie ... I must know ... have you shown that miniature to anyone, told anyone of your suspicions?"

Magpie sat up straighter and crossed his heart. "Not a one," he whispered. "Not a one, I swear, ma'am. There ain't no one on this ship that knows yer real name. Why, they're all wondrin' if yer Mrs. Seaton, but I know the truth. I know yer really Emeline Louisa Georgina Marie, daughter of Henry, Duke o' Wessex, as was."

Emily peeked over her shoulder to scope out the whereabouts of the cooks. "Please promise me this will be our little secret. Say nothing of Mrs. Seaton and the name Emeline Louisa ..."

"Georgina Marie," Magpie finished off triumphantly.

Biscuit approached, his odd eye rolling about as if trying to fix itself upon them, and said, "Pardon me, lass, but thee men, they'll be piped into their breakfast soon and it might not be fittin' they see ya sittin' here."

"I'll be crawling back to my hole momentarily, Biscuit," Emily said tersely, hoping her reply would get rid of him. She waited until he had crept back to his cauldron of porridge. "The miniature, Magpie ... I will get it back to you the minute I—" Her words died on her lips as a sudden realization struck with the force and speed of a cat-of-nine-tails whip.

Good God! Her clothes!

She sprang from her low bucket, her hands fumbling anxiously in the pockets of her white trousers, a fearful look in her eyes. Into the galley came a flood of duty cooks with their ration buckets to begin cooking breakfast for their messmates. Every last one of them gave Emily a long looking over, but in her frenzied state she took no notice.

"Well now, Magpie," whistled one who had to drag his foot behind him, "ye have done well fer yerself!"

"Our young sail maker has risen in the world!"

"Ha, ha, ho, ho."

"Shove off," said the marine sentry.

But it was Biscuit who was more effective in scattering the sailors. He raised his wooden porridge spoon menacingly before them and growled, "Hold yer tongues, ya lubbers, and be mindin' yer manners."

Magpie jumped up from his own bucket, his bandaged head held high, and like a little gentleman took Emily's arm and calmly steered her away from the men's lusty looks, past the marine sentry, and back into the hospital. When they arrived at her corner, he let go of her arm and asked, "What's wrong, ma'am?"

"Oh, Magpie," she gasped, ashen-faced, "your miniature ... it's in the pocket of my other trousers, and ... and Mrs. Kettle took them early this morning to be laundered!"

8:00 a.m.
(Morning Watch, Eight Bells)

THE BOSUN'S MATE'S PIPES resonated round the lower deck, summoning the men to their breakfast. Near the gunroom, Meg Kettle waited until the last of the sailors had scurried past her and run up the ladder before slipping out of the shadows. It was her good fortune to find that the marine sentry had temporarily vacated his prisoner's post. She leaned over the dirty man in the bilboes and grabbed a clump of his greasy hair, yanking his head back. "Time ta wake up, Mr. Lindsay ... Lord, *sir*," she said in derision. Plopping down upon the nearby bench pushed up against the ship's sweating side, she watched the prisoner stir to life. He did so with great difficulty, grunting and groaning and cursing his back muscles, which ached from sitting on the damp floor, and his numb legs, immobilized in the thick irons.

"I've got somethin' int'restin' ta show ya," said Mrs. Kettle, enjoying the spectacle of Octavius's pain.

"Infernal woman, leave me be!"

"Ooooh, but this ya'll be wantin' ta see."

Octavius screwed his head around to face her, rubbing his neck as he did so. "What the devil would *you* have that would interest me?"

"Mind yer tone or I won't be showin' ya." She produced a shiny something from her apron pocket and waved it before him.

Octavius ignored her. "Vile laundry woman! Leave me be."

In one fluid motion—far more fluid than one would think her capable of—Mrs. Kettle leapt off the bench, lifted her skirt, and dealt his crooked spine a savage blow with her booted foot. Octavius gasped for air, as if the woman had held his head underwater a long time. Howls of agony followed.

"Guard, guard, take her away. Take her away!" His voice was shrill and strained like that of a fearful child. "Why doesn't anyone come?"

Mrs. Kettle shoved her face, red and wet with exertion, into his pimply one. "'Cause no one cares fer yer worthlessness any more."

Mrs. Kettle looked pleased with herself as she watched Octavius desperately wrestle with his irons, vainly attempting to free his legs. When finally he gave up his fight and had, for the time, buried his rancour, she slapped her knee and said, "Right, now! Set yer eyes on this here." She placed Magpie's oval miniature into his quivering hands and held the lantern up over his head. "Behold that smilin' face. Now, quick, flip it round."

Octavius wiped at his eyes with dirty fingers and stared at the miniature for some time, turning it over again and again to scrutinize the face and the inscription.

"It's her, ain't it?"

"Who?"

"That *woman* what lies in thee doctor's cot."

"The daughter of Henry, Duke of Wessex, one of King George's many sons? And ... and therefore a niece of the prince regent and the Duke of Clarence?" Octavius snorted like a horse. "Impossible!"

"It's her all right and she's some kind o' princess."

Octavius gave his tormentor an impatient look. "I'll admit to a resemblance, nothing more. I happen to know that portrait painters are never very accurate in their representation of their subject."

"Aye, I suppose yer mother would be havin' a portrait of ya without yer red spots and limp hair."

He disregarded the slight. "I possess a miniature of my *mother* and the artist has succeeded brilliantly in making her look like Boticelli's Venus, when in truth she bears a striking resemblance to a trollop!"

Mrs. Kettle grunted and pointed to the clothing worn by the woman in the miniature. "That woman came on board wearin' thee same blue shirt."

Octavius peered down at the picture again. "It's *called* a spencer-jacket, not a shirt. Fashionable ladies have been wearing them for some time now."

"Oh, we keep up with ladies' fashions, do we now? Harumph! Well, I may not know thee fancy name fer it, but I knows what I see and thee braidin' and design on that jacket's thee same as what that woman were wearin' thee day she set foot on thee *Isabelle*."

Octavius shook his head. "It still doesn't prove that Emily and the daughter of the late Duke of Wessex are one and the same person."

Mrs. Kettle snatched the miniature out of his hands and laid down her trump card. "Aye, then how do ya explain me findin' it in thee pocket of 'er trousers?"

Octavius's mouth opened, his lips framing a silent "O." He drifted into a daze while Mrs. Kettle stood over him, stroking the miniature as if it were a precious, sentimental object. "Ya never know who might be int'rested in seein' this," she said, tempting the wheels in his head to turn. She popped the miniature into her apron pocket, gave it a wee pat, and left Octavius in the dark to consider the possibilities.

In the blue shadows of the animals' stable, Magpie swiftly and soundlessly sank out of sight just as Mrs. Kettle's long swishing skirts swept past him, fanning his face. With Biscuit's milking goat complacently licking his ear, and his heart thumping madly, he listened to her heavy footsteps gradually fade away down the gun deck. In despair, he realized he had come too late in search of the miniature. Mrs. Kettle had already found it, and she was scheming to do something with it—exactly what, Magpie didn't know, but he knew he had to warn Emily and fast. Spying a perfectly rounded lump of dung sitting in a nest of straw by the goat's hind legs, Magpie picked the whole works up and lobbed it like a grenade at the back of Octavius Lindsay's head.

2:00 p.m.
(Afternoon Watch, Four Bells)

"SAIL HO! SAIL HO!"

"Larboard bow ahoy!"

"It's a man-o'-war all right!"

"A mighty big one at that!"

In his cabin, James struggled to raise himself up in his cot. "Dear God! There was a time I thrilled to hear those words. Now they only fill me with dread."

"Stay where you are," said Leander firmly, trying to take James's pulse. "Fly has commanded many ships in his time."

"Hand me my clothes, Lee."

"Your fever has returned and your pulse is weak. Please... stay where you are."

James paid him no heed. He stumbled out of his cot and staggered over to his clothing hook where, with trembling hands, he reached for his white breeches and his blue frock coat adorned with shoulder epaulettes and brass-buttoned cuffs.

"I cannot agree to you leaving your bed in your state."

James mopped his brow. "I've been too long in my bed, Lee. And I am well aware that I may never regain my strength."

"Have you no faith in the abilities of Fly and Mr. Harding?"

"That is not the point!" he replied, with an edge in his voice; then, more gently, he added, "My men need to see me. If we are to face another battle, it will put their minds at ease to have me walk with them above deck."

"That is all well and noble," said Leander, pulling off his spectacles, "but I believe your men would find greater comfort in knowing your health was being restored with rest. As your doctor, I simply cannot approve of you—"

"I will not fight Trevelyan in my bedclothes!" James glared at the doctor for a while until his anger dissipated, then, wearing a look of remorse, he carried his clothes meekly to his desk chair, where he sat down to catch his breath. Slowly he pulled on his breeches, then his Hessian boots, which stood upright on the floor beside him, and finally, his uniform coat.

Leander tucked his spectacles into his waistcoat pocket. "What evidence do we have that it is Trevelyan's ship that approaches?"

James fumbled with his coat buttons, but finding the task exhausting, he shifted his body round to look out through the galleried windows upon the billowing misty-white sea, and fell into a dreamlike state. There was something in his aspect that led Leander to wonder if James's thoughts had travelled home to England. He watched him closely for some time.

"James, why is it the name Trevelyan strikes such fear in you? Granted, two weeks back, his guns inflicted a fearful lot of damage on us, but surely no more than we inflicted upon him."

Beads of sweat ran down James's sunken cheeks, and his eyes never left the sea. "He has an old score to settle with me and has waited a very long time for his revenge. I feared he would resurface again one day; I just never imagined I'd meet him in the Atlantic and find him commanding, of all things, an American ship called the *Serendipity*."

Leander hoped to hear more, but when James revealed nothing

further, he set about collecting his medical chest and made his way to the cabin door. "I will go and question Mr. McGilp for you—see what news there is." Throwing open the door, he found McGilp already standing there, his fist at his forehead in a salute to his captain.

"Mr. McGilp!" cried James, rising to his feet. "Can you tell me? Is she British or Yankee?"

"She's coming from the nor'east, sir. Still hard to tell with the mists and all."

"Bearing down on us?"

"No, at ease and a piece off yet, sir."

"The very minute—*the very minute*—you can identify her colours, let me know."

"Right, sir."

Mr. McGilp hurried off just as the sailing master, Mr. Harding, appeared at the door, red-faced and breathless. "Your instructions, sir?" he rasped.

"Tell Mr. Austen to raise the anchors and unfurl the sails. We must try to harness what wind we can and get to deeper water as soon as possible. Are our repairs nearly complete?"

"Another day or two would have been preferred, sir, but I think we are sound enough to fight ... if need be."

"And time ... how much time would you say we have, Mr. Harding?"

"A good two hours, I'd say, sir—that's if we were to stay put."

After James had shut the door on the sailing master's retreating steps, Leander led him back to his desk chair. Within minutes they could hear the familiar whirl of activity above deck—the call for the hands to weigh anchor and the sound of a fifer piping them to their posts to the tune of "Heart of Oak." Two hundred men alone were needed to raise the thick cables of the main anchor. Eighty-four men, mostly marines, were necessary to operate the twelve bars of the capstan on the fo'c'sle, and several dozen more would be stationed on the gun deck and orlop to handle and stow the incoming, fishy-smelling cable.

"While we wait it out, I must stay occupied," said James, fumbling again with his coat buttons.

"You've eaten nothing today. Could I convince you to take some food?"

"Perhaps a bowl of soup," James said. "I will swallow a bit of nourishment for you, Lee, if you would escort Emily here to my cabin."

"Emily?"

"I would like to question her again." Noticing a mixed expression of interest and alarm on Leander's face, he added, "You may stay for the interview."

"I should like that."

"Shall we say ... in half an hour?" When Leander nodded his agreement, James sighed. "Right then! Now help me fasten these damned buttons."

2:30 p.m.
(Afternoon Watch, Five Bells)

EMILY, GUS, AND MAGPIE sat cross-legged on the floor of Emily's hospital corner reading Jane Austen's *Sense and Sensibility* together. All three knew there had been a sighting, and their anxiety of the unknown was eased somewhat by listening to Austen's fictional tale. Magpie sat with his back erect, his one almond-shaped eye shining in the shadows, his full youthful attention on the story of the sisters named Elinor and Marianne Dashwood. Gus read, his melodious voice loud enough so that Dr. Braden's patients could hear his words as they lay in their cots, though it did not escape Emily's notice that one of his legs was bouncing up and down.

Prior to their reading, Magpie had recounted in worried whispers the scene he had witnessed on the gun deck, and with this intelligence knocking around in her head, Emily sat nervously, one ear to the story, the other listening for the return of Mrs. Kettle with her laundry.

Before long, Leander crept into their corner and, with a nod of his head and an incline of his auburn eyebrows, sought permission to listen in. "I have a bit of time to spare before … before I tend to my next task," he said, as if apologizing for his sudden appearance.

"Oh, please join us, Doctor," Emily said, feeling at once safer with him on the wooden stool beside her.

Gus had barely managed to read a page when Magpie's hand flew up in the air yet again as if he were a schoolboy sitting at his classroom desk and Gus his schoolmaster. "Excuse me, Mr. Walby, but I need to know why Miss Marianne got so sick."

"Magpie, you must stop asking so many questions or we'll never get through this chapter," admonished Gus. "We don't have long, you know."

"It's fine to ask questions, Magpie," Emily said, smiling at his literary enthusiasm.

"All right then," Gus recanted, disliking the thought of displeasing Emily. "While Miss Marianne was staying at the Palmers' home, she took to rambling around their damp grounds, and got her shoes and stockings all wet. The result was she caught a chill and came down with an infectious fever."

Magpie meditated on Gus's answer. "But I don't understand, 'cause me shoes and stockins' are wet all o' the time and I never gets a 'fectious fever."

"What Gus said is true," added Emily softly, "but you also need to understand that Marianne was spiritually exhausted and came close to dying of a broken heart. You see, she had fallen in love with the handsome Mr. Willoughby, and he in turn loved her dearly. In all ways, they were wonderfully suited for one another. But Willoughby had debts to pay, and under the threat of losing his large income, was forced to marry a wealthy woman for whom he did not care. It was his pocketbook he chose over Marianne's love."

Magpie looked upset. "Then who will be marryin' Miss Marianne?"

"For certain it will be Colonel Brandon!" Gus spoke up eagerly this time. "It was him that rode to Barton to fetch Mrs. Dashwood when Miss Marianne was lying ill."

"And although not as dashing or enticing a man as Willoughby,"

Emily continued, "Colonel Brandon is far more honourable, and he adores her."

From her cross-legged position on the floor, she glanced up and was heartened to find Leander smiling down upon her, adoration in his eyes. He started as if emerging from a reverie. "Jane writes well, does she not?" he said. "She always had a talent for writing…"

Realizing his thoughts had been with Miss Austen, Emily's reply was cool. "She does. I have read no better work."

There was an uneasy moment of silence, during which Leander cleared his throat and fixed his stare upon the front cover of *Sense and Sensibility*. Then, standing up, he turned to Gus. "Excuse me, Mr. Walby, before you continue your reading, I have come to inform Emily"—Leander looked right at her—"that her presence has been requested in the great cabin."

An icy chill prickled Emily's spine. Had Mrs. Kettle already shown the miniature to Captain Moreland? She wrinkled her forehead. "More interrogation? Why now? Surely the captain has far more grave concerns on his mind."

"That he does; however, he would like to speak to you before that approaching ship gets too close for comfort."

Gus shut the book, and all three of them pushed themselves up from the floor. Leander swept aside the curtain to let them pass into the hospital. To their surprise, standing amongst the hammocks, holding Emily's cleaned checked shirt and trousers, was Meg Kettle. "Ahh, and what were yas all doin' in there?" Mrs. Kettle asked in a tone that set Mr. Crump into a fit of giggles.

"We was readin' a book!" said Magpie. "Somethin' ya can't and won't never do."

A hush descended upon the room as everyone present gaped at the little sail maker's outburst. Emily placed her hands gently on his thin shoulders.

When she had quite recovered her shock, Mrs. Kettle glared at Emily. "I suppose yer teachin' him yer fancy ways. Readin' a book! Ya 'ave no use fer it, Magpie. Ya won't never rise above yer station, especially now … lookin' like a one-eyed serpent with 'alf a face."

Feeling Magpie squirming beneath her hands, Emily squeezed his shoulders while Leander, standing next to her, looked like thunder. "Mrs. Kettle, your tongue has no place here. I must ask that you leave now."

"And I see ya've fallen under 'er spell as well, Doctor."

"Leave your laundry and turn about!"

Mrs. Kettle hurled the clean clothes at Emily. "There ya be, ya lofty camp follower."

The room echoed with gasps and whistles. Heads rose from their pillows. Mr. Crump wiggled his stump about in raptures. He'd never witnessed such excitement! "Give 'er thee old toss, Doc."

Osmund, none too gently, steered the laundress towards the exit.

"Wait!" said Emily. She stooped to collect her scattered clothes, past caring about the possible repercussions of what she was about to do. All eyes focused on her as she rifled through the pockets of her clean trousers, obviously in search of something, and came up empty-handed. "Mrs. Kettle," she said with all the composure she could muster, "I believe you have something of mine."

Mrs. Kettle shook off Osmund's hold on her arm, her small eyes narrowing, almost disappearing into the folds of her facial fat. "And what would that be?"

Emily stood her battleground, holding onto Magpie again, this time for support. "It was in the pocket of these trousers."

Mrs. Kettle looked uncertain. Several times she swallowed and her fists fiddled in the coarse material of her skirt. Her red face twitched as she cast nervously about, her eyes racing from face to face, her taut stance indicating a desire to bolt from the hospital. But when her eyes finally stopped on Leander, her hunted expression vanished. Giving the side of her head a playful smack, she haughtily exclaimed, "Ahhhh! How could I 'ave taken such leave o' me senses. My sincere apologies to yer *Highness*. Right! In yer trousers pocket it was."

Emily waited, holding her breath, while Mrs. Kettle leisurely reached into the pocket of her apron and jerked out a stained, crumpled piece of paper. Realizing what it was she held up in her fat hands,

Emily watched in horror as a malicious grin appeared on the laundress's lips.

"Ya think I know nothin' of readin', ya imp," Mrs. Kettle spit at Magpie. "Well, hear this!" She shifted into her most amorous voice. "*My Dearest Jane. It is too long since last I heard your joyful voice and walked with you in the gardens at Chawton. I often think of England and the time when we will next meet. More than ever I have need of your comfort and inspiration as already we have twice battled the Americans and our casualties have been too numerous for even this poor doctor to bear. Several of us in the hospital take solace in reading your novel. It has afforded us hours of pleasure. What delightful characters you have created in the Misses Dashwoods. I am particularly taken with Miss Marianne. Would you believe me if I told you that I have recently become acquainted with a true Marianne ...*"

Something in the way Mrs. Kettle read the letter suggested she had memorized its contents. With a dramatic flourish, she dabbed at her eyes and, shooting a meaningful glance at Leander, said, "Such pretty words! 'Tis a pity there ain't more."

Emily forced herself to look at Leander. Her heart sank to see his handsome face frozen in disbelief, his lips moving in silent inquiry, his blue eyes—brimming with devastation—staring back at her.

"Aye, imagine that! Right in 'er very pocket I found yer letter, Doctor!"

Magpie whirled about to face Emily. "What about the miniature, ma'am?"

Emily shook her head sadly.

Suddenly, a burst of cries and bellows came from the men above deck.

"She's Yankee! She's Yankee all right!"

"And a frigate!"

"Clear the decks for action!"

"Lively now, lads."

"Lower the boats."

The drums beat to quarters, instantly plunging the *Isabelle* and her crew into nervous activity. Urgent footsteps pounding overhead and the frantic orders of the unseen seamen sent Emily's heart into her mouth.

"Dear, God, not again!" she whispered.

Gus took hold of her hand and dragged her back towards her canvas corner. "You'll be safe in here, Em."

Emily went in reluctantly, twisting her head around in a backwards glance only to learn that Mrs. Kettle had made her escape and Leander, his cheeks still flushed, was sharpening his surgical equipment for the grisly task that lay before him.

4:30 p.m.
(First Dog Watch, One Bell)

FLY AUSTEN REACHED THE QUARTERDECK and looked about the ship. He was dressed in his freshly pressed blue-and-gold uniform, his body erect, his dark eyes alert. Today his aspect was all business. Wherever his gaze fell, there wasn't one man—from those clinging to the footropes and the tops, to those hugging the rails and manning the guns—whose eyes weren't trained upon the approaching warship. Though she was still a few miles away and resembled a ghost ship emerging from the wispy mists, Fly could plainly see her American colours at her stern. He found James alongside Mr. Harding, holding onto the starboard rail with one hand, watching the ship's movements through his spyglass.

Coming up behind the two men, Fly saluted James and said, "Sir, the men are at their posts and stand ready round the guns."

As he lowered his glass, James looked disheartened. "We haven't had the time to fully repair. What's more, we have neither adequate sea room in which to manoeuvre, nor the wind in our favour, Mr. Austen."

Mr. Harding shifted his weight onto his one foot. "And this is a cursed place to do battle. With very little effort, she could force us back upon those damned shoals."

"We'll not do anything to provoke her," said James determinedly. "We'll wait and see if she fires the first shot." In the company of Mr. Harding, he moved on down the starboard gangway to dispense words of encouragement to the gun crews and yell out final orders to the men and marines in the tops.

Fly pulled out his own spyglass, mumbling words of encouragement to himself, to stay buoyed before the men. *Breathe out, Austen. Remember that Nelson succeeded by breaking with our rigid naval tactics. Perhaps, if we want to save our necks, we should follow suit and try putting our collective imaginations to task.* Lifting the glass to his eye, he studied the looming ship that was still three or four miles away. He could see her cutting a good bow wave beneath her elaborately carved red-and-gold figurehead. Her hull was black with a stripe of ochre-yellow that followed her gunports. The squares of her foresails, plumped up by the strong northeast breeze, glowed in the sun's rays that peeked through the clouds, and resembled large pillows in slipcovers of gold. He watched the tiny figures of the seamen bustling about the decks and climbing the standing rigging to the tops. Near the bowsprit, he was certain he could see the captain himself, a corpulent man in a cocked hat, standing amongst a group of officers. Aware that the whirling mists were finally receding, Fly kept the glass to his eye and made a mental note of the number of guns she possessed. All the while, along the corridors of his mind, there was a pricking sensation—something was familiar about this large ship.

Nearby, the sailors who nervously awaited their next round of orders—Mr. McGilp gripping the *Isabelle*'s wheel, the marines with their muskets ready and aimed, the gun crews and powder monkeys clustered around the great guns on the starboard side of the fo'c'sle, poop, and quarterdeck—never expected to see Mr. Austen, in one sudden movement, toss up his spyglass and throw back his head to howl with laughter.

"Captain Moreland, sir," he called out, addressing all those sweating, eager faces that looked his way, "I invite you to take another look through your glass."

EMILY CAST OFF THE GARMENTS Magpie had laboured to make for her and wiggled into her clean, less formal checked shirt and trousers, determined she would not cower in her corner waiting for the cannons to shake the ship's sides and the agonizing cries of the mutilated men to echo in her ears. When Gus and Magpie had left her to resume their nautical duties, she had attempted to calm herself by rereading passages of Jane Austen's novel, but it was no use. The words in Leander's letter haunted her thoughts and only served to stir up envious emotions for the talented author of *Sense and Sensibility*.

Leaving the security of her corner, she entered the hospital room with trepidation, worried lest there be further talk on the subject of Leander's stolen letter. When the drums had beat to quarters, she had heard great commotion beyond her curtain, but she had not dreamed that every last man had heeded the call, from the marine sentry and Mr. Crump to Osmund Brockley and the loblolly boys. Leander's desk had been transformed into an operating table, with the familiar bloodstained sheet and neat line of surgical tools spread out upon it, and Leander himself was sitting hunched over in the desk chair, scratching notes into his medical journal with a quill pen. Uneasily, Emily stood before him like a child before a stern teacher. "Please, Doctor, I am in need of an occupation."

He pressed his lips together and regarded her over his round spectacles, and without saying a word, lifted up a bucket of bandages by his feet and handed it to her. Emily knew he meant for her to roll them in preparation for their next round of patients. She searched about for the nearest stool, sat down with her bucket, and set about to work, relieved to be doing something useful and delighting in the pleasant musky smell of Leander's closeness. From her seat, she furtively watched his fingers fly over the pages of his journal and his slim shoulders stir in his clean muslin shirt and striped waistcoat as he exercised stiffening muscles, hoping that eventually he would set his eyes upon her.

"I gather my interview with Captain Moreland has been postponed."

He paused in his writing, but did not look up. "It has."

"Yes, yes, of course," she said, hating herself for stating the obvious.

As the silence between them continued, Emily grew more and more jittery, and the pandemonium over their heads seemed at once remote and unreal. At last, Leander lay down his pen. "I thought perhaps you might find respite in reading Jane's book."

She eagerly smiled up at him. "It is not the same without the company of Gus Walby."

"I see," he said absently, as if his thoughts were elsewhere.

"Besides, I cannot help feeling jealous of Jane Austen."

"Why is that?"

Her cheeks turned scarlet. "Because her... her book is so finely crafted, her writing so true. Her accomplishments are an inspiration to all women." Leander nodded thoughtfully before returning to his journal. "And because," she added quickly, "she so obviously holds *your* affections."

The flash of his eyes on her made her shaky and her words tumbled out of her mouth. "Doctor, please, you must believe me. I did not steal your letter. I found it on the floor of the hospital a week back. Osmund Brockley had already stepped on it with his clumsiness and spilled all forms of liquid upon it. It would have been lost altogether had I not picked it up before setting off for the sail room to fetch Magpie's blanket and placed it in my pocket, and when ... when I was forced to return to my cot it remained in my pocket, safe, but altogether forgotten. I swear to you ... I did *not* read it."

Leander shut his journal and leaned back against the wooden spindles of his chair, assuming the aspect of a judge about to exact a punishment. Before long, an expression of amusement brightened his face. "If I were to believe you, Emily, can you tell me truthfully that you wouldn't—at some point—have been tempted to read it?"

She laughed nervously. "Honestly? I cannot tell."

All the clamour and confusion that had crashed above their heads for so long ceased abruptly, as if the peacefulness of the hospital had permeated the entire ship. Together Leander and Emily raised their eyes to the wooden ceiling and strained their ears to catch a sailor's footfall or vociferous bellow.

Emily fidgeted with the bandages in her lap, certain that Leander could hear her heart beating. "Why is there no sound?"

"There is often an eerie calm before battle." He set his eyes once again upon Emily, a sober glint having replaced his one of earlier enjoyment. "You asked Mrs. Kettle to return to you something that was yours. If it was not my letter to which you referred, may I ask what it was?"

Emily was slow to answer, for her mind was muddled. It was tortuous trying to ignore the fact that a Yankee frigate was swiftly bearing down on them, and yet she keenly felt Leander's humiliation at having Meg Kettle scornfully read aloud his letter to Jane. She needed to make amends.

Somehow.

"Mrs. Kettle found two things in the pockets of my trousers early this morning. The first was your letter, the second was a portrait ... a miniature ... of *me*."

"Of *you*?" Leander leaned forward in his chair. "Did you carry it concealed from us when you first came on board?"

"No! No ... the amazing thing is, I found it in Magpie's sea chest, wrapped in his blanket." She watched his face closely. "You see, Doctor, our little sail maker has discovered who I am."

His eyes searched out hers. "And who might that be, Emily?"

With trembling hands, she set aside the bandages and stood up to pace the hospital floor, too worried to meet his stare. "You have most likely heard that prior to Magpie taking to the sea, he was a climbing boy in London, cleaning chimneys in the employ of a Mr. Hardy."

"I have heard something to that effect."

"Three years ago, Magpie was working in the home of my Uncle Clar ... my Uncle William when he chanced to suffer a bad fall. My uncle showed Magpie much kindness, first by throwing his angry, unsympathetic employer out the door, secondly by giving him a large supper—more food than Magpie had ever eaten—and finally by offering him an opportunity to work on a ship. My uncle and his wife invited him to stay with them until a suitable posting was found, and when it came time for him to leave for the sea, they gave him three gifts: a sea chest, a blanket, and a miniature of me that the dear boy claimed he had greatly admired." Emily paused to peer at Leander, only to find that he had not moved, that his gaze still rested on her. "That first evening I came on board the *Isabelle*, Magpie was convinced I was the same woman in his little picture... why, I was wearing the very same blue velvet spencer! But he told no one of his suspicions, and only this morning, when we met together in the galley, did I learn of it myself. Magpie has since discovered that Mrs. Kettle does indeed have my miniature. He saw her showing it to—of all people—Octavius Lindsay."

Leander stretched his arms across his surgery-ready table. "But as she has stolen it from you, we shall simply demand she give it back."

Emily turned to look at him, her dark brown eyes glistening in the half-light. "And by nightfall, every man on the *Isabelle* will know who I am. You see, Doctor, on the back of the miniature, in addition to my full name, there is written my father's name and... his title."

Leander's eyes widened and his lips parted, but he said nothing, only waited.

"I told Captain Moreland when I first came on board the *Isabelle* that my mother died when I was young. She was legally married to my father, but my father's parents did not approve of the match. During my childhood, my father was often absent for long periods of time, but I was well taken care of by various members of his family. Above all else, I adored my Uncle William and his children, and when my father died in 1810, I begged and pleaded to be permanently installed in my uncle's home. Sadly, not long afterward, their home was broken up, my uncle and aunt separated, and Aunt Dora was forced to move into a much smaller home.

"My grandmother was adamant that I live with her in London, and certainly she had enough spare bedrooms to accommodate me, but

I could not warm to the woman who had made my own mother's short life so difficult. Besides, I could not tolerate the thought of vegetating in that household, of being shut up in the company of my grandmother, who was growing increasingly disagreeable, and my poor unmarried aunts, living out my days and evenings cutting out silhouettes, and painting china, and making lace, and doing needlework, having to rely upon visitors to tell me something of the vast world beyond my front door. I was seventeen, almost eighteen, and, as far as I was concerned, free to make my way in the world. To appease my grandmother, I told her I would happily come live with her if she would first grant me permission to have an extended visit with my mother's relations in Dorset. Her answer was a long time in coming, and goodness knows, she made me suffer, but she finally agreed to my wishes.

"My maternal relations were exceedingly amiable, and my days with them were full of fun and adventure. We explored the countryside by horseback and on foot; we went seabathing in Weymouth Bay; took trips to Lyme Regis and Exeter; and climbed the ancient stones on Salisbury Plain. Why, I even glimpsed the Cerne Giant on his green hill." Emily smiled in remembrance and was pleased to see Leander's focused eyes flutter. "Not once, Doctor, did I pick up a needle, or play on a pianoforte, or sit at a whist table. All the while, the thought of returning to London filled me with dread. How could I ever live happily, caged in cold walls of stone, when I had tasted such delights, known such diversions? Determined to prolong my adventure as long as possible, I listened to my cousin's plans to journey to Upper Canada to visit a distant relation who had made his home there some years before, and as I was drawn to the idea of an ocean-crossing, I began scheming to go ..."

Leander, whose right hand had covered his mouth as he listened, spread his fingers to interrupt her. "Emily, in all this, you have brilliantly avoided my question."

"Your question?" she asked innocently.

He angled his head, feigning impatience with her, but when she still didn't answer him he grew solemn and looked troubled. "Who are you ... really?"

Emily stared at the bucket of bandages on her recently vacated stool and summoned the courage to reply. She met his watchful gaze. "I have already told you that my father's name was Henry. At one point in his career, he actually was a farmer. His last name, however, was not George. You see, Doctor, as my grandfather's name is Geo ..."

But Leander did not hear her subsequent words, for they were wrenched away, lost in a shocking hullabaloo of mirthful voices, pounding drums, and thumping noises that flooded the *Isabelle* like a tidal wave, causing the hanging lanterns to swing wildly on their hooks and the ship's oaken timbers to shiver. No sooner had Leander leapt to his feet and Emily blinked at him in wonder when a succession of men blew into the hospital as if propelled by a gust of wind: Mr. Crump and another landsman (who had given the one-legged man assistance with the ladder), both full of chatter and a desire to tell the doctor what had just transpired; Emily's marine sentry returning to his babysitting duties; a poor young sailor who had crushed his hand while his crew readied their gun for battle; and finally, a freckle-faced midshipman with a message for Dr. Braden: "Captain Moreland requests your presence for dinner in his cabin at the start of the First Watch, sir, and sends his apologies for the late hour, but says it will take Biscuit some time to fire up his stove in order to cook a proper meal." Finally it all made sense when Gus Walby clambered down the ladder, calling out, "Dr. Braden! Dr. Braden, sir! You'll never believe it! The Yankee ship ... why, she's not Yankee at all. She's one of ours. She's the *Amethyst*!"

Emily clutched at her chest and allowed a few tears of relief to fall, but as she looked from Gus back to Leander, she found the doctor's attention fully engaged with the sailor and his crushed hand, and her heart sank to the floor. Their private moment had passed.

5:00 p.m.
(First Dog Watch, Two Bells)

MEG KETTLE GRUNTED AND CURSED her way down the ladder that led to the murky orlop deck, trying to lift her long skirt and find the ladder's slippery rungs while balancing a lantern and bowl of stew. The *Isabelle*'s criminal, having been moved below when the gun deck was cleared for action, sat dejectedly in his new irons and raised his head as the blackness around him began to recede. Mrs. Kettle held the bowl high above him and took pleasure in watching him grab for it. "Ya looks like a mangy cur beggin' fer a scrap o' meat."

Octavius's sunken black eyes shone in the lantern-light. "I'm hungry."

With a cluck of disgust, she handed him the stew. "And here ya used ta be so high and mighty, lookin' down yer spotted nose at thee lot o' us."

He wolfed down half his portion of meat and onions before answering in his familiar pompous voice. "Naturally, Mrs. Kettle, for you are a *harlot* and reside in the lowest order of humankind."

Her response was swift. She kicked the bowl from his hands, the chunks of stew flying across the damp floor planks like spinning bits of grapeshot. Octavius howled with anger and attempted to seize hold of her coarse linen skirt.

"Ha, ha," she cried gleefully, dodging his fingers, but soon finding herself breathless, she sought out the comfort of a nearby crate.

Octavius folded his arms across his chest to quell his irritation. He waited for his own breathing to be restored before speaking. "The ship sighting..." He dared to hope. "Is she American?"

Mrs. Kettle shook her scowling face in the shadows. "We would 'ave bin shootin' at her by now, wouldn't we 'ave?"

Octavius gazed upon his bound feet for several moments to hide his disappointment. "Are you still in possession of that miniature?"

"Aye!" She leaned forward eagerly. "What of it?"

He threw her a lingering look of contempt and his intended words died on his lips. It sickened him to have to grovel.

"Ah, be done with ya," grunted Mrs. Kettle, heaving her bottom off the crate and mounting the ladder with her light. Halfway up, Octavius called out to her.

"Mrs. Kettle!"

She paused and lowered her lantern.

"If ... if there should be a Yankee ship on the horizon, would you keep me informed?"

She considered his request for an eternity.

"*Please?*"

"And what's in it fer me, Lord Lindsay?"

He tightened his fists and gulped. "A handful of silver."

Cackling with satisfaction, Mrs. Kettle continued on her way. As darkness settled around him, Octavius flung his unfettered upper body down upon the floor and felt around for his scattered supper, hoping to find it before the rats did.

9:00 p.m.
(First Watch, Two Bells)

A RUMBLE OF LAUGHTER rattled the galleried windows of the great cabin and caused the crystal wine goblets and silver cutlery to jump upon the oak table around which sat James Moreland, Fly Austen, Mr. Harding, Leander Braden, and their honoured guests from the *Amethyst*, Captain Prickett and First Lieutenant Bridlington. Sandwiched between Fly and Mr. Harding was an exalted Gus Walby. He sat with his back erect, marvelling at every word uttered by the important men around him. The atmosphere in the room was exceedingly jovial, and no one seemed to notice that the supper hour was much later than expected. Indeed, the feast before them was one well worth waiting for. Biscuit had insisted upon cooking a joint of beef in addition to the accompaniments of cold ham, roast potatoes, pickled salmon, devilled eggs, sea biscuits, and several boiled lobsters—the latter having been brought on board by Captain Prickett when the two ships finally came alongside one another and were lashed together, making possible a visit between officers and ordinary seamen alike. No amount of badgering on the part of the uneasy officers left in charge had prevailed upon Biscuit to expedite his feast.

"Through my spyglass, I could see your gunports closing up one by one. It was obvious you weren't going to fight us," said Fly to his *Amethyst* friends. "And then, to my astonishment, I saw the Yankee ensign lowered and the British colours raised in their stead."

Mr. Harding wore a wide grin upon his florid face. "My fine Mr. Prickett, what tremendous relief we all felt to see a friend."

"We all knew our chances for victory were slim, as we have hardly recovered from our battle with the Americans a week back," James said, pushing the meat around his plate. Seated next to him, Leander could tell from James's pasty complexion and beaded forehead that he was still feverish.

"Here we inadvertently played a nasty trick on you and still you reward us with a fine supper!" Captain Prickett laughed, his three chins and protruding stomach jiggling as he helped himself to another juicy slab of beef.

"Aye!" said Fly. "It was a battle in itself trying to convince our cantankerous cook to fire up his stove after he'd been ordered, not long before, to douse its flames as we prepared to engage, but a fine supper indeed." He raised his wine glass to Biscuit, who stood behind Captain Moreland's chair, thrilled to be centred out in such distinguished company.

The old cook bowed low before the table. "Me pleasure, gentlemen, me pleasure."

Lord Bridlington clasped his girlish hands together. "We thought it best to fly the American colours until we knew for certain just who *you* were. It's been quite frightening sailing about in enemy waters."

"I am guessing you never made it to Halifax?" said James.

Captain Prickett swallowed a chunk of meat. "No, Mr. Moreland, we never did. We were maybe one hundred miles north of Bermuda when we were shot upon early one morning, in the darkness before dawn. We haven't a clue who it was that attacked us in this most cowardly fashion, but their aim was clean and they caught us completely unawares. We scrambled to fire up our guns, but strangely, whoever it was didn't stick around to finish us off."

"They crippled us for a time, they did, bringing down the tops of our main and mizzenmasts," added Lord Bridlington, speaking to the ceiling as was his way.

"When last we met," said James, "you were escorting three East India merchant vessels. What of them? Were they shot upon as well?"

"No! It was the *Amethyst* that sustained all the damage." Captain Prickett spoke with such vehemence that he spewed bits of beef directly into Leander's potatoes. "But their captains—a fearless lot if you ask me—had no interest in hanging about while we were refitting. They had their orders and their schedules to keep, so we wished them well and sent them on their way."

"Bloody disrespectful it was," said Lord Bridlington, "and here we'd protected them from being fired upon all the way from Portsmouth."

"We hobbled back as far as Norfolk's Gosport Yard," Captain Prickett continued. "There we had the good fortune to find our British friends set up in blockade there. They've locked several Yankee ships into their Chesapeake harbours."

"Ah! Perhaps that explains why we hadn't seen any large sails before yours," said Fly.

Lord Bridlington tapped his long, crooked nose. "There we were, near Gosport Yard, amongst our own and therefore able to safely repair our fallen masts. And there it was we met a friendly fisherman who passed the word you'd done battle with the *Liberty* and were refitting off the Carolina islands. Once the *Amethyst* was patched up, we were ordered to seek you out and, if possible, offer you aid."

"We are truly grateful," James said warmly.

With that, the men switched their attention to Biscuit's banquet of beef and roast potatoes—with the exception of Gus Walby, who was far too excited to eat a mouthful, and who, throughout the conversation, had sat quite still, his hands folded in his lap, his blond head bobbing from officer to officer as they delivered their enthralling words. As they supped, the ensuing discussion covered a variety of topics from the health of King George III (he was as mad as ever), to the invigorating news of the recent victory HMS *Shannon* had achieved over the USS *Chesapeake* on June 1st beyond the capes of Boston Harbour (a glimmer of hope and pride after a bitter succession of naval defeats), and finally, to the science of war wounds. The men were most interested in drawing out Leander, whose mind was evidently hovering elsewhere, for he had not yet contributed a word to their spirited chatter. But as the doctor was in no frame of mind to discuss dissection and amputation and trepanning, the subject was soon spent. The meal came to an end and Biscuit and his Jamaican mates carried in five more bottles of French wine (from a store of several hundred bottles that, according to James, had been taken from the hold of a captured French frigate in '07) for the diners' after-dinner pleasure. The cook uncorked two of them, and poured the contents round—including a "wee taste" for Mr. Walby—before slipping out the door and affording the men some privacy.

James raised his glass. "To our ships at sea."

"Our ships at sea," the others repeated, raising their glasses as well, the rich red wine swirling about and reflecting candlelight as it was carried to their lips.

James held up his glass a second time. "To the health of our King George."

"King George's health."

"Hear, hear."

All fell quiet as they enjoyed the bouquet and flavour of the captain's stolen wine.

"Oh, I just remembered something!" said Captain Prickett in a spray of words and spit, chewed bits of food this time striking the side of Leander's face, forcing Gus to stifle his rising laughter. "I have some intriguing news from our comrades blockading Gosport Harbour!"

James looked up quickly from his untouched meal.

"You'll remember, Captain Moreland, that at our last meeting in Bermuda, I told you the story of Captain William Uptergrove of the *Expedition*—an old friend of yours, as I recall—coming upon the debris of a burned merchant vessel some fifty miles southeast of Halifax?"

James, who had been rapidly wearying and was ready for his bed, hiked himself higher in his chair. "Aye, I do. Have you more information?" Seeing James's sudden interest, Leander swivelled in his chair, hoping for a better view of the *Amethyst*'s captain, and some advance warning of more flying fragments of food.

"Well, as we heard it, the doomed vessel was known as the *Amelia*. And apparently, it was a Yankee frigate called the *Serendipity* that destroyed her."

"My God!" cried James. Fly's dark eyes brightened as he too leaned in closer.

"The captain's name was Thomas Trevelyan."

James mopped his brow. He and Fly exchanged a significant glance, which did not escape Leander's notice.

"Now you'll remember me telling you that Uptergrove reported there being only three survivors from the *Amelia* before she was robbed and burned. It turns out there were many more. Uptergrove himself picked up an elderly woman, a little child, and an unconscious young man, all of whom were found clinging precariously to a bit of debris in the water, and sailed them back to England."

"And the others?" asked Fly and James together.

"Once back in London, the old woman had sufficiently collected her wits to carry herself—without delay—to the Board Room of the Admiralty in Whitehall where she insisted upon telling her tale directly to the Duke of Clarence. She subsequently informed Clarence that she'd seen, with her very own eyes, her young mistress, a strapping sailor named Bun Brodie, and several other men forced from the defeated *Amelia* and taken prisoner by Captain Trevelyan himself."

Mr. Harding turned quickly to address Captain Moreland. "Isn't Bun Brodie the name of the man now tending our sails, sir?"

"It is, Mr. Harding." James took a moment to courteously explain to an astonished Captain Prickett and Lord Bridlington how it was Mr. Brodie came to be on the *Isabelle*. He did not, however, divulge anything about the woman they had on board, and with a warning glance at his men—and another aimed especially at Gus, whose saucer eyes and quivering mouth gave the impression he was about to burst—discouraged them from volunteering this information. When James had finished his explanation, Leander spoke up. "Can you tell me, Captain Prickett, the old woman's young mistress, what of her?"

Captain Prickett, his face flushed with fine food and spirits, looked very pleased with himself. "The Duke of Clarence is offering a handsome reward for her safe return to England, Doctor, as she is the only daughter of his now deceased brother, Henry, once known as the Duke of Wessex. She is called Emeline Louisa."

There was a moment of silence as everyone digested the intriguing information, Captain Prickett, his eyes round and vivid with anticipation, enjoying each man's reaction in turn.

Mr. Harding, whose mouth had fallen open, exclaimed, "She is the daughter of the Duke of Wessex and the niece of the Duke of Clarence? No wonder our Admiralty agreed to give the old woman a personal audience and take seriously her claim." He shot a glance at James, who furtively raised a finger to his lips.

"She is therefore a granddaughter of our King George!" added Lord Bridlington.

Gus gasped. "That makes her a princess!"

"She is, young man." Bridlington giggled. "Although there's so much illegitimacy in our monarch's family, it's not clear whether the Duke of Wessex was actually married to Emeline's mother. Most likely, they enjoyed the same kind of an arrangement as the Duke of Clarence and his Mrs. Jordan. How many illegitimate FitzClarences did they breed together?"

All of the men sniggered at Lord Bridlington's remark, except for Leander, whose handsome face lost its colour as it dawned on him who had been sleeping behind the canvas curtain in his hospital all this time. "Captain Prickett?" he asked in a tight voice, "do you have any idea where this Emeline is now?"

Captain Prickett shrugged. "Still on the *Serendipity*, I'm supposing. Word is getting around briskly that there's a reward for her safe passage home. All of our poor sailors are quite determined to find her, hoping to make up for the pathetic lack of prize money in this ridiculous war."

"Do you have any understanding why Trevelyan would have taken her prisoner in the first place?" James asked, his faded blue eyes unnaturally bright. "Did he know who she was?"

Captain Prickett shook his head as he refilled his wine glass. "I regret I cannot say, but if he did, he would certainly have congratulated himself for having taken such a superb prisoner of war." He gulped his wine and held up one of his sausage fingers to the men. "Oh, one more thing, gentlemen. Should it be your good fortune to again come upon the *Serendipity*, be forewarned that the lady in question is travelling under the name of Mrs. Seaton."

Leander looked as if he had been dealt a physical blow. "She is ... married then?"

"It would seem so, Doctor Braden," said Lord Bridlington, eyes cast upwards. "The wounded man Captain Uptergrove found in the sea and carried back with him to England was a Frederick Seaton, and as he was travelling with Emeline Louisa, I daresay he was her husband."

10:30 p.m.
(First Watch, Five Bells)

There was a gallant English ship
A-sailing on the sea,
Blow high, blow low,
And so say we:

And her Captain he was searching
For a pirate enemy,
Cruising down along the coast
Of the High Barbaree.

Emily could lie in her cot no longer. The music, clapping, thumping of dancing feet, and men's voices raised in hilarity above her head was much too blaring and invigorating for sleep. Normally, the crew would have been abed in their hammocks long ago, but tonight they willingly relinquished a few extra hours of rest to revel with their mates from the visiting *Amethyst.*

At the start of the First Watch, the hospital had emptied, Osmund, the loblolly boys, Mr. Crump, as well as the other dozen or so patients having either rushed or limped off to "drink like fish" while they could. Before leaving her alone (with not even her marine sentry, who in any case neither desired nor had been ordered to keep her company on such a night), Osmund informed her that "Dr. Braden would be carousing in Captain Moreland's cabin until late" and that she'd have complete privacy to "seek amusement in bathing or in the officers' toilet." But as Emily found these options unappetizing, she was determined to join in the jollity above deck, figuring the men would be too intoxicated to recognize a woman in their social circle.

Emily threw on the white pants and sailor-blue jacket that Magpie had sewn for her, tied on her red polka-dotted scarf, rolled her pale hair up into one of Leander's felt hats, slipped on her silk shoes, then slipped them off again, preferring to go barefooted. Tingling from head to toe, she fled the hospital, savouring a freedom she had not tasted since setting off to the orlop a week ago, as excited as if she were en route to a soiree. She hurried through the empty galley as quickly as her sore ankle could manage, past Biscuit's cold black patent stove and the silent guns that sat before their sealed gunports, and headed towards the aft ladderway near the wardroom, preferring to make her entrance on the less-populated quarterdeck.

Not a soul did she meet until the harsh light of a single lantern revealed the outline of the closed wardroom door ahead and up drifted the sound of two familiar voices, speaking in unfamiliar hostility. As noiselessly as possible, she ducked inside the pantry, where on oak shelves were stored the officers' tableware, silverware, and crystal goblets. She dropped to her knees and crawled into a corner hole. With her heart pounding like the sailors' drums overhead, she peeked around a stack of china bowls and saw Fly, looking stiff and uncomfortable in his dress uniform, and Leander, leaning against the wardroom bulkheads, dressed in a short brown frock coat, his white cravat untied and hanging loosely upon its lapels.

"For God's sake, Lee, I did *not* know," Fly said emphatically to his friend, whose pale face was hauntingly desolate as if he'd received some bad news.

Leander raised his head. "Do you take me for a fool? Do you really expect me to believe that? I caught the knowing looks you shared with James at supper. It was quite evident you both knew more. Earlier, James told me he wished to speak to her again, but I never suspected that new information had come to light, and that you, my old friend, had been privy to it for some time."

Fly exhaled heavily. "The morning after we fought the *Liberty*, we interviewed Bun Brodie. It was then he told us of his being on the *Amelia* when she was savagely attacked by Trevelyan, and him being taken prisoner along with a woman named Mrs. Seaton."

Leander looked hurt. "That was a week ago! And knowing how I feel, you didn't think this bit of intelligence important enough to tell me?"

"Even if I suspected that Emily may be the said Mrs. Seaton, I had no way of knowing for sure. James and I had hoped to hear as much from Emily's own lips, we just didn't get the chance to—"

"You're saying you knew nothing of Emeline Louisa, King George's granddaughter, before hearing of her tonight from that insufferable Captain Prickett?"

"Nothing! And I believe Mr. Brodie himself knew her by no other name."

"My God! She's a married woman!" Leander's voice was hoarse with emotion. "Not only that, she is royalty. Royalty! With the entire

British fleet, and perhaps the Yankee navy as well, searching for her so they can fill their filthy pockets with prize money!" Leander looked at him dejectedly. "All this time spent wondering!"

"War or no war, there must be hundreds of women sailing the Atlantic. We have no definitive proof that Emily is the same woman."

"Think of it, Fly. The lady left hints for us along the way: calling herself Mr. George, telling us her father's name was Henry, speaking of ships, and her nightmares. It's no wonder she was plagued with nightmares—taken in the night, several crewmen killed, dozens of innocent children drowned. I believe she ... she tried to tell me ..." There was a crazed glint in his eyes as he pushed his body away from the bulkheads with one foot. "Now I know the truth."

Fly put his right hand upon Leander's slumped shoulder and thrust his face into his. "We do not have the full story yet, my friend. There are still many mysteries surrounding our Emily. Let us go and find her and give her a chance to refute our suspicions."

Leander stood there wavering a moment, then massaged his weary face with his slim fingers and quietly said, "No! I've been a fool. It's best I no longer concern myself."

Emily withdrew into the crushing clutter of her hiding spot and hugged her knees tighter still to her chest. Her heart cried out to him. Rocking back and forth, despair and bile rising in her stomach, she started to shiver as waves of suffocating anguish passed over her again and again. She felt cold, miserable, numb, and lost. Before long, she heard Fly and Leander's echoing footsteps, and realized they had parted in different directions, and as she listened to the hollow sounds, it struck her—like the bullet from Trevelyan's ship—that Leander was walking away from her.

Tuesday, June 15

6:30 a.m.
(Morning Watch, Five Bells)

THE SLOW, DELIBERATE FIVE BELLS of the Morning Watch shook Emily free of her troubled dreams. Opening her heavy eyes, she saw the thick column of a mast rising before her, and beyond its gently waving topsail, ghost-stars winked in the brightening sky. The red sun was just beginning to peek over the eastern horizon and its striking rays spread a rich crimson colour onto the bit of sea it touched. Travelling in its midst as though through a fire, with all her sails set in the light breeze, was the *Amethyst*, far enough away now that the gold letters of her name, painted onto her stern, were no longer visible to the naked eye.

Shivering in the morning chill, Emily sat up to rub her frozen feet, suddenly remembering she was on the mizzenmast's platform and recalling, too, the sad events that resulted in her having sought sanctuary there. She scanned the mizzen's yards and rigging and couldn't believe her good fortune in finding she was totally alone. Surely one of the sailors would have stumbled across her as he climbed to the yards in the night; but perhaps when the celebratory revelry of the evening before finally came to an end, no one was fit to climb the high ropes. Peering over the side of the platform, Emily spied the men far below, going about their business on the quarterdeck.

Mr. McGilp had both hands on the *Isabelle*'s wheel, his weathered face turned to the sea and one ear angled towards Mr. Harding, who seemed in a jolly mood despite having trouble balancing himself on his one foot as he spoke at length to the coxswain. Beyond them, on the larboard side of the ship, rows of barefooted seamen, their trousers rolled up to their knees, scrubbed the gritty quarterdeck with square holystones, and up through the crisp air came the grumpy voices of two sailors who Emily was certain were Morgan Evans and Bailey Beck.

"Me knees are aching. And, ooooo, me back!"

"Quit your bellyaching, you dumb ox, you're giving me a headache."

"I'll be havin' no pity fer ya. Yer head's achin' on account of all yer dancin' on the barrels and doin' cartwheels around the deck and drinkin' a month's worth o' the grog last night."

"And I have no pity for your old scrawny knees, so shut up and keep your head down. Here comes the officer of the watch, that little squib, Walby."

Emily couldn't help grinning at their banter and the sight of Gus Walby, who strutted before the labouring men, his young chest puffed and proud in his midshipman's uniform. But soon her grin faded. In another half hour, the sleeping crew would be called from their beds, and Osmund would barge into her hospital corner with sea biscuits and jam only to discover she wasn't in her cot. Her brief moment of freedom would, as usual, soon end. Emily hugged the solid topmast, took several breaths of the fresh salty air, and tried to take pleasure in the rising sun. Through the puckered sails of the mainmast, she caught sight of Captain Moreland standing alone beside the starboard rail, his spyglass trained on the expanse of sea that lay to the north of the *Isabelle*. He cut a lonely figure in the morning light, wraith-like with his cream-coloured breeches and shirt and yellow-white hair. Devoid of his uniform and the great height of his captain's hat, he appeared shrunken, less formidable, and apprehensive. Feeling sadder still, Emily stood up, stretched, and gazed several feet up to the mizzen crosstrees, determined to reach them before returning to the hospital.

Careful with her footing, as the platform wood was slippery with dew, Emily grabbed onto the mizzen's topmast shrouds and began her ascent, thankful that she'd dispensed with her silk shoes, relishing the sensation of falling backwards as she climbed higher and higher. She ignored the throbbing pains that still plagued her shoulder and ankle, and instead filled her head with inspiring remembrances of her youthful days when she'd managed to clamber up the shrouds on her father's ships when his attentions and those of his officers were engaged elsewhere.

Upon reaching the crosstrees, over a hundred feet from the deck below, she spread herself onto their latticed shelf to catch her breath. She then drew herself up into a ball, peeled off Leander's felt hat, and turned her face into the wind to feel its caress on her warm cheeks and through her hair, hoping its sough would whisk away the noise of the clamouring sailors below. She watched the departing *Amethyst* ply the glowing waters and tried to lift her spirits by recalling the lively scenes of the night before as the crew of the two lashed ships had celebrated together on the *Isabelle*'s deck. With envy, she had watched the drunken dances, amusing games, Magpie's flute-playing, and rousing singsongs from her platform perch, and had fervently wished she'd been among them, swilling her own small mug of grog in an effort to slow her heart's nervous shudder and rid her mind of melancholy thoughts.

Tearing her eyes from the *Amethyst*, her quick glance swept the upper deck again, stopping on Leander, who stood curiously amongst the swabbing crews, wearing the same dishevelled clothes he'd had on the previous evening, shading his eyes with his hands as he leaned back his auburn head to look upon the mainmast. As it was the bosun's responsibility to inspect the ship's sails and rigging, Emily pondered what possible interest the doctor would have in any one of the *Isabelle*'s towering masts. Curious, she followed his movements along the quarterdeck to the ship's wheel where, with a nod, he greeted Mr.

McGilp and Mr. Harding, then up the short ladder to the poop deck where he walked to its aft bench and angled his head upwards a second time to search the length of the mizzenmast. Emily felt a tingle dance down her spine, wondering if he'd seen her curled upon the crosstrees like a proud eagle minding its lofty nest. She shifted away from his gaze to hide her long, blowing hair beneath the abandoned felt hat.

With a small smile playing upon her lips, she waited for him to call out to her, and as she did so, her dark eyes fell upon the blue world that lay forever beyond the *Isabelle*'s wake. She squinted into the shimmering vastness until a shape suddenly appeared on the horizon. With a jerking motion, she sat upright, her fingers tightening around the rough edges of her latticed platform, and endured the sick feeling that resulted in the explosive quickening of her heart. In the far distance, emerging from the morning mists, were the distinctive white sails of three ships.

7:00 a.m.
(Morning Watch, Six Bells)

THE QUARTERMASTER turned over the sandglass and rang the bell six times, and as the echo of the last toll drifted away, the bosun's mate in his deep, penetrating voice called out, "All hands ahoy. Up all hammocks ahoy."

Alongside the aft rail of the poop deck beneath the blowing British colours, James stood in the company of Fly, who'd been quietly summoned from his bed the moment his captain had spotted the three ships.

"They're still far off, sir," said Fly, unhappy with the worry lines on James's face. "It'll be hours before they catch up to us, if ever they do. Shouldn't we feed the men before we beat to quarters?"

James glanced about him distractedly to find the seamen who'd been cleaning the quarterdeck now standing and craning their necks over the ship's sides to catch a glimpse of whatever it was the captain and Mr. Austen were looking at through their spyglasses. Finally he said, "Aye, you're right. Feed them first." He raised his spyglass for yet another look. "The one in the middle is definitely larger than the others and not sailing as quickly. Let's hope it's nothing more than a frigate escorting two merchantmen. But there is something worrying in their aspect. It's my guess we are being chased."

"Should they prove to be the enemy, sir, we can sail towards Norfolk where, as Captain Prickett informed us, our fleet is blockading the Chesapeake. We will find friends there."

"But the winds, Fly, they are soft, and the tides, they're with us now, but should we change direction and go northwest rather than northeast . . . ?" James straightened himself up, snapped shut his spyglass, and pursed his lips. "Right then! We can . . . we can at least try to harness more wind." He strode across the poop deck to its fore rail. "Mr. Harding, if you please," he called out in a voice that sounded stronger than Fly thought him capable of. The sailing master was waiting expectantly for his orders beside Lewis McGilp at the wheel on the quarterdeck below.

"Sir?"

"Have the bosun put out the word for the captains of the tops and their crews. Muster the skilled men you can and have them unfurl every last sail we've got." With a brief nod, Mr. Harding hobbled off on his task. James then spun around to address Mr. Tucker, who had just thrown the log line out over the *Isabelle*'s stern and was now timing her speed with the aid of a small sandglass. "What is our speed, Mr. Tucker?"

"Three knots, sir."

"Slow as molasses. We'll soon bring that number up." James watched as men from the swabbing crews familiar with the workings of the sails began their ascent up the rigging to unfurl the reefed topgallants and royals, and he saw Mr. Harding disappear down the main hatchway to search out the bosun and more men to go aloft. Satisfied, he then waved at the officer of the Morning Watch, Gus Walby, who had been leaning over the larboard rail, scanning the distance behind the *Isabelle*, and was now standing tall on the deck, his hands clasped behind his back, bright eyes firmly focused on the ship's two senior officers.

"A moment of your time, Mr. Walby."

Gus dashed up the short ladder to the poop deck. "Sir?"

"You have the best eyes of anyone on this ship," said James, smiling. "Take my glass and tell me what you see."

"Thank you, sir." Gus took the spyglass and lifted it to his eye. After a moment of soft grunting and speculation, he said, "Two frigates, sir, and one smaller ship ... I believe ... I believe it's a brig."

An astonished James stared at the boy with fatherly affection as he was handed his glass back. To Fly, he said, "Your student, Mr. Austen, does you proud."

Fly looked down upon the fair-haired midshipman and gave him a wink.

"And its colours, Mr. Walby. Are they discernible?" asked James.

"I cannot see anything flying from the tops, sir, and their stern flags are obscured by their sails."

James laid a blue-veined hand on Gus's small shoulder before crossing to the starboard rail, where he paused to gaze after the diminishing *Amethyst*. Fly and Gus followed him and watched as his eyes fell upon the flag locker beneath the taffrail.

"Mr. Walby," he said thoughtfully, "as we are not a flag ship, I have no flag-lieutenant. I wonder then if I could trouble you to run up the mizzenmast and signal to our friends on the *Amethyst* that we need help."

Gus's cheeks reddened as he struggled to contain his excitement.

"And perhaps," James added, "you could ask Mr. Stewart—if his arm is no bother to him—to assist you in hoisting the flags."

"Right away!"

The boy was halfway to the ladder down when James stopped him.

"Mr. Walby?"

"Sir?"

"Remember, one hand for the ship, one for yourself."

"Yes, sir!" Grinning, Gus raised his fist in salute before setting off like a full-sailed ship in a storm to fetch Midshipman Stewart.

Heartened by James's burst of energy and seeming return to his old self, Fly smiled at him. "Are you feeling better, sir?"

The good humour James had manifested in the presence of Gus Walby vanished as he studied the progress of the approaching ships. "Not at all." He fell into a trance-like state for several seconds before adding, "Feed the men, Fly, then beat to quarters and clear the decks for action."

"Will you get some sleep then, sir?"

"No. But I'll be in my cabin ... composing a letter to my wife."

8:00 a.m.
(Morning Watch, Eight Bells)

IN WHAT LEANDER PERCEIVED as the most unappetizing corner on the orlop deck, Meg Kettle lay in her cot, moaning and clawing at her blankets, her puffy eyes closed, spittle lodged in the creases of her mouth and running down her moist face. He hung up the lantern he'd brought with him and set down his medicine chest on a small shelf by her bed whereupon she had displayed her prized possessions. It was difficult for Leander not to compare her to a rabid dog, nor to gag at having to breathe in the fetid air that emanated from the laundress's unwashed body. Opening his chest to begin preparing a stomach-settling tonic—as he supposed in advance of his examination that this would ease all that ailed her—Leander studied the jumble of tarnished buckles, watches, hairbrushes, bags of tea, jars of pickles, bits of cheap jewellery, embroidered handkerchiefs, shillings, china cups, candle stubs, and silver spoons, the majority of which, he suspected, were gifts from the sailors for her services, stolen from the captain's table and the *Isabelle*'s storerooms. He hoped to spot amongst them Emily's miniature.

"Oooo, 'twas good o' ya to come see poor Meggie, Doctor," she said in a weak, crackling voice as if she were on her deathbed. "I always hoped ya'd one day come to me bed. When I sees ya swimmin' with thee men, I always admires yer handsome buttocks, and I think to meself I should be invitin' ya down here fer a wee bit o' kicky-wicky."

"Mrs. Kettle," said Leander crisply, his back to her, "it is my understanding that you had a poor night and have been sick to your stomach."

"I 'ave, Doctor. Me head's a poundin' and me insides, they're a churnin'. Ooo, here it comes agin. Grab me bowl there quick."

Leander fetched the wooden bowl at the foot of her cot and held it to her mouth to catch the gush of yellow liquid that was laced with the distinct odour of rum.

"Perhaps too much drink last night?" he asked, taking away the offending bowl and offering her a dampened cloth.

"Why, I drinks too much ev'ry night, Doctor. Nay, this be a different feelin.' 'Aven't kept me vittles down fer a week now."

For a moment Leander studied his moaning patient, then moved in closer to check for fever and take her pulse, and while he held her plump wrist in his hand, he furtively searched her bed and blankets for any lumps that might indicate hidden objects. Seeing nothing suspicious there, he looked around her little corner, his eyes settling on the bulging duffle bag hung upon an iron hook in the shadows.

Mrs. Kettle stopped her groans long enough to give him a queer look. "I ain't an idiot, Doctor. I knows what yer about."

"I beg your pardon, Mrs. Kettle?"

"Yer lookin' about fer that miniature, ain't ya?"

"I am counting the beats of your heart."

"Then why ain't ya lookin' at me?"

Leander, who found it easier to look upon bleeding corpses, could not think of a reply.

"Quit pretendin'. Ya can't fool thee likes of Meggie Kettle." She groped beneath her blankets, dug in and around her bosom, and pulled out the little painting. "Go on! Take a good long stare at it. It's that woman what lies in yer cot, all right."

"I have no interest in it," he said solemnly, tearing his eyes away, "although I have been informed it wasn't given freely to you; that it was stolen. You haven't forgotten that stealing is a punishable offence on this ship?"

"That don't bother me none 'cause when they comes round lookin' fer it, they won't finds it. And they can't very well punish me, can they, Doctor, if they can't finds it?"

Biting his lip, Leander finished taking her pulse, gently lowered her wrist, and twisted round to reach for the cup of prepared tonic. Turning back, he met the miniature head on, Mrs. Kettle having thrust it up temptingly before him. His heart sank as he recognized Emily's dear, smiling face—there couldn't be a truer likeness of her anywhere—her pale gold hair, and the blue velvet jacket she wore (surely the same one she had on when Gus Walby first spotted her adrift in the sea). Seeing his flicker of discomfort, Mrs. Kettle clapped her hands together. "It ain't no secret amongst thee men how ya feels about 'er. Osmund Brockley tells me ya won't let no one near 'er 'cept Magpie and Gus Walby; that yer besotted with thee wench."

"'Wench' is a word I might use to describe you, Mrs. Kettle, not her," he said in monotone. "Now, if you'd kindly give me the miniature, I will see that it is returned to its rightful owner and say nothing of its having been stolen to Captain Moreland."

Mrs. Kettle shook her head at him, narrowing her eyes suspiciously, and shoved the precious stolen object back into her shirt.

Leander gazed at her intently, unshaken by her defiance, and held out the cup of tonic. "Drink this. It should ease the vomiting."

Still eyeing him, Mrs. Kettle took the cup from him, drained its contents, wiped her mouth with the back of her hand, and finally glowered up at him. "Even if she did fancy ya, she'd never be allowed to marry yer kind, bein' a king's granddaughter and all... and you, nothin' more than a naval surgeon. She's outta yer class." She lay back on her flat pillow, looking pleased with herself. "Nay, thee only way ya can 'ave 'er is by ... is by tacklin' 'er in thee sail room like young Octavius Lindsay done. Ho, ho, ha, ha, ha."

Tears of mirth poured from her eyes, mixing with the white spittle on her lips, and as Leander watched her guffaw like a drunken sailor, he was struck with an overwhelming desire to dump her from her grubby cot onto the damp floor—where a host of vermin was sure to find her—grab Emily's miniature, and race off with it. Instead, he stuffed his trembling hands into his apron pockets, took a deep breath, and forced a smile.

"Rest if you can, Mrs. Kettle, and I'll be back later to examine you more closely, if I may."

She dabbed at her eyes with a bit of her blanket and blinked up at him. "What? To rifle through me bosom?"

"Certainly not!"

"What fer, then?" Suddenly she looked more anxious. "Ya didn't poison me, did ya?"

"No! But I suspect you may be with child."

10:00 a.m.
(Forenoon Watch, Four Bells)

THE MOMENT THE MEN were done eating, James ordered them to clear the decks and get to their action stations "in the event those three ships prove to be our enemies." With the *Isabelle* abuzz and reverberating with activity, Gus Walby sat precariously upon the mizzen top crosstrees, tightly gripping the captain's telescope in one hand and a length of secured rope in the other, looking across at the main and foremasts and down upon the decks to watch the sailors, landsmen, officers, and marines alike preparing for battle: placing scuttlebutts of drinking water at intervals, puddening the yards (to prevent them—should their supporting ropes be severed—from falling upon the men), wetting and sanding the decks (to avoid slippage on the inevitable rivers of blood), putting up the splinter nets for protection against flying bits of oak, piling grape and shot beside each of the guns, cleaning pistols, and stacking poleaxes and pikes. Gus could see the captain of the marines giving his men their orders, Captain Moreland and Mr. Austen plotting their strategies on the poop deck, and Mr. Harding alongside Mr. McGilp at the wheel devising navigational manoeuvres to suit the prevailing wind conditions; and as the men all went about their tasks, the fresh morning air circulating round the ship rang with their laughter, chatter, songs, orders, and oaths.

"What is our speed now, Mr. Tucker, if you please?"

"Five knots, sir."

"It better be them Yanks this time. I'm out fer a bit o' blood today."

"Looks like it'll be three against one."

"Then ya better 'ave writ yer will."

"What fer? I ain't got nothin' ta will ta nobody."

"Might as well fight 'em 'cause we can't carouse with 'em. Drained our barrels of grog last night."

"England expects and all that."

"Don't forget your old shipmate, faldee, raldee, raldee, raldee, rye-eye-doe!"

Gus had been through the drill enough times now to know that the same flurry of activity would be abounding on the unseen upper and gun decks. Biscuit would be dousing his breakfast fires, Dr. Braden sharpening his surgical tools, the gunner handing out muskets, and men taking down the bulkheads and canvas screens. Those with no immediate occupation would be writing letters home to their loved ones—or their wills—and in her hospital corner, Emily would be steadying her nerves with the aid of Jane Austen's book.

Gus was just about to climb down the mast to report to the captain when his heart skipped a beat. Dr. Braden—of all people—was climbing up the mizzenmast towards him.

"Doctor," he called out in alarm. "What's wrong, sir?"

Leander, shoeless, stockingless, and climbing in a loose shirt with sleeves rolled up to his elbows, paused in his ascent to catch his breath, and smiled up at the young midshipman. "Several times now I have been dared to climb the ropes, and I thought it as good a time as any to try my sea legs."

Gus widened his eyes in disbelief, thinking the doctor's timing inopportune. "You will be careful, sir. Please don't fall."

"It is not my intent to fall, Mr. Walby." Leander continued climbing. "I have often heard Captain Moreland tell you men to keep one hand for the ship and one for yourself, but as I'm no sailor, I think it best I keep both hands for myself." He reached Gus's platform and peered down at the little men scurrying about the decks far below his bare toes.

"You're over a hundred feet up here, sir."

Leander grinned. "I will fare better without that knowledge, thank you, Mr. Walby." He hooked his arms around two sturdy ropes. "I'm not fond of heights, but climbing up here for pleasure is one thing. To work on a daily basis upon these bits of rope suspended over nothing is quite another." Seconds later, he exclaimed, "Why it's magnificent up here!"

As Dr. Braden, his face flush with exercise, enjoyed the air's salty tang and beheld the snapping sails and shimmering horizons, Gus watched him closely, relieved to see the doctor in good spirits, especially after last evening's dinner conversation, when he had seemed desolate and withdrawn. In silence the two fell to watching the approaching ships, and when Leander lifted his face to Gus again, the jubilant glint had left his eyes.

"I have not taken leave of my senses, Mr. Walby," he said soberly. "Finding myself with little to do, I volunteered to come up here to retrieve your intelligence. And—" He paused to produce a small napkin-wrapped bundle out of one rolled-up sleeve. "I brought you breakfast. Two biscuits and some cheese."

Gus accepted the food. "Thank you, sir. How kind of you."

"Now, what have you found out? Any word from the *Amethyst*?"

"Mr. Stewart and I hoisted the flags for assistance some time ago, sir, but she's not answering, and I fear she's too far away now to see the signals."

"Is it possible she has no lookouts on duty?"

Gus grimaced. "That would be unwise, sir, particularly in enemy waters."

"Indeed," said Leander, but he wondered how any of the sailors could have resumed their duties after such a night of revelry. "Tell me then, Mr. Walby, what more can you see of the three ships?"

"Definitely two frigates and a brig, sir. And they're gaining on us, travelling much faster than we are."

Leander gazed into the distance. "Is their nationality evident?"

"Aye, sir, they're American."

"Are you quite certain?"

"I just witnessed the colours being raised on one of the frigates."

"Any chance she may be flying false colours?"

"No, sir. Not this time."

Leander raised his brow in question.

"The markings on one of the frigates are familiar," said Gus. He lowered his voice. "I'm sure of it, sir. It's Trevelyan's *Serendipity*."

11:00 a.m.
(Forenoon Watch, Six Bells)

WITH HIS WHITE, HAIRY ARMS folded belligerently upon his chest and an unhappy expression fixed on his bronzed, withered face, Bailey Beck planted his feet in the small area on the orlop where Jacko, the *Isabelle*'s shoemaker, did his work creating, sewing and repairing the sailors' footwear. "Ya lubber! Ya told me ya'd have 'em ready at three bells and now I hear the six bells. Do ya figure I don't mind fightin' them Yankees in me bare toes?"

There was a scowl on Jacko's usually cheerful face as he sat on his low stool, polishing one of two silver buckles for a pair of newly minted shoes that lay atop his pile of leather pieces on the dusty floorboards. "Makes no difference to me," he replied as evenly as a ship in the doldrums. "We'll all be keepin' the company o' Davy Jones before thee day be done. I heared 'em sayin' there be three ships comin' after us. Yanks they be, and I doubt they'll be lookin' to trade fish and jokes with we Isabelles."

"Lost yer nerve, 'ave ya, Jacko?"

"Lost it long ago, when I lost me leg." Jacko rubbed his wooden peg as if he were stroking a faithful dog. "I ain't like ya, Bailey. Ya fear nothin'."

Bailey's angry face softened. "The guns can't hit ya here below the water, man. Ya ain't got nothin' to worry about."

"I do if them Yanks board us. I ain't as fast with me dirk as I once were."

"Don't go blamin' yer lost leg fer that. Blame yer prodigious fat belly." Bailey cracked up, but seeing that Jacko did not share his enthusiasm for the insult, he wiped his eyes and reassumed a serious aspect. "Aw, anyways, 'twon't come to that. We'll blow all three of 'em outta the water with our heavier guns, ya'll see." He cuffed Jacko in good fun across the head. "So quit fussin' with them foppish shoes and finish mine up first. Ain't no one on this ship needs a pair o' dandy shoes like them."

"They be fer Emily. I told her I'd knock her up a decent pair so she don't 'ave to wear them blue silks."

Bailey looked at his old mate with surprise and was contemplating another wisecrack when Jacko quietly added, "If I don't see ya again, would ya see the young miss gets 'em?"

11:30 a.m.
(Forenoon Watch, Seven Bells)

"Alls I'm askin' fer is two minutes with 'im without ya hangin' about."

"It wouldn't be right, Mrs. Kettle," said the young marine standing sentry over the unfortunate Octavius Lindsay. Rather than being returned to the gun deck, which had been cleared again for action for the second time in twenty-four hours, Octavius had been left in irons outside the slops room on the dank orlop. The uncertain-looking soldier kept spinning around to see if anyone was lurking in the darkness.

"No one's about. All thee men was called to stations."

"W-e-e-e-l-l-l."

"Won't be no harm done. I 'ave no key to unlock his chains."

"All right, then. But two minutes only."

"That's a good lad and fer yer trouble ya can visit me sometime in me cot," she cooed, reaching out her arms to him.

"I'd—I'd rather not, Mrs. Kettle," he sputtered, crimson colour flooding his face as he took a step backwards.

"Be off then, ya fool."

The flustered marine shot off along the orlop deck like a frightened colt, coming to a halt only once he was well beyond the laundress's reach, though still in sight of his prisoner.

"Ho, ho, ha, ha," chortled Octavius, bent over his locked legs. "You'd be far better off bribing green boys with your silver spoons and necklaces, Mrs. Kettle, than offering up your flesh." He tensed, expecting a kick in the ribs, and when none was delivered, was shocked to find the laundress in a serene frame of mind.

She bestowed upon him her sweetest smile. "There be three Yankee ships chasin' us. Just what yas was hopin' fer. Here. Take it and hides it where ya can." She handed him the miniature with a sidelong glance towards the marine who had occupied himself poking around the sail room. "Won't be no one lookin' fer it here." Mrs. Kettle then pulled a quill pen and piece of paper from the pocket of her skirt.

"Hell! What's this for?"

"I wants ya to write somethin' out fer me and I'll come back fer it when I can. But know this... I 'spects to be rewarded roundly fer helpin' ya—that is, if we ain't dead in a few hours."

12:30 p.m.
(Afternoon Watch, One Bell)

EMILY SAT ALONE on a stool in the empty hospital, Jane Austen's *Sense and Sensibility* opened but ignored upon her lap, a loaded pistol at her feet, staring at the ladder that led up to the fo'c'sle deck and praying that Leander would soon come back. The hours of agony and suspense that had passed since the three ships were first sighted had left her numb, and now that the threat was known—a greater one than ever the *Isabelle* had faced—she no longer felt fear, only a desire, above all things, to speak to Leander before the guns began to fire and his hospital filled with the dead and dying.

To her surprise, it was not Leander but Morgan Evans who climbed down the ladder. He pulled off his knitted hat, ran a hand through his hair, and gave her an awkward little bow before glancing about the hospital. "Excuse me, ma'am, for interrupting your reading..."

Emily laughed, rising with the book in her hands, relieved to have some company. "Oh, you are interrupting nothing. I haven't been able to concentrate since I heard the fife and drums for quarters."

A bit of red crept into Morgan's cheeks as he shifted from one foot to another. "I've—I've come to ask a favour of you."

"Do you need me to help unfurl a few sails or fill up the guns with powder?"

Morgan grinned, his eyes looking everywhere but at Emily. "You'd be too late for all that. Everything that can be done is done." He fiddled with his hat and stayed on the opposite side of the hospital, keeping between them Leander's desk, which was once again transformed into a surgical table. "I know that you're a clever one, ma'am. I once overheard you reading a story about two sisters to Mr. Walby and Magpie."

Emily stared at him in surprise. "Thank you, Mr. Evans."

"You see, ma'am, I can't read. I always meant to learn, but there never seemed to be the time nor anyone around that could teach me."

"But your way of speaking—I always thought you were well educated."

"My mother took great pains to teach me to speak properly, and she had the best intentions to provide me with a good education herself, but she died when I was a boy, in childbirth along with her baby."

"I am sorry."

"What I want to say, ma'am, is that, well, I've been on a ship of some kind for seven years now. I didn't set out to be a sailor. I learned carpentry work in my hometown of Swansea in Wales, so I could help my sisters keep the house and pay the mortgage. But this one night, when I was fourteen and supposed to be long in my bed, I sneaked out of the house, and along with a friend of mine, we stole into the local tavern to scrounge a few drinks. Beg your pardon, ma'am, I know it's not something you would do. It was on my way home, when I was alone, I suddenly found myself surrounded by a press gang."

"You mean those naval ruffians who scour the countryside, forcing men of all ages to work on their ships?"

Morgan nodded. "It seems someone had tipped them off that I had some skill with a hammer and nails. They asked me the name of my ship, and when I told them I wasn't connected with any ship at all and never had been, they beat me about the head and carried me off to the docks, where they threw me into the hold of a large frigate. Well, you see, I'm almost twenty-one, ma'am. That was seven years ago and I don't think my sisters know whatever became of me. Most likely they believe I was spirited away."

"You haven't been home at all since you were fourteen?"

"No, ma'am." He glanced shyly up at Emily.

"And this favour you have come to ask of me?"

He cleared his throat and straightened himself up as if trying to summon up courage.

"I was wondering if you could write a letter to my sisters for me, Brangwen and Glyn they are, informing them of my whereabouts these past several years."

Seeing his hopeful expression, Emily felt a sudden constriction around her heart.

"I would ... I would be delighted, Mr. Evans."

2:00 p.m.
(Afternoon Watch, Four Bells)

THE FIRST SHOT ERUPTED from the *Serendipity* like a steaming volcano blowing its top.

Clinging to the lower mizzenmast platform, Gus could smell its cold metal, feel its shiver, and hear its ominous drone as it fell, short of its mark, into the empty ocean behind the *Isabelle*'s stern. Its shocking suddenness caused him to drop the captain's telescope, and a young sailor working above him to lose his foothold on the topsail yard. As fate answered, the sailor was able to grasp onto the shrouds before falling to a certain death on the unforgiving deck below. The telescope did not fare quite as well; with an unsettling crash, it landed at Captain Moreland's feet, its glass shattering and the shards cast spinning across the poop deck planks. Without a flinch, James kept his composure to address his anxious gun crews hunched over their cannons, itching to light their guns in reply.

"Hold your fire, men," he cried. "For God's sake, hold your fire." His command was repeated again and again around the ship, and when the guns stayed silent, he muttered a word of thanks, for he was not certain what action to take. His men, with their hearts in their mouths, stared at him, waiting for the word. Beneath the fluttering British flag on the poop deck, James, Fly, Mr. Harding, and Leander stood in a semi-circle, consulting navigational charts and closely watching the movements of the enemy ships—the *Serendipity*, a second frigate, and an accompanying brig—that now loomed, three abreast, a mile off the *Isabelle*'s stern.

Realizing that James was undecided in his tactics, Fly spoke up. "Sir, if we turn the ship broadside, we're prepared to fire four successive rounds. With a little luck, we may rip open one of their hulls."

"But we are too heavy to out-manoeuvre those three ships," said a jittery Mr. Harding, bouncing back and forth from foot to stump. "Why, by the time we swing her round, they'll have raked our stern, or worse still, shot our own hull full of holes."

In mute silence, James calmly flicked away the glass bits of his broken telescope with his boot.

"With respect gentlemen," said Leander hesitantly, "do we not have greater gun power, having more and heavier guns than either of those two frigates or that brig?"

"We do, Doctor," said Fly, "but despite bolstering our numbers with the men taken from the *Liberty*, we are still seriously short on skilled sailors, and therefore, not all of our seventy-four guns will see action. In comparison, those ships possess one hundred guns between them."

Mr. Harding shook his head sadly. "And with these light winds, we can't hope to match their speeds."

"But surely this Trevelyan is not interested in just sinking us here in the Atlantic?"

"Nay, Doctor," said Fly. "He would more likely be wont to humiliate us by taking us a prize and leading us triumphantly into one of his nearby ports, an American flag hoisted over ours."

James gazed around the *Isabelle* with affection. "It is not my intent to send my men to certain death today, nor to humiliate them; however, the simple truth of the matter is that Trevelyan knows the *Isabelle* well. He is fully aware of her capabilities and encumbrances."

"What about trying negotiations, sir?" asked Mr. Harding, his round, red face lighting up hopefully. "We—we could return the sailors we took from the *Liberty*, and sweeten the deal with the return of the girl."

James pulled his eyes from his ship's standing rigging and proud sails to glance past his sailing master at Leander, who had turned very pale. "Where is Emily, Doctor?"

"In the hospital," Leander answered slowly.

"Think of it, sir," said Mr. Harding, a bit too quickly. "They may bite at the prize money she will bring, and agree to leave us be."

Leander stared at James in disbelief. "Surely you don't—you don't mean to offer Emily up to Trevelyan?"

"What are our chances here, Doctor?" cried Mr. Harding. "Would you have us all perish for the sake of one woman? She may be our only hope."

"You surprise me, Mr. Harding," said James in a cold, reproachful voice. "A seasoned warrior such as yourself." He took several paces from his companions and wavered alone on the *Isabelle*'s stern with his back to them, staring unseeing at the *Serendipity*.

Closing his eyes, he allowed his mind to drift across the Atlantic to England. For several wonderful minutes he dwelled in a pleasant reverie filled with light and beauty and the love of family and friends until the cries and calls from the enemy ships intruded upon his consciousness, yanking him back to the terrible reality of the moment. Quietly and privately, James tucked away in his heart the precious memories of the Yorkshire moors, his wife's dear smile, and the loveliest sound in the world, the laughter of his six children. "I will give Trevelyan nothing," he said to the wind, blinking away a solitary tear. "Besides, it is me he wants, and for nine long years he has waited for just such an opportunity." He swung around to face his waiting officers.

"Lee, find Emily and take her down to the orlop. In the event Trevelyan has heard of our admiral's *reward* for her, hide her there, wherever you think appropriate."

Leander looked dazed and uncertain.

"Go! Now!"

Fly leaned into him and gave him an encouraging smile. "But don't linger too long, Doctor. We may soon need you to wield a sword." Leander snapped his mouth shut, cleared his throat, grinned self-consciously, and hurried off.

When he was gone, James removed two letters from the inside breast pocket of his uniform coat and held them out to Fly. "Should the outcome be ... I would rest easier knowing ..." He stopped, and began again. "There is one addressed to my wife and another to you. I have attempted to answer all your questions regarding Trevelyan. Just know that he was connected with the ugliest episode of my life."

Fly accepted the letters with a comprehending nod. Silent seconds passed away before he was aware again of the vigilant eyes surrounding them. "Sir, the men ... they are prepared to fight. They understand nothing of handing over prisoners in order to be left alone."

James sighed. "I know that, son." He raised his head to yell at Gus sitting up high on his platform. "Mr. Walby!"

"Aye, sir?"

"Get down from there this instant and get yourself below." He turned to Fly again. "How far off is Gosport Yard, where our friends are set up in blockade?"

"We are not far off now, sir."

"Let us pray they hear our guns."

"Sir?"

With restored conviction and resolve, James settled his blue bicorne upon his head, and in a voice robust enough for all to hear cried, "Shall we give it a try, Mr. Austen? Shall we have a go at them?"

Understanding his captain's meaning, Fly beamed. "Aye, sir!"

"Broadside!"

"Broadside it is, sir!"

"Turn her round, Mr. McGilp," James bellowed to the coxswain, as he climbed sprightly down the ladder to the quarterdeck, "and let her fly."

A roar of approval swept the *Isabelle* fore and aft as the energized men, seeing Captain Moreland striding with purpose down the deck towards the bow, high colour in his sunken cheeks and a glowing smile upon his lips, realized that he meant to fight. Fly followed, desperately trying to keep up to his revitalized leader, and was cheered to see the sailors' reactions to the news. Mr. Crump gripped the larboard rail and showed his joy by dancing around on his one leg while Biscuit swiped the air several times with his cutlass. Bun Brodie released a guttural sound not unlike a foghorn and lifted a laughing Magpie high over his copper-coloured head. Bailey Beck clapped Morgan Evans on the back, almost knocking him off his feet, then pumped his arm in an enthusiastic handshake. The scarlet-jacketed marines all raised their muskets to their eyes, and the sweating gun crews rallied round their cannons and carronades on the larboard side of the ship, waving their rammers and fists in the air, ready to pour the gunpowder into the firing holes.

And the *Isabelle* turned her head slowly into the wind.

Within minutes, a second blast ripped from the *Serendipity*. This time it hit its mark, smashing into the mizzen topmast, snapping it in half and sheering away the lower platform, catching Gus Walby unawares on the ropes below and cruelly slinging him into the sea.

3:00 p.m.
(Afternoon Watch, Six Bells)

LEANDER SAID NOT A WORD throughout their journey from the hospital to his private cabin, located between the captain's storeroom and the spirits room on the orlop deck. When finally he spoke, his tone was detached and formal, as if he were seeing Emily as a patient for the first time. "You're to stay here." He unlocked the low, thin door, held high the lantern he carried, and stood back to let her pass into the room. "I am sorry for the dampness and the strong smell of fish."

Emily glanced miserably around his cramped quarters, which contained nothing more than a shabby hammock, a small bookshelf, and two wooden pegs on which he had hung a few articles of clothing. It was obvious to her why Leander preferred to sleep in the hospital. She stole a glance at him and her heart sank. He stared back at her, his features rigid, his eyes blank, as if she was not there at all, and solemnly he said, "I will not pretend that our situation is not serious. There are three of them to our one."

"The *Amethyst*—?"

"Our signals to her for assistance went unanswered."

"Will you not allow me to stay in the hospital, Doctor?"

"It is Captain Moreland's wishes—his orders—that you ride out the battle down here."

"Would I not be put to better use helping you with your patients?"

"I—the men would only be anxious for your safety. You'll be better off down here."

Hearing the misstep in his speech, she scanned his handsome face, willing him to gaze upon her with adoring eyes as he once had, only to be disappointed when he blinked several times and looked away. A brooding silence fell between them. Emily's arms dropped to her sides in defeat. She bit back her stinging tears in an effort to conceal her hurt and fear from him. Long, awkward moments passed before she broke their silence.

"Would you leave me the lantern? I do not like the darkness."

"Of course," he said, placing it on his bookshelf next to a slim volume of Robbie Burns's poems. He gestured towards a small purple bottle slipped in amongst his books. "Should things get ... intolerable, you might find a sip of that will help." He frowned and started as if suddenly remembering something. Reaching into the pocket of his brown frock coat, he pulled from it a folded slip of parchment and held it out to her.

"Is it another letter to Jane you would have me read?" Emily asked.

"This one is for you."

Emily glanced up sharply, daring to hope.

"There—there is information that has recently come to light," he continued, his eyes full of sadness, "information gleaned from Captain Prickett and Lord Bridlington of the *Amethyst* with whom I had the privilege to dine last evening. It is the very best of news. Read my letter and take comfort in it, and know that you do have a life worth living."

Emily looked puzzled. "You *tell* me this, Doctor, yet I hear no joy in your voice. What of that?"

From the far reaches of the orlop, a voice suddenly called out, shattering the unsettling stillness around them. "Dr. Braden? Are ya down here, sir?"

"I am, Mr. Brockley."

"And will ya be along, then? The hospital—I'm worried it'll soon be full, sir."

"I am coming straightaway."

Emily snapped in exasperation. "You are always needed somewhere! Why, I can hardly complete a sentence let alone a conversation in your company without someone listening in or pulling you away or beating to quarters or drowning or needing you to stitch up their bloody head! And now ... you are needed *again*." With a sharp intake of breath, she caught herself, regretting her words.

Leander lifted his chin. "There are many things I cannot change and that is one of them."

She sighed and shook her head. "Doctor, will you not stay a moment? I should like to hear this good news from your own lips."

"I should go." He bent his tall frame to pass through the low door. Out in the darkness of the deck, he paused, briefly, before setting off, firm resignation evident in his stride.

A forlorn emptiness pressed down on Emily as she watched him go, disappearing bit by bit into the obscurity like an elusive dream. He was nothing more than a grey shape in the black shadows when a thunderous explosion ripped through the air and the *Isabelle* pitched and groaned with a hit. Panic arose in her breast as she listened to the crew's suppressed but distinct outpouring of horrified anger in the distance. In the furore, she was certain she discerned the chilling words, "*man overboard*." Her pulse accelerated with anxiety for the *Isabelle*'s crew. They were no longer faceless, nameless sailors; they were her friends, companions, brothers she had never before known, cherished substitutes for her lost parents. Her family.

"Who is it that has fallen now?"

Cold dread coursed through her veins as she realized, with a battle looming, a rescue of the poor soul would be impossible. The *Isabelle* shuddered as her larboard guns boomed and jumped in answer to the enemy blasts. Emily imagined the men falling dead, bloodied and torn apart by grapeshot, or worse still, alone and injured on the deck, pleading piteously for help that would be a long time in coming, if ever. Her mind raced to Morgan Evans, who only minutes before had said good-bye to her in the hospital after he had haltingly dictated a touching letter home to his Welsh sisters. She thought of Fly Austen and Captain Moreland running steadfastly about, assuring, assisting, and encouraging their men while standing in the direct line of enemy fire, and of little Magpie, his head still in bandages, and dear Gus Walby, proudly wearing his bicorne, both of them heady with adrenaline as they carried out orders and fought alongside the older men. Wild-eyed, she peered into the spreading gloom for a final glimpse of the one man she cared for above all others, and hysterically she cried out, "Leander!"

For a moment, there was a haunting silence, as if the battle had ended and all hands were lost, then at last she heard the welcoming echo of his returning footsteps. He soon appeared in the dim illumination of her lamplight, an expression of expectation on his face, staring at her with wide eyes as her own filled with tears.

"I cannot bear this coldness between us any longer," she choked out. "I—I have relied so completely on your friendship these past weeks. I am well aware that I may not see you again. Will you—could you not at least shake hands with me?" She extended her trembling right hand as the tears started down her face and whispered, "Would you leave me thus?"

He stood stock-still, his auburn brow etched in sorrow, and for the longest time said nothing. Only when the pervasive wails of war intensified did his words at last tumble out. "If I had not heard the name of Mrs. Seaton and learned of your background and parentage and understood the reason for your unhappiness and nightmares; if everything was different, if everything was put right in the world—had we been born in the same circles—not opposite ends of the earth—and I wasn't simply a ship's doctor—then—then—I would never leave you."

It was Emily's turn to be rendered speechless. She gave him a tentative smile and her eyes never wavered from his face.

He nodded towards the letter she held to her breast and gently said, "I cannot stay long, but I shall stay here while you read it."

Tearing it open, she hungrily swept its contents.

Dear Madam;
Should we not have an opportunity to speak again in private I feel compelled to inform you that I am now aware that you are the granddaughter of King George and will henceforth address you as the Princess Emeline Louisa. I can only speculate what unfortunate circumstances resulted in you being taken prisoner on the Serendipity *and now understand why it was you were travelling across the ocean under the name of Mrs. Seaton. But know this—it has been my pleasure and an honour to care for your wounds these past weeks. You have proven to be a most affable and courageous patient.*

Rejoice in the knowledge that your lady-in-waiting and your husband, Frederick Seaton, were rescued from the wreck of the Amelia *and are safely home in England under the care of your Uncle William, the Duke of Clarence. It is my hope that this news will safeguard you from your blackest hours.*

I bid you Godspeed,
Your Faithful Servant,
Leander Braden.

Emily's fist tightened around the letter and her shoulders sagged as she fell against the cabin door, sinking to her knees, murmuring thanks like the tranquil sea after a tempest. Transfixed in happiness, she sat there until her spent sobs had turned to laughter and eagerly she looked up at Leander. "I travelled under the name Mrs. Seaton for no other reason than for my safety. Frederick Seaton is my cousin. He is not, nor ever shall be, my husband."

Leander's lips parted in surprise.

"There is so much that I need to tell you, Doctor. So much that I need to explain. Give me a chance to tell you about myself and when you have learned all, tell me there is some hope."

"Hope? When we belong to such different worlds?"

"It is your world, not mine, to which I wish to belong."

Leander stared at her in mute elation, then dropped down next to her. There he lifted her little white hand that bore the scars of her leap from the *Serendipity* and, closing his eyes tightly, held it to his cheek, then to his lips, letting it linger there. When he opened his eyes again, their sea-blue colour was more striking than ever, and the fine lines around them crinkled in mirth. He seemed as content as he had been that gusty morning when they had sat together on the *Isabelle*'s waist within the shelter of the smaller boats.

"God willing, I will meet you later, up high on the mizzenmast's platform, and there we will talk and watch tomorrow's sun rise." He searched her face as if trying to memorize every one of her features, and his own broke into a teasing smile. "Your pistol, Princess Emeline, keep it with you at all times. I suspect you know how to use it."

He rose and bowed to her respectfully, as he would have had he made her acquaintance in a lavish ballroom, allowed his gaze to fall on her another moment, and was gone. Emily shrank back against the door and waited until the guns and desperate cries above had swallowed the wrenching sound of his departing steps, then dragged herself beneath Leander's bed where she wept unrestained tears of joy.

4:00 p.m.
(Afternoon Watch, Eight Bells)

BEFORE EVEN A FULL HOUR had elapsed, the roar, rattle, and thunder of battle had rolled away with the white clouds of the June day, leaving in its place a suffocating pall of acrid smoke that swirled around the *Isabelle* like a grey-black blanket trying to hide her terrible destruction from her enemies. Rudderless, mastless, she bobbed about on the wine-red waves like a dead sea-creature. All about her was profound silence except for the stifled groans of the wounded who lay in pathetic heaps, crumpled and traumatized, upon the bloody decks, and a single white gull that tumbled through the smoke, squawking eerily, like a bird from another world.

James lay still, near the bowsprit where he had fallen, his breathing laboured, trying to focus on the gull as it cheerfully swooped and glided around the ruins of his once-proud masts. He kept his eyes skyward, afraid of what he might see if he lifted his head to search the decks. He could smell charred flesh and feel the stickiness of the blood that ran in rivulets along the planks, seeping into his cream-coloured breeches, and he tried to convince himself that neither belonged to him. He would have to get himself up soon—*stand tall on the deck*—as the men needed him now more than ever. They required direction and a calming word. The enemy was approaching. He could hear their excited shouts as they clambered into their small boats to cross over and board the *Isabelle*. James attempted to raise himself up, but he couldn't breathe properly, nor could he move his legs, or his arms, or any part of his body.

He lay there helplessly as the American boats pulled nearer and nearer, unable to do a blessed thing, except dwell with forlorn thoughts. *Is this how it would end, then? No victory, no glory, no prize money, no lofty comparisons made to Lord Nelson back home in England; his family forever having to bear the shame of his ignoble defeat at the hands of a British traitor?* James twitched and tasted blood in his mouth, and from somewhere far away, heard a voice calling to him.

"Captain Moreland! Sir!"

It was Fly's voice, but James could not see him clearly. Fly appeared over him suddenly, faceless in the darkness, and there were two others at his side, one weeping profusely.

"Hold on, sir, and I'll get Leander." Fly's voice had a strange hoarseness to it.

"No!" James began to cough and he had to wait until his spasms had passed. "No. There will be others who need the doctor's attention. I will wait my turn."

He felt himself being gently lifted from the wet deck and carried away, although in which direction they were headed he could not guess. He tried to hold onto their voices, which grew more and more distant with each step.

"Biscuit! Take the captain to his cabin."

"Ach, but sir, it's bin shot out … awful mess in there. Glass all over thee place and thee furniture, why it's nothin' but rubble."

"Take him there in any case." Fly then lowered his voice. "Magpie, quit your snivelling this instant! Tell Dr. Braden to meet me in the great cabin. Run!"

"Fly?" James called out, feeling an overwhelming desire to go to sleep. "My letters, do you have them?"

"Aye, sir. They are safe."

"I—I regret that first time a few weeks back, allowing Trevelyan to get away. Perhaps I should not have concerned myself with wind and repairs; perhaps I should have gone straight back after him."

"But, sir, you had no idea it was Trevelyan's ship."

"No." James sighed. "Still …" He lifted his faded blue eyes to the sky once again. "I ask for your forgiveness."

He could see quite clearly now and watched as the white gull, having grown tired of the cheerless wreck, swooped down the length of the *Isabelle*'s decks towards her taffrail, circled her shattered mizzenmast and the tattered British colours that still fluttered from her stern, and finally soared through the smoke to search for the sun.

4:20 p.m.
(First Dog Watch)

MAGPIE PAUSED MIDWAY on the ladder down to the hospital to wipe away the tears that poured from his eye, trying to carry out Mr. Austen's orders to be brave and stand tall. He didn't feel brave at all. Below him was a hellish scene. A heap of bleeding men sat slumped over and dazed on the hospital floor, looking as if they had been hastily dumped there from the deck above like a bucket of refuse hurled from a second-storey window. Some had their heads so covered in gore that he had no idea who they were; others had arms and legs hanging unnaturally from their bodies. Magpie shuddered and felt his stomach heave. It was worse than any nightmare he had ever had.

"Move along, boy," shouted a sailor at Magpie's head. "Git outta me way."

Magpie dangled precariously to one side of the ladder as the sailor, carrying a hysterical gunner with a badly burned back over his shoulder, swept past him and into the congested hospital. Magpie took a deep breath and followed the sailor, keeping his eyes on the ceiling planks, having no desire to see the writhing mass of miserable men who coughed and cried out at his feet, nor the devastation of Emily's little corner, which had taken a hit through its gunport. What remained of her canvas curtains shivered in the sea breeze that blew through the gaping hole in the ship's side, bringing with it wafts of unwelcome smoke. Standing in the middle of the mayhem was Dr. Braden, hunched over his gruesome operating table, periodically raising his voice with orders and advice for Osmund Brockley and the loblolly boys, as well as for Bun Brodie and Biscuit, who both claimed some knowledge of medicine and had therefore agreed to stay and help him with his wretched work.

"Sir?" Magpie stood patiently by Dr. Braden's side while he performed an amputation, keeping his eye averted from the doctor's red-stained arms and the frightening tools he held in his hands, and the mangled mess spread out upon the table before him. When the doctor finally set his eyes on him, Magpie was unsettled by their haunted look. Raising himself up on his tiptoes, he whispered, "Mr. Austen was hopin' ya could come to the great cabin to examine Captain Moreland. He ain't doin' so good."

Dr. Braden straightened himself and slowly looked all around him, pausing thoughtfully on what was once Emily's corner. "Tell Mr. Austen . . . I will come."

As Magpie emerged from the woeful hospital onto the fo'c'sle deck, he found Morgan Evans standing before him, his face blackened with soot, his knitted hat gone, carrying Bailey Beck in his arms. Magpie didn't like the way Bailey's white head was slumped against Morgan's chest, nor the hysterical note in his own voice as he cried out, "Mr. Evans, sir!"

Morgan's reply was strangely subdued. "I've told you before, you don't have to address me that way."

Magpie grasped Morgan's upper right arm and looked up at him. "Would ya help me find Mr. Walby?"

Morgan didn't answer. A pained expression crept into his eyes as he shifted the weight about in his arms.

"Please, sir?"

Morgan's lips began moving silently, as if he were speaking in a trance, and the only thing Magpie could understand was, ". . . that second shot from the *Serendipity* took the mizzenmast down and him with it. He's gone."

With his precious load, Morgan hurried away towards the ladder down to the hospital, leaving Magpie alone. Bewildered, the little sail maker stumbled to the starboard rail and hung his head over the ship's side, gulping at the air. His eye fell below to the accumulation of battle debris that knocked up against the *Isabelle*'s hull—bits of barrels, shredded sails, and lifeless sailors—and he followed its path out beyond the smoke into the far water, upon which the sun still shined. Aware of the gentle rise and fall of the ship, he clung to the rail and thought about Emily, and Jane Austen's book, and tried to recall all the delicious things Mrs. Jordan had fed him for supper that fascinating first night in the Duke of Clarence's home. The sounds around him had no meaning: the ringing of the ship's bell, the roaring requests for assistance with the wounded, and the shrilly cries of the Americans as they made ready to board the *Isabelle.*

After a time, Magpie shoved himself away from the rail. He wiped at his runny nose and aimlessly started walking, and though he was bumped and jostled by those scurrying around him, he kept his head down. Near a carronade, still scorching from employment, he discovered an officer's spyglass, lying forgotten on the red deck. Magpie bent over to pick it up, and as his hand closed around it he looked out again upon the azure sea. The water was calm and the winds running northeast were light.

4:30 p.m.
(First Dog Watch, One Bell)

THE SURVIVORS LINED THE SHIP'S RAILS, making way for the boarding party of sixty or so American officers and marines who moved across the *Isabelle*'s quarterdeck like a creeping pool of blood. With heavy hearts and vacant eyes that stared from weather-beaten faces, they wordlessly watched. Mrs. Kettle hovered near the *Isabelle*'s wheel, away from the men. She didn't like the look of the *Isabelle*'s crew—their sloping shoulders, and arms that hung uselessly at their sides—and chose instead to concentrate on the Americans, stretching her neck to catch the first glimpse of the Yankee captain around whom Bun Brodie had spun countless yarns. A long time passed while each of the boarders made his way up the ladder aside the ship, and she was certain that the last of them to step onto the quarterdeck was Captain Thomas Trevelyan himself.

Though not the pirate with flowing beard, peg leg, and flag—bearing skull and crossbones—that Mrs. Kettle had imagined, her knees still wobbled as she looked him over. He was a giant of a man with straw-coloured hair that stuck out in untidy bits from beneath his cocked hat. He had hideous eyes and a scarred, pockmarked face that reminded her of someone mouldering in his grave. Mrs. Kettle would hate to have encountered his kind at night in a London alley-way. Before the remnants of the *Isabelle*'s crew, he rose up, hands on his hips, a smirk on his sunken face, looking around with satisfaction at the ruin he had wrought.

The marine lieutenant at Trevelyan's side straightened his round infantry hat and hollered at his assembled soldiers. "Forty-six of the *Liberty*'s crew are prisoners on this ship. Seek them out, have them muster on the quarterdeck, and prepare for their transport to the *Serendipity*."

Trevelyan addressed one of his officers. "Mr. Smith, strike all the bunting and raise our colours. She may not be worth the powder to blow her to hell, but she's our prize now." He took several more steps, his eyes flicking over the crew that shuffled backwards as he leaned into them, before halting in front of Midshipman Stewart.

"Where is your captain?"

The flush-faced teenager struggled to clear his throat. "He's in ... in the great cabin ... sir."

Mrs. Kettle steadied her nerves with deep breaths as Trevelyan strode in her direction. Her left hand sought out her abdomen and she stroked it absently while her right fumbled at the neck of her shirt. Smiling prettily, she plucked a folded note from her bosom—the one she had asked Lord Lindsay to compose for her. She stepped forward, and held it out to Trevelyan, her heart beating rapidly when his eyes flashed over her form.

"Whom do we have here?" he asked with condescension. "The cook?"

"Nay, sir. Meggie Kettle, the laundress."

He glanced down at the proffered note. "What's this?"

"If ya please, sir. I needs ya to read it. If yer Cap'n Trevelyan, as I'm supposin', ya'll be findin' whot's in it mighty int'restin'."

Squinting, he studied her a moment, then snatched the note and skimmed its contents. When he was done, he crumpled it up triumphantly in his fist and his lips twisted into a smile. "Well, Mrs. Kettle, it seems the *Isabelle*'s more valuable than I thought."

CLUTCHING HIS MEDICAL CHEST under one arm and buttoning his clean shirt with his free hand, Leander kept his head down and hurried past the ship's wheel towards the great cabin. He stopped short when one quick glance up revealed the destruction ahead. The cabin's galleried windows had been blasted away; one wrong step would send him plunging into the sea. Scattered about the once-fine space were fragments of Captain Moreland's private papers, maps, and logbooks; his oak table and red velvet chairs had been reduced to pathetic piles of scrap and material. The only thing that had survived the barrage of Yankee shot was Captain Moreland's hammock, which was still swinging with the ship's serene rise and fall, and as Leander observed the spreading stain on its side and the still form lying within, he realized he had arrived too late.

"I am sorry for wasting your time," said Fly without lifting his head. He was sitting on the floor with his back resting against one of two remaining bulkheads, staring blankly at an opened letter that lay across his knees.

"I too am sorry … for your loss." Leander eyed Fly, looking for signs of injury, but he saw nothing significant beyond a few cuts that still bled through tears in his breeches. "Will you be all right?"

Fly breathed in and out heavily and looked up. "I understand the hospital took a hit."

"It did. It came through the gunport and it …" Leander couldn't finish his sentence.

"James never agreed with your philosophy of having your hospital on the upper deck. He always figured you and your patients would be safer on the orlop."

Leander's lips disappeared into a thin line and he nodded. "If there is nothing I can do here, I must get back."

Fly's stare fell upon the rusty stains on Leander's forearms. "Aye. But as I'm not sure when we may have another private moment—as there is little time left—I wonder if I could delay you." He held up the letter. "James asked that I read this if ... if things did not go well."

Leander set his medical chest on the floor beside Fly, lowered himself upon it, and gazed expectantly at his friend. Fly shot a furtive glance at what was once the main entrance to Captain Moreland's cabin, then began to read in a low, dull voice as if he were delivering a sermon to an empty church.

"Dear Mr. Austen. I realize that what I am about to relate is a subject I should have taken up with you long before now. I had hoped there would be time for you to hear my tale from my own lips. The following is not a story of which I am proud; in fact, I have spent the past nine years trying to forget it ever happened, and I thought I had almost succeeded. In putting off the telling of it, I employed every excuse: our occupation with the prisoners from the Liberty, *Lord Lindsay's shameful affair, and my lingering illness. I believed that—nay, I prayed—we would not meet Trevelyan again; leastways, I did not expect him to appear again so soon after our initial engagement. If I am justified in only one respect in writing—and not speaking—of this sorry business, it is that I will leave this world with the comforting knowledge that I have documented the details, of which, God knows, you will most certainly require somewhere down the road."*

Fly injected some inflection in his voice as he started in on James's story.

"In May of 1803, I was commanding the Isabelle *along with Henry, the Duke of Wessex. As you know, war had broken out once again with France, and I was ordered to assist in blockading the French port of Brest. We ended up in blockade for several months and it was most difficult on the crew. In addition to their regular duties, they were expected to undergo daily drills, intercept coastal convoys intent on supplying Brest, search the seas for any French ships returning from the West Indies, and, of course, watch the movements of the French frigates holed up in the harbour lest they be sent out on a*

clandestine operation or try to escape under cover of night. For all of us, the most difficult task was just trying to stay afloat offshore in all sorts of bad weather.

"The long weeks bobbing on the waves, battling nothing but the weather, took their toll. Supplies of fresh food ran low, the men naturally were not allowed any shore leave, and they were given only a drop of grog—Wessex and I wanting to keep them all sharp-witted as we worried they may have to give chase at any time. The result was that tempers flared and fights broke out amongst the men.

"One of the most troublesome amongst the crew happened to be a young lieutenant named Thomas Trevelyan. Trevelyan had recently been elevated in the world, as his step-father, Charles DeChastain, a man of great wealth and power and an earl no less—Trevelyan's widowed mother had already been married to DeChastain for thirteen years—had finally legally adopted Trevelyan, making him one of his heirs. Consequently, Trevelyan figured, despite his age and inexperience, he should be on equal footing with the son of King George and me, the lowly Captain Moreland. Trevelyan argued every decision, every order. Wessex wanted him punished for his continual insubordination, but I did not, as I understood the crew's conditions were unbearable at times, and my own spirits had sunk very low. To exacerbate the situation, Trevelyan's twelve-year-old half-brother, Harry DeChastain, was also on board. He was a midshipman and he adored his older brother. Trevelyan's discontentment and belligerent disposition had a profound effect upon him."

Fly pushed his body away from the bulkhead, jumped to his feet, and began pacing through the remains of the room, keeping his eyes averted from the cot as he continued to read.

"In late March of 1804, the Isabelle *was badly damaged in a gale, and when it had passed over, we were forced ashore to do repairs. Early one morning, while we were anchored off a lonely stretch of the French coast, six of the crew deserted in one of the ship's small boats. Trevelyan and his little brother, Harry, were amongst the deserters. When it was discovered they were gone, Wessex ordered several crew members to set out in the remaining boats and find them. Miraculously, since the morning was quite foggy, they did. Fear-*

ing severe punishment, two of the deserters jumped overboard and drowned. The other four were brought back to the ship, tied to the grating, and before the assembled crew summarily given 300 lashes apiece. On my insistence, Harry was given half that number, but despite the lesser punishment, his back swelled up like a charred pillow and an infectious fever set in. For two long weeks, he suffered cruelly, finally dying on his thirteenth birthday.

"Trevelyan recovered—physically—but he was a changed man. He went about his business, did as he was told and questioned nothing. Wessex figured he had learned his lesson; I figured he was just biding his time. Five months later, in early September, the Isabelle *received orders to give chase to a French frigate returning from the West Indies. Away from the company and security of the other British ships in blockade, Trevelyan led a mutiny. He had Wessex and me locked into our cabins, then killed three of the* Isabelle's *officers, as well as my faithful steward, threw their bodies overboard, and endeavoured to take over the ship. While we were being held hostage, Wessex and I tried bargaining with Trevelyan, promised to hear his grievances, and grant a pardon for the mutineers. We both swore on a bible to make changes in exchange for our release and a return of the ship to our command. When a week had passed and our ship was again close to the French coastline, Trevelyan finally yielded and agreed to end the mutiny. I was fully prepared to make concessions and attempt to bring about better conditions for our men, but as Wessex had the advantage of birth and position over me, I was forced to bow to his authority. Wessex refused to make any concessions whatsoever and instead ordered that the mutineering ringleaders be strung up on a yardarm and Trevelyan be shot.*

"In the early hours of the morning upon which the executions were to take place, as eight bells tolled the end of the Middle Watch, Trevelyan, with the help of unnamed accomplices, was released from his irons. He then attempted to set the Isabelle *afire. In the ensuing disorder, he threw himself and a hatch cover overboard, floated to shore, and disappeared into the French countryside. This time, he was not caught."*

Fly folded up James's letter and looked at Leander for the first time since his friend had entered the room.

Leander rose slowly from his medical chest. "I do not understand.

Why is it no one seems to have heard much of this mutiny when its details are as horrific as those of *Spithead* and the *Nore*?"

"For the simple reason that there was no court-martial, only a simple inquiry. James goes on to write that given the political weight of Wessex, and the fact that Wessex and he had determined their own punishments for the deserters and mutineers on the *Isabelle*, the admiralty chose to keep the affair private. Over the years, there have been hundreds of single-ship mutinies that have vanished into the sea mists with no record. All that remains here are the recollections of those men who were aboard the *Isabelle* in March of 1804, and … I just happen to know of one such man."

"And who would that be?"

"Bun Brodie. He was sailing with James at that time. The man was lucky enough to be with Nelson at Trafalgar, but despite this honour, Brodie told James that he had admired him more."

Leander gazed pensively at the visible sea through the broken ship wall. "In all these years, did James never hear another thing from Trevelyan?"

"In his letter he states that the Royal Navy suspected Trevelyan's successful escape was aided by the French themselves, in exchange for information regarding our orders and manoeuvres, and that he had fled to the United States; but no, James never heard another thing until a few weeks back when Emily told him that it was Trevelyan who commanded the *Serendipity*."

"So Trevelyan blamed James and Wessex for the death of his brother."

"Aye, it would seem so, and for subsequently ruining his life. Branded a traitor, he would not have been allowed back in England to collect any forthcoming titles, and more importantly, his inheritance."

"And he took Emily prisoner as a kind of posthumous revenge against her father, and the moment …" Leander raised his voice, "the moment he learns that the ball from Mr. Clive's pistol didn't kill her, that she's in fact on board with us, he'll take her prisoner once again."

Fly nodded in agreement. "Precisely."

Pulling his glasses from his face, Leander screwed his eyes shut and rubbed the auburn stubble on his face. "But if Trevelyan fled to the United States nine years ago, how ... how would he have ever known that the only child of the Duke of Wessex was a Mrs. Seaton travelling to Canada on board the *Amelia*?"

"Perhaps he was tipped off," suggested Fly. "Perhaps he had spies, someone watching her movements in England, especially once her father had died."

A lengthy silence fell between the two. Finally Leander said, "Emily knew nothing of Trevelyan's desire for vengeance."

"How can you be certain of that?"

"I just am." He slipped his glasses back on his nose and bent down to gather up his chest. "We will speak again ... as soon as it is possible," he said with urgency in his voice, "but I must go." With a half-hearted smile, he faced Fly and extended his right hand to him. Wordlessly, they shook hands, then Leander hurried away.

He had only just disappeared from view when, from out of the corner of his eye, Fly saw him returning, walking slowly backwards towards the spot he had just departed. Wheeling about to question his friend, Fly discovered five men encircling Leander, dressed in the red, white, and blue uniforms of an American captain and marines. There were telltale signs on the faces and clothing of the four marines that they had recently seen action, but the scars on the captain's face were old ones, and his clothes looked new: his breeches were still white, his epaulettes gleamed gold, and his uniform coat was freshly pressed. It looked as if he had just put them on before boarding the *Isabelle*. He barely glanced at Fly as he pushed past Leander into the shell of the great cabin, and said nothing while he kicked aside bits and pieces of Captain Moreland's personal belongings with his boots and examined the room's wreckage, pausing on the contents of the reddening cot. He stepped heavily towards it and stared at James's silent form, his expression never changing even as, in one fluid motion, he grasped the ivory hilt of James's sword, which lay across his dead body, and slipped it into the black leather scabbard at his left hip. When his lips at last moved it was to utter a single word. "Pity."

It was only then that Fly knew for certain the identity of the American captain standing before him; he was not from the second frigate, nor the Yankee brig, but the man who commanded the *Serendipity*.

Leander, his brow furrowed with impatience, stepped towards Trevelyan. "I must take my leave, sir. There are dozens below in my hospital awaiting my attention."

Trevelyan swung around, the heels of his boots grinding shards of Captain Moreland's broken crystal goblets into the floorboards as he did so. He gave Leander a prolonged stare. "Well, then, they will just have to wait. Your services, Dr. Braden, are now required on *my* ship."

6:00 p.m.
(First Dog Watch, Four Bells)

THE GUNS HAD STOPPED FIRING two hours ago. Emily had heard the ship's bell ring out the half-hours, but she knew from the eerie hush on the *Isabelle* that the outcome had not been in their favour. She'd given up sipping Leander's rum and re-reading his letter and rocking herself back and forth long ago. There was nothing left to feel now. If he could have, Leander would have returned to her long before, or at least sent Gus Walby or Magpie in his stead. But no one had come, and there had been no voices or footsteps outside the small cabin where she lay sprawled in a daze on the damp floor. She had heard what she guessed were small boats knocking up against the hull, had tried to convince herself they belonged to the *Isabelle*, but if she was wrong and they did not, how long would it be before ... ?

Emily lifted herself unwillingly from the floor, angled her head and listened; still nothing but a rhythmic beating sound against the hull and the occasional muffled voice in the distance. The lantern's candle was waning, its flickering light projecting her huddled silhouette upon the sweating timbers of the room. Soon she would be left in utter, suffocating darkness. With this realization an image of faceless forbidding figures rose before her, causing her to shudder with such fear that she sprang to her feet and began pacing the cramped perimeter, alternately wringing her hands and pulling at her long hair.

Was there another place to hide, then? In the *Isabelle*'s hold perhaps? But what if they sank the ship? What if Leander finally did come looking for her and she wasn't there? Could she disguise herself with some of his clothes and wend her way above deck, there to run up the shrouds or blend in with the men and endure whatever punishments the Americans inflicted upon their lot? With whitened knuckles, Emily tore Leander's frock coat and felt hat from the hanging pegs, pulled on the coat, fumbled with its two buttons, and shoved her hair up into the hat; all the while she was sadly aware of their evocative smell.

Then she froze.

There was a knock at the door. She spun round and stared at it in horror before calling out in a low voice, "Leander?"

"Aye," came a whispered voice, "it is me."

A warm wave of relief passed over her as she swiftly unlocked the door and threw it open. She blinked into the blackness, unable to see a thing besides the dying light in Leander's cabin. A thick hand caught her around the wrist and jerked her forward with such roughness that her hat rolled off and she dropped her letter. Something cracked. She cried out as her arms were wrenched behind her and her hands tied tightly together with rope. The sound of her pounding heart was painfully amplified in her ears, as were the grunts of satisfaction muttered by whomever it was binding her wrists. There were others standing nearby—she could tell from the pervading stale air and shuffling steps on the wooden deck. As Emily fought to gather her wits, a light appeared from the spirits room and with it the bulky shape of Mrs. Kettle. She grinned at Emily and broke into a gale of laughter, and when she was done, dabbed at her eyes. "I knew ya was hidin' in thee great doctor's cabin all thee while."

Emily gazed at the laundress with cold resentment.

"Ya see, prisoners ain't left on the gun deck durin' battle. They be tossed down here on thee orlop. It was *him* what saw Dr. Braden leadin' ya here." Mrs. Kettle cocked her head behind her, and Octavius Lindsay—no longer fettered in irons—stepped into the light of her lantern.

6:30 p.m.
Out at Sea

AS HE ROWED FARTHER and farther away from the *Isabelle*, Magpie forced himself to keep his eyes glued to the little whirlpools created by his oars. He liked the way they gathered energy and took on a life of their own: swirling the sea-greens and blues together, then spinning away from his cutter, like miniature ships without sails. He could not bring himself to look at the three ships hovering in a semi-circle to the south of the *Isabelle*, nor could he look at the *Isabelle* herself, having already witnessed too much. The Yankee colours now flew in exultation above the British ones on the *Isabelle*'s broken masts, strangers in strange uniforms swarmed her decks, and gaping holes in her hull reminded him of hideous mouths opened in agony. It was a miracle she was still afloat.

Magpie blinked at the June sun just beginning to climb down from her lookout in the sky and tried to take pleasure in the white gulls that squealed and frolicked high above his head. It had been easy enough leaving the *Isabelle*. All of her small boats had been lowered into the sea long before the battle began, to be towed astern as a precaution against their being blown to bits and becoming a hail of deadly splinters that would slice through the fighting crew. With all the confusion on the quarterdeck, no one had seen him scramble over the taffrail and shinny down the towrope that led to the skiff, the smallest of the three cutters—an easy task for someone who had once been a London climbing boy. Biscuit had seen him, though, not long after he had happily been relieved from the hospital. It was Biscuit who had hastily thrown together for him a small duffle bag that contained a blanket, bandages, a wineskin of water, and a day's supply of sea biscuits, and had then released the towrope after Magpie was safely seated in the cutter and had picked up the oars.

"If thee Yankees don't capture ya and toss ya in thee supper stew, ya might wanna stay out there. Ya may be safer in thee sea than here on thee *Isabelle*," Biscuit had said while giving him a lift over the taffrail. "Keep yer bandages dry if ya can; ya don't want no infection settin' in. And whatever ya does, don't eat them biscuits all at once." As Magpie had started down the rope, Biscuit saluted him.

Handling the oars was not an easy task for Magpie. The cutter normally required four men to do the rowing, and his arms and back ached as they never had before, his hands were bleeding, his legs felt numb, and there was a bad pain in his head. As he set down the heavy oars to rest, he wished Biscuit had come along to share the work.

Taking up the spyglass, he looked north again. The dark smudge on the horizon—the one he'd noticed when he had first set off—was definitely larger than before. Did he dare hope? Sighing, he picked up the oars. If the Yankees didn't notice his boat out on the waves, if the winds and the sea stayed calm, and if his body held out, he would soon be there.

6:30 p.m.
(Second Dog Watch, One Bell)
Aboard HMS *Isabelle*

MORGAN EVANS WEARILY CLIMBED the ladder from the hospital onto the fo'c'sle deck, squinted into the golden evening light, and drew a long breath of sea air. He had waited a long time for Dr. Braden to come back after being summoned to Captain Moreland's cabin, and while waiting, Morgan had occupied himself helping Osmund Brockley with the injured. But Dr. Braden never returned and there was little he could do for those who required an amputation or a bullet extraction. Morgan forced from his mind disturbing pictures, especially that of Bailey Beck's old eyes as he breathed his last.

The smoke of war had passed away now and the sun sparkled on the calm waters of the Atlantic as if mocking the fact that a violent event had just taken place. The weather decks and yardarms hummed with the activities commonly seen following an enemy encounter. Morgan could see Bun Brodie climbing the mainmast rigging with a roll of sail slung over his shoulder, while dozens of sailors were already aloft stripping the torn sails from their yards. A crew of men was hoisting the small boats from the sea to swing once again on their davits until they were next needed. The guns were being cleaned and stored, and everywhere repairs were underway. Along the larboard rail, Maggot and Weevil were sewing the dead into their hammock coffins, and weaving throughout their dismal part of the ship was Biscuit, carrying a tray and muttering oaths in between the times when he stopped to offer a mug of coffee to one of the American officers. Standing on the quarterdeck was a sober-looking Fly Austen, giving his men their orders, though not in his usual robust voice. If it hadn't been for the pervasive horde of shouting American officers and marines, their hands poised on their muskets and swords, and the strange, muted quality that lingered amongst the men, Morgan could have believed all was right with the *Isabelle*. Unable to look upon the long line of bodies laid out on the larboard gangway, he inched his way instead along the crowded starboard rail towards the quarterdeck, where he overheard Midshipman Stewart reporting to Mr. Austen.

"Sir, all the boats are up; however, it appears the skiff is unaccounted for."

Fly replied with a sideways glance. "Perhaps a casualty of war, Mr. Stewart."

Fly's glance then shifted and fell on Morgan. There were lines on the commander's face Morgan had never noticed before, and in his right hand he carried a book that Morgan supposed was a bible.

"There you are, Mr. Evans! Collect your hammer and nails if you please. We've been instructed to patch up the ship and ready ourselves for sailing as soon as possible." His tone was sarcastic.

"Where are we sailing to, sir?"

"To Hell's harbour."

Morgan looked past Fly at the flag of stars and stripes that fluttered from the *Isabelle*'s stern and understood. "Aye, sir." As an afterthought he added, "Captain Austen."

As there was no pleasure to be taken in the tribute, Fly looked away and, assuming exuberance, pointed aft of the *Isabelle*'s waist. "Perhaps, Mr. Evans, before you dash off, you might wish to witness the spectacle that is about to unfold on our fine decks."

Morgan turned his head in time to see Meg Kettle tramping up the ladder from the upper deck in the company of two American marines. She had a wide grin planted on her face as she swayed down the deck in a relaxed manner, swinging a bag of what Morgan figured must be her possessions, and chattering merrily away to her escorts even though they said nothing in return. As she passed by certain men she recognized, she winked or bobbed her head or, in some cases, blew them a kiss.

"Why, sir, would they want the likes of her?"

"Why? To do their laundry, of course, Mr. Evans," Fly replied dryly.

Following on the heels of Mrs. Kettle was Octavius Lindsay. He walked freely behind her, his dark eyes troubled by the sun's strong glare, but he held his unshaven face high and the arrogant sneer of old was once again visible on his pale features. While the marines set about putting Mrs. Kettle and Mr. Lindsay into the small boats for transportation to the American frigates, there arose from amongst the onlookers a groan that sounded like the cries of a pod of wounded whales. Morgan craned his neck to view the object of their outpouring, but at first could only see the jackets of four marines. When he saw Emily—her eyes ablaze with fear—despair tugged on his heart. Unlike Meg Kettle and Mr. Lindsay, her hands were tied behind her back and she was being pushed along the deck with the point of a musket's bayonet, often faltering and having to endure the guffaws of the enemy.

In agitation, Morgan again addressed Fly. "Is there nothing we can do, sir?"

"Not a thing, Mr. Evans."

Morgan couldn't stand to watch any longer. He turned away sadly and fled below deck.

7:00 p.m.
(Second Dog Watch, Two Bells)

"Pick it up. Move along," came the gruff command. It was followed by a sharp jab between Emily's shoulder blades, hitting dangerously close to her healing bullet wound, and she cried out in pain. When the wave of agony had subsided, her swollen red eyes looked towards the *Isabelle*'s men. They had all paused in their chores to watch her as they had done that first night she came on board; only then, she had been carried, safe in the arms of Morgan Evans, and the expressions on the men's faces had been curious and kind. Now she could only read guilt and compassion in them. She lifted her chin in defiance, avoiding glances at the destruction around her, at the dead sailors arranged in their hammocks at her feet, and at the figure of Trevelyan himself, lurking by the break in the larboard rail where, in a few moments, she would be lowered into a waiting boat and rowed away from the *Isabelle* forever. A solid line of armed, blue-jacketed marines kept the sailors back. Emily searched the faces that peeked out between arms and bayonets and the heads that bowed as she passed, hoping to catch a glimpse of those known to her.

Before long, she was standing, weak-kneed, near the *Isabelle*'s open rail-edge, peering across at the anchored brig and frigates, feeling Trevelyan's eyes boring into her back like the jabs of the Yankee bayonets.

"Emily!"

She swung her head in the direction of the cry, and found Morgan Evans, his face overspread with a deep red, looking at her with his hopeful eyes. He tried to draw closer, but was thrust back by two marines. He then shot his arm through a barrier of crossed muskets and with a bob of his head urged her to take the gift he held out in his hand. She gazed down at the black leather sailor's shoes with the shiny silver buckles, and her eyes blurred with tears. She twisted her head to the marine at her back. "Please take them for me." With a look and cluck of disgust, the marine snatched the shoes from Morgan's hand and stuffed them into the pocket of her borrowed coat as if they were soiled handkerchiefs. When Emily again looked up at Morgan, he gave her a naval salute and with an audible catch in his throat said, "Mr. George, sir." All too soon his face was lost in the jostling throng.

"Prepare the chair," shouted Trevelyan, referring to the contraption on a pulley that would be used to lower Emily to the boats.

"Wouldn't it be easier if you just tossed me overboard?" she asked, keeping her eyes fixed on the American ships. "Or perhaps you—you could ask Mr. Clive to shoot me again?"

She heard Trevelyan click his tongue against the roof of his mouth. "Madam, our Mr. Clive is neither a reliable nor steady marksman. I would not think to trouble *him*."

She moved away from him to watch in anguish as the chair was manoeuvred into place for her, acutely aware that an escape was impossible. In time, a gentle pressure on her shoulder roused her from her miserable reverie. It was Fly who stood next to her now, his face tired and troubled, holding out his sister's well-thumbed volumes of *Sense and Sensibility*.

"Perhaps it is worth a second reading," he said quietly.

"Most certainly it is," she replied, giving him an encouraging smile as he slipped the slim books into the empty pocket of her coat. Despite Trevelyan's nearness, she leaned in closer to Fly.

"Mr. Austen, you have been most kind to me. For that I will always be grateful." She fixed her eyes as steadily as she could on his. "Is the doctor—well?"

A softening of Fly's features told her he was.

Her voice quivered. "Could I then impose on you once more to deliver a message to him for me?"

Fly bent his head to hers. "You may be in a better position to deliver that message yourself, Emily," he whispered.

Her eyes narrowed in question, and she was about to ask, *Whatever do you mean?* when her arm was seized from behind and she was shoved towards the waiting chair.

"For God's sake!" Fly shouted at Trevelyan in restrained exasperation. "Could you not at least untie her hands?"

As Emily was roughly hustled into the chair and another rope secured around her waist, Trevelyan gave his snide reply. "Mr. Austen, you should know that a good captain never gives those he cannot trust a second chance, even if that person is one's *intended* wife."

Emily stiffened. His words invaded her brain like a malignant infection. There was an awful moment of silence that preceded Trevelyan's command for the chair to be lowered. As it lurched and dropped, Emily trembled and felt herself growing ice-cold. She saw nothing, heard nothing, and could only think that this is what it must feel like to be lowered into one's grave. By the time her chair reached the waiting boat, hands scrambled to unfasten the rope at her waist, and smirking officers and sailors openly scrutinized her, but she was hardly conscious of them. She sat on the front few inches of the aft bench of Trevelyan's barge, her hands still tied behind her, her back to the *Isabelle*'s great hull, and closed her eyes, refusing to look ahead at the three ships that would take her who knows where, unable to contemplate what was to become of her. Soon she felt the boat rock and knew that Trevelyan was positioning himself on the bench opposite her.

"Away, then," he yelled. The oars fell into the water with a jarring splash and the barge rolled away from the *Isabelle*. Within seconds of their departure, a voice called out urgently to Captain Trevelyan from the *Isabelle*'s decks.

"Sir, the *Serendipity* has signalled to us of a sighting: two ships, perhaps ten or so miles to the north of us."

"And their nationality?"

"It is uncertain at this time, sir. Do you still wish to take the *Isabelle* a prize?"

For the first time since being paraded from her ship, Emily looked directly at Trevelyan, only to find him drawing his fingers back and forth across his chin, and staring at her with those strange eyes of his. She stared back, determined—though it sickened her—to hold his hostile gaze.

His immediate reply was loud enough for all to hear. "No! Raid her hold, take what able-bodied men you want and then—since I have achieved what I came here for—you can burn her."

Emily's stomach churned with horror. Her heart was so full that she could not speak. But Trevelyan, as if he had all the time in a world that was at peace, not war, leaned forward and stroked her hair as he would his pet dog.

"Perhaps, madam, once you are settled on the *Serendipity*, we can order you a bath."

7:00 p.m.

Adrift in the Atlantic Ocean

When the small cutter finally pulled alongside the fallen mizzen-mast, Magpie let out an agonized wail. Gus was sprawled across the timber debris and its torn topsail like a discarded doll, his legs submerged in the sea, his back twisted, and his arms—swollen and blackened with bruises—hooked around the mast-stump. Only his face had escaped the ravages of his calamitous fall—angelic still and gently caressed by the watery fingers of the Atlantic.

"Mr. Walby?"

When there came no reply, an undaunted Magpie shoved the spyglass down the neck of his shirt, grabbed the length of rope lying beside him on the bench, leaned over the gunwale, and fastened a portion of the mast's rigging as securely as he could to a metal hook on the bow of his boat. Then he climbed out of the skiff onto the mizzenmast wreckage, locked his legs around the stump, and inched his way along it until he arrived at Gus's head. Wondering how best to rouse him, Magpie gingerly tousled his damp hair and said, "Sir! I'm rescuin' ya, sir."

He waited awhile, but there was no response to his voice or his touch. There was nothing but a still form lying beside him.

Magpie started shaking uncontrollably. A crushing pressure squeezed his ribs, as if he'd been jammed between two cannons, and he couldn't breathe. His soot-stained fingers sought out his crumpling face as he lowered his head to his knees. "I'm sorry. I'm sorry I didn't row fast enough."

He stayed huddled over Gus on the fallen mizzenmast, listening to the quiet lap of the sea as it nudged their little floating island farther still from the *Isabelle*. So great were his feelings of desolation, he no longer cared where the low waves carried him. He thought of playing his flute, but it was still in the skiff, rolling about on the ribbed bottom, and he did not possess the strength to retrieve it. Instead, he stretched his body along the mast, and made the decision to die next to his friend.

It was a loud cry that awoke Magpie with a start. Raising his head in sleepy confusion, he gazed about in gloomy recollection. The *Isabelle*!

Blue-black smoke slithered up and around her standing masts and spewed from the gaping wounds in her hull. Magpie pulled the spyglass from his sodden shirt and tried to steady his hands long enough to see through its magnifiers. Instantly he understood the significance of the sailors' scramble to lower the cutters from their davits, the urgency with which they descended the yards and the tops, and the chaos that abounded above deck. Before long, the men, with no option but to take their chances in the sea, would be throwing themselves off the rails.

With a rallying shot of adrenalin, Magpie bolted upright. "Mr. Walby," he said, "we gotta go back. I ain't gonna leave ya here alone."

Slowly, reverentially, he began to unwrap Gus's bruised arms from their embrace of the mast, and had successfully freed one when he heard an odd sound. He tensed, wondering if it had come from the debris knocking about in the water, or a sea creature, or was simply a product of his imagination. His eyes darted about, fully expecting to light upon a nearby school of dolphins. As he began working on Gus's other arm, he heard it again: a human-sounding yelp of pain. This time there was no mistaking its source.

"Yer alive, sir!" he shrieked.

Gus's eyes flickered, then opened. "I'm cold."

"Oh, Mr. Walby ..." Magpie's voice broke. He tugged at his arms again.

"No! Leave me. I'm broken—most everywhere, I think. Leave me here."

"I won't, sir," shouted Magpie. "I've brung a blanket and some water." With his chest bursting now with happiness, he chattered on, his words tripping over one another, informing Gus of how he would make him better by feeding him freshly baked biscuits and fixing up his broken bones "just like I seen Dr. Braden do it" and how he would carefully haul him into the cutter where he could get dry.

"And then I'll play 'Heart of Oak' on me flute!" Magpie broke into sudden, shrill song. "*Come cheer up my Lads, 'tis to glory we steer ...*"

Gus closed his eyes again. "Save yourself and go back."

Magpie, his back to the dying ship, knew there was no sense in telling Gus of the terror on the *Isabelle*. "I won't, sir." He glanced to the north again and his heart quickened, for he was now certain that it was two sails he could see on the skyline. "But if ya can see fit to look through the glass with yer good eyes and all, ya might tell us what ya see." He waited anxiously for the waves to swing the mizzenmast in a north-facing direction, and then held the glass before Gus's right eye. "There now, Mr. Walby, give us a squint."

Gus stared at the horizon for what seemed to Magpie an eternity.

"What d'ya see, sir?"

Finally, Gus raised his head a bit and began to laugh—his laughter weak at first, then an outpouring of explosive sobs. "I'm certain of it, Magpie! Two ships—one of them—why, I know her colours!" he gasped, tears streaming down his whitened cheeks. "It's our good friend, the *Amethyst*!"

10

Wednesday, June 16

6:00 a.m.
(Morning Watch, Four Bells)

"It's useless!"

"Abandon the pumps!"

"Get to the boats!"

"There's no time! There's no time!"

In a haze of horror, Emily watched the twisted fingers of the brilliant flames engulf the Isabelle*'s careworn masts and rapidly consume all in its way—tarred rigging, torn sails, tinder-dry planks—with the brutal vitality of an exultant beast pouncing upon its prey. Faceless figures, as black as the bitter smoke that filled her nostrils, panicked around her, running for only God knows where. Emily feverishly searched the seething mob of sailors, hoping to recognize the features of a loved one, but the glowing furnace refused to make distinctions between the night and its fearsome shadows.*

"Fire the starboard guns."

"Lower the larboard boats."

"Mr. Evans! To the stern at once!"

"The fire—it'll soon reach the magazine!"

Though she could not see Fly Austen, Emily could hear his voice, hoarse and spent, above the shouting and raging roar of the inferno. His sharp orders were everywhere—now fore, now aft, now amidships—and she called out to him, but he did not reply. Headlong, she ploughed into the crush of frantic bodies and battled her way towards the ship's foredeck, desperate to find the hatchway that would take her down to the hospital.

Perhaps there she would find Leander.

From the bowels of the ship, a shot of flame whooshed before her like a fiery giant, blocking her way, knocking her backwards upon the scorching planks. Fleeing feet trampled and stumbled over her. She gasped as the severe knocks to her body tore open the skin on her forehead and ruptured anew the bullet wound in her shoulder. Blood poured down her face, filling her eyes and her mouth.

Boom! Boom! Boom!

The starboard guns were fired off in rapid succession, ferociously shaking the Isabelle *and everything that still clung to her decks. The larboard boats began their precarious descent into the darkened water, while bits of burning spars and shroud rained down upon the desperate men who lowered them, setting several afire. The men shrieked and darted about in a ghastly dance before hurling themselves overboard. Emily, unable to breathe, unable to scream, lay paralyzed and helpless near the mainmast, holding her ears in a vain attempt to shut out the appalling bedlam.*

After long, terrifying moments, someone stopped to help her. She felt a small, warm hand slip into hers, pull her to her feet, and guide her to the starboard rail.

"Gus? Magpie?" she cried, addressing her shadowy saviour. But, before her eyes, the small hand and its owner slowly shrank away, then disintegrated, as if never really existing in the first place.

Desperate to escape the severe heat, Emily hung her head over the rail and contemplated a plunge into the heaving blackness below. The deck beneath her feet groaned and began to buckle. No one fled past her now; Fly Austen's shouting had long since ceased. The roar and snap of the fire as it ravaged the Isabelle *was the only sound that struck her ears. Now all was ablaze, the flames leaping around her like a swarm of striking snakes.*

Suddenly Leander was there. He was untouched by the fire, except for its reflection that glowed in the depths of his eyes. His gaze was steady, reassuring, as he extended his hand towards her. Intense happiness flowed through

Emily's veins as she loosened her grip on the rail and turned to meet him. Her fingertips were almost touching his when he moved away, as if an invisible hand were dragging him backwards into the fire. It was then that a tremendous explosion ripped through the Isabelle, *thrusting the ship's pathetic remains upwards, above the sea's surface for a moment, before slamming her down, down upon the eternal waves ...*

Emily's eyes flew open. She was drenched—drenched with sweat and tears. Her heart was beating with the speed of a hummingbird's wings and her chest hurt. She sat up in her cot and struggled to slow her laboured breathing. For the fourth time that long night, she had dreamt about the *Isabelle*. It was in flames and Fly Austen had tried with steadfast determination to organize the men and maintain some semblance of order as it burned around him. Someone ... perhaps Gus or Magpie ... had helped her up when she had fallen on the quarterdeck, and Leander—Leander had been there, smiling, holding out his hand to her. But the fire was everywhere and there had been a thunderous noise that caused the decks to collapse down upon one another and he had been wrenched away from her, cast into an abyss.

Leander.

In painful recollection, Emily squeezed her eyes shut and began to tremble violently in the dimness of her tiny cabin. If only he would come to her now, pass through the canvas curtain and soothe away her nightmares with his tonics and his dear company. But the door to her quarters—her new quarters on Thomas Trevelyan's ship—was locked, and the *Isabelle* was gone, burned to the waterline, her crew presumably dead or scattered.

It was more than Emily could bear, this incessant, frenzied speculating about who might have survived and who had not. Briefly, before being taken from the *Isabelle* by Trevelyan and his marines, she had seen Fly Austen and Morgan Evans, and therefore knew they had escaped harm during the confrontation with the American frigates—but had they survived their ship's final destruction? And what about the others? Of them, she had no real news at all. Those on Trevelyan's *Serendipity* were forbidden to speak to her. She knew there was someone on duty outside her locked door. She could see the heels of a pair of boots in the space between the door and wooden planks of the floor—the same space through which they had passed a tray of stale biscuits hours before—but no one had answered her calls or cared about her grief.

In need of fresh air, Emily crawled out of her cot, mindful of her swollen ankle and aching shoulder. She clambered over the still-warm cannon that sat silent below the cot, negotiated her way round the network of thick ropes that held it in place, and finally pushed open the heavy gunport. A cold sea-spray met her face with a sharp slap, but despite its sting, she filled her lungs with the early morning air and gazed out over the grey swells towards the faint glimmer of light between the dark horizon and the black wall of clouds hovering above it. She stuck her head out the gunport, welcoming the freshness from the surging sea and the wind that tossed the straight strands of her hair about her shoulders. She forced herself to breathe deeply until her pounding heart slowed. But nature could not diminish her sorrow, and desiring only to sleep, she closed up the heavy port, jumping back with a start as it fell into place with a thud and plunged her cabin once more into semi-darkness.

Using the gun's ropes for assistance, Emily groped her way back towards her cot and was almost at her destination when her bare feet tripped over objects that had been relegated to the wet floor ten hours ago when she had first been thrust into this unfamiliar cabin. Kneeling down, her shaking hands felt about for the pair of leather shoes with the gleaming silver buckles, and the precious volumes of Jane Austen's *Sense and Sensibility*. In her crouched position, she pressed them to her breast until she heard the ship's bell clang four times—6:00 a.m. Listless, she scrabbled to find her footing on the cannon, and tumbled into her cot. There she set the shoes and volumes down beside her pillow, wrapped herself into her blanket—a frock coat that held a faint musky scent within its voluminous folds—and let her tears come again.

There would be no sunrise this day.

6:30 a.m.

At Sea

"Sir? Captain Austen?"

Fly Austen struggled to open his heavy eyelids as the dread of his troubled dreams began to recede into the void of his subconscious. Who was speaking to him? He was so exhausted, so wet and cold and hungry, that he could not tell. And where was he? There was a rocking motion beneath him, but no ceiling over his head. He sat up—his back screaming in pain as he did so—to cast his sleepy eyes around him.

It was early morning. He was in a small boat—a cutter—bobbing about on dull waves under a leaden sky that was spitting cold rain. With him, crowded into the boat, were eighteen indistinguishable men, all with soot-blackened faces. Some, with discernible wounds, slept, while others gazed at nothing, perhaps, like him, trying to reconcile the events of the last several hours. Every one of them was soaked to the skin and they huddled together to steal what warmth they could from their neighbouring comrades. Floating nearby were two more cutters and one larger pinnace, each carrying roughly the same number of exhausted, wet men, and each towing—by means of ropes and discarded shirts—bits and pieces of charred timber on which were sprawled another handful of survivors. One young lad had even lashed himself to an empty chicken coop to ride out the waves.

Fly rubbed his eyes as if trying to banish the dismal scene before him. Was this all that was left? In his fitful dreams, he had been able to save his men from the burning *Isabelle*, but this ragged bunch, drifting on the waves as helplessly as a bullet-ridden bird, spoke the true tale. As bitter awareness filled his dark eyes, he turned them towards Morgan Evans, who tried a second time to rouse him with his words.

"Captain Austen?"

Fly nodded wearily as his glance flickered over his meagre fleet. "Aye?"

"They've spotted us again, sir."

"Who has?"

"The *Amethyst* and the *Expedition*. I beg you to look behind you, sir."

Fly twisted his sore body in order to follow Morgan's finger and squinted at the two murky sails, running towards them from the north.

"They're still a few hours off, but—we're sure of it—they're on their way, sir."

Fly recalled sighting the two British ships before Trevelyan had set the *Isabelle* afire, but as the flames' guiding glow had been extinguished and darkness had settled on the sea long before their arrival, they could be of no assistance to the poor souls, with nothing to cling to, who had cried out most piteously for help.

Fly winced. "How many of us are there, Mr. Evans?"

"Seventy-five in the boats, another twelve in the water, sir."

"But there were so many on the *Isabelle*."

"I was told there were four hundred of us in all, sir." Morgan hesitated. "Four hundred and one if you include Miss Emily."

Fly gave the carpenter's mate a grim smile as he made a tremendous effort to stand up. With his boots splashing in the several inches of seawater that had poured into the cutter, he examined the boats and floating timbers of the once-proud *Isabelle*, and the men who remained. Had they been able to lower the large launch and the second pinnace before the fire engulfed them, many more lives could have been saved. And the skiff, it could have carried a few more, but its fate was unknown long before Trevelyan's men and their torches had done their contemptible work. In the bow of the surviving pinnace, Fly noticed the unruly mop of hair that belonged to Biscuit. "You there, Biscuit! What the devil are you about?"

The old Scottish cook raised his woeful face from his hands, wiped at his whiskery cheeks, and reluctantly met Captain Austen's stare. "Canna help me sobbin', sir. Ya see, I lost me stove, me old reliable

Brodie stove. She be keepin' comp'ny with a pod o' queer sea monsters by now, no doubt."

"Brighten yourself up and tell me what provisions we have amongst us."

"Why, none, sir, none at all. No food, no water. Ya see—there weren't no time, sir."

Fly clenched his fists to fight the gnawing thirst and hunger that caused him more agony than his back. He didn't want to have to think, let alone lead men. He would gladly lie back down in the cold water that slithered up and down in the cutter's belly if only he could sleep and forget.

Morgan and a few of the others who were still alert looked up expectantly at Fly. They waited. At last Fly took a deep breath and stepped up onto the cutter's bench, balancing himself on his weary legs.

"Men! We must work together. We must stay occupied. These boats... each one of them should be fitted with sailing gear." He forced an injection of fervour into his strained voice. "If there is mast and canvas to be found—raise them! If oars—lower them! And for goodness sakes, find something with which to bail this infernal seawater! If we can pull together, our reward just may be a hot breakfast." He peered at the approaching ships through the rain that now fell harder, and to himself added, "so long as, this time, Providence is on our side."

Friday, June 18

9:00 p.m.

Sunset at Sea

WITH HIS RED SCARF tied around his bandaged head, a shirtless Magpie grunted as he lifted the oars from the calm waters and laid them to rest with a heavy thump on the gunwales. He then pulled his bare feet up onto the skiff's middle bench and sat cross-legged to watch the sun fall from the western sky. Under normal circumstances, he loved to watch the burning orb as it gradually disappeared, leaving in its wake an afterglow of pearl and rosy pinks, but now he was relieved to see the last of it. This day had been harsh. The sun's penetrating rays had been relentless and had burned his skin. There had been no water to drink, the contents of the wineskin given him by Biscuit long gone. The last two days, though stormy and frightening, had afforded drops of water from the low-hanging clouds. He had eagerly caught them on his tongue, and in his hands to give to Gus. But today there had been nothing.

The air already felt cooler. Soon it would be dark. Magpie didn't like to think of it. There were such strange sounds heard at night. Throughout the past two, he had slept uneasily next to Gus, under a tent of canvas he'd fashioned from the boat's stowed sail, fancying he heard shouting voices and the creaking timbers of ships passing by. Again and again he had bolted upright, his heart pounding with anticipation, hoping to see the *Isabelle* and his buddies hailing him with their swinging lanterns as they stood lined along the rail. It was never the *Isabelle*. It was never anything at all. Worst were the sounds—real or imagined—that he could not identify: cries and groans, murmurs and gurgles that caused his shaking body to break out into gooseflesh. Frightening, fanciful images had whirled about in his head like a waterspout. But as the sky had been without stars or light of any kind, the black-cloaked night had refused to share her eerie secrets.

"Is there anything left to eat?" Gus whispered from under his blanket.

"Oh, I'm sure of it," Magpie said cheerfully, reaching for his duffle bag and rummaging about inside. "I'll find us some biscuit."

Yesterday they had been lucky. Gus had suddenly remembered the breakfast Dr. Braden had brought to him on the mizzenmast platform the morning of the *Isabelle*'s last day. Luckily he'd never gotten around to eating it and it was still there in his pocket. Seawater had annihilated the two biscuits, but the fat square of cheese was still edible.

Magpie felt Gus's hopeful gaze on him as he pretended to search for food. Wrapped in a blanket under the canvas tent, Gus had both arms dressed in crude splints that Magpie had created using strips of cloth from his own linen shirt and the ribs of a crushed barrel he had located wedged under the skiff's aft bench. Being certain that Gus also had a broken right leg, he had applied a longer splint to it, with the aid of a boarding pike found fastened to the innards of the boat's larboard side.

"How many days has it been?" Gus asked, the light having left his eyes when Magpie's search proved fruitless.

Old Bailey Beck had once told Magpie about stranded sailors who carved X's on the tree trunks of their uninhabited islands to keep track of time. He well knew how many days it had been, but he'd scratched time markers anyway on one of the skiff's planks just in case.

"Four."

Gus tried lifting his head. "And can you see land?"

"Please don't try gittin' up, Mr. Walby. Ya'll heal quicker if ya stay put."

"Are there any boats to be seen, then?"

Magpie peered into the gathering gloom on the horizons. Yesterday he thought he'd seen thousands of sails in the whitecaps on the rough sea. Now all was calm and flat and the distances were frighteningly empty. His hesitation in replying was answer enough for Gus. When he spoke again there was a note of anxiety in his voice.

"Can we raise a sail, then, Magpie?"

"There's no mast to be had, Mr. Walby. I kin only row, but I ain't very strong."

"Which way are the winds blowing?"

"From the north."

"And the currents—which way do they flow?"

"Can't rightly tell, Mr. Walby, on account of me bein' a sail maker, not a sailin' master. Mr. Harding, though, could tell us, if he were here."

"But he's *not* here!" Gus turned his head away. "I don't know—I don't know if I can hang on much longer."

"Oh, but ya gotta, Mr. Walby. Ya just gotta hang on."

Gus stared blankly at the canvas walls of his shelter; his voice was hollow. "Was it all just a dream then, Magpie? The two ships I saw through the glass? What—what of them? You never said."

Magpie's weary mind raced. *What could he answer?* He had lost sight of the *Amethyst* and her sister ship the night the *Isabelle* had been burned. He laughed nervously. "Oh, no, sir. They be on their way fer us still, I'm sure. Tell ya what, if ya just sleep now I'll ... why, I'll try catchin' us a fish fer supper."

There was a disquieting cast in Gus's watery eyes as he fixed them on Magpie, but he nodded and soon drifted off. The moment Magpie heard his even breathing, he seized the spyglass that lay against his bare left foot and stared through it, long and hard, trying to will a ship to come into view. There was no sight of land or sail, marine life or bird, anywhere, but he kept on staring through the glass anyway, until the sky's colours had completely faded and a rolling fog appeared, creeping silently over the water like a phantom flotilla. Magpie was about to crawl into the open-ended tent alongside Gus when he heard a low thud at the skiff's stern, as if something had struck it.

For a moment, he sat paralyzed, trying to think what it might be: a big fish, a bottle with a message inside, a sea creature intent on making him his supper, perhaps? Whatever it was wouldn't go away. It continued to knock insistently against the stern the way a sailor used to knock on his sail room door on the *Isabelle*. Quietly and carefully, Magpie made his way aft so as not to disturb Gus's slumber or upset the boat, and when he had kneeled down upon the backbench he peeked over the side.

What he found there caused his stomach to heave. He covered his mouth to stifle his shrieks and his one eye began streaming from the stench, but he could not look away. It was a dead sailor, come to meet his own kind. His face was burned beyond recognition and it appeared something in the sea had been gnawing it. His body was horribly bloated, his clothes taut and torn, and astoundingly, his hat was still on his head, sitting low on the thick waves of his chestnut hair. Across the front of the black felt hat, embroidered on a faded blue ribbon, were the words "HMS *Isabelle*."

Magpie had seen his ship burning from afar and guessed the outcome. This sailor had come, like a human dispatch, to confirm the worst. With a terrible fascination, Magpie stared at the mangled body until his fear subsided and his insides settled enough for him to fetch his flute from the pocket of his trousers. He put the instrument to his sunburned lips and began piping a tune that the Duke of Clarence had taught him to play—a piece called "Grazing Sheep" (or something like it), composed, he'd been told, by a man named Bach a long time ago. Its beautiful notes calmed him. When the tune was done, he reached down into the dark water, lifted the hat from the dead man's head, and, despite the stench and dampness, placed it on his own. Then, putting his fist to the hat's brim in a final salute, he gently nudged the unknown sailor away from the skiff, back into the waves.

Midnight
(First Watch, Eight Bells)

Aboard the USS *Serendipity*

"WITH RESPECT, DR. BRADEN, you look very tired, sir."

Leander was sitting at the small table in the surgeon's cockpit, updating medical notes in the journal that had belonged to the *Serendipity*'s former physician. He took off his spectacles and raised his sore eyes to find his assistant standing over him. The young man's forehead, partially hidden by wisps of fine, black hair, was furrowed with lines of concern. Leander wondered if the lad had seen eighteen years.

"I am, thank you, Mr. Norlan. Are you off, then?"

"I wondered, sir, if you might like to accompany me above deck for some fresh air. I know it's late, but the air down here is particularly stagnant, and I believe ... I believe Captain Trevelyan said it was quite all right for you to go up after dark."

Aye, being the nocturnal beast that I have become, thought Leander, standing up to stretch his muscles, which had not been exercised in days. His entire body hurt, the result of having assumed a permanently hunched-over position on this American ship where, around the clock, it seemed, he had performed amputations, extracted grapeshot, examined throats, set broken limbs, and mixed tonics for this foreign crew. The low beams of the orlop deck suited the man who stood less than five feet; it was hellish for one who stood over six.

Leander looked at Joe Norlan, whose features at times reminded him of someone he once knew, though he could not say whom. He spoke like an Englishman and there was often a certain expression in his hazel eyes, as if he were communicating some secret code he hoped Leander would soon crack. If a second opportunity were afforded, he would gladly exchange conversation with the young man. Not tonight, though. Tonight he longed to be alone.

"Perhaps another time. I need you well rested and alert in the morning."

There was a hint of disappointment in Joe's voice as he said, "Good night then, sir," and left the cockpit.

Leander closed the medical journal and picked up a lantern to take a last peek at his patients as they slept on their flat wooden cots, and gave a few instructions to the loblolly boy whose duty it was to stay the night with them. Then, wearily he climbed the ladder to the lower deck where his light cast long shadows across the congested field of hammocks that stretched before him, each filled with the rounded form of a snoring sailor. He headed aft, towards the two rows of tiny cabins that lined both sides of the ship, and stopped before his own door, the very last one on the starboard side. Despite his fatigue, he knew sleep would not come, and suddenly he wished he'd taken Joe Norlan up on his invitation.

With a change of heart, Leander retraced his steps and trudged up a second ladder, which brought him to the gun deck. Gazing ahead into the gloom, he caught sight of a group of idlers, playing cards and swilling mugs of what was most likely grog at a lowered table between two large guns that had last seen action against the *Isabelle*. The scene reminded him of Bailey Beck and Morgan Evans and their penchant for late-night gaming. Surprised, the men paused in their play to watch him. Leander greeted them with a nod of his head. Uncertain whether they should speak or salute in reply, the men raised their mugs to him instead. As Leander slipped away into the shadows of the deck, he heard one of them say, "Never seen the like afore! Why, he stitched me up and took care o' me like I were one o' his kind!"

His companions laughed.

"Did ya figure he'd bleed ya dry and drink yer blood, then?"

They returned to their game, while Leander, hidden from their prying eyes, paused beside the steps that led above deck and leaned his auburn head against a post to gaze upon the warren of cabins belonging to Captain Trevelyan. Earlier today he had overheard one of his patients whisper, "The cap'n keeps 'er locked up next to him, and he don't allow no one to talk to 'er." She was somewhere before him, then, only a few feet away. Leander imagined he could hear the soft rise and fall of her breathing, and he lingered there until the ship's bell announced midnight and the beginning of the Middle Watch. The card players snarled as they threw down their cards, and scraped their benches and boxes along the floorboards as they rose to head out to their stations. Nearby, a door opened, and Leander, though he knew he should push on, stood transfixed, imagining—hoping—it might be Emily who emerged. His hopes were dashed when the glow of his lantern revealed the last person he expected to see.

"Well, well! If it isn't the good doctor!" said Octavius Lindsay, a slow grin suffusing his pimply face.

Leander's glance flickered over Octavius's new uniform. He wore the coat and carried the hat of an American naval lieutenant. Leander was tempted to reply, "I see you have very quickly been raised in the world, Mr. Lindsay," but decided against it.

"Tell me, Doctor—how is life in the bowels of the *Serendipity*?"

"I have a bed, food, and a young assistant who learns quickly. I have no complaints."

"That is good news indeed! Of course, if you did, Captain Trevelyan would hear none of it." He lifted his chin and pushed past him to take the first step of the ladder up, and having gained it, sneered down upon him. "You'd like to know where *she* is, wouldn't you?"

Leander shoved his hands into the pockets of his waistcoat and unflinchingly met the younger man's cold stare, noting with satisfaction that the lieutenant was the first one to look away. With a dismissive snort, Octavius hurried up the ladder, closely followed by the gang of gaming sailors. Leander stepped aside to let them pass, and when he was alone again, gazed sadly upon the captain's silent quarters. He began the journey back to his own cabin, opting for the stagnant air on the lower deck rather than subjecting himself to the repugnant air that now certainly wafted above.

12

Sunday, June 20

8:00 a.m.
(Morning Watch, Eight Bells)

EMILY FROZE. Was that someone knocking at her door? Surely whoever it was had mistaken her cabin for that of the captain; unless it was Trevelyan himself, come to root her out of her dark hole. She moved away from the open gunport, where she'd been standing since dawn, and turned to stare at her door, as if expecting it to be suddenly kicked in. In the five days of her captivity, no one—not even Trevelyan—had come for her, or spoken to her. Her meals of soggy biscuits, jellied soup, and cold coffee had all been shoved under the door, and her only visitors were the occasional cockroach and the waves that crashed against the ship's hull. Were it not for the shouts and laughter and activity of the men, the striking of the bell, and the incoherent whisperings next door in the captain's cabin, she would swear she was alone on this floating prison.

Much to her surprise, her door creaked open, but rather than the expected Trevelyan or threatening gang of musket-brandishing marines come to order her about, a teenaged boy sidled in. With one curious, darting glance he absorbed the contents of her room—

including herself—and finished with a lengthy stare at the silver-buckled leather shoes she now had on her feet. He was dressed in a grey shirt and loose-fitting trousers, and his tea-coloured hair fell about his shoulders and into his large, round eyes. His mouth hung open, most likely because there were too many protruding teeth inside, and the nose above it was long and bumpy. He was painfully thin and, from the scarlet stains on his cheeks, Emily guessed he was also painfully shy.

"Sorry to disturb ya, Miss. I'm—I'm just gonna bring in yer basin fer washin' in."

"Who are you?"

"The cap'n's faithful servant, Miss."

"And *are* you faithful?"

"I do me best, Miss."

"Where is Mr. Lind?"

"Oh, Mr. Lind was ripped up pretty good by flyin' glass that day a ways back when ya leapt from the cap'n's windows durin' the battlin'. We couldn't do nothin' for him, so we pitched him over the side."

"While he was still alive?"

"Cap'n Trevelyan says it was the merciful thing to do."

Emily, looking aghast, shook her head to banish that image. "Do you have a name?"

"If ya wants, Miss, it's Charlie, though ya might hear the men call me Fish."

There was no need for Emily to ponder the origins of his nick-name. She made no remark, having no interest in introducing herself to this strange boy.

"The cap'n told me I weren't to speak to ya none, Miss. I was just to bring in yer wash basin and a bit o' soap." He disappeared out the door, but soon returned, dragging a basin of green water that gobbled up her entire floor space. "The men will soon be attendin' church service on deck, Miss, so no one'll be peekin' in at ya."

"I should hope not."

Charlie reddened.

Thinking Trevelyan was rather tardy in carrying out his demands that she bathe, Emily said, "And why is it I'm *now* expected to sit in a basin of cold water?"

Charlie glanced at the open door and lowered his voice. "It's not fer me to be tellin' ya why."

Emily's stomach knotted with fear, once again sickened by the recollection of Trevelyan's sinister words spoken to Fly Austen before he had forced her from the *Isabelle*. He had referred to her then as *his intended wife*! Feeling behind her for the cold metal of the gun, she sank down upon its carriage. "How—how old are you?"

"Thirteen, Miss; fourteen come August."

"And where is your home?"

He looked surprised.

"Well? Are you from Boston? New York? Norfolk?"

"No one's ever cared to ask afore, Miss."

"Did the American navy steal you from a British ship?"

"With respect, Miss, it's the British doin' the stealin', not the other way round."

Emily angled her head and raised her eyebrows.

Charlie pushed the hair out of his eyes. "It's Salem, Massachusetts I'm from, and if yer int'rested, Miss, I could show ya where it is on a map."

"I know how to locate Salem on a map."

"Me apologies, Miss; I figured ya might have some learnin'."

Without warning, an enormous officer with a florid face filled the doorway and glared at Charlie. "What the devil are you about, Fish, er, Mr. Clive?"

Charlie wilted. "Just leavin', sir."

"I should hope so, Mr. Clive." The officer scrutinized Emily from head to toe, raised one bushy-black eyebrow in a pompous manner, and moved on.

"Good-bye then, Miss." Charlie turned to sidle out.

Emily felt a constriction in her chest. That door would close again and heaven knows when it would next open. She had so many questions. Maybe this boy—maybe he had some information about the *Isabelle*.

"Will you come again?" She had not intended to sound so eager.

"Of course, Miss, to collect yer wash basin." He doubled his thin body over in a clumsy bow and slipped away.

Emily returned to stand watch by the open gunport. She looked out upon the colourless waves as she unbuttoned her shirt and eased out of it. Her fingers then sought out the healing bullet wound in her shoulder and as she gently caressed the rough layers of new skin, a gurgle of laughter burst from her lips. "I've just met the fearsome Charlie Clive!"

Noon
(Forenoon Watch, Eight Bells)
Aboard HMS *Amethyst*

THE BULK OF CAPTAIN PRICKETT of HMS *Amethyst* spread out like an oak tree, overshadowing Fly, who sat quietly, drinking his coffee, upon a wooden crate on the poop deck near the taffrail.

"Mr. Austen, so wonderful to see you up and about, my good man. I drink to your restored health and to the health of your miscellaneous men." The captain lifted his own china cup to his red lips and drained the contents, which curiously did not possess the aroma of coffee. He then grunted with satisfaction and peered over the taffrail into the foggy gloom.

Fly's gaze slid from the corpulent captain to the misty weather decks where he spotted a few of his Isabelles working contentedly alongside their *Amethyst* compatriots. "I thank you for all you've done, sir."

"I'm just sorry we couldn't have saved a few more of you," Prickett said with a concerned shake of his big head.

You could have if you had heeded our signals for assistance, Fly was tempted to retort.

"Well, now, time for dinner. Will you join me, Mr. Austen? Bridlington and I are most anxious to have a good, long chat with you."

"I wonder, sir, if I may defer your kind invitation. I'm afraid I find myself with no appetite."

"By all means. But you must eat, Mr. Austen, and keep up your strength. I'll have my cook bring a morsel to you here. God knows when this outrageous fog will lift. It'd be damned impertinent of the enemy to come upon me while I'm enjoying muttonchops and fish pie. You *will* keep a sharp eye out, won't you, Mr. Austen?" Without giving Fly a chance to answer, he hiked his breeches up over his girth and started off. But his ever-roving eye soon caught sight of Morgan Evans and Biscuit climbing the steps to the poop deck.

"Ah, now, here come the two you sent for, Mr. Austen. Such affable characters! I've a mind to take the Scottish cook off your hands since *you* won't have need of him any too soon. Ha, ha!"

"Sir, you are welcome to him, though I'll warn you his culinary skills leave much to be desired."

Fly nodded at Morgan and Biscuit as they loped past Captain Prickett towards him. He had not seen any of his men since the Wednesday afternoon of their rescue, when the *Amethyst* had hove to in order to pick up the straggling survivors, for he had immediately been taken below to the surgeon, suffering from burns and exhaustion. In the meantime, Morgan and Biscuit had washed up nicely, having been the recipients of new slops. Fly was shocked to see such a gleam in Biscuit's orange hair—dazzling against the white of the sails and the swirling sea mists—and happy that Morgan again wore a shirt, as his last one had been sacrificed to bandage up the burned flesh on Fly's back—an injury, he'd been told, caused by a fiery, falling spar that had struck him. The two men halted before him, with Biscuit standing behind Morgan, who saluted.

"You passed the word for us, sir?"

"I hope yer feelin' better, Cap'n," added Biscuit, leaning over Morgan's shoulder. "We've all been missin' ya, sir."

"Much better, thank you." Fly looked up gravely at Morgan. "Those hard hours, Mr. Evans, during which we pulled towards the *Amethyst* and the *Expedition*, you made me aware of our numbers, though I confess I had no desire to know the names of the men sitting alongside me in those small boats. I ask that you tell me now."

Morgan, aware beforehand that this was the reason he was being summoned, held out a sheet of parchment on which were written—in an elegant cursive script—the names of the eighty-seven survivors of the *Isabelle*. "I took the liberty of asking Lieutenant Bridlington for his assistance with this, sir."

Fly set his mug down on the deck and took the sheet from Morgan. He took a quick glance down the list, then reluctantly examined it a second time.

"Our sailing master, Mr. Harding?"

"No, sir."

"Our purser, Mr. Spooner?"

"No, sir."

"Mr. Tucker? Mr. Harris? Mr. Crump? Old Bailey Beck?"

"Ach, nay, sir," said Biscuit, putting his hand on Morgan's shoulder.

"Young Gus Walby?"

"You may recall, sir, that Mr. Walby fell from the mizzen at the start of the battle."

Fly nodded absently and sighed. The only names he recognized on the parchment, besides his own and those of the two standing before him, were Lewis McGilp, the coxswain, Jacko, the shoemaker, Maggot and Weevil, the Jamaican brothers, Mr. Stewart, the midshipman, and Osmund Brockley, Dr. Braden's assistant.

"What about our little sail maker?"

Biscuit stepped forward. "Now funny ya should ask about wee Magpie, sir. Ya see, afore thee Yankees did their boardin', I set him inta thee skiff with a few rations. He were bound-bent on findin' Mr. Walby. Might be he did just that. Might be they was both picked up."

"Aye."

"Well, yas never kin tell, sir."

"You never can tell," echoed Fly, without any of Biscuit's enthusiasm.

"Trevelyan took some of our men, sir," said Morgan, "though I don't know who or how many. And … and Dr. Braden and Emily are on the *Serendipity*, prisoners perhaps, but hopefully safe."

"And Mr. Lindsay and Mrs Kettle too," Biscuit added cheerfully, "though yas might not be carin' much fer their kind."

Fly folded up the list of mainly ordinary seamen, landmen, and boys, and rose to his feet. "If you please, Mr. Evans, beg a quill and more parchment from Bridlington for me. The Admiralty and Parliament will be expecting to receive a full account of the circumstances surrounding the loss of our ship, and I shan't keep them waiting any longer."

"Aye, sir, but you might be interested to know that it'll be some time before you'll be meeting with anyone from the Admiralty."

Fly gave him an expectant look. "Why is that, Mr. Evans?"

"Well, you see, sir, we're not heading north to Halifax, nor are we returning to England."

Fly looked up at the squared sails and around at the fog that shut in the *Amethyst* like an ethereal curtain-wall. "Then where is it we're headed?"

"South, sir. To find the *Serendipity*."

Afternoon

Adrift in the Atlantic

MAGPIE WAS NOT SURE what time it was. He was not even sure what day it was. His brain was as foggy as the cold, eerie mists that moved around the skiff; as thick as the rolls of canvas that were once housed in his little sail room on the *Isabelle*. Too weak to sit upright, he lay across his bench on his side and stared at the oars resting in their locks, trying to encourage his lungs to provide enough wind power for him to blow into his flute. Playing a tune was the only thing that eased the misery of the wrenching spasms in his stomach. Gus had been awfully quiet for a long time now. Magpie supposed he was only sleeping, but had no energy to crawl into the tent to make certain by checking his pulse.

Perhaps today the skiff would enter shallow waters beside an island or hit a scattering of rocks near a shore. If the fog would go away, perhaps he'd spy a fishing vessel or a merchantman, one close enough to hear him call out for help. He didn't want to think about an American frigate or a pirate ship finding them, but he'd happily board their vessel and be clapped in irons if they would just give him something to eat. No longer could he bear to imagine the feast that the Duke of Clarence and his wife had once set before him—the succulent roast of pork and scrumptious baked bread pudding. It only made his pains worse, as if the unknown creature that had gnawed on the dead sailor had now sunk its teeth into his belly. There was a dull pain in his head too, where his right eye used to be, but he could ignore it. His innards, however, would not afford him such luxury. He lifted his flute to his lips.

It would have to be today.

3:00 p.m.
(Afternoon Watch, Six Bells)
Aboard the *Prosperous and Remarkable*

PROSPER BURGO scratched the top of his head where he had gone bald and cursed the fog that shrouded his brig, the *Prosperous and Remarkable*. He wrapped his long fingers around the ropes on the bowsprit and inched along the spritsail yard. Then, leaning his body into the light breeze, he listened.

"What ya hearin'?" asked Pemberton Baker, Prosper's jack-of-all-tradesman.

"I dunno. Might be me 'magination, or might be I'm hearin' music."

"Might be yer losin' yer mind."

Prosper twisted his neck to glare at Pemberton, who stood on the foredeck, peering up at him on his precarious perch. Soon, however, a sunny smile had replaced his scowl. "Ya ox! I lost me mind long ago! Nay! Listen! Shhh! There be music out there!"

Pemberton bent his short, stocky legs, tilted his thick torso forward, and cupped his right ear. At length he grunted. "There's naught but thee gentle wind's whisper."

Prosper made odd gurgling sounds in his throat. "Ya lubber! I bet I kin recognize thee tune afore ye."

The men in the fore rigging, hearing Prosper's challenge, stopped working, cocked their heads, and after a time offered up their own conjectures.

"Nay, Prosper, 'tis only the wind."

"Or a ship's bell?"

"Should we be beatin' to quarters then?"

"Nay, 'tis a seagull."

"Or one o' Ma Carey's chickens."

"Birds, ya say? Are we nearin' land? Toss the lead again, Jasper."

"Yer all puddin' heads, thee lot o' yas," said Prosper. "What kinda sailors are ye anyway when ya can't recognize thee strains o' 'Can o' Grog'?"

The men all laughed and broke into song. "*When up the shrouds the sailor goes, and ventures on the yard ...*"

Prosper raised his hand. "Shush all o' yas." The men shut their mouths and watched with interest as their commander set his facial features into listening mode and poked his head here and there into the fog like a hen pecking at the ground for kernels of corn. After a short while of intense silence, he shocked them all by crying out, "Ah hah!" and scrabbled down from the spritsail yard. "Turn this beast around, ya lubbers," he yelled, jumping down onto the deck and sprinting aft along the starboard rail, all the while gesturing vigorously at the moving mists.

"What is it?"

"What 'ave ya seen?

Prosper's fringe of thinning curls flew about his ears as he wheeled about to face his men with a grin. "Why, I've seen a flute-playin' devil lyin' in his coffin and I 'spose it be common courtesy we pick 'im up."

3:00 p.m.
(Afternoon Watch, Six Bells)
Aboard the USS *Serendipity*

IT WAS MID-AFTERNOON when Charlie Clive returned to Emily's cabin to fetch the basin. He sidled in at her invitation to enter, and once again took a darting glance around her accommodation before bowing to her as she lay in her cot. Sitting up, Emily noticed the lad had taken a brush to his hair and had tied a blue-and-white striped scarf around his thin neck. In his arms, he carried a heap of dresses. As he stepped towards her, one of them fell to the floor. Emily was reminded of the day, a few weeks back, when another small lad had come to her, proudly bearing a bundle of new clothes.

"Mr. Clive," she said in a deadened voice, "there is no need to bow."

"Oh, but Miss, I were told to bow afore all ladies of genteel birth."

"Who told you that?"

"Me ma."

"And why would you imagine I was genteel?"

"The men, they say yer highborn, though none of us knew it last time ya was on our ship." He looked ashamed suddenly, and Emily wondered if he'd known that his revered captain had had a fondness for ordering her about like a servant. "Besides, Miss," he added, peeking up at her through his hair, "I kin see it in yer bearin'."

She sighed. "What's that you have there?"

"Clothes fer ya, Miss."

"I *have* clothes, Mr. Clive."

"These are from the captain."

"Tell him I don't want them." She pulled Leander's coat around her shoulders.

"Yer to dine with him at eight bells, Miss, and he said he don't want ya sittin' at his table in men's trousers."

"Tell him I'll not dine with him. My regular fare of soggy biscuits is quite adequate."

Charlie's round eyes grew larger. "I can't tell him that, Miss."

"Why not?"

"No one speaks to Cap'n Trevelyan in that fashion."

"Well, *I* do, Mr. Clive." With a dismissive shrug she slid down into her cot and turned her back to him. "You can set the clothes down, but I will *not* wear them."

Charlie cleared his throat, but made no attempt to leave. At last Emily rolled over and questioned his insolence with a frown. His cheeks reddened as he stooped over to grab the washbasin by its handle and began dragging it towards the door. Refusing to meet her eyes, he said, "The captain told me, Miss, if ya didn't put these clothes on fer dinner, he'd come right in here and do it fer ya."

3:30 p.m.
(Afternoon Watch, Seven Bells)

IN THE SURGERY, Leander hesitated before the canvas curtain that separated him from his next patient and shot a quizzical look at his young assistant.

"Are you certain you don't want to handle this one on your own, Mr. Norlan?" he whispered, pulling his spectacles from the breast pocket of his black apron.

"Quite certain, sir."

"You would gain much in experience in dealing with her complaint."

Joe looked appalled. "Please, sir, she frightens me, really. And I know very little of her—of her parts."

"If you hope to become a doctor one day, you'll have to familiarize yourself with female parts."

"You're speaking in terms of studying my medical books, of course, sir?"

"Of course." Leander averted his face to hide his amusement. "Now stay close, as I may require reinforcements." He placed his spectacles on his nose and plunged through the curtain.

Mrs. Kettle lay groaning on a flat wooden cot that hugged the ship's side, her fat arms thrown across her face. Upon hearing him approach, she popped opened one eye. "What a good man ye are and a sight fer me sore eyes and limbs."

Such a greeting would have warmed Leander's heart had it been forthcoming from anyone else besides the former laundress on the *Isabelle*. "Are you well, Mrs. Kettle?"

"Please call me Meggie, Doctor. I likes it when thee men call me Meggie." She groped about to catch and squeeze his hand.

"Are you still troubled by an unsettling of your stomach? Shall I prepare another tonic for you, *Mrs. Kettle*?"

She quit her moaning and raised herself up on one arm. "What I needs is a long rest."

"I see. Have you, then, forgotten my instructions to curtail your vigorous habits for the sake of your unborn child?"

Mrs. Kettle flopped back upon her cot. "I 'aven't time fer no kicky-wicky with thee Serendipities, Doctor. Cap'n Trevelyan himself keeps me occupied day 'n night."

Leander stared at her over his glasses. "May I ask the nature of these occupations?"

She looked indignant. "Why, I were expectin' to be raised in thee ranks and he's got me launderin' hammocks and slops and yards o' canvas."

"But, Mrs. Kettle, laundering was your occupation on the *Isabelle*."

"I knows that, but oooh, thee sails be heavy and thee hammocks—so foul-smellin'—and me back aches so and me head constantly pains me."

"Shall I beg a word with Captain Trevelyan and, if I should be so lucky as to be granted an audience, suggest that, given your circumstances, he engage you in gentler pursuits?" Leander wondered why he should do anything on behalf of this woman.

Her little eyes brightened and she smiled sweetly. "Would ya, Doctor, fer me? Tell 'im to get rid o' that little whelp, Charlie Clive, and I'll do his personal biddin.'"

Leander clasped his hands behind his back. "And if he is not agreeable to that?"

"Tell 'im I'll do anythin' that doesn't call fer stinkin', back-breakin' labour."

"I shall try, though I cannot promise you anything."

She thrust out her lower lip. "If he's ugly, remind 'im he owes me a favour and Meggie always comes collectin' on 'er favours."

Intrigued, Leander was about to question her further when she surprised him by bounding out of her cot with all the robustness of a bull. She wiggled her toes into her shoes, swept aside the bit of canvas, and briskly waddled past Joe like a duck being chased by the farmer intent on having it for his supper.

With rounded eyes, Joe watched her flee. "Captain Trevelyan owes *her* a favour, sir?"

Leander compressed his lips. "I wonder..."

4:00 p.m.
(Afternoon Watch, Eight Bells)
Alongside the *Prosperous and Remarkable*

MAGPIE LOWERED HIS FLUTE and stared up at the assortment of strange faces gawping down at him from the side of the blood-red ship that had inexplicably materialized out of the mist. Being light-headed, he couldn't discern if the ship was large or small, its crew friend or foe. Rippling in the light wind high on one mast was a pennant upon which two lengthy words were painted in black, though he did not know what they meant.

Magpie tried to warn Mr. Walby, but he choked on his words and could only lie there helplessly and watch as a shadowy figure mounted the Jacob's ladder tossed over the ship's side and climbed down towards them. When the figure reached the last rung, it vaulted into the skiff, landing squarely in its centre without upsetting it whatsoever. Magpie peered up at the man who now hovered over him. He was bald save for a fringe of long curls about his ears. His skin was red and deeply lined, and he wore a loose-fitting shirt, open at the neck. "Are ya a pirate, sir?"

"Not officially," said the man.

"An enemy, then?"

"That all depends."

Despite his weakened state, Magpie was able to detect a charitable glint in the stranger's squinty grey eyes as he squatted down next to him, and gently raised his little head off the bench. Then, yanking a wineskin from his belt, the stranger held it to Magpie's blistered lips. "Now drink slowly, me little man."

"Bless ya... bless ya, sir," sobbed Magpie. He took a few sips of water while the stranger eyed the bandage on his head.

Soon the man's notice fell to the black felt hat with the embroidered banner perched atop Magpie's duffel bag. "By Jove!" he cried,

"Here I'm thinkin' yas were a young devil acquainted with grog, when in fact yer from thee *Isabelle*. Come aboard me *Prosperous and Remarkable* and tell us yer tale."

Magpie pointed towards the skiff's bow. "Please, sir, could ya see to Mr. Walby?"

The stranger peered into the canvas shelter, and seeing Gus in all his splints asked, "Did ya 'ave a fight with this poor scalawag and he wound up losin'?"

"Oh no, sir. Mr. Walby got knocked up fallin' from the mizzen."

For some time the man crouched over Gus, and when finally he emerged from the shelter, he hollered up at his ship. "Pemberton, ya jackanapes!" A stocky fellow with a pudding face appeared at the rail. "Have thee bo's'n's chair lowered and ready me surgeon's table. There be two little men here that require some tendin' to."

4:00 p.m.
(Afternoon Watch, Eight Bells)
Aboard the USS *Serendipity*

EMILY SAT STIFF AND TENSE at the captain's table waiting for Trevelyan to appear. Behind the empty chair facing her stood two servants, Charlie Clive and a dark-skinned fellow named Beans. Charlie kept his eyes lowered to the floor, but Beans's bright, brown eyes were glued to her, making her feel all the more uncomfortable. She kept her own gaze fixed upon the feast spread out on china dishes before her: roasted ham, salt-fish pudding, pork pie, white biscuit, and a bottle of French wine. The aroma of the steaming ham aggravated her terrible hunger, and were she alone, she would have carved herself a chunk of it.

When the door at her back jerked open and heavy steps entered the great cabin, Emily flinched. She knew from the anxious expressions on the young boys' faces that it was Trevelyan; she herself recognized his odour, and could feel his eyes boring into the top of her head. There was a clanking noise as he put away his sword, and a spray of droplets as he removed his rain cloak. Emily looked up as his looming figure came into view and watched him seat himself across from her. He said nothing, his thin lips a determined line in his bloodless face, but a slight nod of his head brought Charlie and Beans round the table to serve him his supper. Once his plate and wine goblet were filled, he began eating, and Emily watched his hands, scarred like her own, cut his meat and lift his goblet to his lips while her own stomach howled for decent nourishment. Between mouthfuls, he glanced at her, but was well into his meal before he spoke.

"Serve yourself, madam. You have no servants here."

"I am not hungry."

Charlie's face fluttered with astonishment. Beans still smiled. Trevelyan sipped his wine, his eyes roving over her hot face before dropping beneath her chin to inspect her garments. She was wearing Leander's coat and had left it open a crack so he could see she had put on one of the dresses Charlie had brought to her.

"I am wondering at you wearing a man's frock coat, madam, when we are heading south and the humidity is on the rise."

"Of all I possess, this coat is the dearest."

"And obviously not your own. I thought perhaps a dress would flatter your figure much more than the common slops in which you came on board."

"Why would I require to be dressed in a more flattering manner when you have me imprisoned in a closet?"

"Is there a problem with your lodging? Would you prefer to hang your hammock on the gun deck with the men?"

"My *lodging* is quite satisfactory. I would, however, feel less a prisoner if I could stretch my legs at least once a day."

Trevelyan looked amused. "Oh, but you *are* a prisoner: a most valuable one. Have you forgotten the United States is at war with Britain, or are you a typical woman who cares nothing for and cannot comprehend politics?"

Emily dug her toenails into the soles of her shoes. "Is that the reason you came back with a bloody fleet to pounce upon the *Isabelle*—only to retrieve me because you'd discovered that I was a valuable prisoner?"

There was no emotion in his eyes as he regarded her. "I knew you were valuable property, madam, when I first learned you were planning to cross the Atlantic on the *Amelia*."

Emily had difficulty concealing her shock. "And ... and for this reason only you destroyed the *Amelia* as well as Captain Moreland's ship?"

Trevelyan emptied the bottle of wine and swirled the ruby liquid in his goblet for the longest time. When he spoke again his tone had changed. "I would have thought, madam, that lying about suited your disposition and habits."

"I have never been one to lie about, sir."

"Yes. I recall you polished my silver very well during your last stay with us, which I found surprising; for I was certain, despite the fact that your English home—*your palace*—must have been filled with the stuff, the task was quite foreign to you."

Emily's blood boiled. "It may also surprise you, *sir*, that I have never lived in a palace."

His head rolled to one side. "Old King George never installed his son, Henry, and your poor mother in an apartment at the Queen's House or St. James's or Windsor Castle?"

"He did not."

"Astounding!"

"And I am rather astounded that *you* are even acquainted with my father's first name."

Trevelyan leaned forward, placed his elbows on the table, and rested his chin on his upturned hands. "I was once well acquainted with your father, *madam*."

"Really? Were you a *servant* of his?"

Trevelyan mused a moment and his eyes wavered in recollection, but he did not dignify her question with a reply. He downed the rest of the red wine, and at length said, "I would have been quite happy to share the contents of this bottle with you."

"It was easy to resist the temptation. You stole that wine from the *Isabelle.*"

He grinned. "I did! And no doubt Captain Moreland stole it from the hold of one of his French prizes, but as *he* has no further use for it, I hate to think of it going to waste."

Emily's pulse quickened. "What does that mean?"

"Oh! I forget. You know nothing of the *Isabelle*'s fate."

"*You* forget. I was there when you ordered her burned."

His eyes narrowed. "That's right, madam, I burned her to the waterline and her sorry hull is on the bottom of the Atlantic, in water so black and so deep no one will ever find her again."

His words cut with all the force of a whip. She closed her eyes for a moment and drew in a deep breath. "And... and what of her men?" With a throbbing heart, she watched Trevelyan push back his chair and rise to his feet. He grabbed a piece of ham, stuffed it into his mouth, and chewed on it fiercely before turning to nod at Charlie and Beans, who immediately moved to clear the table. He then strode to the wall where he'd hung his rain cloak and sword, took only his weapon, and headed towards the cabin door.

"Mr. Clive, when you are done, take madam back to her *closet,*" he said, opening the door. Then he turned to Emily. "Your Captain Moreland was torn apart by our grapeshot. When I boarded his ship, it was my misfortune to find him dead in his cot, though bleeding still like a stuck pig."

Emily covered her mouth to strangle her cry.

"For services rendered, we did *rescue* two of your Isabelles: one surly youth named Mr. Lindsay and a cow called Mrs. Kettle."

Emily twisted in her seat to confront him, but could only whisper, "Is that it? Is that all?"

His eyes grew more distant as he gazed down at her, and there was a twitching in the flesh of his face. The door shut behind him, and Emily sat there in disbelief, her eyes shining with tears. Rain knocked upon the newly installed gallery windows at her back, and the ship's bell clanged once, its resonance hurting her ears. Charlie and Beans said nothing as they tiptoed around her, removing the dishes and the remains of the supper. The still-warm aroma of meat and pastry and pudding tormented her.

After wiping her wet cheeks with a sleeve of Leander's coat, she let her gaze fall on Trevelyan's desk, the very one she had pushed in front of the door three weeks ago to bar entry to the *Serendipity*'s marines whilst she made her escape from out the blasted stern windows. There had been nothing atop his desk then. Now it held two gold-framed miniatures. The first was a painting of a young boy, perhaps eleven or twelve years old, with sandy hair and dark, merry eyes. The second one brought a lump to her throat. It was Magpie's little painting of the daughter of Henry, Duke of Wessex—Emeline Louisa Georgina Marie.

Near Midnight
(First Watch)

THE FIRST KNOCK intruded upon Emily's dreams of her childhood home in England, but did not wake her. The second was louder, more insistent. She lifted her head off her flat pillow and sleepily called out, "What is it?" Her cabin was as black as tar. She could see nothing, and when no one responded, her heart began to race.

Sitting upright, Emily listened to the wind whistling around the *Serendipity*, and to the shouts of the watchmen, which sounded like the cries of those lost at sea. Her cot was swinging more wildly than normal, and rain pounded on the timbers around her. Recollecting the happiness of her dream, she felt an oppressive sense of sadness. It had been ages since she had visited a place of sunshine and happiness in her dreams.

Once more she called out in the night, this time with fear in her voice. Still no one answered. After a few anxious minutes, Emily heard a swishing sound, as if someone had passed something under her door, and soon her cramped quarters became redolent with a mouth-watering aroma. By now used to finding her way around in complete darkness, she scrambled out of her cot and over the cold cannon, falling on her knees to crawl the remaining distance. Her groping hands discovered a wedge of pork pie wrapped in paper. In the darkness, she filled her mouth with the savoury pie, and only once she had food in her stomach did she pause again to listen. Someone was still standing on the other side of her door. She was certain of it. She sensed his presence, was certain even she heard his breathing. Lying flat on the clammy floorboards, she put her face near the gap under the door and whispered, "Charlie? Is it you, Charlie?"

Still nothing.

"Thank you."

Somewhere beyond her cabin another door opened and Emily could hear muted voices approaching. In a flash, whoever had come to her with food, stole away.

13

Monday, June 21

Noon
(Forenoon Watch, Eight Bells)
Aboard the *Prosperous and Remarkable*

THE MOMENT MAGPIE opened his one eye to the new day, he drew a sigh of relief. There, in the low cot next to him, nestled in the forepeak of Prosper Burgo's brig, was Gus. His face was as wan as a morning moon, and his arms, resting on a plaid blanket, were bound in fresh splints, but Magpie could hear his even breathing, and was so happy he hadn't died in the night and Prosper's crew hadn't had to heave his lifeless body over the side of the *Prosperous and Remarkable*. Peeling back his own blanket, Magpie got to his feet and went above deck in search of the commander, thinking it was only proper to thank him for all his kindness.

The day was dull and warm and a humid rain fell. Magpie trudged the unfamiliar flush-deck, pausing now and again to ask passing sailors if they knew the whereabouts of Captain Burgo. Finally, one of them pointed towards the bow.

"He often stands there, lookin' fer fat merchantmen with holds o' valuable cargo."

The only ship Magpie had ever been on was the *Isabelle*. In comparison, Prosper's brig was diminutive, and congested with clutter and livestock pens. Only two masts rose up over its small decks, on which fifty or so men roamed—not one of them dressed in a proper uniform—and he'd counted only fourteen guns in all. Inching his way fore, Magpie found himself distracted by the new sights and the curious, hardened faces of the crew. It was no surprise to Magpie that Prosper found him first, magically appearing before him when he hopped down from the fore rigging with his spyglass in hand. Setting his fox-like features in a frown, he scrutinized the fresh bandage on Magpie's head. Being, among other things, the ship's surgeon, Prosper himself had meticulously applied it the night before.

"'Bout time yas were roused, Magpie. Ya come on board, gulp down me vittles, tell me yarns about thee *Isabelle* and *Serendipity* and some wench named Em'ly, and then ya go sleepin' right round thee watch. Do ya fancy I'm runnin' a hostelry here?"

"No, sir, but I didn't sleep too good in the skiff."

Prosper turned and shouted, "Mr. Dunkin, ya scoundrel! Find our little friend here a raincoat o' sorts." To Magpie, he said, "Now don't be callin' me *Sir*. I prefers thee sound o' *Prosper*."

"But aren't ya the captain?"

"I'm thee owner o' this here brig!"

"But ya give the orders, don't ya, sir?"

Prosper shrugged. "That I do! And I 'spect me men ta obey me. If they get foolhardy I pitch 'em overboard, or fix thumbscrews ta their sensitive parts, or I leave 'em on a deserted island where they starve ta death—*slowly*."

Magpie looked out upon the dreary seas and wondered if he'd be spending the rest of his life with Prosper Burgo. He didn't like the sound of those thumbscrews! Reluctantly he followed Prosper down the deck, frightened by the red and purple veins that rose on the man's face whenever he roared out his commands.

"There's a wind come up, ya bunch o' ruffians. Square away thee yards. You there! Clear out this pen. It reeks. You lubbers sittin' on yer arses can move these barrels below and earn yer supper. Pemberton, ya galoot, bring me and Magpie here a mug o' chocolate." Prosper paused to take in air and assumed the ship's wheel from Pemberton Baker.

"Have ya spotted any fat merchantmen, Mr. Prosper?" asked Magpie in a small voice.

"Nay! Plenty o' fishin' vessels, but there ain't no merchantmen to be seen. I was hopin' these warmer waters would be crawlin' with 'em. Ya see, they're all holed up in them northern harbours thanks ta yer Royal Navy, and it's been kinda hard on me fortunes o' late."

"What will ya do when ya see one?"

"Why, I'll give 'em chase, board 'em, cut up their crew, and seize their ship."

"Yer a pirate, then?"

"Nay!" He lifted his stubbly chin to the wind. "Me *Prosperous and Remarkable*'s got a letter o' marque."

"What's that?" asked Magpie, as the scoundrel named Mr. Dunkin helped him into a hooded poncho.

"It's a piece o' paper given ta me by me governor allowin' me ta rob enemy ships at will."

Magpie's eye shot open. "Yer not Yankee, are ya, Mr. Prosper?"

"Yankee? I woulda strung ya up—and yer friend, despite his afflictions—if I be Yankee."

Magpie's hand flew to his throat.

"Nay! I'm from Quebec!" continued Prosper. "Born in thee Magdalen Islands, smack dab in thee mighty St. Lawrence."

"I ain't never heard o' those places, Mr. Prosper."

"Hmm! Guess I'll have ta take ya there one day, but only after I've plundered a few fat merchantmen and kin afford ta rest fer a spell."

"Where're we now?"

"We'll soon be raisin' Charleston. Intelligence tells me there ain't many o' yer British ships blockadin' these parts ... and that Trevelyan's *Serendipity*'s bin seen headin' this way." He rubbed his chin thoughtfully. "I gotta hankerin' ta meet yer Em'ly."

An icy ripple danced down Magpie's spine. "Oh, Mr. Prosper, if

Emily's on the *Serendipity*—and I don't know it fer sure, I'm only thinkin' Trevelyan took her agin—ya wouldn't think o' hurtin' her?"

Prosper turned his ruddy face to the sea and grinned from ear to ear. "Nay, me little man. I wouldna think o' it."

1:30 p.m.
(Afternoon Watch, Three Bells)
Aboard the USS *Serendipity*

EMILY LOOKED UP from Jane Austen's book, alerted by the heightened excitement on the quarterdeck beyond her door. The *Serendipity* was slowing down. For the past two hours she'd been engrossed in reading by lantern-light, positioned on the floor with her back leaning against the coolness of the cannon, and during that time she'd heard frequent calls to "heave the lead," and replies that revealed the water depth was gradually diminishing. More recently, she'd heard orders for "all hands aloft" and "shorten sails" and "anchor down."

Picking herself up off the floor, she tossed the book onto her pillow and struggled to open the gunport, the windy, rainy conditions having made it necessary to keep it closed until now. To her delight, the *Serendipity* was sitting broadside to a sizable town. Towering church steeples, terraced homes, impressive buildings, wharves, and warehouses materialized in the mists beyond a harbour full of ships. Emily raised herself up on the cannon's carriage so she could stick her head farther out the port. The rain had stopped and the winds had died away. There was a mucky, marshy smell in the air, curiously mingling with the fragrance of flowers. In the harbour lay moored countless bobbing vessels: fishing boats, cutters, merchantmen, cruisers, frigates, sloops, brigs, barques—she couldn't even put a name to them all—and in no time the *Serendipity* herself was moored in the shallower waters. Listening to the commotion as the men, amid much laughter, prepared to lower the boats, Emily discovered her own spirits lifting.

It had been almost three months since she had set sail from England, three months since she had last stepped on firm ground. She longed to touch trees and smell flowers and jump into a feather bed with fat pillows. It didn't matter to her that this strange town was likely part of the United States; she still wondered what it had to offer. If she could wander through its streets, would she find bookshops and bakeshops and dressmakers, and perhaps an inn that did not serve its patrons hard biscuits and jellied pea soup?

With envy, she watched as two cutters, each carrying twenty or so men, drifted into view from around the *Serendipity*'s stern, the oarsmen eagerly setting the oars into their locks while their mates cried out, "Huzzah!" in anticipation of the delights and entertainments that awaited them and their hard-earned shillings. Emily couldn't believe so many men had been granted leave to go ashore all at once, for she knew this sort of arrangement would not be tolerated amongst the captains and commanders of England's Royal Navy. No sooner had she tucked away that thought when, to her further surprise, the ship's launch rounded the bow with another twenty-five on board! It plied through the waters beneath her, so close she could read amusement in the sailors' eyes as they beheld her leaning out the gunport.

Trevelyan stood at the stern of the launch, his eyes haunting in that expressionless face of his. He was outfitted in his dress uniform: a dark blue jacket with startling white trim and flashing gold buttons, and bright white breeches. "Lay on your oars," he shouted at his men, and they immediately ceased their rowing so that he could address Emily. He lifted his black bicorne from his matted hair and, in a voice as flat as the now-calm waters of the harbour said, "Madam, would you care to accompany us to William's Coffee House for a meal, and have drinks later at McCrady's Tavern?"

Without thinking, Emily's reply leapt from her lips. "Yes! Please! I would like that."

Trevelyan raised his eyebrows a notch. "Very well, then, find yourself a means of transportation and we'll look forward to your company in town."

Emily's face flushed as the men cackled and hooted, their heads and shoulders shaking with mirth as the launch rowed past her. Trevelyan pressed his hat down on his head and called for the oarsmen to pull harder. His men refocused on their tasks, all of them that is, but one. *He* continued to stare up at her, a smirk upon his lips. It was easy to recognize him, despite his new, borrowed uniform and the confidence that overspread his pockmarked face. Try as she might, she would *never* forget Octavius Lindsay.

Emily slunk backwards into the shadows of her cabin, away from his probing eyes, and silently screamed at her stupidity. Her fist struck out at the wooden wall behind her, and with a howl, she collapsed to the floor in pain. There she drew her knees up to her chin and had a good cry, unaware of the sounds of bells and voices and screeching gulls around her. When her tears were spent, she lay still, her eyes absently roving over the confines of her cabin, her thoughts wading through a pool of anguish and apathy. A few inches from her damp brow, a stray sunbeam had found its way in through the open port. She reached out and placed her throbbing hand in the little circle of warm light that quivered on the floorboards. A sudden determination emboldened her to pick herself up off the ground and gaze out again. Trevelyan and his merry lot were now nowhere to be seen. She imagined they had arrived at one of the wharves and were now boisterously descending upon Charleston. She gazed up at the sky. There was an opening of blue in the parting clouds and a sunny sparkle on the spire of a white church. She glanced below, to the place where Trevelyan had addressed her from his launch, where the water now quietly licked at the hull. Her eyes shifted to the bobbing boats nearby, and finally rested upon the enticing skyline of the town.

Nightfall could not come soon enough.

7:00 p.m.
(Second Dog Watch, Two Bells)

JOE NORLAN WAS ABOUT TO CLIMB down the ladder to the waiting pinnace, but changed his mind when he caught sight of Leander leaning on the rail at the back of the ship, seemingly absorbed in the liveliness of the Charleston Harbour. "Just a minute," he called down to the sailors who waited with anticipation to push off. They grumbled their acquiescence as Joe hurried along the deck to the spot where Leander stood. Upon reaching him, he cleared his throat and somewhat shyly asked, "Sir? Would—would you care to come with me?"

When Leander looked at Joe, he seemed confused, as if he'd been dreaming of someplace far away and had not yet returned. He was unshaven and looked as if he hadn't slept in days. "Where is it you're going?"

"Into Charleston, sir. I haven't been off a ship in months; not going to miss my chance now." Joe nodded towards the soldier who stood rigidly a few feet behind Leander. "You can bring *him* with you, sir."

Leander smiled wanly. "Yes, apparently I'm allowed more freedom as long as I have Mr. Morven in tow."

"Well, then?"

"Well, then, I—I haven't a clean shirt to wear."

"You've no time to change even if you did, sir. Will you come, then?"

Leander hesitated, looking embarrassed. "I'm afraid I have no money. The little I once had went down with the *Isabelle*."

Joe slipped his hand into the pocket of his trousers and jingled a few coins. "I've plenty for the two of us; well, at least enough to buy us a decent meal."

While the sailors bellowed at Joe, "Hurry up, or thee boat's leavin' without yas!" Joe pleaded with the sullen-looking first lieutenant in charge to grant Leander shore leave. "Neither of us have enough money to get into much mischief, sir, and we can keep an eye out for the lads who will."

The first lieutenant considered a minute, his bushy-black eyebrows dancing up and down, and his lower lip thrusting in and out all the while. At last, a laugh burst from his fleshy face. "Did you figure, Mr. Norlan, that you and Dr. Braden can take liberties with our captain away from his ship?" He shoved Joe towards the ladder that dangled down the ship's side. "*You* can go. But your friend here is required to stay on board to stitch the busted heads of those that'll be swinging from the rigging tonight."

10:30 p.m.
(First Watch, Five Bells)
Aboard the *Prosperous and Remarkable*

THE EVENING WAS BALMY, and the silver-crescent moon sailed in and around starry beacons and banks of pearly clouds. The lights of Charleston twinkled in the distance, beyond the bouncing black masts and lanterns of moored vessels in the harbour. Prosper had lowered his distinguishing pennant, doused his lights, and anchored his *Prosperous and Remarkable* as far out in the water as was possible; that way, should there be any trouble, he could do a quick disappearing act. As they had slipped in under cover of darkness, Prosper was relieved they hadn't grounded on a sandbar or rammed into Sullivan Island and smashed through the new brick walls of Fort Moultrie. And he certainly hadn't desired to bump into the back of a British cruiser that might be silently lurking, waiting like an alligator in tall reeds at the mouth of the harbour to give chase to any fleeing Yankee frigates. While the cutter was being prepared for its descent into the murmuring water, Prosper addressed his small crew.

"Now, I'll only be takin' a few o' yas. Don't wanna stir up no suspicion, and I knows what happens ta most o' yas when ya down a few too many—ya start blubberin' 'n' boastin' somethin' fierce. Now, we don't need no trouble." He swung round and crouched down to speak to Magpie. "You run and tell yer friend yer goin' inta town with old Prosper so he won't worry none about ya."

Magpie was stunned. "Yer takin' *me* to Charleston?"

"Aye! I'm takin' ya on yer first reconnaissance adventure! But yer gonna hafta leave that hat behind. Should anyone see that needle-worked '*Isabelle*' on it, they might just pitch ya into their dank dungeon under thee Exchange House. Trust me, they have nasty ways ta make a man talk in there. Ya hurry, now!"

A thousand thoughts crashed through Magpie's mind—not the least of which was the prospect of dungeons and Yankee thumbscrews—and his heart boomed like warring cannons as he hastened below to the forepeak where he and Gus kept their cots. Charleston was a Yankee town! What if someone pointed him out as an enemy of President Madison's? Would they pitch him into their damp dungeon? How did Prosper figure he could escape if all those ships lying in the harbour took after him? And what did that big word, "reconnaissance," mean? As he stowed away his hat under his cot, there was such a rush of emotions coursing through Magpie he could barely breathe.

Gus was awake, staring at the ceiling beams. There was more colour in his cheeks than there had been at noon, but his eyes were now feverish with fear.

Upon seeing Magpie, Gus cried out, "Where are we? Who's the man that put these new splints on me? I swear it wasn't Dr. Braden."

Gus had been delirious the previous day when Prosper had carried him onto his brig, and during those awful days drifting about in the skiff, knowing how it would upset him, Magpie had never once mentioned the final fate of Captain Moreland's ship.

Magpie attempted a smile. "That was Prosper Burgo what looked after ya, sir. And we're on his ship, the *Prosperous and Remarkable*! He's from Quebec and he's been lookin' after ya real good."

Gus still looked fearful. "We've stopped. Are we in Halifax?"

"No, but we're somewhere."

"Where?"

"Well, sir, some place called Charleston."

"Charleston?"

"Aye!"

"We're in South Carolina?"

"Aye, I suppose that's where it be, but everythin's gonna be all right. And I'm goin' ashore with Prosper fer a bit to do some ... well, to do some explorin', so rest up. Pemberton Baker will look in on ya. Prosper calls him a jackanapes and a galoot, but he's really a kind sort o' fellow."

Gus's forehead wrinkled and twitched as if he were trying to make sense of it all, and Magpie worried he was going to ask more questions—questions he didn't have the nerve to answer right then and there. Chewing on his lip, he was relieved when Gus lowered his gaze and lapsed into a thoughtful silence.

"Well, then, I'll be seein' ya, sir."

Magpie lunged for the ladder up, but stopped mid-step when Gus called out, "Wait!"

Swinging around, Magpie watched his disabled friend strain to lift his head from his pillow.

"Magpie," he whispered, "just in case ... ask Mr. Prosper for a gun."

10:30 p.m.
(First Watch, Five Bells)
Aboard the USS *Serendipity*

THE WALLS OF EMILY'S CABIN vibrated with celebratory sounds: flutes and fiddles, singing voices, dancing feet, clapping hands, and drunken laughter. The sailors still aboard ship, not having had the good fortune in securing shore leave, had been allowed to engage in other diversions tonight on their own home deck. It was the first time, in all her accumulated weeks on the *Serendipity*, that Emily had heard such unbridled festivity in the evening. Ever since the ship's arrival in Charleston, boatloads of bedraggled men, women, and children had come boisterously rowing out to meet their ship, waving baskets of food, bottled spirits, letters, and care packages. For hours Emily had rested her head against the gunport frame and watched with envy as the visitors had eagerly scrabbled up the ship's ladder (or been hauled up like harpooned whales on bosuns' chairs), and embraced their lovers and loved ones at the rail with shrieks of joy. In an effort to buoy her own spirits, she had pictured herself among them, imagining her own reunion with Leander Braden: his warm arms drawing her close, his searching, sea-blue eyes sending shivers through her.

The celebrations were now in full swing, and while the entire world danced upon the weather decks, there was no time to lose. Charlie had just left her, having come to collect the crumbs of her boiled beef and cheese supper. "I won't be comin' back no more, Miss. I won't be bringin' ya yer meals no more. I'm gonna be learnin' the sails," he had mumbled as he hesitated by the door with her tray. His protruding mouth had opened expectantly as if he had hoped she might make a fuss and demand an explanation. But Emily's mind had long since strayed from the *Serendipity* and the affairs of her sailors. When the door had closed behind him, she felt certain that no one would hear her furtive movements in her dark hovel nor give her another thought until morning.

Emily gazed out the gunport at the wafer moon that glinted upon the calm harbour, and searched the water to make certain there were no boats returning to or leaving Trevelyan's ship at this late hour. With the coast clear, she changed into her favourite clothes, which she had arranged upon her cot earlier. Her fumbling fingers pulled on the now-stained rumpled trousers and sailor-blue jacket that Magpie had sewn for her, and tied her neck-scarf around her head to conceal her plaited hair. She then groped about under her bed for her leather shoes and, finding them, held them in her shaky hands a moment, smoothing the silver buckles with her thumbs. They had to be worth something! Quickly she rolled them up into a paisley shawl that she had found amongst the clothes Charlie brought in to her the previous day, stuffed the lot down the front of her jacket, and felt her way to the cannon carriage. It would have been so much easier had the cannon not been lashed so closely to the walls surrounding the gunport, but even if she could untie its solid ropes, the gun was far too heavy to clear away.

Her body tingling with excitement, she mounted the carriage and, closing her left arm around the gun's mouth, reached out to steady herself against the port's framework so that she could hook one leg over the ledge. The crescent moon had now slipped behind a quilt of clouds and low growls of thunder echoed in the distance, but she did not care. Her eyes and mind were fixed on the distant lights of Charleston. Fighting to maintain her precarious balance, she raised her other leg to the ledge and had both legs dangling over the side of the *Serendipity* when lantern light and the stink of an unwashed human suddenly filled her cabin.

"Ho, ho! What's all this about?"

The unexpected voice caused Emily to teeter and her heart to lurch like a ship in a storm. With a desperate cry, she struggled to steady herself so she could jump from the gunport, but the intruder was too swift. A strong slippery arm caught her around the waist, dragged her across the thick lashings, and dropped her to the floor. Tears of pain sprang to Emily's eyes as her back struck the wheels of the carriage. Her head swooned as she peered up at her adversary who thrust the harsh lantern light into her face.

"Won't thee cap'n be int'rested in knowin' ya was tryin' to escape again," taunted Meg Kettle, grinning like a gargoyle.

Behind the elated washerwoman came a hoot of laughter. A shadowy bare-chested figure in dungarees hovered by the door. He dumped a ditty bag, a hammock, and heap of linen blankets upon the floor and smiled at Emily, who winced in pain beside the cannon.

"Can't say I blame ya for tryin' to escape, Miss. Ya must 'ave been informed in advance that ya was to share a bunk with Mrs. Kettle." He placed his fist to his temple in a mock salute and slipped away, leaving the two women alone with one another.

11:00 p.m.
(First Watch, Six Bells)
Aboard HMS *Amethyst*

LONG AFTER CAPTAIN PRICKETT, Lord Bridlington, and their senior officers had sought their beds, Fly Austen stayed behind in the *Amethyst*'s wardroom to write. Through the thin canvas screens that divided their small cabins and flanked the rectangular oak table at which he sat, Fly could hear the mumbles and snores of the men as they slept soundly, thanks in part to the hearty multi-course supper Biscuit had forced them to eat. Pushing back his chair, he stretched and wandered over to the galleried stern windows. Still there were no lights to be seen out there, save for the haunted moon that spilled its path of brilliance across the purring waves.

Fly felt in his breast pocket to make certain he still had the two letters James Moreland had given to him before his death. One of them he would post the first opportunity he got; the second he would have to safeguard at all costs. Fly searched the dark regions beyond the moon's glow. It wouldn't be long now before they raised Charleston.

"Sir?"

Fly swung round. Morgan Evans was standing in the wardroom doorway, looking somewhat bleary-eyed. At first, Fly had difficulty recognizing the younger man without his old familiar knitted hat pulled down upon his shaggy hair. "Mr. Evans! I apologize for summoning you this late and disturbing your rest."

"Actually, sir, I was up playing cards with some of the lads, and losing, so I was quite relieved you wanted to see me."

"I need you to do something for me," Fly said gravely, offering Morgan a chair, "and unfortunately this might be the only chance we'll have to talk without an audience in attendance." He motioned towards the officers' cabins.

Morgan sat down and watched Fly seat himself opposite the table from him.

"I have great respect for your judgement, Mr. Evans, and I value your honesty. As you happen to be my senior crewman on this ship, I would ask that you read over this statement." He slid a sheaf of papers towards him. "When you are done, give me your pronouncement on its accuracy."

Morgan shifted on his chair. "I'd be honoured to, sir, but I can't read. I can't read, nor can I write."

Fly retrieved his papers, and without embarrassing Morgan further, said, "Well, then, lend me your ear awhile." Pouring the last of the coffee from the silver pot into his cold cup, Fly gulped it down and in a subdued voice began reading his account of the events of June 15, 1813. As he listened, Morgan closed his eyes and relived all the excitement, fear, and horror of that dreadful day. A thousand poignant images flashed through his brain: carrying Bailey Beck down to Dr. Braden when already his life had drained from his old body; Magpie's crumpling face when he learned Gus Walby had fallen from the mizzen at the start of the battle; the bloody ruins of Captain Moreland sprawled across the deck; the gaping, jagged hole in the hull where Emily had once lain; and *her*, bound and being dragged towards the exultant Trevelyan, like a condemned person about to meet the gallows' executioner. He could clearly see the ghastly stumps of men stretched out in agony on the operating table, smell the inferno that obliterated his ship, and hear the roar and hiss of her wreckage slipping beneath the waves. And how he could still taste the cold! They were so cold that night, sitting beaten, dazed, and hungry in the small boats, the driving rain adding to their misery.

When at last Fly was done, he looked up to see Morgan's eyes glistening, and, keeping his own eyes averted, patiently waited for the younger man to speak.

"Aye, sir, that's pretty much how I—I recall it," Morgan said, nodding his head. "There's just one thing—with respect—you've mentioned how we signalled to the *Amethyst* for help once we realized our situation. It should have been quite easy for Captain Prickett to turn around at once. How do you account for him not answering us?"

"I cannot account for it at all," Fly said, dropping his voice to a whisper. "But it is a detail I must include. Had they come back in time, we wouldn't have been so badly outnumbered, and perhaps could have saved the ship. No doubt the Admiralty will have questions for Prickett and his officers."

"But they've been so kind to us, sir."

Fly felt his breast pocket again. His gaze fell absently upon his coffee cup, and when at last he spoke his voice was so disembodied, Morgan was not certain the question had been posed to him.

"Was there something more I could have done?"

Wishing to bestow words of comfort, Morgan blurted out, "The lads are itching for a crack at Trevelyan, sir, and hope we catch up to him soon."

Fly's brow darkened as he raised flinty eyes to Morgan. "We will, Mr. Evans, and rest assured, they'll get their fight."

Midnight
In Charleston

MAGPIE WAS MISERABLE. This was the fifth tavern Prosper had brazenly marched into since their little party from the *Prosperous and Remarkable* had landed in at the wharves a little over an hour ago. Without exception, the walls of every drinking establishment had hummed with boisterous chatter on the subject of Captain Thomas Trevelyan's triumphant arrival in Charleston, and every Yankee sailor had lapped up the often-false details regarding HMS *Isabelle*'s demise. Magpie would have given his remaining eye to scream out, *Lies! Trevelyan were a coward! Bringin' down Cap'n More-*

land's brave crew like he were stalkin' a fox, employin' three ships to do the deed. Oh, to do so would have given him so much satisfaction. But every so often Prosper had shot him a warning glance, and while they strolled between taverns, he threatened to toss him into "that dank dungeon" beneath the imposing Exchange building if he so much as opened his mouth.

Magpie had grown weary of the women in their tight-fitting gowns, petting him on the head as if he were a puppy, or pushing him aside, and the strangers with purple noses and stale breath, shoving their queer faces into his, demanding to know how he'd come to lose an eye. More than anything, he wished to return to Prosper's brig to check on Gus and crawl into the little cot beside his. The problem was, Prosper, having been intrigued by all the talk of the booty Trevelyan was alleged to have stolen from the *Isabelle* before setting her afire, insisted on getting a look at the man firsthand before making his way back to their cutter.

Magpie sat in the front window of a red-brick tavern off a cobblestone alley near the wharves, listening as Prosper talked with a woman whose breasts were more awe-inspiring than Mrs. Kettle's. Their other crewmen had spread out to take their refreshments in opposite corners of the establishment so they could eavesdrop on the rum-soaked sailors who raised their tankards and voices in conversation and contention at their heavy square tables. Magpie's tired eye wandered around the room. Candle and lantern light danced upon the sailors' faces. Some played at cards, some drank sullenly, while others squealed with mirth as they pinched the bottoms of the female servers or pulled them down onto their laps for a kiss and a cuddle. The arched fireplaces that dominated the room lay empty. It was still so humid at this late hour that no additional warmth was required. The room reeked, filled with a pungent mixture of sweat, liquor, and brine, and Magpie was thankful for the open window next to him and the light rain that fell on the cobbled streets.

A server stopped at their table to refresh Prosper's tankard.

"Just warnin' ya, sir, we won't be servin' much longer."

"Fine!" Prosper smiled, lifting his ruddy face from his companion's heaving bosom. "Then I won't be drinkin' much longer." He flipped a silver coin at Magpie. "Get lost fer a bit, ya wee jackanapes. Go git me somethin' worth eatin'." Magpie was happy to leave, not wishing to know the nature of the pranks Prosper and the woman were playing at beneath the oak table.

It was a long time before anyone paid him any heed at the bar. He was about to give up when a young black girl, busy stirring something in a steaming copper pot on a stew stove, turned her dulled eyes upon his coin.

"Ya won't git much fer that," she said, wiping her damp brow before handing him a small loaf of bread. Magpie shrugged and stepped away from the bar with Prosper's meal—only to find a giant of a man blocking his way. He seemed to tower up to the tavern's ceiling. He was hatless, his hair the colour of harvested straw, and on his thin frame he wore a rain cloak that dripped streamlets upon the tavern's flagstone floor. In his large, scarred hands he held a mug of ale, and sharing a drink with him was another man, dressed in white breeches and polished Hessian boots. The two men were engrossed in a conversation and had no idea they had pinned Magpie to the bar. Knowing Prosper would be impatient for his supper, Magpie made an attempt to skirt around the tall man, but the moment he glimpsed the face that belonged to those breeches and boots, his eye nearly popped out of his bandaged head. Thinking his knees would buckle beneath him, he cowered against the oak bar and quivered like a mouse cornered by a cat, with no alternative but to listen to their exchange.

"Sir, when your business is done here in Charleston, where will you go next? Have you been issued new orders?"

"No, I have not. But even if I had been, I would not heed them. I am setting my own course now." He raised his mug. "After all, with my recent success, I do not expect my actions to be questioned by Secretary Jones."

"In what direction shall we be sailing, sir?"

"North. I plan to seek out the Duke of Clarence. My spies tell me that the minute he received word his niece had been taken prisoner after the sinking of the *Amelia*, he asked permission from his brother, the regent, and Lord Liverpool to put to sea with a few escorts and undertake a mission to rescue her himself." The tall man gave a low snigger. "How very *admirable*."

"Will we head to Halifax then, sir?"

"Perhaps, or we just might be lucky and find the old boy patrolling the waters around Bermuda."

"Sir, your prisoner ... might I be so bold as to ask what you plan to do with her?"

The tall man gulped down his drink and wiped his mouth on the damp sleeve of his cloak. "You will know of my plans soon enough. For now, know this: so long as she is imprisoned upon the *Serendipity*, I have ... insurance."

"I am pleased for you, sir."

"Thank you, Mr. Lindsay. You have served me well."

"It was and *is* an honour to serve you, Captain Trevelyan."

Captain Trevelyan?

Hearing the name, Magpie gasped as if he'd been struck with a ramrod. That was it! He could linger there no longer. Reaching out blindly, he pushed past the two men, but in a flash Trevelyan's dark eyes were on him. He raised his arm and shoved Magpie backwards, causing him to lose his balance and trip over Mr. Lindsay's feet.

"Damnable foundling," said Octavius, inspecting his boots as if checking for scuffs.

The minute Mr. Lindsay's eyes beheld Magpie, tremors of surprise ruffled his pimply countenance, but when he had quite recovered from shock, he seized Magpie by the shirt collar. "How the *devil* did you come to this place? Who brought you here?" His suspicious glance roamed the crowded room.

Trevelyan raised an eyebrow and hunched over to glower at Magpie, droplets from his cloak soaking into Prosper's loaf of bread. Magpie was too terrified to answer, his mind now busy imagining that Mr. Lindsay would march him down a lonely back alleyway and fix thumbscrews to his private parts to make him talk. His only hope was that Prosper would pull his face out of that woman's bosom long enough to see that he needed saving.

"This worthless mongrel was the *Isabelle*'s sail maker, sir," said Mr. Lindsay, tightening his hold on Magpie's shirt.

Magpie thought he was going to be ill.

Trevelyan was as serene as if he were greeting a friend. "Well, then, Mr. Lindsay, we must bring him back to the *Serendipity*. If we seize him up to the shrouds, he might have a few tales worth hearing."

"Or we could treat him to a miscreant midshipman's caning, sir."

"Better still, we could feed his fingers to the local alligators."

Up came Magpie's stomach, his colourful, half-digested supper of oyster stew, corn pone, and plums spewed forth, splattering all over Captain Trevelyan's cloak and Mr. Lindsay's shiny boots. Both men jumped back in annoyance, knocking over a server and her liquor-laden tray. As tin and pewter connected with the floor's flags, shrieks of surprise and dismay rent the tavern air. In the chaotic din that ensued, Magpie recognized Prosper's provocative roar.

"Ya wee jackanapes, run fer it *now*!"

Dumping the sodden loaf of bread into the putrid puddle frothing on the floor, Magpie scratched and clawed his way through the smelly tangle of sailors and flew like grapeshot towards the tavern's front door.

"Stop that foundling!" shouted Trevelyan behind him.

"Don't let that mongrel escape!"

"There he is! Grab hold of him!"

As he fled for his life, his terror turned his mind to mush; still, up ahead, he was able to distinguish Prosper Burgo in the mob. As if it were commonplace for Magpie to have enemy soldiers upon his heels, Prosper sat sedately at his table, one arm draped around his companion's voluptuous shoulders, his head wobbling about on his scrawny neck, his back teeth now well-afloat. Fearing he was on his own, Magpie fixed his eye on the opening tavern door as he dodged grasping hands and leapt over legs meant to trip him up. And as he bolted past Prosper, he was certain he heard him say, "I'll follow ya when thee way be clear."

Tuesday, June 22

1:00 a.m.
(Middle Watch, Two Bells)
Aboard the *Prosperous and Remarkable*

GUS'S EYES FLEW OPEN, the sudden noise having awakened him. Pemberton Baker was still sitting near his cot, whittling away at a chunk of wood with a small knife, his features unremarkable and placid in that large face of his.

"Was that cannon-fire, Mr. Baker?"

"It were only a clap o' thunder. And it's *Pemberton*. We don't much stand on formalities round here."

"But are you quite certain? It was so loud!"

"Common thing in these parts ... thunderclaps."

"Is Magpie back?"

"Nay! Whisht now and go to sleep."

Alarmed, Gus lifted his head from his pillow. "Shouldn't he be back by now? What time is it?"

"Close to two bells in thee Middle Watch."

"You don't think anything has happened, do you?"

"Nay! Yer friend's as safe with Prosper Burgo as with God." Pemberton returned to his whittling. "Sleep now. Thee more sleepin' ya do, thee sooner ya'll be leavin' yer cot."

"Why aren't *you* in bed, Mr ... Pemberton?"

Another rumble of thunder rattled the brig's timbers. Pemberton studied his knife. "Not sleepy. But I'll be goin' soon; me bed's over yonder. You whisht now."

Gus closed his eyes and tried to summon slumber, but the thunder frightened him, booming all around as if the *Prosperous and Remarkable* were under siege. He turned his head to watch Pemberton work, digging and paring away at his chunk of wood, the tiny shavings falling like crumbs onto the bent knees of his beige trousers. Then, raising his eyes to Pemberton's wide, blank face, he whispered, "Would you stay awhile and talk to me? I should like to hear what became of the *Isabelle*."

3:30 a.m.
(Middle Watch, Seven Bells)
Aboard the USS *Serendipity*

PULLING THE HOOD of his borrowed rain cloak over his head, Leander stepped onto the weather decks of the *Serendipity*. Instantly, the rain found his face, but he welcomed it after the heat and oppression of the ship's bowels. The decks were empty except for the glum souls on watch and a handful of others who had earlier been celebrating a bit too heartily and had simply dropped before they could stumble off to their beds. On a discarded heap of canvas, he spotted a sleeping Meg Kettle, snuggled up with a snoring sailor, both of them oblivious to the pelting rain in the happiness of their makeshift bed. It was perhaps fortunate that Trevelyan and his new toady, Octavius Lindsay, had made plans to spend the night in Charleston.

With a pounding heart, Leander wandered to the part of the ship where Emily was housed. Flashes of lightning revealed the area around her cabin to be clear; no one stood guard there now. Nevertheless, in the event he was stopped and questioned, he had invented an excuse and, for insurance, brought his medical chest along. As he neared his destination, he strode past two sailors who were busy clearing the upper deck of the filth and clutter from the night's carousing. Both of them nodded in his direction, nothing on their worn-out features indicating they thought it amiss that the British doctor should be wandering near the great cabin in the middle of the night.

Leander studied the closed doors before him. Rattling snores filled the air, though he could not pinpoint their origin, as the walls of the cabins were nothing more than flimsy sheets of canvas stretched upon frames of wood. Thanks to information provided by one of his patients, Leander now knew where it was that Emily lay, and twice now he had spied young Charlie Clive coming out of her cabin, carrying a tray. He moved towards her door and quietly set his medical chest on the floor by his feet. Then, reaching into his coat pocket, he pulled out the package of bread and meat that Joe Norlan had kindly brought back for him from town. He knocked once and took a step backwards to listen. Inside her cabin there was movement—of that he was certain—but to his dismay the snoring suddenly stopped. Had his knock awakened a nearby officer? Hardly daring to breathe, he waited, but when nothing happened, he grew restless.

"Emily?" he whispered into the night. "Emily, it's me."

The long-awaited reply—one word mumbled in a sleepy voice—caused him both joy and physical pain.

"Doctor?"

Faint with excitement, he called out again. "I'm right here at your door. I've—I've brought you some food."

"Why, Doctor, was ya lookin' fer me?"

Whirling about, Leander came face to face with Meg Kettle. She stood there, one hand on her prodigious hips, the other rumpling her untidy hair, a jubilant expression pressed upon her fat cheeks. She snatched away the meat sandwich and sank her grey teeth into it. Then, producing from her apron pocket a key that she dangled before him, she unlocked Emily's door and, keeping her eyes on him, squeezed her bulk into the cabin. "Doctor," she said, chewing with her mouth open, "it's a bit late fer me to be entertainin' visitors, if ya knows what I mean."

Leander reddened. "This—this is *your* cabin?"

"'Tis *now*, so shove off or I'll report yer mischief to Cap'n Trevelyan when he returns." She slammed the door in his face.

Thunderstruck, Leander remained rooted to the floor timbers, unable to comprehend this disastrous turn of events. *She* was there, a few feet from him, a bit of canvas separating them, yet he could do nothing. The two sailors were now watching him. By lantern light, Leander could see sportive smiles upon their faces. Retrieving his medical chest, he reluctantly left Emily in the hands of Meg Kettle, and with his head held high, brushed by the sailors, ignoring their mirthful clucks. His fingers tensed around the handle of his medical chest and determination burned in his breast. Sooner than later, he would find another opportunity.

5:00 a.m.
(Morning Watch, Two Bells)
Aboard the *Prosperous and Remarkable*

OUT OVER THE OCEAN there were still muted bursts of thunder, but the driving downpour that had knocked for ages against the sides of the *Prosperous and Remarkable* next to Gus's head had finally ceased. Lying in his cot, Gus waited for Magpie to strip off his sodden clothing and pull on the oversized muslin shirt that Prosper had donated for his night attire. He was anxious to hear about Magpie's explorations in Charleston, but didn't dare tell him he'd been awake for ages, listening for the sound of his familiar step.

"Why are you back so late?" he snapped.

Magpie hopped into his cot, drew his knees up to his chest, and pulled his thin blanket around him. In the light cast by the lantern that hung near their cots, Gus could see that Magpie's cheeks were aglow and his eye sparkled, and when he finally spoke in a loud whisper, his words tumbled out in a breathless, jumbled torrent. "Oh, sir, when we come back here, I wanted to see ya straight off, but Prosper was insistin' he change me bandages. And then he was wantin' to ask me hundreds o' questions 'bout Cap'n Trevelyan and Octavius Lindsay."

Gus was aghast. "Trevelyan? Mr. Lindsay? Why?"

"Oh, sir, you'll never guess—I saw them, in a tavern near the docks. And Trevelyan stands eight feet high and ya wouldn't like the looks o' him. He's got the eyes o' Lucifer and his hands—they're all cut up like a farmer's plough runned him down. And Mr. Lindsay—I don't understand it, sir, 'cause the last I saw him, he were clapped in irons on the *Isabelle*, but—well, he's workin' for Trevelyan now. And ya see, while I were gettin' Prosper somethin' to eat, I heared them usin' big words I didn't understand and talkin' 'bout Halifax and Bermuda and the Duke o' Clarence comin' to rescue Emily."

"*Emily*?"

"Oh, sir. She's alive. She's on the *Serendipity*, just like I guessed. Just like I told Prosper. But then I got real scared and threw up me supper all over Trevelyan and Mr. Lindsay's boots, and they didn't much like that so I had to run fer me life. And, sir, we ... we had to wait 'til the wharf were clear o' Yankees afore we could get to the cutter and come back. I kept on thinkin' 'bout that dungeon, and I were so distressed, I couldn't stop me tears. Prosper told me again and again to quit me snivellin' or he were gonna feed me to the alligators. They 'ave alligators in these waters, sir, with big teeth! And I didn't like the thought o' alligators eatin' me legs. All the while it were rainin' and I had to keep hidin' and watch out for Trevelyan and Mr. Lindsay and the soldiers runnin' around, hollerin' and chasin' us with their muskets, ready to shoot us dead." He stopped to take in air.

Gus could see Magpie's body trembling beneath his blanket. "You must slow down and tell me everything from the very beginning."

Magpie took a deep breath and was about to try again when Pemberton's firm voice sounded in the darkness. "Lads! Pipe down! Out with thee lantern. Thee call fer hammocks up will come afore ya know it. Whisht now!"

Scurrying from his cot, Magpie quickly blew out the lantern candle and came to kneel beside Gus's head. "Sir, afore I tell ya 'bout what I saw and heared tonight," he whispered, "I gotta tell ya 'bout the *Isabelle*. Ya gotta know it first."

"I do know," said Gus, glad that Magpie could not see his welling tears. "Pemberton told me everything—that is, everything he'd learned from *you*. He said you didn't know what happened to the crew, because—because you'd come away in the skiff—to find me." Gus's throat closed up and he paused until he once again had full command of his voice. "He did tell me how you came by that embroidered hat you keep under your cot." Gus felt Magpie's warm hand close around his forearm, beneath his splints.

"Oh, sir, I wished ya'd never had to learn the truth. I wish we was on the *Isabelle* still, sittin' in Emily's corner readin' that book and Dr. Braden smilin' upon us and Mr. Crump makin' wisecracks from his hammock. And Prosper's biscuits aren't nearly as tasty as them what Biscuit used to bake." Magpie began to weep.

"Start from the beginning, Magpie."

But Magpie's weeping only grew louder until at last Pemberton raised his voice in warning. "If ya don't stop yer blubberin,' I'll toss ya overboard meself, and trust me, them alligators ya don't fancy none will be sure ta find ya."

Magpie mewled and made a dash for his cot. But soon he was feeling his way back to Gus's head. "Sir, I promise, I'll tell ya everythin' after I sleep a bit. But ya gotta know now. Come first light, we're leavin' here, and Prosper ... well, he's all fired up and plannin' on goin' after Trevelyan the first chance he gets."

7:30 a.m.
(Morning Watch, Seven Bells)
Aboard the USS *Serendipity*

EMILY OPENED HER EYES from her night of dreams to find her lower back aching and Meg Kettle standing over her, a broad smile on her thin lips.

"'Bout time ya woke up."

Emily sat up in her cot, rubbed life into her face, and frowned as she surveyed the grubby hammock that was newly hung so close to her own. As if reading her thoughts, Mrs. Kettle said, "It were Cap'n Trevelyan's idea t'ave thee *ladies* bunk together."

"Mrs. Kettle," said Emily with restraint, "one would hardly consider you a lady."

"Ooo, and ya think *yer* a right smart lady! Jumpin' outta ships and wearin' trousers and drinkin' with thee Isabelles and sleepin' with all thee men in Dr. Braden's hospital?"

Emily did not give her the satisfaction of a reply. She gazed past Mrs. Kettle, wishing she were alone to remember the voice that had called out to her in the night. It had seemed so real and so close. She closed her eyes for a second, pulling the coat that had been *his* up around her shoulders.

"Get a move on. Ya won't be layin' 'bout today."

Emily threw Mrs. Kettle an impatient glance. "I'll get up when I want to."

"Nay! Today ya 'ave work to do."

Emily lifted her chin. "I beg your pardon?"

"It's yer punishment fer tryin' to escape last night."

"I would have thought being forced to share my cabin with *you* was punishment enough."

Mrs. Kettle made a snuffling sound. "Yer to do thee men's washin."

"With you?"

Mrs. Kettle's hands found her hips. "Nay! Won't be findin' Meggie doin' laundry no more."

"Why not? Has Trevelyan finally decided to reward you for being a traitor?"

A muscle in Mrs. Kettle's cheek quivered. "I bin given a promotion."

"Really? Shall I address you from here on as yeoman of the *bedsheets* or perhaps as captain of the *heads*?"

"Think yer comical now, don't ya?"

"Mrs. Kettle, I doubt there's a uniform on this ship large enough to fit your frame."

Mrs. Kettle compressed her lips and flounced her hammy arms across her chest, but Emily, having no interest in hearing the details of her shipboard promotion, scrambled from her cot and pushed up the gunport. Rain and sea spray blew into the tiny cabin, invigorating Emily's warm face. She filled her lungs with the clean, salty air, and massaged her lower back as she gazed longingly towards Charleston.

"Shut that," growled Mrs. Kettle.

"I will not."

"Ya'll get me hammock all wet. Now shut it."

"I will not! I cannot breathe in here. You reek like a manure patch."

Mrs. Kettle took a menacing step towards Emily. "Ooo, if I'd a knife, I'd cut yer bold tongue from that white throat o' yers." Emily swung round and stood her ground before the open gunport, meeting the older woman's stare dead on. They glared at each other until the whooshing sound of a tray being passed under the cabin door diverted Mrs. Kettle's wavering glance.

"Yer breakfast!" trilled an unfamiliar voice.

Scurrying to collect the food, Mrs. Kettle said, "Git dressed and be quick with yer gruel. Come eight bells, ya'll 'ave yer white hands in a tub o' saltwater."

The thought of leaving her small prison—especially now that it was redolent with the essence of livestock—lifted Emily's spirits. Having endured endless days of nothingness, she was ready to embrace any form of occupation and would not have complained even if ordered to draw the weevils from the ship's biscuit barrels. Suppressing her anger with Mrs. Kettle, Emily watched as she gobbled her buttered biscuits and foraged about in her ditty bag.

"Were you speaking to Dr. Braden last night?"

Mrs. Kettle gave Emily nothing more than a wary glance.

"I—I thought I heard his voice."

The laundress let loose a gurgle of laughter along with a spray of biscuit bits. "Dr. Braden? Where did ya get thee notion?"

Emily felt her confidence wane. "He said he had brought me some food."

A pompous smile crossed Mrs. Kettle's sweaty face. "Ya daft girl. 'Twere a dream only. Yer precious doctor's lyin' on thee ocean floor."

8:00 a.m.
(Morning Watch, Eight Bells)
Aboard HMS *Amethyst*

BISCUIT HUMMED A SCOTTISH TUNE as he set upon the captain's table a steaming pot of chocolate, a dish of marmalade, toast, and a freshly baked salt-fish pie. Fly frowned at Biscuit. Humming had not been allowed in the presence of Captain Moreland at mealtimes, but Captain Prickett, who was busy stuffing his linen napkin into the collar of his shirt, did not seem to mind the impertinence. "Biscuit, tell me, my good man, what's in the pie?"

Biscuit clasped his hands behind his back and cast a grave gaze upon the stern windows as he rhymed off the ingredients. "Soused herrings, oysters, halibut, lobster, potatoes, herbs, parsnips, pepper and salt, oh … ah …" He paused to show off his greenish teeth. "And a pinch o' rum."

Captain Prickett smiled his delight. "Well done, Biscuit. Now cut me and Mr. Austen a generous slice of it, then fetch the spiced cake you baked last night."

"Ya'll be wantin' cake fer breakfast, sir?"

"Most certainly. The day's chores already lie heavy on me. I need to be fortified with tasty sustenance." Captain Prickett spread a dollop of marmalade onto a half piece of toast, popped the whole works into his mouth, and studied his guest as he chewed. "How are you faring this morning, Mr. Austen?" he asked when Biscuit had left them.

Fly, who was about to take his first bite of pie, lowered his fork. "I am well, sir."

"And that scorched back of yours?"

"On the mend. These past few days of rest have helped immeasurably. I thank you for the reprieve in not sending me straightaway to work in the galley with Biscuit."

"Biscuit is quite capable of performing wonders with very little assistance."

"I am glad you are finding his service satisfactory. With all due respect, his performance was not quite as impressive on the *Isabelle*, but then Captain Moreland and his officers provided Biscuit with nothing more than the most basic of victuals."

"Where I, Mr. Austen, insist that my officers pay handsomely for their provisions, as food is my one joy."

As Captain Prickett eagerly dug into his pie, Fly took the opportunity to pop his waiting forkful into his mouth.

"I have other plans for you, Mr. Austen," Prickett said between bites. "That is why I wished to dine with you alone this morning."

Fly watched his face expectantly, but had to wait until the pie was dispensed with to hear more.

"You are aware, Mr. Austen, that we raised Charleston earlier this morning."

"Aye! I could see the town in the distance when I rose from my bed, sir."

"Hopefully, we find Trevelyan here, and if not in Charleston then in the general vicinity, though we may have to search as far south as

Savannah or even St. Augustine. We have gleaned information from two fishing vessels that claimed they passed a ship fitting the *Serendipity's* description. Now, if I were Trevelyan, and I had something to celebrate—in this case, the taking down of Moreland's ship—it is to Charleston that I would head. After all, it is known as the Paris of the American South for good reason."

Fly listened intently to his host. "What about blockades, sir? Are any of our ships watching the harbour mouth?"

"We haven't the manpower to properly blockade these American ports, Mr. Austen, and what we do have is concentrated in the north, just south of New York. We are totally ineffectual down here. It's about time our ships moved south in larger numbers."

"Sir, are we close enough to get a good look at the ships anchored in the harbour?" Fly strained his neck to catch a glimpse of Charleston through the great cabin windows, but his vantage point afforded him only a scene of rolling waves.

Prickett thoughtfully sipped his cup of chocolate. "Of course it is necessary to keep a safe distance and this rainy weather doesn't give us the best visibility."

Feeling suddenly restless, Fly asked, "What are you proposing to do, sir?"

"Hang about a few days, see whether Trevelyan's *Serendipity* does slip out of the harbour."

"And if he does, sir?"

"Well, now that's where you come in, Mr. Austen.

"Sir?"

Prickett cleared his throat. "You've had experience with this Trevelyan, Mr. Austen. You know his tactics, his games, and more importantly, how fast that ship of his can sail."

"Aye, I have gained a brief familiarity, sir."

Prickett shifted his bottom about in his chair. "You see, Mr. Austen, I've spent the past two years escorting merchantmen about this ocean, bullying potential predators with the *Amethyst*'s sheer size and her long guns. Call it luck, call it misfortune, I cannot recall when I last fired a broadside at anyone and, heaven forbid, had the fire returned;

notwithstanding, of course, that cowardly early morning shot we recently withstood." He poured himself a second cup of chocolate. "For the most part, my men are experienced seamen, though they've had little opportunity to become a well-drilled crew. And I'm afraid *I* am not a fighting captain."

An awkward silence followed, during which Fly was forced to listen to Prickett slurp and extol the virtues of his hot drink. Finally he took the initiative. "Sir, are you asking me to assist you with your campaign against Trevelyan?"

"Assist? Nay! I'm asking that you *lead* it."

Fly set down his knife and fork and handed Prickett an incredulous stare. Prickett looked sheepish, but his familiar joviality soon returned the moment he spied Biscuit entering the great cabin with the spiced cake. "Ah! There you are. Cut me a generous slab of that, will you now?"

12:30 p.m.
(Afternoon Watch, One Bell)
Aboard the *Prosperous and Remarkable*

MAGPIE COERCED A CHUNK OF MEAT down his throat. He had lost his appetite—due to the roughness of the sea and also to the company he was keeping. If it weren't for the presence of Prosper and for his kind invitation to join his messmates for a meal, Magpie would have quietly carried his plate back to the corner he shared with Mr. Walby. He peered up at the men who sat around the mess table, swilling their dinner's ration of grog, and eating their salted beef and boiled potatoes with their fingers. Though not having been intimately acquainted with them, Magpie was aware that a few of the Isabelles had had diseases of the mind or appetites for petty thievery, but these Prosperous and Remarkables were a different breed altogether. He had seen the likes of them before—at night in London, where they could be found lingering in rotting doorways down damp, foul alleyways, preying on passersby, dragging them into dark recesses, and murdering them for the few coins in their ragged pockets. Most of those who sat around him now had queer body parts—cracked teeth, maimed arms, missing ears, tattooed faces—and all of them had a peculiar brightness in their gaze. The man on his left had huge hands and shifty eyes, and a nose that looked like a tumorous strawberry. The way Magpie saw it, Prosper must have invited him to the table thinking he fit in with the bunch, having only one eye in his head. He shuddered as he sat on a chest at the head of the table and grabbed for his mug, praying the grog would settle his stomach, which had been home to a knot the size of an anchor since early the previous day. To avoid eye contact with the fearsome faces that surrounded him, he huddled over his plate and waited for the ship's bell that would herald the end of the dinner hour.

"Taken nineteen prizes since thee start o' this war," said Prosper, jabbing his knife in the air, "and, by Jove, I'd likes ta 'ave an even twenty."

"Aye, it's bin a while now, Prosper," said the tattooed sailor at the end of the table. "I miss thee feelin' o' me cutlass cuttin' some gullet."

The man with shifty eyes who sat next to Magpie's left elbow spoke up. "D'ya recall two months back, comin' upon that brig—what was it? Portuguese? French? Austrian? No matter. D'ya recall? And I roughed their captain up good and pitched overboard them what got in me way. And them wenches in their silk gowns—how they screamed shrilly, enough to uncleave barnacles from thee hull—and begged us to kill thee men but spare them."

"And did ya?" Magpie's question was barely audible.

"Nay, pitched them in too."

"Ya galoot," hissed Prosper. "'Twere a waste. I coulda thought o' other things ya coulda done with 'em."

The men broke into laughter and slammed their fists in approval on the solid oak of the tabletop, causing the pewter plates to dance.

"Is it true then, Prosper? Are ya goin' after Trevelyan?"

"Aye! Heard his men in Charleston talk o' silver, weaponry, and hundreds o' casks o' French wine in thee hold." Prosper swivelled his head towards Magpie. "And … a comely lass named Em'ly in thee great cabin."

Magpie's heart stopped. He looked fearfully from Prosper to the man on his left that had boasted of pitching wenches overboard. "Ya—ya won't harm her, sir?"

The man leaned over and thrust his strawberry nose into Magpie's flushing face. "Nay. So long as she don't git in me way."

A second round of hilarity rocked their small table, the noise so loud it frightened Magpie. He had to tug on Prosper's sleeve to get his attention. "But, the *Serendipity*'s a lot bigger than the *Prosperous and Remarkable*. And Trevelyan's got hundreds o' men and sharpshootin' marines and lots o' big guns."

A smug smile sprang to Prosper's lips and his eyelids fell to halfmast. "Nineteen prizes, little man, nineteen of 'em." His good humour suddenly changed to a scowl. "Magpie! Swathed in them bandages, ya look weak in thee head. 'Twould serve thee *Prosperous and Remarkable* well if I was ta fix ya up with an eye patch."

There, finally, was the bell.

Prosper rose to his feet and cuffed the heads of the two men on either side of him.

"Have yas finished fillin' yer faces, then? Better look lively, ya band o' ruffians! Won't be bobbin' forever in these waters with no purpose, ya know. Soon, we'll be goin' after our prize. And accordin' ta Magpie here, yer gonna see fightin' on thee seas in thee rare style o' David and Goliath."

As the men advanced from the mess table and headed out to their stations, Magpie whispered, "May the saints preserve us—every last one o' them."

1:00 p.m.
(Afternoon Watch, Two Bells)
Aboard the USS *Serendipity*

EMILY SEARCHED THE WASHING LINES fixed between the main and fore shrouds for space on which to hang her last load of linens, muslin shirts, neckcloths, silk stockings, and cotton trousers. She then set her laundry basket down on the deck beneath the foresail, gave her back a stretch, and wiped the sweat from her brow with her shirtsleeve. The sky was still overcast, threatening more rain, but between puffs of ocean breeze, the day was hot and sticky. Emily did not mind the weather. Nor did she mind that her ankle was hurting, her hands were red and roughened (the unhappy result of being submerged for hours in tubs of warmed saltwater and lye soap), or that her muscles were crying for mercy, having been shocked into use after weeks of inactivity. Her physical ailments were small nuisances compared to the pleasure of being out-of-doors, working alongside the Serendipities. The colourful scenes in the harbour and of distant Charleston were an agreeable change from the confinement of her dark cabin. Though physically drained, she felt stronger mentally, better than she had in days.

Bending down to pick up a pair of damp dungarees and two forked clothespins, Emily spotted the striking figure of Bun Brodie and his distinctive copper-coloured pigtail out of the corner of her eye, coming along the deck with a roll of canvas slung over his shoulders. She had seen him earlier, labouring above her on the yards, replacing sails for most of the day with the help of young Charlie Clive. They did not dare speak to one another, for Meg Kettle hovered nearby, keeping an eye on her every movement, making certain Emily did not converse with any of the sailors, although it was quite acceptable for *her* to lick her lips provocatively and make eyes at them. But this time, as Bun Brodie passed by Emily, he smiled and whispered "Mrs.

Seaton" in greeting, before taking his heavy load up the shrouds. Emily could not keep her heart from quickening. With the exception of Meg Kettle and Octavius Lindsay, Bun Brodie was the first of the Isabelles she had seen on the *Serendipity*. If... if Trevelyan took him, did she dare hope—despite what Mrs. Kettle had said that morning—might he have taken others as well? At the very least, Mr. Brodie might be able to tell her what had become of Captain Moreland's crew. Locking away the flame of hope, Emily looked up at Charlie, standing tall beside Bun Brodie on the foreyard, only to find him gazing down upon her. Though the lad's facial features rarely fluctuated, he acknowledged her with a wave before setting to work unfurling the new sail.

Deep in happy thought, Emily pinned the remaining clothes onto the already congested lines, unaware that Trevelyan's launch had returned to the ship. Suddenly hearing his distinctive voice only a few feet from where she worked gave her a fright, but as the deck was teeming with all manner of activity, and she, outfitted in hat and trousers, must have blended well with the crew, Emily hoped he had not yet recognized the new washerwoman. Keeping her back to Trevelyan, she listened with curiosity to his conversation with Octavius Lindsay.

"Why am I only hearing of this now, Mr. Lindsay?"

"Sir, you—I had no idea where you were lodging in town."

"How many of them were there, besides that little mongrel that vomited on my rain cloak?"

"Hard to tell, sir. They scattered... ran down different alleyways and streets."

"Did you watch all vessels leaving the harbour?"

"We did our best, sir. At dawn we rowed from ship to ship to question and search the crews, but we came up empty-handed. Perhaps, whoever it was, they took their chances and slipped away in the dark."

"There is still daylight, Mr. Lindsay. Search again. Take the launch and twelve or so marines with you, and this time, make certain you upend all chests and run a sword through every ditty bag. That little mongrel could be hiding anywhere. He could be on anyone's ship.

But before you dash off—I have brought Mr. Humphreys with me from town. See to it that he is provided with accommodation below deck."

"Mr. Humphreys, sir?"

"The chaplain."

"Aye, sir."

Emily laughed to herself as she hung up the final articles of laundry. Few men of the sea had religious leanings. Was Trevelyan about to seek God and salvation with the help of this Mr. Humphreys? She scooped up her empty basket, then while she waited a moment, giving Trevelyan time to quit the deck, a stomach-churning thought struck her. Feeling faint, she turned around slowly. But *he* stood there still, his strange eyes having found her. Whatever thoughts he had in his head, they were hard to read. His thin lips parted and Emily braced herself for what surely would be a disparaging remark related to her present occupation; instead, he lifted his gaze to the foresail that billowed above her head, and called out, "Mr. Clive, are you contented with your new situation?"

For a moment Charlie appeared bewildered and delayed his reply as if he weren't certain his captain had singled *him* out. "Aye, sir."

"And does it surpass serving up biscuits and tea to common wenches?"

Charlie's eyes shyly met Emily's upturned ones. "I—I suppose so, sir."

"And have you mastered the shrouds, Mr. Clive?"

Charlie's head rose higher on his skinny neck. "Oh, aye, sir."

"Show me then."

"Sir?"

"Climb down and I will observe your abilities."

Perched high up on the yard, Bun Brodie and the men assisting him in replacing the foresail followed Charlie's cautious descent with amusement until the lad had landed safely on the deck between Emily and Captain Trevelyan.

"Well done, Mr. Clive," Trevelyan said with no enthusiasm. "Now this time I will watch as you climb to the foretop and back. But as I require improvement in your speed, I will suggest a contest and provide you with an opponent."

Those within earshot of the exchange broke off their chores and crowded round to witness the impending spectacle, including Meg Kettle. Emily's mouth went dry when Trevelyan's eyes dropped on her like an axe and remained there as he spoke in a voice for all to hear.

"Men! Ten years ago I had the *privilege* of watching a young child race up the ratlines on HMS *Isabelle* as her proud father looked on. Perhaps today, *she* will bewitch us with another brilliant performance."

Astonished, Emily could only gape at Trevelyan as she tried to make sense of his words. Cold dread rushed through her body as the spectators—encouraged by Trevelyan's rare display of good nature—drew closer.

"But, sir, that was a very long time ago," said Emily, trying to gather her scattered wits.

"Yes," Trevelyan responded flatly.

"I've not had much *opportunity* of late to climb ropes."

"I was told you were spotted sitting upon the mizzen crosstrees the morning of the *Isabelle*'s last day. Did a great eagle carry you there?"

Emily glanced at Mrs. Kettle and was inflamed to see a glowing smile upon the woman's glistening features. Quickly, she turned back to Trevelyan.

"I have never made a habit of participating in *such* contests, sir."

Trevelyan sloped his body towards her until barely an inch separated their faces, then he tilted his head to one side. "Well, madam, you can begin now. I believe—given your unorthodox upbringing—you shall relish this novel adventure." He stepped backwards to smile at the crowd.

Feeling helpless, Emily wavered. She prayed no one would see the tremor in her hands nor hear the pounding of her heart.

"C'mon now, Miss."

"Show us what yer made of."

"Give Charlie a lickin'."

"Aye, thee whelp needs a good thrashin'."

"Nay!" Meg Kettle yelled out. "'Tis thee other way round."

With the men's raucous laughter ringing in her ears, Emily—dazed and distressed—pulled off her hat, threw it into her empty laundry basket, and set the basket down upon the deck. Then she squared her shoulders and slowly began rolling up the legs of her trousers.

Noon
(Forenoon Watch, Eight Bells)
Aboard HMS *Amethyst*

FLY AUSTEN LOWERED HIS SPYGLASS to address Captain Prickett and his first lieutenant, Lord Bridlington, who stood alongside him on the starboard rail, looking out over Charleston.

"It appears there are three larger ships in the harbour; perhaps they are frigates, perhaps one of them is Trevelyan. It would be ideal if we could move in closer to shore to get a better look."

Surprise crossed Lord Bridlington's face. "But if we were to do that, in a heavy ship such as ours, we may ground on a shoal and some of the smaller vessels would then come after us and board us, and if they were to gain control, what would become of us?"

Captain Prickett raised his hand to silence his senior officer. "Mr. Austen," he said, lowering his voice so the men working around him could not hear his words, "tell me what course of action we should assume and *I'll* pass the word to have it carried out."

Beneath the bow of his bicorne, Lord Bridlington's eyes widened.

"Thank you, sir," said Fly thoughtfully. "There is a sloop flying under our colours hove to near Sullivan Island. It might be wise to attempt communication with it."

"Imagine our Admiralty sending nothing more than a sloop to watch this part of the coast. The Americans must be having a good laugh at our expense," grumbled Prickett. "Consider it done, Mr. Austen."

"Also, sir, I wonder if we could—as soon as possible—put to sea. With your permission, I should like the gun crews to practise their drills, as you yourself admitted this morning that it has been a long while."

Captain Prickett glanced around his ship and nodded in agreement. "Right! I will arrange for it, Mr. Austen."

Lord Bridlington's eyes darted between his captain and Fly. "If gunfire is heard onshore, won't the enemy get the notion that we are issuing a challenge of sorts?"

Captain Prickett hiked his breeches up around his prodigious belly. "That's exactly what we are doing, Mr. Bridlington. If Trevelyan's holed up in there, we'll root him out... if he's any kind of a man, of course."

Captain Prickett clapped his jumpy officer on the back and led him towards the nearest hatchway, leaving Fly shaking his head in wonder as he watched after them. Left alone, he ambled along the rail, pausing every few feet to squint again through his spyglass. There were myriad vessels sailing in and out of the Charleston harbour; most of them appeared to be harmless fishing boats, though the *Amethyst* was too far away for Fly to confirm it one way or the other. He stayed there for an hour, accepting a cup of tea and a roll from Biscuit, but speaking to no one else as he continued his watch over the harbour. Engrossed in his thoughts, he took some time to recognize Morgan Evans loitering nearby, still unaccustomed as he was to seeing the young man without his distinguishing wool hat. "Mr. Evans!"

Morgan put his fist to his forehead in salute. "Beg your pardon, sir, I didn't mean to disturb you."

Fly regarded Morgan with fondness, his mind wandering to thoughts of his own baby sons back home in England. Were they to mature into young men the quality of Mr. Evans, he would be a proud father indeed. Fly wondered how Morgan was coping without the company of his old mate, Bailey Beck, and whether the horror of Mr. Alexander's drowning still troubled him. He desired to inquire, but believing himself to be yielding to softness, returned his attention instead to the sea. "What is on your mind, Mr. Evans?"

Morgan shifted from foot to foot as he always did when he was nervous. "We've seen you watching the harbour for hours now, sir, and wondered if, by chance, you'd observed what's running along the larboard rail?"

Fly's black eyebrows shot up. He swung round to search the waters beyond the *Amethyst*'s waist and, without hesitation, strode to the opposite rail, raising his spyglass as he walked.

"We've been keeping our eye on her for a while now, sir," said Morgan, hurrying to catch up to him. "There aren't many ships that boast a hull the colour of blood. If I'm not mistaken, we've seen this one before."

Through his glass, Fly watched the two-masted, square-rigged brig bearing down on them, though still a far piece away. "My guess is you are not mistaken, Mr. Evans. The Atlantic is a vast ocean with millions of square miles of water to traverse; chance meetings are a rarity, and yet we meet again."

"What's his game, sir?'

"Damned if I know, Mr. Evans."

1:30 p.m.
(Afternoon Watch, Three Bells)
Aboard the USS *Serendipity*

LEANDER LEFT THE CABIN belonging to Mr. Morven, the marine, having tended to the man's unfortunate injuries, sustained during a fall down wet steps, and set off on a quest for food, as he had missed taking his dinner. He had just begun walking towards the galley when an outburst of laughter resounded above deck. Curious, and without the impediment of Mr. Morven attached to his hip, Leander sprinted up the nearest ladderway to investigate. He could see a hundred or so Serendipities encircling the foremast, and hear Captain Trevelyan's voice rising above the carefree commotion, though he could not make out his words. Joe Norlan soon spotted him standing there and waved him over.

"How is your patient, sir?" Joe asked.

"He has a bump on his head."

"Inflicted by *you*, sir?"

Leander smiled wryly then motioned towards the crowd. "What's all this?"

"You're just in time. We're in for a rare delight. Captain Trevelyan has set a contest between—oh, shush—the fun begins." Joe's eyes flew to the shrouds, leaving Leander none the wiser. But before long, two figures appeared on the ratlines. The assembled sailors clapped, whistled, and hooted their approval as the figures climbed. Their noise attracted the notice of those on ships moored nearby, some stopping to watch.

"Up ya go."

"Faster, man!"

"Cap'n Trevelyan has thee watch set on ya."

"Ya won't live it down if ya get beat, Fish."

Leander turned to look at Joe, whose face was flushed with enjoyment. "It's Charlie Clive?"

Joe nodded, his eyes never leaving the climbers.

"I wasn't aware Charlie was acquainted with the ratlines. And who is it with him?"

So enthralled was Joe in the competition, he did not reply. Leander exhaled his disgust and began pushing through the spectators. He detested this kind of contest and the cheap captain's pride in the speed with which their men were able to scale the ropes. By the time Leander had shouldered his way to the edge of the crowd, one of the climbers was nearing the foretop. Trevelyan turned his head towards him and their eyes locked, mutual loathing evident in their brief glance.

"Doctor Braden!" he called out, reinstating his gaze on the climbers. "Are you impressed with *her* skills?"

The implicit message in Trevelyan's words sent Leander's eyes scrambling up the shrouds. From this new standpoint, he could see the familiar plait of gold hair swinging over the shoulders of Charlie's competitor. "Dear God," he whispered, his pulse escalating.

The jostling onlookers continued urging them on, their voices echoed by several spectators out in the harbour.

"She's gainin' on ya, Fish."

"Look ahead now! Don't look down."

"Faster now!"

Charlie was the first to reach the foretop, and seeing that Emily was well behind him, he lingered long enough to bestow a victorious smile upon the spectators. Cries of "Huzzah" erupted around Leander, causing him even greater alarm. Seemingly spurred on by the Serendipities' support, Charlie launched into his descent and in no time had passed Emily just as she reached out to touch the foretop's platform. Seeing her take one hand off the lines, Leander shouted, "Be careful!" The men guffawed and slapped Leander on the back in fun; however, no sooner had the words escaped his lips when, to his horror, Emily slipped and lost her footing. An anxious murmur rose up as those standing on the deck beneath her dangling legs followed with trepidation her fight to maintain a hold on the ropes and restore her footing. Leander broke out in a cold sweat; he bolted instinctively towards the shrouds, but Trevelyan stopped him. "There's no point in *both* of you breaking your necks."

"C'mon, lass," yelled the sailors.

"Holdfast."

"You can do it now."

"Every hair a rope yarn, that's you, Miss."

Powerless to help, Leander thought his chest would burst as he watched her struggle. After long, agonizing moments, a scream of exertion rent the harbour air as Emily hauled herself up and once again had her feet firmly on the ratlines. But likely weakened by her struggle, she stayed put and leaned her head against the security of the ropes. As all eyes were glued to her efforts, few witnessed Charlie's fall. It all happened so fast. He had been so close to the end of his race, but before anyone even realized he had gotten himself into trouble, he hit the deck with a ghastly thud. He lay there on his back at Trevelyan's feet, his limbs splayed unnaturally across the deck, blood trickling from his nose and right ear. His large eyes searched the concerned faces that closed in around him, as if looking for their approval, and his mouth went into spasm as if he were trying to speak. Leander knelt beside him and laid a hand on the lad's thin shoulder, knowing there was nothing he could do for him. Joe Norlan and Bun Brodie soon appeared and crouched down near the lad's head.

Charlie became agitated and hoarsely he cried out, "Miss ... Miss?"

Aware of Charlie's misfortune, Emily was slow in descending the ropes. Once down, she clambered off the shrouds and fell onto her knees beside the boy, her chest heaving with emotion and breathlessness. There was a crazed look in her brown eyes that moved feverishly over the boy's broken body. She was no more than three feet from Leander yet she had no idea he was so near; her concentration was exclusively with Charlie. His heart full of anguish, Leander silently watched her take one of Charlie's hands in hers, their clasped hands raw and blackened with tar from the ropes.

"You soundly beat me," she said.

Charlie's eyes brightened and a hint of a smile tugged at his mouth. But in a matter of seconds, his brow had furrowed. "I need ya to know ... I didn't shoot ya, Miss."

Emily smiled through her tears. "I know. I've long known." Charlie choked up blood, the sight of which caused her distress, though realizing he had more to communicate, she leaned over and put her ear to his trembling lips. "If yer ever in Salem, tell me Ma ... I was comin' up in the world."

"I will." Emily squeezed his hand. "For you, Charlie."

His spasms ceased, his face relaxed, and his eyes stared sightlessly up the foremast. Emily tugged the red kerchief from her neck, used it to gently wipe the blood from his face, then tucked it inside his torn shirt. Her head fell onto her heaving chest as a brooding silence descended upon the men who, seconds before, had been in a celebratory mood. Leander could hear questions shouted from the nearby ships, the cry of the seagulls as they circled the anchored *Serendipity*, and Emily's quiet sobs. The rain came again, a few drops at first, but soon falling steadily, dimpling the pool of Charlie's blood that crept slowly along the deck. The sailors dispersed, some returning to their posts, others seeking shelter below. Only a few remained: Joe, Bun Brodie, Meg Kettle, and three other young lads who were likely the dead boy's messmates. Leander sensed Trevelyan standing over them, and peered up to see the man gazing upon Charlie's body as he would a dead rat.

Unable to contain his smouldering anger, Leander lashed out. "This should *never* have happened."

Trevelyan regarded him coolly. "Yes. It's a pity the wrong climber fell."

Emily stirred and lifted her face; her haunted eyes instantaneously sought Leander's. She looked disoriented, as if she did not know where she was, or whether the moment was one in which to grieve or rejoice. Her head shook slightly as she stared at him in disbelief, her lips soundlessly forming questions. The rain mingled with her tears and caused loose tendrils of her hair to attach themselves to her crimson cheeks. A slight frown played on her forehead, then, gradually, a gleam of affection appeared in her eyes. Endeavouring to suppress his own strong emotions, knowing his features betrayed all, Leander longed to be rid of those who gaped down upon them in fascination.

Emily's glance stayed fixed to Leander's face, and when at last she spoke, her voice was scarcely a whisper. "I am so tired. Is—is this all a dream, then? Have you been right here with me, all this time?" She released Charlie's little hand and reached for Leander's, but Trevelyan, witnessing the gesture, stepped between them. His orders pierced the lament of the pouring rain. "Dr. Braden, remove this corpse and its debris from my deck."

Emily levelled a look of disdain at Trevelyan. A muscle worked in his scarred cheek as he reciprocated, his gaze equally as disdainful. "Mrs. Kettle, have your worthless washerwoman take down the laundry at once and hang it below."

Out at sea, thunder rumbled like distant guns in battle.

15

Thursday, June 24

10:00 a.m.
(Forenoon Watch, Four Bells)
Aboard the *Prosperous and Remarkable*

"MR. WALBY!" CRIED MAGPIE as he flew down the ladder and into the forepeak, holding his embroidered *Isabelle* hat to his head. "I got the best news for ya. Prosper wouldn't allow me to be sayin' anythin' afore now."

Gus was sitting up in his cot, reading a book that Pemberton Baker had found for him—a moth-eaten copy of Boswell's *Life of Johnson*. Seeing that Mr. Walby had been laughing, that his face was glowing with enjoyment, Magpie stopped in his tracks. "What's so comical?"

"Did you know, Magpie, that Dr. Samuel Johnson believed that being in a ship is like 'being in a jail, with the chance of being drowned,' and that 'a man in a jail has more room, better food, and commonly better company.'"

Magpie pursed his lips. "I don't like the part 'bout drownin' but I don't think I'd find better comp'ny in jail than what I got here, sir."

Gus gave his friend a warm smile. "The eye patch becomes you."

"Ya don't think I look like a pirate, do ya, sir? Like Captain Kidd or Blackbeard or one o' them fellows?"

"No, but you do look *dauntless*. I don't think many will take up a quarrel with you." Gus set down his book. "What's your news?"

"Since Prosper says yer doin' real good now, Pemberton's gonna take ya up on deck so's ya kin see fer yerself."

A pensive look crept into Gus's eyes. "Is the *Isabelle* sailing again?"

"She won't never sail again, sir. But this sight'll sure cheer a soul up."

Pemberton was as good as his word and soon arrived on the scene. With the help of Magpie, whose job it was to make certain Mr. Walby's splints didn't knock up against the ship's timber sides and cause the patient undue distress, he carried Gus up into the sunshine. At their posts, the Prosperous and Remarkables greeted Gus as he journeyed aft in Pemberton's strong arms to the taffrail where Prosper was waiting for them next to an elaborately carved ebony armchair and matching hassock. "Mr. Walby," he said with a flourish of his arms, "this is so's ya kin view thee world in comfort while on deck."

Once ensconced in his special chair, Gus, whose expression had been so full of joy from the moment he alighted into the warmth and brightness of the day, grew suddenly sombre, his face darkening like a rain cloud. Seeing a large ship a mile or two off their stern, its white sails obscuring any other identifying features, Gus stiffened. "That's not Trevelyan, is it?"

"Nay," said Prosper. "Trevelyan's still holed up in thee harbour, quakin' in his boots 'cause he knows ole Prosper's waitin' on him. We bin circlin' that one out there fer a few days now."

"Is it a merchantman that you're aiming to board?" Gus asked, uncertainty in his voice.

Prosper chuckled. "Nay! We're gonna save our resources fer *thee* prize, though it be killin' me men. There be plenty o' merchantmen comin' from thee harbour and no one ta stop 'em."

Magpie's eye rounded in excitement as he handed Gus the spyglass he had found abandoned on the *Isabelle*'s deck that final day. "Squint through the glass, sir. What d'ya see?" As Gus's arms were encumbered with splints, Magpie held up the glass for him.

"Why, it's the *Amethyst*!" Gus stared at Magpie. "Why didn't you tell me this before?"

"We weren't certain 'til this mornin', sir," said Magpie, beaming. "When she run up her colours, we knew she were British, but vis'bility's bin poor with all o' the rain, and she made sure she kept her distance from us 'cause Prosper refused to make it known what he was about. Besides, Mr. Walby, yer the one with the keen eyes. Yer the one what woulda known fer sure."

"What do you suppose she's doing down here?" asked Gus, peering again through the glass.

"On blockade duty, most like," suggested Prosper.

"She's bin goin' out to sea for thee past two days to shoot off her guns," added Pemberton.

"I like to think she's come lookin' fer us, sir," answered Magpie in a small voice.

Prosper and Pemberton howled with laughter. "There won't be no one lookin' fer thee likes o' yas. Far's anyone kin tell, yer inside Jonah's whale."

Magpie grimaced, not liking that image of his presumed departure.

Prosper rested one hand on Gus's shoulder. "Rest here fer a spell. We'll fetch yas fer dinner. And then both o' yas kin mess with me."

Gus waited until Prosper and Pemberton had wandered out of earshot. "Does that mean I get to meet his band of ruffians?"

Magpie nodded. "Aye! They're a frightful lot, but ya'll fit right in, sir, with yer busted limbs and all."

Gus watched the *Amethyst* in silence for several minutes. "Magpie, are you thinking what I'm thinking?"

"Likely, sir."

Gus peered up at his friend. "Do we *dare* think it—do we *dare* hope …"

"… there be Isabelles on board?" Magpie finished.

6:30 p.m.
(Second Dog Watch, One Bell)
Aboard the USS *Serendipity*

ANGRY VOICES ROUSED EMILY from her rest. As she shuddered awake, Jane Austen's book slipped from her lap. Reading had become her only means of distraction, but the fresh sorrows of the past two days had left her as spent as a shipwreck, and now, as never before, sleep came so easily. Leaving her cot quietly so as not to disturb the slumbering Mrs. Kettle, who required rest before tackling her twilight recreation, Emily put her ear to the flimsy wall of mounted canvas that separated her space from Trevelyan's quarters, hoping to follow the conversation, or at the very least, identify who was arguing with the captain. Regrettably, she could hear nothing more than the angry intonation and inflection of the words being spoken. Mrs. Kettle's rum-induced snores were enough to rattle the ship's timbers. Her ear was still to the wall when Trevelyan himself came to fetch her.

"Dress yourself appropriately, madam, and be in my cabin in five minutes."

"For what purpose, sir?" asked Emily, clutching her chest from the shock of his sudden appearance at her door.

He gave her a humourless smile. "Why, for a glass of wine and some conviviality, of course."

She quickly changed into a roughly woven earth-coloured dress from Charlie's collection of castoffs, and overlaid it with Leander's coat. Upon entering Trevelyan's cabin, her heart endured another shock, for standing by the stern windows, staring out upon the harbour that glittered in the waning sunshine, was Leander. Hearing her step, he glanced round expectantly. His face was suffused with colour, likely the result of his heated words with Trevelyan, but the stony expression in his eyes softened the moment they beheld her. Emily felt her own face flush and stood there like an awkward schoolgirl at a country ball, aware that Trevelyan was closely watching their behaviour as he poured claret into three glasses.

"Drink up, madam," he said, handing Emily her refreshment. "You have a moribund look about you." He turned to Leander. "As for you, Doctor, you must drink to forget those things you *cannot* change." Lifting his own glass to his lips, Trevelyan planted his feet and allowed his eyes to travel freely over Emily. "You amaze me, for the day is exceedingly warm, yet you insist on wearing that frock coat."

"It gives me great comfort, sir," she said, meeting Leander's eyes. An endearing smile played upon the doctor's lips, but all too soon he returned his gaze to the harbour, leaving Emily overcome with sadness. For days she had prayed that his life had been spared the sinking of Captain Moreland's ship. Discovering him here, so close, had filled her exhausted heart with joy, but since that time there had been no opportunity for them to speak alone. Now it seemed as if those precious weeks on board the *Isabelle* had never taken place. Leander was still far away—on one of those distant ships that sailed on the cloudless blue horizon beyond the windows—and all that remained to torment her was a ghostly shadow.

Trevelyan interjected her forlorn thoughts with a snort. "*I* will choose what you wear tomorrow."

Wresting her eyes from Leander, she gave Trevelyan an empty glance. "Why is that, sir?"

"I shall not *marry* you wearing another man's frock coat."

A contemptuous laugh burst from Emily's lips. "I shall not *marry* you at all. I *loathe* you."

"Seeing that our feelings are mutual, we should get on quite well."

"I would prefer to be flogged with a cat o'nine tails, sir."

"I shall arrange it for you, madam ... with pleasure." Trevelyan helped himself to a plum from a bowl of fruit on his table and sank his teeth into it. "I have brought with me a Mr. Humphreys from town. He hopes to travel with us as far as Boston. In exchange for his passage, he has agreed to conduct the ceremony."

"Sir, I have no intention of marrying you. You do not interest me."

"It may surprise you, madam, that beyond your family connections, I have *no* interest in you."

Emily's retort was swift. "It does not surprise me at all, especially as you keep Mrs. Kettle and ... Mr. *Lindsay* ... so close to your side."

Leander had turned from the windows to watch her, his hand in a fist before his mouth. Emily's hand shook as she raised her glass to her lips, fully expecting to feel the back of Trevelyan's hand cut across her face; instead, he finished eating his plum and examined her as he would the bilge water in his hold.

"There is no impediment that I know of. You are not married, though you travelled on the *Amelia* under the guise of Mrs. Seaton."

Emily sniffed at him and lifted her chin. "But, sir, you have not posted the banns."

"That will not be necessary."

"I am not twenty-one."

"Your parents are deceased. You have no guardian on this side of the world, and I have already secured what I need to make it legally binding." Trevelyan raised one eyebrow. "You're not betrothed to an indulgent prince from the Continent now, are you?"

"I am not," was her terse reply.

Trevelyan's eyes wandered in Leander's direction. "Or, perhaps, to an inferior ship's surgeon?"

Emily could not bear the look that had crept into Leander's eyes. "No, sir."

"Good! For that might distress poor old Queen Charlotte, the Prince Regent, and your miscellany of uncles."

"I can assure you their distress would be far greater if I were to marry a fiendish captain from an enemy fleet."

"Oh, I think they shall be quite pleased with the arrangement. You see, madam, although you may be unaware of it, I am well connected, almost as well as you are. And as I am my *English* father's rightful heir, I intend to return to London to collect my fortune—one way or another—with you as my wife."

Emily rounded on him. "If you are who you say you are, sir, it bewilders me that your behaviour towards your *countrymen* has been anything but exemplary. It bewilders me that you are commanding an American ship and not an *English* one. Furthermore, as we are totally unsuited for one another, I am quite puzzled that you should *require* a granddaughter of the King as your wife."

Trevelyan walked over to his desk. Still there was nothing more upon its polished surface than the two miniatures. He picked up the one of the young sandy-haired lad, and smoothed the gold of the frame around the boy's smiling face with his fingers, quite as if he had forgotten that he was not alone. When he had replaced it again, he muttered, "I *shall* require it."

So profound was the silence that fell upon the great cabin that Emily jumped when a sudden knock sounded at the door. A breathless young messenger appeared, asking for Leander.

"Beg yer pardon, sir, Dr. Braden's needed below in the surgery."

Emily turned her head to find Leander's eyes fixed upon the miniature of Emeline Louisa. As he slowly set down his glass, she saw his lips part and heard him take a deep breath. Then he looked at her, as if for the last time.

"If you have something more to say, Doctor," intercepted Trevelyan, "make it fast and be on your way."

With all the composure he could muster, Leander replied, "I thank you for the wine, sir, and for the wisdom of your *counsel*."

The door closed quickly behind him. Emily's dark eyes flashed at Trevelyan. "Your *counsel*?"

Ignoring her, Trevelyan seated himself at his table. "The moment the winds and tides are in our favour, we will leave this place, and tomorrow Mr. Humphreys shall marry us."

"You forget, sir, you do not have *my* consent," snapped Emily.

"Madam, should you choose to be difficult, I shall deliver your *compatriots* to officials in the Navy Department."

"My compatriots?" Emily hesitated a moment, unsure of what he meant. "You are welcome to hand Mrs. Kettle and Octavius Lindsay over to your *officials*. They deserve to rot in prison."

"I refer to your Isabelles that sit in my gaol."

Emily's mind raced. Was he telling her the truth? She had seen Bun

Brodie. Was it possible there were others? Were Gus and Magpie—those two dear souls—languishing in the *Serendipity*'s filthy hold?

Pouncing upon her uncertainty, Trevelyan added, "And of course there is your *esteemed* Doctor."

Emily's wavering confidence drained away. "But you—you require Dr. Braden's services on your ship."

"I will do what I must to get my way."

Feeling the sting of tears, Emily was slow to reply. "Sir, I cannot pretend to understand the nature of your former crimes against your country; however, my guess is your more recent traitorous offences, namely those against the *Amelia* and *Isabelle*, will cost you dearly. I doubt you will ever be allowed to set foot again in England."

Trevelyan poured himself another glass of wine, leaned forward over his table, and clasped his hands under his chin. "Then, madam, neither will you."

16

Friday, June 25

6:30 a.m.
(Morning Watch, Five Bells)
Aboard HMS *Amethyst*

THE EARLY MORNING MISTS were beginning to recede around the *Amethyst* as she stood out to sea under her topgallants. Near the bowsprit, Fly Austen was captivated with the shimmering orb of orange on the eastern horizon as he searched all round, looking for that elusive ship with the blood-red hull. At this hour, there was no sign of it. Captain Prickett and Lieutenant Bridlington, who were keeping him company on his watch, were more captivated with their bowls of cold fish soup, recently delivered to them by a cantankerous Biscuit.

"I would have preferred hot soup, Mr. Austen, but already the day is a warm one," said Pickett, beads of sweat dripping down his cheeks as he downed spoonfuls of the brown, oily stuff.

Put off by the smell of both Prickett and his breakfast, Fly wheeled about to face the harbour where, despite the distance, he could see a few sails beginning to stir. "At least there is relief in the winds, sir. Perhaps they bode well for a sea battle."

Bridlington looked alarmed.

Prickett nodded in agreement. "Tell us your thoughts, Mr. Austen?"

"Now that we have had it confirmed that Trevelyan does indeed lie anchored beyond, I question the wisdom in further delay."

"But, Mr. Austen," said Bridlington, "this suggestion of yours—to issue him a challenge—is a disquieting one. The *Amethyst* is a ship of seventy-four guns. Trevelyan's frigate boasts no more than thirty-six. It would be dishonourable to challenge a ship with inferior gun power."

Fly had to stifle his impatience with the first lieutenant; they had already discussed the subject at length last evening in the wardroom. "Mr. Bridlington, of course you are aware that when it comes to single-ship action, much has to be taken into consideration, beyond the gun power of the opposing ships. The *Serendipity* is a much younger ship, she is well manned, her crews are well drilled, and her sailing ability is far superior to ours." Fly compressed his lips. "Moreover, her captain is foolhardy and would undoubtedly be the first to issue a challenge if he had an inkling who was watching him."

Bridlington sought Prickett for help. "Sir, we are not ready for this."

Prickett hiked up his breeches. "No one is ever prepared to be shot to pieces. Toughen up and resist being a milksop."

Bridlington reddened and looked offended, but neither Fly nor Prickett paid him heed, for at that precise moment energized voices pierced the calm morning air.

"Sail, ho! Sail, ho!"

"That ain't no fishin' boat."

"For certain that's a frigate."

Fly peered up at the masthead. To his pleasant surprise, sitting astride the foreyard, helping to make repairs to the stirrups, was the ubiquitous Morgan Evans. Catching his attention, Fly called out, "Is it him, Mr. Evans?"

"It's him all right, sir."

Fly tossed the sulking first lieutenant a smile. "Well, now that our plans for a challenge have been thwarted, let us see how well the *Amethyst* handles herself in a chase."

Bridlington's eyes were frozen in fear, but Prickett threw away his soup bowl and launched into action. He stomped around the quarterdeck with his hands on his heavy hips, barking orders that sounded as if his guns were already firing. "All hands aloft. Make sail, lads, and be sure to chain those yards. Where's the bo's'n? Wake the sleepers, man! You there, see to the netting. There'll be no Yankees boarding my ship today. Pass the word for Biscuit. We must all be fed before clearing the decks for action." Fly watched in amusement as the stocky captain administered every direction, so unlike the smooth chain of command that had been prevalent on Captain Moreland's ship.

The *Isabelle.*

Though he would never admit it to Bridlington, Fly felt his own fears, his own anxiety, and for reassurance, reached into his coat pocket to touch James's letter. Prickett soon rejoined him at the bowsprit, as his voice was now quite spent. "Tell me, Mr. Austen," he said hoarsely, trying to assume a bold stance, "*are* we ready?"

Fly's thoughtful gaze scoured the decks and masts of the *Amethyst*. Though the scurry of activity was anything but organized, there was a contagious buzz of excitement in the air. "Not at all, sir, but our men—they are extraordinarily exuberant."

10:00 a.m.
(Forenoon Watch, Four Bells)
Aboard the USS *Serendipity*

EMILY LEANED OUT OF THE GUNPORT as far as she could. The ship was astir; something was about, and she was determined to find out what. Unable to sleep past dawn, she had witnessed the rising sun, Mrs. Kettle's grumbling early departure from their cabin, and the *Serendipity*'s progress as it slipped out of the harbour and blithely glided past a sleepy British sloop that was lying to near Sullivan's Island. Now, however, the sailors all seemed to move with quickened steps and there was more talk than normal, though Emily could not make out the significance in their shouted words. With a sarcastic shake of her head, she wondered if all the fuss was in honour of her upcoming *nuptials*, or if indeed there was a looming threat. From her vantage point, she could tell they were sailing in a northeasterly direction, but the sea was empty. If something was following in the *Serendipity*'s wake, she could not see it. Her mind's eye envisioned a fleet of twelve ships coming for her, the *Isabelle* leading the way, and Captain Moreland standing fearlessly above her bow waves, intent on rescuing his friends and having his revenge. But even her imagination could not create a perfect image, for she knew that, if cornered, Trevelyan would not surrender without bloodshed.

The cabin door opened and closed. Wheeling about, she found Meg Kettle with the breakfast tray. The laundress set the food down upon the wooden stool and slipped out the door again. When she returned the second time, she was carrying what looked like an elegant dress box. "Aren't ye a lucky one," she snarled.

"And why is that?" Emily said, her voice flat.

Mrs. Kettle blew a strand of greying hair out of her eyes, then eagerly lifted the lid from the box as if she were opening a Christmas gift addressed to her. She pulled out a crisp new chemise and a dress of fine white cotton with satin embroidery, and held them up for inspection. "Cap'n Trevelyan picked 'em out hisself in Charleston."

Emily glanced indifferently at the dress. "And that makes me lucky?"

Mrs. Kettle returned the clothing to the box with such tender care one would think she was restoring baby birds to their nest. She then placed her hands on her hips and scowled at Emily. "It's more than ye deserve, I say. And look! See what he ordered up fer yer breakfast."

Emily looked over the tray laden with sweet rolls, butter, strawberry preserves, cold ham, spiced nuts, cream, and steaming coffee. This morning she would have preferred her usual ration of tea and gruel. "I marvel at Trevelyan's *gifts* to me at this late hour," she said. Wandering over to the tray, she picked up the mug of coffee, then returned and sat upon the cannon carriage. "The feast is all yours, Mrs. Kettle. I have no appetite for it."

Without hesitation, the older woman stuffed a sweet roll into her mouth, grabbed a handful of spiced nuts, and stood back to scrutinize Emily with her little eyes. "Savin' yer *appetite* fer other things, are ye then?"

Emily glanced away, her ears alerted to the increasing commotion beyond the cabin walls. But Mrs. Kettle resumed her heckling. "Look at ya, sittin' there, full o' self-pity."

"Self-pity? You are quite mistaken, Mrs. Kettle. As I am the *luckiest* of women alive, my temperament can only be interpreted as a testament to my immense disappointment that I will *not* be wed in the garden of a Charleston mansion, nor will I be able to wear magnolias in my hair, and eat an iced layer cake."

The laundress watched Emily closely, squinting now and again as she crunched on her spiced nuts. "Bet yer face would be all smiles if ya was marryin' thee doctor."

Emily wilted. Unable to summon enough energy to reply, she gazed out the open port at the small wave-like clouds that drifted by, and kept her painful thoughts to herself.

"Thee poor doctor! So melancholy is he. Why, just now it was, I passed him by, comin' out o' thee cap'n's cabin," said Mrs. Kettle. "He were movin' real slow, like a man about to face thee gallows."

Though she longed to hear something—anything—of Leander, Emily sat there silently, refusing to be drawn out.

Mrs. Kettle spit into the cabin's corner. "Yer nothin' but an ingrate! Ya bin indulged yer whole life. Why, I would give away me unborn child to be marryin' thee likes o' Cap'n Trevelyan."

"Keep your child, Mrs. Kettle, and take Trevelyan," said Emily quietly, turning from the open port to face her. "You are welcome to him."

Mrs. Kettle stopped chewing, and gaped at her.

A sharp knock rattled the cabin door, mobilizing Mrs. Kettle into action. She snatched another roll and cried, "That's it! Ya gotta hurry! Thee cap'n's waitin' on ya."

"Waiting? Wh—what? Now?"

"He wants thee weddin' over, just in case yonder ship gets too close and he's gotta clear thee deck."

Emily's heart accelerated. "What ship?"

"Thee one behind us wavin' all manner of British flags and unfurlin' her full complement o' sails."

Emily flew to the gunport.

"If ya don't git yer dress on, I'll give ya a good wallop," said Mrs. Kettle, as if speaking to a child.

"Where is the ship? I cannot see it. How close is it?"

When Emily refused to budge from the gunport, Mrs. Kettle stormed towards her and started pulling at her shirt. "Looks like I'll be dressin' ya meself."

Emily pushed her away. "Leave me be! I *shall* not wear Trevelyan's gift."

"Ya foolish wench, ya can't git married in yer trousers."

"I can! I will!" Emily turned away to conceal her tears and scanned the horizons, standing on tiptoes to lean farther out the port. There! There it was! She could see a crescent of its billowing white sails against the serene blue sky. Her hands tingled with nervous excitement. If only she could tell Leander. But then, if he had just come from next door, perhaps he already knew. So preoccupied was Emily watching the ship's progress that she forgot about the laundress. Investigating her whereabouts, she found the cabin door ajar and Mrs. Kettle standing next to it, holding her silver-buckled shoes, Jane Austen's books, and Leander's frock coat in her fat arms. There was a spiteful gleam in her small eyes.

"Git into yer dress ... now."

A sick, sinking feeling shook Emily to the core. "Only if you return ... what is mine," came her faltering reply.

There was a shuffling sound beyond the door and Trevelyan's tall figure came into view. His eyes peered through the crack and latched onto Emily's frightened ones. Mrs. Kettle shook her head and let out a long, low cackle of laughter.

11:00 a.m.
(Forenoon Watch, Six Bells)
Aboard the *Prosperous and Remarkable*

GUS LISTENED. There was a great deal of bumping and banging, scraping and scurrying going on above his head. Prosper's men all seemed to be moving around the weather decks with single-minded strides; Gus could hear them grunting and swearing at one another as they laboured. What he wouldn't give to know what was about. But Magpie had been gone since breakfast and the wait for his return seemed like forever. The heat of the morning was making him sweat like the damp timber walls, and his wool blanket made his legs itchy. He cursed aloud the splints that supported his broken body. In his short life, he had never had to spend so many endless empty days in bed. If only his cot rested beside a gunport as Emily's had on the *Isabelle*. If only he could sit in his special chair near the taffrail to catch the sea breezes and vicariously take part in all ship activity. If only someone would stop by for a visit or read to him to help pass the hours—well, anyone with the exception of Prosper's fearsome messmates. Having become acquainted with them yesterday, Gus not only doubted the Prosperous and Remarkables knew their letters, he wasn't certain he really desired their company.

At last Magpie appeared, wearing his *Isabelle* hat and twitching like a bundle of nerves. Gus pounced on him. "What have you been doing all this time?'

"Mendin' sails, sir," he said breathlessly. "There's piles o' them what needs mendin'."

"What news of the *Amethyst*? Is Prosper planning to communicate with her today?"

Magpie dropped down onto the nearest stool. "Oh, Mr. Walby, we're not sailin' near Charleston no more."

Gus's disappointment was severe. "Where are we, then?"

"In a big, empty cove, sir, beside a bit o' marshy coast."

"That's not very helpful, Magpie."

"I tried askin' Prosper, sir, but he's in a foul mood this mornin'. He's struttin' round the deck, peerin' through his spyglass, mumblin' 'bout missed opportunities and the storm what's comin'."

"Storm? At breakfast you said there were blue skies."

"Aye, but the winds are pickin' up and there be some ugly-lookin' clouds about."

Gus sighed. "I guess I won't be allowed up on deck this afternoon?"

"Yer chair's been cleared away along with the livestock pens, 'cause the men—they're stackin' their muskets and cannon balls."

"Have we sighted an enemy ship?" The words were scarcely out of his mouth when he heard the men begin their task of taking down the gun deck walls. Their audible chatter left him in no doubt: they were clearing for battle. Magpie and he were staring transfixed at the bustle beyond their cots when Pemberton lumbered down the ladder.

"C'mon now, Gus. I'm takin' ya below, 'neath thee waterline with yas."

"What about Magpie?" cried Gus, as Pemberton plucked him from his cot.

"Magpie's got some fightin' to do, and if we form a boardin' party, Prosper wants him coverin' his back. You whisht now and don't worry none 'bout him."

As Pemberton, with Gus in his arms, hurried towards the ladder to the lower deck, Gus glanced uneasily back at his friend, only to see that beneath his *Isabelle* hat and eye patch, his little face had gone green.

11:00 a.m.

Aboard HMS *Amethyst*

"EVEN IF WE WERE TO SEND our shirts and linens aloft, we wouldn't have a chance in hell of catching up to him," said a disheartened Fly to Captain Prickett and his senior officers as they all rallied beneath the *Amethyst*'s foremast. "Unless, of course, we dump every one of our guns and cannons into the sea."

"We *can't* do that, Mr. Austen," protested Lieutenant Bridlington.

"It was only said in jest, Mr. Bridlington." Fly looked at each of the officers in turn. "At the very least, we should continue following him. I believe we will have our chance—perhaps just not here, not today."

"If we *were* to catch up to him, Mr. Austen," Prickett said, puffing out his uniformed chest, as if trying to appear taller, "what *would* you do?"

Fly studied the gathering grey-blue clouds overhead and thought of the dear friends Trevelyan had on board. "I would like to blow him out of the water with our countless guns, but I cannot. We *must* take care. The trick is to simply disable him and hope that nature does not finish him off."

11:30 a.m.

(Forenoon Watch, Seven Bells)

Aboard the USS *Serendipity*

THE RISING WINDS wrapped Emily's wedding dress around her legs and carried her unbound hair in all directions as she stood trembling behind Trevelyan at the *Serendipity*'s wheel. The sailors on their yards, as well as those hanging from the rigging and clustered around their guns, openly gaped at her—they all knew of the ceremony that had just taken place in the great cabin. But she no longer cared about their curiosity or what thoughts might be racing through their heads. At her back stood the ever-present Meg Kettle, still cradling Emily's treasures in her arms like a newborn babe. She could feel the older woman's eyes boring into the back of her head, and hear her muttering obscenities, but she would not acknowledge her presence. Trevelyan stood before her, engrossed in discussions with his sailing master, the coxswain, and Octavius Lindsay, the latter of whom frequently threw pompous airs her way. Feeling as if she had been bled dry, Emily kept her face averted from them all and her eyes locked on the sails of the British ship that followed, still too far off for its cannon fire to find its mark.

"We was sailin' close to the wind, sir," said the coxswain, "but the winds are shiftin', comin' from the east now."

Trevelyan gazed upon his majestic masts. "Then the sails must be set accordingly. How far have we come from Charleston?"

"About twenty miles, sir," replied the sailing master.

"And what is our present speed?

"Last reading was five knots, sir."

Trevelyan ran his scarred hand over his mouth as he observed the trailing shadow on the sea. "Keep up all sails, all squares, fore and aft, including the royals, until I tell you otherwise."

"Do you not think we should put further to sea, sir?" asked Mr. Lindsay.

"No," said Trevelyan. "I wish to sail close to shore."

"But, sir, if these winds strengthen," said the sailing master, a note of concern in his tone, "that may be dangerous. These parts are full of shoals and unpredictable currents."

"I will consider it when the storm breaks and our visibility is diminished. In the meantime, take frequent soundings. Toss the lead every fifteen minutes and check the nature of the sea bottom with the charts."

"Why all this concern over winds and shoals and currents?" It was Emily who spoke out. The sailing master and Mr. Lindsay scowled at her impudence; Trevelyan, on the other hand, seemed intrigued. He folded his arms across his chest and set his chin, waiting for her to continue.

Emily plucked the wild strands of her hair from her eyes. "I do not understand why you don't simply stand and face the enemy that follows you."

"Because I have *other* business that concerns me," said Trevelyan, "and have no interest in wasting time and grapeshot."

"As you have no reinforcements at your side, are you afraid of losing this time?"

The sailing master and the coxswain exchanged looks; Trevelyan spoke calmly as ever. "Hardly."

Emily tossed her head. "Have you forgotten we're in the midst of a war? Heading north, your chances of running into another British ship will only increase."

Trevelyan's jaw worked for a time before he answered her. "So will my chances of sighting more American ships." He swung around fully to face her straight on. "Would you reconsider your eagerness to engage that British vessel if you knew who it was standing beneath its foremast?"

Recalling her own fanciful daydream about Captain Moreland, Emily was thrown off guard. "Sir?"

But Trevelyan would not enlighten her. He nodded at Mr. Lindsay. "And as you met with no success in tracking down that little *mongrel*, I will wager *he* is most likely standing alongside."

By now Emily had lost the thread of the conversation. Unable to provide a rejoinder, she stayed silent and suffered the snickers behind her.

Trevelyan waved his finger at Mrs. Kettle. "You there! Take madam below. The slop room or one of the storerooms should suffice."

Should the guns start firing, Emily could not bear being below in the darkness. "No!" she cried out. "Let me stay here."

Trevelyan gave her a thorough looking over. "In that white dress against these darkening skies, you will be a sitting duck. I cannot afford to have you strewn about in messy pieces upon my quarter-deck, especially not on my *wedding* night."

The men within earshot enjoyed a hearty laugh at Emily's expense. Mrs. Kettle appeared at her elbow, chuckling away. "C'mon then—*Mrs. Trevelyan.*"

The laundress might as well have shot a pistol off at Emily's ear as address her by that name. In desperation, she pleaded, "Please, sir, please don't send me below. I promise—I will stay out of your way."

Trevelyan remained unmoved. "Take her away, Mrs. Kettle. But before you go, relieve your arms of that *rubbish.*"

Thrilled to be the centre of attention, Mrs. Kettle pranced to the larboard rail where, with obvious pleasure, she scattered Emily's possessions into the winds. In a matter of seconds, the buckled shoes and beloved books were lost, swallowed by the swirling waves. Leander's frock coat was more defiant. It was carried by the winds and sailed high, reaching the heights of the topgallants, before descending in a slow dance to the sea. Watching it, Emily went numb. But there was no time to grieve.

"Larboard bow, ahoy!" came the cutting cry from a topman on the mainmast.

"Sail in sight!"

"Looks like a privateer."

"And carryin' British pennants and colours."

Any vestiges of amusement instantly evaporated from Trevelyan's face. He swore and seized Mr. Lindsay's spyglass to study this second ship that had appeared out of nowhere. "Where the *devil* did he come from?"

"A concealed cove maybe, sir?" offered the coxswain. His face, turned towards the shoreline, was frozen in alarm.

"I daresay he was waiting for us," said the sailing master quietly.

Giving no further thought to his new wife, Trevelyan sprang into action, roaring orders at his attending men as he criss-crossed the weather decks. Struggling to keep up to him was an ashen-faced Mr.

Lindsay, tugging on the stand-up collar of his borrowed uniform coat.

Mrs. Kettle pinched Emily's forearm and forced her towards the ladder. As they descended to the ship's bottom, the first crack of cannonfire echoed around them.

Noon
(Forenoon Watch, Eight Bells)
Aboard the *Prosperous and Remarkable*

ON THE FOAMING WAVES, the *Serendipity* loomed like a white whale over the *Prosperous and Remarkable*, a mere bouncing dolphin in comparison. Magpie could not fathom how Prosper imagined he could bring down Trevelyan's mighty ship, but already he'd sent off a warning shot that he meant business. The winds were causing problems, and the rains, though nothing more than a drizzle, had made their unwelcome appearance. Prosper had told Magpie that in order to manoeuvre around the *Serendipity*, they couldn't go straight at her; they would have to sail south, close-hauled, and come up behind her or risk being battered upon the lee shore. Magpie didn't like the sound of this and wished he were on that big ship in the distance—the one flying British colours from her mastheads; the one Prosper speculated was the *Amethyst*.

Like a puppy, Magpie followed Prosper around, uneasily carrying the two dirks with the portentous eighteen-inch blades that Pemberton had given him as if they were hissing hand grenades. As always, he was unsettled by the red and purple veins that popped up on Prosper's balding head as he spit out instructions like tobacco juice.

"Pemberton, ya jackanapes, take thee wheel from this lubber. Mr. Dunkin, ya scoundrel, see ta them gallants. Reef 'em up or else we'll soon be findin' ourselves sittin' broadside ta thee Atlantic." Prosper gave Magpie a backwards glance. "Keep up, lad. When we board, ya can't go wandrin' off. And sheath those cursed blades, will ya. I don't fancy one o' 'em stickin' into me backend."

Magpie did as he was told, then hurried to catch up to Prosper, who was disappearing down the ladder to the gun deck. "How many guns do ya 'ave, Prosper?" he asked breathlessly.

"Fourteen, twenty-four-pounders!" exclaimed Prosper proudly.

"And how many men?"

"Fifty-five, includin' you and Gus."

"And how many tons is the *Prosperous and Remarkable*?"

"'Bout one hundred, give or take a ton. Now stop annoyin' me with all o' yer nonsense."

Magpie's eye was as round and bright as a silver crown. "But the *Serendipity*'s gotta be seven times that."

Prosper stopped abruptly beside the galley stove, stooped over Magpie, and with all the confidence in the world, whispered, "Just watch me go. I'll show ya how it's done." He straightened himself, shoved his soiled shirtsleeves up his tanned arms, and hollered at his men, who were circling around their guns, waiting. "Right, then, ya bunch o' puddin' heads, I'm gonna take thee wheel and bring yas up behind Trevelyan. Thee first chance ya git, blow his rudder ta hell."

Noon

Aboard the USS *Serendipity*

THE INSTANT MRS. KETTLE had shut the slop room door and suspended her lantern from the low ceiling, Emily's heart began pounding in her ears. Fighting to control her mounting panic, she searched her new cage. It smelled heavily of salt and tar, and its slimy walls were covered with makeshift shelving, all crammed with clothing for the sailors. Emily jumped when something warm brushed past her ankle. Whatever it was scuttled away from her into the murky regions beyond the lantern's glow. Unable to stand still, and desiring to be as far away as possible from Mrs. Kettle, Emily unhooked the lantern and carried it with her to the farthest end of the rectangular room.

"What're ya doin'?" demanded the laundress, who hovered uncertainly near the door.

Emily ignored her inquiry and wrested a pair of dungaree trousers and a stripy, open-collared shirt from the shelf labelled "Boys," then cast about until she spotted a neatly folded stack of neckcloths, selecting a black one for herself.

"*Those* be reserved fer funerals," said Mrs. Kettle tartly.

"Then it is most appropriate, for *I* am in mourning." Emily set the lantern down on a shelf and quickly stripped down to her chemise, leaving her wedding dress in a disarray of ghostly white at her feet. She wiggled into the shirt and trousers, and loosely knotted the black neckcloth around her shoulders. With a ceremonious flourish, she picked the wedding dress up off the sodden floor and hurled it at Mrs. Kettle with as much vehemence and zeal as the laundress had hurled her possessions overboard. When it landed on the woman's surprised face, Emily broke into a fit of laughter. "A gift for you, Mrs. Kettle, since you *so* admired it."

Mrs. Kettle clawed at the dress as if it were a substantial spider web, and—once revealed—her fat face flared with anger. "Cap'n Trevelyan don't fancy ya wearin' sailors' trousers," she growled. "Git yer dress back on. I'm to deliver ya, thee way I took ya."

Emily snatched a heap of clothes from the shelf at her back and angled her head in challenge. One by one, she flung an assortment of footwear, vests, jackets, and trousers at Mrs. Kettle, who howled in protest as if being bombarded with musket balls. It was an agreeable distraction for Emily until the heel of a shoe struck Mrs. Kettle's forehead and the woman exploded. "Ya wanton witch!" Hiking up her coarse skirts, she bowed her head and charged at Emily like a steaming, snorting bull in a ring. Fortunately, Emily was far swifter in her movements and leaped out of the way in time, leaving the beast to collide heavily with a portion of shelving, dislodging it completely from the walls. Down it came, striking Mrs. Kettle with a hefty thump upon her hunched back and pinning her to the floor.

Emily laughed, barely able to breathe. "Oh, Mrs.—Mrs. Kettle, if only Trevelyan knew that his deadliest weapon was here in the slop room. If only he could ramrod you into his cannons, imagine the damage you could deliver to the hulls of enemy ships."

For several moments, Mrs. Kettle lay there stunned. Then her caterwauling began. "Oooo! Now ya done it, now ya *really* done it. Me back. Me head. Me poor babe. All broke fer sure. Oooo!"

Brushing away her mirthful tears, Emily sidestepped the prostrate form and made for the door. "Are you bleeding, Mrs. Kettle?"

"How's would I know with me face pasted to thee floor?"

"At least we know your tongue is still intact… Tell me where I can find Dr. Braden."

Above their heads on the upper deck, voices yelled out, "Stand clear! Steady now! Fire! Fire!" The *Serendipity*'s guns boomed and recoiled violently on their carriages, the reverberating shudders passing through Emily, who had to reach out to steady herself against a shelf.

Mrs. Kettle's shrill voice shot up an octave. "If ya leave me here, squashed like a decayin' rodent, so help me I'll kill ya. I'll rip yer royal head from that white neck o' yers. Thee minute I'm standin', I will."

"Don't tempt me," Emily shot back. "You deserve no better than to be left here to fester and rot."

The penetrating cries that followed were more dreadful than the blaring echoes of cannonfire. Emily repeated her question, this time more firmly. "*Where* is Dr. Braden?"

Mrs. Kettle's reply rushed out of her mouth like a swift-moving stream. "Ya'll—ya'll find 'im nearby. Thee door ain't locked. But leave thee lantern be! I'll—I'll not be left here in thee gloom with hairy creatures crawlin' 'bout me parts."

2:00 p.m.
(Afternoon Watch, Four Bells)
Aboard HMS *Amethyst*

FLY AUSTEN READIED HIMSELF to climb down the ladder to the waiting launch that bobbed vigorously in the waves alongside the *Amethyst*'s hull. The ship's two pinnaces and three cutters had already set out towards the rudderless *Serendipity*, full of jubilant men still hoping for a true crack at the enemy. Behind Fly, Captain Prickett and First Lieutenant Bridlington strutted about the quarterdeck, as if *they* had been solely responsible for paralyzing the American ship.

"I cannot believe our good fortune, Mr. Austen," cried Bridlington. "Not only did we barely fire a shot, barely was a shot returned. The commander of that small brig—whoever he may be—is *truly* remarkable."

"I've never seen such fine seamanship, the way he came up on Trevelyan's tail like that," exclaimed Captain Prickett. "Root the man out, will you, Mr. Austen? I'd like to meet the fellow and have Biscuit fix him a celebratory feast with all his favourites—and mine, of course."

"I will, sir. But we must hurry. In a matter of minutes they will be attempting to board the *Serendipity*."

Captain Prickett did not seem concerned in the least. "One false move from Trevelyan," he laughed, "and he'll receive another blast from us. This time we'll bring down his mainmast!"

Fly started down the ladder, feeling the pain of his injured back as he gripped each rung. Captain Prickett peered over the rail. "We must claim her a prize, Mr. Austen. Raise the English ensign over hers, and sail her into Bermuda, nay, better still, into Halifax. Well-wishers will be greater in number there."

Fly was too tired to inform Prickett that the prize was not theirs to take; he had more pressing matters on his mind. Once settled in the launch, he laid his hand lightly on the shoulder of Morgan Evans who, at his request, was manning one of the oars. "Mr. Evans."

Morgan's mouth was pressed into a thin, grim line. "Aye, sir?"

"Let us away, for we have friends to find." As Fly turned his face towards the *Serendipity*, he noticed Biscuit sitting there, his odd eye rolling about in his head. "Captain Prickett will not be pleased when he discovers you've abandoned his ship and his galley."

"I'm comin' with yas, Mr. Austen," said Biscuit. "Anyone what tries to harm thee lass will be feelin' thee point o' me cutlass between their shoulder blades."

2:30 p.m.
(Afternoon Watch, Five Bells)
Aboard the *Prosperous and Remarkable*

THERE WAS A TREMENDOUS SHUDDERING of oak timber as the *Prosperous and Remarkable*'s larboard fore crashed against the *Serendipity*'s starboard quarter. A very smug Prosper Burgo, his wispy curls plastered to his ruddy face by seaspray, whooped with joy.

"Right now, ya scoundrels, lash thee ships together," he bellowed. "Toss thee grappling hooks. Boarders! Stand ready, and if ya haven't already, gather yer pistols, pikes, and tomahawks. Topmen! Ready with yer grenades and stinkpots."

"What are stinkpots?" asked Magpie, wearing his *Isabelle* hat, his hands quivering on his dirks.

Prosper grinned. "Little combustible jars what emit a nasty, suffocatin' smoke when they's pitched at thee enemy."

"Shouldn't ya be stayin' here to command yer own ship, Prosper?" Magpie was still hoping to shirk the boarding party.

"And miss all thee fun? Hell, no. I'll be leadin' thee charge." Prosper swung around to address his men, who had their muskets aimed at the American ship. "Keep a close lookout fer sharpshooters and any foolhardies what try to blow a hole in me *Prosperous and Remarkable* while we're away *visitin'*."

Magpie's eye drifted past the *Serendipity*'s fallen foremast and snarled rigging to the *Amethyst* beyond, lying like a mystic vision in the angry waves less than a mile off. The sea was too rough for her to open her lower gunports, but those on her upper and weather decks were pointed at the *Serendipity*, and her boats, though a piece off, were pulling towards them. Still, Magpie's heart skipped several beats. A number of Serendipities had already abandoned their quarterdeck guns; Magpie could see them fleeing towards the fore hatchway. A few of them, in their eagerness to escape capture, swept over the bow and into the heaving sea. Trevelyan and his senior officers were nowhere to be seen. Magpie fancied they were lying in wait below, oiling thumbscrews as they plotted an ambush.

Well, this was it.

Inhaling the moist salty air through his nose and exhaling through his mouth, Magpie joined Prosper and his band of ruffian boarders—twenty in all—as they hustled, roaring like ancient warriors, across the *Prosperous and Remarkable*'s gangway and over the bulwark of the *Serendipity*, landing upon her bloody quarterdeck. Overhead, musket balls whistled, and grenades and stinkpots rained down upon the *Serendipity*'s fore and aft decks, their acrid smoke encircling the boarders in a black hell.

"If ya kin keep me alive 'til I find Trevelyan," Prosper barked over his shoulder, "we'll go searchin' fer yer Em'ly. Stay close now." He cocked his pistols and headed straight for a menacing mob of Americans running at them, brandishing pikes and hollering war cries of their own.

Magpie gulped and followed.

Just prior to 2:30 p.m.
Aboard the USS *Serendipity*

As the Serendipity pitched and rolled, and the world two decks up screamed with cannonfire and commotion, Emily nervously watched Leander. Huddled unsteadily over his table, his shoes slipping in the streams of blood running across the floor and filling the cracks between the timber planks, he was operating on a poor sailor who had begged him to try and save his leg, which had been split open by a hail of jagged splinters. At Leander's side was his assistant, Joe Norlan, holding the railing sailor down as the scalpel cut into his flesh. Without looking up, Leander suddenly called out, "Emily, please, I need more sand."

It was a relief for Emily to escape Mrs. Kettle, who was sitting upright in her hammock, moaning and cussing, apparently having forgotten that she'd been diagnosed with a badly sprained neck and ordered to rest. If it weren't for Leander, Emily would have happily *wrung* her neck to silence her. Prying the laundress's sweaty, grasping hands from her arm, she hurried to fetch a tin of sand from the large barrel lodged in the lower section of the medicine cupboard, and sprinkled the contents around Leander's feet. Stirred by his closeness, she lingered as long as she could. There was a troublesome tightness in her chest and her stomach boiled with fear, but, for his own part, Leander spoke and moved about so calmly one would think he was working in a garden and not in an overcrowded surgeon's cockpit where the reeking air was rife with doleful lamentations.

"You don't have to stay in here if you don't want to." Leander's words were like a tonic to Emily. Biting back tears, she met his gaze. "There is no place on earth I would rather be, Doctor." A faint smile crossed his lips in reply as he returned his attention to his patient.

Averting her eyes from the sailor's gory leg, Emily picked up the water bucket and carried it over to the waiting group of wounded men on the floor, leaning against one another in various states of consciousness. Crouching down beside them, she helped each one bring the water ladle to his lips. Only one man among them seemed alert. He watched her closely, his normally bright, probing eyes dulled by his preoccupation with his injury. Emily was acquainted with few men on the *Serendipity*, but she recognized this young man with the dark skin. It was Beans, who, alongside Charlie Clive, had served Trevelyan dinner the first night she had been summoned to the great cabin.

"Obliged, Miss—Mrs. Trevelyan," he said, clutching a burned arm to his chest.

"It's *Emily*, just Emily," she gently replied.

Beans stared back at her blankly.

"Could you tell me what is happening up there?" she asked, once his thirst had been quenched.

"It's a hellish place. Fer a bit we was bein' harassed by a puny brig. It managed to come up on our tail, shoot our rudder away, and sail off before the cap'n could even fire a broadside. We did what we could, but the *Serendipity* don't steer too good with a busted rudder. And that big ship—the one followin' us—caught up, close enough to take down our foremast."

There was flutter in Emily's heart. She had heard the others speak of "that big ship" as the *Amethyst*. "If all is lost, why are our guns still firing?"

"'Cause," said Beans, "the cap'n says ain't no one gonna take him alive."

Having overheard their conversation, Mrs. Kettle squealed from her bed, "I told yas! I told all o' yas! We're all gonna die."

Leander's admonishment was in earnest. "Restrain yourself, Mrs. Kettle; otherwise, I'll be forced to dispose of you in the slop room."

"Don't matter, Doctor," she bawled. "We're all goin' down, just like thee *Isabelle*."

"Mr. Norlan," said Leander, frowning, "in the cupboard you will find a tangle of unclaimed stockings. If necessary, stuff one down her throat."

"Right, sir," said Joe, fighting to maintain his hold on the wounded sailor who spewed blasphemy as Leander rubbed salt into his leg gashes to guard against infection.

The *Serendipity* twisted and moaned, as it had not before. The oil lanterns jumped on their hooks. A cry rose up amongst those who were still conscious. They lifted their eyes to the low ceiling, and their bodies tensed. At first, Emily worried that the winds had thrown them upon a barrier of shore rocks.

"I knows that sound," said Beans, as if he were commenting on the weather. "They's placed alongside us. Soon they be boardin'."

A profound sadness descended upon the surgery. All was deathly silent until Mrs. Kettle continued her pronouncements of their imminent doom and a fresh round of wounded Serendipities limped or were carried through the door. Catching sight of them, Leander's shoulders sagged, but he worked on, doing what he could for these men, although they were not his own. The cannons were quiet now, but cracks of musket fire and exploding grenades filled the air, and Emily thought she could hear the clash of swords. Above the din came an ominous noise of rhythmic pounding. Below, in the hold, the shouts of the men manning the pumps rose in anxious volume as did the cries of the carpenters trying in vain to pack oakum and bits of cotton and wool into the hull's gaping seams.

Her stomach sickly with the stench of burned flesh, Emily moved wearily towards the ragged newcomers, discovering Octavius Lindsay among them. Giving herself a moment to collect her thoughts, she offered the water ladle to the others first, but when at last she came to him, *he* was the one who had difficulty meeting her eyes.

"It is … fitting … Mrs. Trevelyan," he said haltingly, "that you should serve me last."

Emily hardened her stare, not wanting to look down at the appalling dark stain around his belly that had deepened the blue of his officer's jacket. "Given the affected nature of our relationship, it is a wonder I am serving you at all."

"I am quite used to being served last."

"Why is that, Mr. Lindsay?"

"I am my father's eighth son." He snickered and raised the water to his lips with his quivering, bloodstained fingers, then thought better of it. "Is it some form of poison to finish me off?"

Emily shook her head. "It will help a little while you wait."

Octavius observed the other waiting men, perhaps silently taking note of their number, and slowly eased himself back against the surgery wall. "My confidence would be greater if it were simply one of my arms or legs ..." His voice trailed off and his eyes fixed themselves on nothing in particular. Gone was the bravado he had displayed only a few hours earlier as *she* had stood in wretchedness by the ship's wheel, having endured a sham of a wedding ceremony with a man she despised. Yet, despite the ruin of his once-white breeches and crisp uniform, his Hessian boots were unsullied, and reflected the lantern light over Leander's table.

"I wanted a career in law, you know," he said suddenly.

Deliberating the wisdom of staying with him, Emily finally asked, "Why, then, did you choose the navy?"

"For the simple reason that the *choosing* was done for me." He coughed, and once he had recovered, an odd laugh burst from his lips. "If someone had told me I was going to find the King's granddaughter by my side near the end, I—I might have lived my life differently."

"How so, Mr. Lindsay?" Though her voice was challenging, the lump rising in her throat perplexed her. Cognizant of his spreading stain, she waited patiently for him to continue, but he had turned his head to the wall and closed his eyes, his features locked in a wince. Emily looked to Leander, who was now applying bandages to the badly burned torso of a powder monkey, the sound of the young lad's sobbing agony only precipitating her lump to rise higher.

A violent pitch of the ship caused the *Serendipity*'s cargo to shift and several of her guns to break free from their binding tackles, the grinding, thumping clamour of it all striking fear in the men as if an explosion were about to blow them to bits. Emily was thrown up against the medicine cupboard and onto the floor. Leander and Joe unhooked the lurching lanterns seconds before a shocking torrent of water hurtled into the surgery like the flow of a tide, sending the wounded sailors—those of them who could—scrambling for the ladders.

Mrs. Kettle went hysterical when she found she could not get out of her hammock. "I needs to get outta here," she shrieked. "I needs to tell 'em I ain't Yankee."

Cold water swirled around Emily's legs. Every part of her ached and it was hard to breathe, for two dead sailors—their eyes staring into eternity—had pinned her to the cupboard. Beside her, a young sailor vomited, and panicking voices filled the air.

"The guns! They're poundin' our sides."

"There's too much water!"

"Abandon the pumps."

"We're founderin'."

"Every man—every man fer himself."

"Joe! Grab hold of Mrs. Kettle! You there, are you able to stand? Carry out whomever you can."

Wedged between the cupboard and the wall, Octavius looked over at her, fear plainly written on his boyish face. Emily blinked back at him, astonished to think he was likely her age. "Give me your hand, Mr. Lindsay," she said, surprised by her own words.

His breathing came in dreadful snatches, his coal-black eyes welled up with tears and he stared around him in despair.

"Come!" she insisted. "Perhaps you may still have your career in law."

He did not reach out to her. Instead, his hand disappeared into his blood-drenched jacket. When it reappeared, he was wielding a small pistol. Emily froze in horror, knowing all too well what he was contemplating. She tried to plead with him, but her mouth would not move. Slowly, he cocked the trigger. Tears ran down his pimply face as he lifted the gun's barrel to his temple. Silently, his lips moved. "I'm sorry, Mother," he seemed to say as he pulled the trigger. Emily's body convulsed as if the shot had ripped through her and not him. Crumpling against the solid mass of the cupboard, she gasped for air, trying to shut out the image of his shattered skull.

The gun blast heightened the hysteria in the surgery. Around them, the *Serendipity* whimpered like a wounded animal. The water level rose. The rhythmic pounding continued its funereal lament. In all the confusion, Emily sensed Leander nearby. Working quickly, he hauled the heavy bodies off her, locked his arm around her waist, and yanked her to her feet. She could see that his jaw was set, his feverish eyes fixed on the way out. "You must get out of here," he cried, leading her to the ladder, already clogged with frantic men climbing for their lives.

3:30 p.m.
(Afternoon Watch, Seven Bells)
Aboard the *Prosperous and Remarkable*

ALONE ON THE ORLOP DECK of the *Prosperous and Remarkable*, Gus sat rigidly in his elaborately carved, ebony armchair, his ears fixed on the clash and pandemonium far above. Pemberton had given him a lamp so he would not be left in the dark, but its oil was sputtering, and with the brig leaning on its larboard and knocking up against another ship—at least that is what he guessed—he was having difficulty holding on to it. Should it fall from his precarious grasp—no, no, he would not allow his mind to travel there. Though the ship's bell was no longer ringing the half-hours, Gus estimated it had been at least four hours since Pemberton had brought him down here. He had no idea what was happening, nor could he understand why it was all taking so long. Not knowing made it impossible to slow the disquieting beating of his heart. If the outcome were not a good one, would anyone remember he was hiding out in the brig's bottom?

Like the feeble gasp of a dying mouse, the lantern went out.

Gus's distraught voice stabbed the darkness. "Magpie? Prosper? Pemberton?" When no one came, he broke down and wept. He couldn't help it. He was certain that any minute now Trevelyan and his dogs would come creaking down the ladder and…

"Help! Help! Please!"

He waited and listened, straining to hear something beyond the hammering of his heart. But hope faded when there came no reassuring replies, no hastening footsteps—only the lonely sounds of the muttering bilge water and the suffering ship that wreaked havoc with his head. No longer could Gus sit tight. With one tremendous effort he propelled himself out of the chair, screaming in agony as he did so, rolled over the hassock, and landed hard on the scummy planks of the orlop, jarring his broken body. He lay there for a moment, waiting for the overwhelming wave of pain and nausea to subside. Then, using his unsplintered forearms, he dragged himself to the ladder.

3:30 p.m.

Aboard the USS *Serendipity*

EMILY THOUGHT SHE WOULD SUFFOCATE in the crush. She clung to Leander's arm for dear life as he pressed forward on the ladder, determination transfixing his handsome features. Behind them, Joe Norlan escorted the sobbing Mrs. Kettle. Emily muttered a prayer of thanks that she was not following the laundress's rump up to the next deck; it was bad enough that their progress was slowed by the many wounded who required assistance. Those who could not get a foothold on the ladder had already broken into the closets where Trevelyan housed his liquor. Happily, they uncorked their stolen bottles and guzzled the contents, the odd charitable sailor offering a swig or two to those hanging onto the ladder. Others stood about, seemingly unconcerned by the rising water, eating bread and cheese pilfered from the food storerooms.

When at last they reached the lower deck, Emily was shocked to find it deserted, except for a half-dozen or so men who were rummaging through ditty bags or sitting alone with their belongings, fingering coins, combs, letters, and silhouettes of loved ones. Nevertheless, the areas surrounding the ladders to the gun deck were seething with sailors who hoped, sooner or later, to gain the weather decks. The ship continued to list, no longer able to completely right itself. Emily gritted her teeth and kept her eyes forward. Her anxiety was impossible to ignore, but she took some comfort in feeling Leander's hand on her arm.

As they jostled their way up the ladder like a herd of cattle en route to the slaughterhouse, Bun Brodie spotted them, and in his gravelly accent yelled out, "Give me yer hand, m'am." With his strong right arm he hoisted Emily to the deck as easily as if she were a bucket in a well. At Joe's urging, Bun did the same for Mrs. Kettle, though imperilling every muscle in his back as he did so. Once Leander and Joe had rejoined them, they stayed close to Bun, for he was reassuringly armed. Together they surveyed the final set of steps, watching in alarm as the aft hatchway became blocked with brawling men. Leander yelled for them to head fore. They dashed along the gun deck, kicking aside the scattered debris of battle—powder horns, shot, sponges, wads, ramrods, cartridge cases—and dodging the cannons that rolled dangerously about, rupturing the ship's sides with their pounding weight. But when they came upon the wounded, huddled in tattered heaps where they had fallen, Emily slowed down, unable to look the other way. Their piteous pleas for mercy cut into her like a surgeon's knife.

"Can we help them, Doctor?"

Leander tugged her forward. "I'll come back for them."

As they approached the fore hatchway, three Yankee sailors threatened them with their long sabres.

"Go on!" shouted Bun, shielding them with his immense frame as they began their ascent.

Leander lifted Emily up the ladder and hissed "Don't look" in her ear. But his warning came too late. Out of the corner of her eye, she saw Bun shoot one of the sailors, and as he levelled his pistol a second time, one of the two remaining sailors, enraged by the loss of his friend, viciously hacked at Bun's right arm, severing it completely. The gushing blood struck Leander in the side of his face and coated the wooden rungs under Emily's feet like a grisly form of paint.

Reaching the main deck, they discovered Joe and Mrs. Kettle were no longer with them. Certain that Joe could take care of himself and his objectionable charge, Leander insisted they press onward. Swiftly he scanned the smoke-shrouded deck, as if assessing the best escape route. A small brig was lashed to the starboard rail of the listing *Serendipity*, and a gang of men was labouring furiously to cut the ropes of the grappling hooks that held the brig up on a precarious angle. Off the *Serendipity*'s larboard bow, Emily sighted a collection of boats plucking men from the sea, and in the dreary distance, a waiting ship. "Doctor," she said, pointing, but Leander had already seen them and was pulling her in their direction. They scrambled over the bulwark and were steadying themselves on the slender ledge of the fore chains on the exterior of the hull, holding tightly to the railing—enemy shot had razed the standing rigging—when Emily suddenly lifted her head to listen. There was no mistaking the eager young voice that called out to her.

"Emily! Em! Em!"

Ignoring Leander's protests, she spun around and searched the knot of men locked in hand-to-hand combat in and around the splintered remains of the foremast. There was Magpie, his felt hat pushed down upon his dark curls, his lost eye hidden behind a black patch. He was hopping about on the broken bowsprit as if it were scorching hot, waving two impossibly long dirks. No more than four feet from him, standing taller than the others, was Trevelyan, his face a grimace of indomitability as the blade of his sabre crashed down again and again upon his enemies. Around the imposing captain, four of his officers and marines were locked in a clash of swords with, among others, a sure-footed, florrid-faced man with fox-like features, and—Emily could hardly believe her eyes—Fly Austen.

"Good God!" gasped Leander when he too recognized his old friend.

Emily's hands were riveted to the rail. Though each jab and slash of the men's steely weapons pierced her heart, she could not tear her eyes away. Leander let go of the rail and drew Emily to him, his hands on her arms hurting her now, his eyes burning into hers.

"That ship out there is the *Amethyst*; the boats below are theirs." He dropped his voice and spoke fervently. "This is the *one* thing I can do for you."

Emily wavered in the fore chains, the water roiling at her feet, and sadly turned to the ghastly scenes that played with a strange clarity on the sloping deck. Faces of men she remembered from the *Isabelle* were fighting alongside Fly and Magpie. There was Leander's loblolly boy, Osmund Brockley, his bulky frame moving slowly, awkwardly, but fending off sabre strikes quite expertly with his pike, and the coxswain, Lewis McGilp, baring his teeth as his cutlass thrust upwards into the trunk of a Yankee marine. And there was Biscuit, spitting out the bone-chilling battle cries of his Scottish ancestors as he cut a path to Trevelyan.

Leander, his eyes gleaming with anticipation, eased his grip on her arms and waited for her to jump to her freedom. Death and destruction closed in on them like the choking smoke of the battle. Stifling a sob, she laid her weary head against his heaving chest.

"I—I need to know what will become of you, Doctor."

With a quick indrawn breath, he gazed down at her. "I will be right behind you."

Emily shook her head, knowing he would first see to her safety, then steal a sword from a dead sailor to join his childhood friend in battle and perhaps in death. Behind them, the engagement raged on, Emily finding it sickeningly hypnotic despite her fear that, when she looked up again, she might find Magpie's small body drawn and quartered upon the bowsprit. Rolling her head around on Leander's breast, she found Magpie still jumping around and thankfully intact. It was Mr. Austen who was in trouble. In numbed horror, she watched as Trevelyan raised his sword and struck Fly with the side of its cold blade, and with his boot shoved him sprawling upon the deck. Trevelyan set his bloodless lips in a determined line and aimed his pistol at his victim, limp with resignation at his feet, as powerless as his namesake caught in a spiderweb. Then suddenly, as if reconsidering his options, Trevelyan swivelled his head and hooked his haunting eyes onto Emily's, his morbid grin an indication he was savouring his advantage over her compatriot. He did not carry out Fly's execution; instead, he swung his long arm around in a sweeping semi-circle and pointed the gun in her direction.

Then he fired.

Emily sensed time grinding to a halt, as it did in her nightmares, the ones in which she tried desperately to flee dark, sinister, unnamed shapes. Dazed, she could not immediately comprehend why Leander, having made no sound at all, had collapsed against her, nor why his shirt, already soiled with the dried blood of his patients, now had a patch of bright red creeping across the left shoulder. Clasping him gently to her, Emily stood still by the rail and watched helplessly as Trevelyan again raised his pistol.

Magpie flew from the broken bowsprit, landing on all fours behind Trevelyan like a tiger about to pounce on its unsuspecting prey. The scream that now burst from his chest was otherworldly, a plaintive yet bloodcurdling snarl that sprang from deep inside him. In one sprightly motion, he plunged his dirks deep into Trevelyan's thighs, sending the stupefied captain stumbling and staggering along the littered gangway. As Trevelyan's legs buckled beneath him and he dropped to the deck, something dislodged from the breast pocket of his uniform coat and shot across the red, weathered planks towards Emily, like a messenger frantic to deliver its final message. Although her glimpse of it was a brief one, she could see it was the gold-framed miniature of the young lad that Trevelyan had set next to her own painted portrait on his desk. It was the last thing Emily saw on the *Serendipity*.

Groaning and twisting in its death throes, the frigate slipped farther into the Atlantic, throwing Emily and Leander, their arms loosely entwined, from the fore chains and into the swells that tried, like cold, grey hands, to pull them down into a watery grave. As the men had fought on the deck, so Emily fought to prevent Leander from disappearing beneath the punishing surface. Ignoring her exhaustion and the pains that tortured her ankle and shoulder, she tightened one arm around his waist and kicked towards the nearest boat, which was now rowing towards them, the men in it having raised a shout when they spotted her. Recollection of another time when Trevelyan's pistol had been accurately aimed at her back fuelled her desperate strokes.

"Hold on, Doctor, please hold on," she spluttered, the waves crashing over her head. "This I can do for *you*." Leander gave her one long look of admiration, then shut his sea-blue eyes.

It was only after Morgan Evans had pulled them from the sea and given his oars over to another so that he could cloak Leander in a relatively dry blanket and hold on to him—as he had once held on to her—that Emily turned her back to the silent, staring men, covered her face with her hands, and allowed herself to cry.

7:00 p.m.
(Second Dog Watch, Two Bells)
Aboard HMS *Amethyst*

EMILY SET ASIDE THE LETTER that Fly Austen had handed her while she waited in the sanctuary of Captain Prickett's great cabin. She had neither the desire nor the composure to assimilate the details of what Fly had described as Trevelyan's private war—not now, when her thoughts belonged exclusively to another, much more worthy subject. Mentally and physically exhausted, she was thankful to be alone, thankful for the clean change of clothes, and thankful to be surrounded by the healthy timbers of a friendly ship.

Swinging her trousered legs up onto the cushions of the bench below the cabin's stern windows, she hugged her knees to her chest and gazed upon the place where, hours before, the Atlantic had swallowed the battered *Serendipity*, and where its tiny nemesis, the red-hulled *Prosperous and Remarkable*, still rocked triumphantly in the tranquil waves. The sky had cleared and the clouds that now sailed overhead were white and cottony and had blown together to form dreaming castles and majestic mountains. In the west, an evening sun spread beams of scarlet and gold upon the waves, enabling the boats belonging to the *Amethyst* and to the small brig to continue their task of picking up survivors. Emily had been relieved to learn that there were a great many.

As she watched the victorious and the vanquished sitting side-by-side in the boats below the windows, Emily's eyes misted. She could see the Amethysts and the Remarkables offering biscuits, meat, water, and even the rarity of cigars to the appreciative Serendipities, and she knew that once on board, they would be further provided with clothes, medical attention, and, eventually, camaraderie. She tried to recall what grievances had provoked their animosity—nay, their war—in the first place, and wondered if the men below, should they be questioned, could even name them.

Viciously they had fought against one another, had been only too happy to lop off limbs, mutilate young faces, and even snuff out lives, but when it was all over, the victorious treated the vanquished with an unspoken regard, as their own. It was as if their minds had cleared when the smoke of battle had cleared away, and they realized that, though a wide sea stood between them, they really were just the same: men of flesh and blood who shared the same language and sheltered the same dreams within their breasts.

There was a quiet tap on the door and Fly Austen entered, sending Emily's thoughts crashing back to the present. She rose to meet him, her eyes round with apprehension.

"They are still operating on him," Fly said softly. "I wondered if you might like some company while you are waiting."

Emily exhaled a nervous sigh and began wringing her hands. "Thank you, Mr. Austen. What I should really like is to be with him."

"I understand, but this man, Prosper Burgo, insisted he could not be distracted by a princess of England while he worked on 'thee esteemed Doctor Braden.'" Fly attempted to smile. "Mr. Burgo's quite a character, really. Apparently he's taken a shine to our old laundress."

Emily gave Fly an incredulous stare. "Not Meg Kettle?"

"One and the same. Apparently, he found her in the waves, her ample skirts keeping her afloat, and was quite proud of himself for 'rescuin' such an affable lady.'"

Emily sniggered. "He'll soon find there's nothing affable or ladylike about Mrs. Kettle. If it weren't for the growing babe in her womb, I…" But what did it matter now? Why bother telling Mr. Austen the *real* reason Meg Kettle had been invited to join Trevelyan's crew before he burned the *Isabelle*? Perhaps he already knew why.

Fly studied the floor at his feet. "I wonder what became of Octavius Lindsay? He has not been brought in on any of the boats."

Incapable of reliving his last moments, Emily relegated his lonely death to the farthest corridors of her mind. "Let us not speak of Lord Lindsay at the present, Mr. Austen. I am much more interested in knowing if *you* are quite well."

"I have sustained a few wounds, but I am told I will live." His smile faded as he peered out the stern windows. "Trevelyan could so easily have run his sabre through me or finished me off with his pistol. I am guessing it was his hastiness to get to *you* … that saved my life."

Overcome by a chill, Emily began rubbing her arms. "And tell me, Mr. Austen, will Leander live?"

Fly gently steered her to one of Captain Prickett's armchairs before answering. "They are doing what they can. The *Amethyst*'s surgeon is with him, and so is a young assistant named Joe Norlan, with whom I believe you are already acquainted. And I have it, on very good authority, that Prosper Burgo is more than competent."

Emily bit her lip and nodded her head, but his words did little to ease her suffering.

Fly blinked and turned his head away, and began studying the contents of Captain Prickett's cabin. "Did you look at the letter?" he asked after a time, not meeting her stare, but in a tone that suggested he was relieved to set aside the sorrowful subject of his friend.

"No. Not yet. I'm afraid I am quite distracted."

"Read it when you can. I believe—I believe it will afford you some answers."

Emily glanced up at him with wan interest.

"Captain Moreland wrote that letter in the hours before he died so that I would have an understanding of Trevelyan's thirst for revenge, of the hatred he harboured for both James and your father, Henry."

Emily thought of the gold-framed miniature and a mystifying shiver passed through her worn body. "Did the root of his hatred have something to do with a young lad with ... sandy hair and merry eyes?" she asked, enunciating the words of description.

Fly's eyebrows jumped up. "It did indeed! Trevelyan's younger brother, Harry ... he blamed them both for his death."

"Dear Captain Moreland," said Emily wistfully. "I remember the doctor telling me—when I would not divulge my full name—that I could keep my secrets as long as I was in no way endangering the lives of the Isabelles." Her voice broke. "I did not know."

"Read the letter and I will be here to discuss it with you."

Emily drew a deep breath. "And where is Trevelyan now?"

"Below, surrounded by ten of Captain Prickett's men and their muskets. You will never again have to fear him."

Leaning back in her chair, Emily gave a sardonic laugh. "I would rather Magpie's dirks had killed him rather than disabled him, Mr. Austen. You see, I never wanted the title of *princess*, I never *was* Mrs. Seaton, but now—in the days since we last met—I have *become* ... Mrs. Trevelyan."

Fly stood unmoving, his mouth open in surprise.

"It was never my ambition to become so, Mr. Austen. I endured it for the sake of the men that Trevelyan claimed he had taken from the *Isabelle* and locked in his gaol, and for that dear soul now fighting for his life."

A look of compassion crossed Fly's face. "Evidently, there is much we need to catch up on, much we need to share, but there will be time to do so, later."

"Thank you, Mr. Austen. You have always been so kind to me."

As they sat silently, both gazing out the bright windows, a ray of scarlet sunlight found Emily. She closed her eyes and basked in its rosy warmth as it played upon her upturned face. The sounds of life on board the ship that until now had seemed strangely muted suddenly intruded upon her thoughts. Calls were made requesting food and hammocks and the bosun's chair to help those onto the ship who could not climb the rope ladders. Emily could hear someone—perhaps it was Captain Prickett—gruffly questioning the whereabouts of Biscuit, as his presence was required immediately in the galley. It was Morgan Evans who replied, saying something about Biscuit being delayed as he was occupied at the present with a special task. Hearing Morgan's voice and knowing the young man had safely come through the tragic events of the past weeks gave Emily's weary spirits a lift.

Perhaps encouraged by the slight curling of her lips, Fly pressed his fingertips together and wrinkled his brow. "I wonder, Emily, are you feeling up to greeting a few visitors?"

"You are now going to tell me who lives so that I shall know who we have lost? Will I be able to bear it?" she whispered, gripping the arms of her chair.

Fly closed and opened his eyes in an exaggerated nod. "I believe so." He called out to those apparently waiting behind the cabin's door. Given the signal, they burst open the door, wreaking havoc on its fragile hinges. In sauntered Biscuit, carrying a large tray. He had cleaned up nicely since Emily had last seen him; his thatch of orange hair was combed off his forehead and his prominent chest hair buttoned up respectably inside a smart muslin shirt.

"Wee lass," he cried out, one eye looking at her, one eye looking for her, "I brung ya a pot o' tea and a pile o' fresh biscuits to celebrate yer safe return."

Emily laughed. "Baked with a pinch o' sugar and a shot o' rum, I hope?"

"Ach, 'tis thee only way." Biscuit set the tray upon Captain Prickett's polished table and stepped aside to make way for the next visitor, who swooped down upon Emily like a ghost in the trailing tails and balloon-sleeves of a shirt that had obviously not been tailored to fit him. He moved so swiftly towards her chair that her brain could not make a positive identification until he was in her welcoming arms and hugging her fiercely.

"*Magpie*!" she cried, embracing him in return, her cheek pressed against his thick dark curls. "My little Magpie," she cooed, rocking him gently, as the men looked on, visibly moved by their joyful reunion, Biscuit dashing away a few stray tears.

When at last Magpie lifted his head to look up at her, his young face was fluttering with excitement like topgallant sails in a fresh breeze. "Do ya like me eye patch, Em? Do I looks like a pirate?"

Emily caressed the reddened, puckered skin beneath the black patch. "Not at all. You look like the hero of an epic tale ... *my* hero."

Magpie beamed from ear to ear, his smile warming Emily like the descending sunlight that poured into the cabin, and he threw himself into her arms for another embrace, holding on to her for such a long while that Fly had to clear his throat. Magpie's curly head shot up again, his face overspread with a blush. "Oh, Em," he said, jumping back, "we got another surprise fer ya."

"What is it?" she asked, excited by the boy's infectious enthusiasm.

Together Fly, Biscuit, and Magpie all turned on their heels and shot broad smiles at the open door. Emily's brilliant eyes followed theirs. A gurgle of emotion erupted from her lips as she slowly rose from her chair. Standing before her in the doorway was a stocky, pudding-faced man she had never seen before. But in his arms he carried Gus Walby.

10:00 p.m.
(First Watch, Four Bells)

EMILY HESITATED before stepping into the *Amethyst*'s narrowing forepeak, where Leander was lying in a low cot next to the open gunport. The space was a poignant reminder of the corresponding forepeak on the *Isabelle* where he had once had his hospital, and where she had once been his patient. At his bedside stood Fly Austen, Joe Norlan, and two other men she did not know—though one looked familiar—conversing with one another in hushed, reverent voices.

Emily recalled the bittersweet hours she had just spent in the company of Magpie and Gus, delighting in their happiness at being reunited with her, awestruck by their miraculous rescue at sea, and marvelling at the tales they recounted of Prosper Burgo and his salty band of ruffians. In their exuberance, neither boy had asked questions about her final imprisonment on the *Serendipity*. Perhaps it was intentional on their part, or perhaps they simply possessed too many exciting stories of their own to relate; either way, she was grateful, for she needed no reminders of Charlie Clive, her marriage to Trevelyan, the loss of Jane Austen's book, and the gun blast that had hastened an end to Octavius Lindsay's short life. Though the lads' stories had proven to be a wonderful diversion, Emily had stiffened every time footsteps echoed near their private corner lest it be a bearer of bad news. Yet Fly, when he had finally looked in on their little party of three, had been quick to allay her fears with a significant nod of his head and the words, "He's awake and asking for you."

Emily massaged her face, hoping to exile her worry lines and inject some colour into her pale, swollen complexion, then she swept into the forepeak, her eyes latching at once onto the cot. Without a word, the four men tiptoed past her, Fly offering a smile of encouragement and the *familiar* one, an impudent grin painted upon his weather-beaten features, conducting a head-to-toe inspection. When they had departed, Emily sank down upon a wooden cask already positioned next to Leander and brooded over his ashen complexion and wisps of auburn hair curling upon his damp forehead. Her eyes fell to his shoulders—bare with the exception of the bandages—and traced his slim, freckled arms that lay at his sides, continuing down the lines of his long legs visible beneath a light linen sheet. Her desire to lie beside him was so strong that she was certain he must have heard her sharp intake of breath. Blushing, she returned her gaze to his face and the look in his eyes—so full of affection—warmed her insides and deepened her spreading colour.

She laughed unsteadily. "Were they common butchers, or did they fix you up nicely?"

"Between the three of them, they fixed me up nicely," said Leander, his voice husky. "Thank goodness for the man they call Prosper Burgo."

"He's the one who rescued Magpie and Gus from the sea and took care of them," said Emily, examining his bandages.

"I should like to hear all about it."

"I *will* tell you ... only later, Doctor, not now."

Leander lifted his right hand and felt his left shoulder. "I suppose Trevelyan wished his ball had struck lower or had found his *intended* victim."

No, Emily thought sadly, her eyes filling with compassion, *Trevelyan knew that in striking you he was dealing me a deadly blow*. "I worried you would bleed to death before someone was able to help you. Did the ball splinter bone or take in a fragment of your shirt?"

Leander smiled up at her, perhaps impressed by her knowledge, but he soon grew solemn. "We can't be certain, though infection is always a concern."

Not wanting to dwell on the subject, Emily cheered her voice. "Well, then, Doctor, once you are up and around, I will offer you *my* left shoulder to lean upon."

"And how is your right one faring?"

"Aside from occasional achiness, it is quite well."

"I am glad of it. And that ankle of yours?"

Emily sighed. "In order to heal it properly, I'm afraid I'm going to have to rest for weeks on end."

"That won't be easy for you, though you *are* welcome to stay here with me. Perhaps we could employ Prosper Burgo to provide us with his own special tonics to ease our complaints."

"Of all things, Doctor, I should like that ... I should like to stay." A tear started making its way down Emily's cheek and, for a time, she could not speak. "Mr. Austen has informed me that, first thing in the morning, we shall be sailing for Bermuda. It is believed that my Uncle Clarence is there, awaiting news of me." A slight frown appeared between Leander's eyebrows, but his eyes never left her face. "I must return to England to testify against Trevelyan. He will have to answer for the *Amelia* and the *Isabelle*."

"And for his treatment of you."

Emily turned her face from him. "Mr. Austen assured me that if I go to England, my uncle would do everything in his power to secure an annulment for me. But I told him that I would not leave until I knew for certain that you were going to live."

"I will live, Emily."

She took a deep breath. "You say that, yet I must be certain."

"You *must* return to England, if not for yourself, then for all those that lost their lives at the hands of Thomas Trevelyan."

Overcome with restlessness, Emily suddenly leaned forward on her wooden cask. "You once told me that I had been spared from perishing in the sea because I had a great deal of living left to do."

"I have no doubt that there are a legion of adventures awaiting you, for *you* seem to thrive on them and *they* seem to find you. You are an extraordinary woman. I've never seen your like before and probably never will again."

"Do you not see, Doctor?" she said with a whine in her tone that she detested. "I am afraid of returning to England."

"What is it you fear?"

"I fear the empty, meaningless existence that awaits me there. I will be placed in my uncle's guardianship or, worse still, he'll hand me over to my grandmother, and every waking moment of my life will be mapped out for me." Emily pressed her hands between her knees and began rocking back and forth. "The moment I am released from my fraudulent marriage, every effort will be made to marry me off again. My mornings will be spent playing the pianoforte and learning my French lessons; my afternoons will be passed in the company of hairdressers and dressmakers; and my evenings in salons and assembly halls. I am *not* interested in being celebrated for my elaborate hairstyles and exquisite gowns."

Amusement curved Leander's lips. "It sounds like a life most women would relish."

"If you were not injured, Doctor, I would throw something at you."

Emily's words were playful, but her feelings were not. "Why is it so easy for you to pretend you do not understand what I am trying to find the words to say?"

He angled his head on his pillow, as if hoping for a better view of her.

"If I return to England now," she continued, one hand covering her mouth, "I fear I will never see you again. You left me once before, Doctor, with hope burning in my breast. If you would only give me that hope again—if I knew you wanted me to return—I would find the ship that would bring me back to you."

Leander reached out to touch her free hand, which lay in a fist on her lap. "Emily, the reality is, I am a ship's surgeon, a lowly doctor in the Royal Navy. I have nothing to my name. I possess no land, no house, no family wealth—" He gave a sarcastic laugh. "Not even these few articles of clothing are mine. I do not have the means to offer you the life you deserve."

"The life I deserve, Doctor? *I* chose to leave behind all the trappings and comforts of my life as the granddaughter of King George when I boarded the *Amelia* for Upper Canada all those weeks ago." Emily slid off the cask and knelt beside Leander's bed, entwining her fingers with his long slender ones. "All that I ask is to have the life I hunger for—one that is far away from London. I long to become a learned woman as you are a learned man. I want you to be my teacher and allow me access to your library of medical books. Let me—let me train as your assistant and help you with the men when they are ill or wounded, and if my home should be on the sea, it makes no difference, so long as I may lean on you and feel your arms around me whenever I am in need of comfort."

Leander gaped at her as if he expected her to laugh and proclaim her words to be nothing more than a salve to speed his healing. After a time, he raised his head from his pillow. "Is this truly what you wish for, Emily?"

"Those hours, those days on the *Serendipity*, Doctor, when I thought you had gone down with the *Isabelle*, they were the worst of my life.

You must know; I cannot bear to live forever wondering where you are, whether or not you are safe."

The intensity in Leander's eyes startled her. "And, you must know, Emeline Louisa Georgina Marie, that, above all else, I completely… love and adore you."

17

Friday, July 2

4:00 p.m.
(Afternoon Watch, Eight Bells)
Aboard HMS *Amethyst*

PAUSING BEFORE THE LOOKING GLASS nailed upon the wall of Captain Prickett's great cabin, Emily contemplated her reflection. She hardly knew herself. It had been a long time since she had curled her long hair and adorned her head with a bandeau—in this case a blue one to match her blue-and-white-striped morning dress. Magpie had sewn it for her from the fine yards of fabric Prosper Burgo had produced from the hold of the *Prosperous and Remarkable*, stolen a while back, he had smugly admitted, from some "fat, forgotten merchantman." As usual, the young sail maker had done wonders with his needle, making pretty little puffs on the long-sleeved gown that tightly wrapped her from neck to wrists, but fell loosely below her bosom. His creation had left Emily speechless and certain the lad could become a sought-after dressmaker once his naval career ended; her suggestion had awakened a dreamy glow in Magpie's eye. Though she would have preferred to wear loose-fitting trousers and a short jacket, she doubted her uncle would recognize—or be pleased to find—her dressed like a sailor, with her hair an untamed tangle completely at the mercy of the capricious winds.

Through an open gunport, she could see her uncle's ship, its sails furled, its myriad pennants—including the flag of the Duke of Clarence—flapping in the Bermuda breeze from the highest points on its three masts. In the clear turquoise waters around it lay anchored a flotilla of smaller ships, and beyond, the grey rocks and dark green wind-swept shrubbery of Ireland Island. She took in great gulps of sea air, then glanced around Captain Prickett's cabin, where she had taken up a pleasant residency for the past week—at least during the hours when she was not found in the forepeak, supplying food and affection to its one precious occupant who, with each passing day, grew stronger under her watchful eye.

Full of regret and trepidation, she left the great cabin and made her way towards the break in the larboard rail where a row of men had formed, like a receiving line at a ball, to speak their parting words to her before she was taken the short distance across the harbour to her uncle's waiting ship. Hundreds of heads swivelled the moment she was spotted crossing the quarterdeck, the men stopping in their tracks to mark her steps, some of them raising their hats to her, some bestowing a naval salute. By now she was accustomed to their eager displays of curiosity and felt such goodwill towards each and every one of them—regardless of whether he was a true compatriot or had been born on this side of the Atlantic—that she wished they could all return to England with her.

Amazed that her wobbly knees were able to carry her, she walked slowly, acknowledging as many as she could, so pleased whenever she recognized a face she had once known upon the *Isabelle*. There was Osmund Brockley, Lewis McGilp, Jacko, Mr. Stewart, the red-haired midshipman, and Maggot and Weevil—all of them beaming their biggest smiles. Prosper Burgo was there too, his arm still draped around a complacent Meg Kettle, which astounded Emily, for the man had now been acquainted with "thee affable lady" for a full week. Emily had hoped that—somewhere in the crowd—she might see Mr. Crump, Mr. Harding, Bailey Beck, Bun Brodie, Captain Moreland, and even Octavius Lindsay, but she never did.

Arriving at the place where she was to descend to the *Amethyst*'s launch, Emily found two sailors strapping Gus Walby and his splints into the bosun's chair. He alone would be making the journey with her. The thought of his dear company in the weeks ahead had sustained her during the darker moments of the past few days. At the rail stood the forlorn figure of Magpie, watching Gus as he was lowered to the rocking launch. Overwhelmed by the woeful scene, Emily turned away from it to address the waiting men.

Biscuit stood at the nearest end of the farewell procession. He placed a paper bundle in her hands and winked his straight eye at her. "I baked 'em fresh this mornin'. Ya won't find nothin' like 'em on thee admiral's ship."

"Thank you, Biscuit. Thank you for everything."

He bowed low and clumsily before her, and upon straightening himself up, said, "Stay well, lass."

Beside the Scottish cook, shifting from one foot to another, was Morgan Evans, a new knitted hat sitting at a jaunty angle upon his head. "Mr. Evans," Emily said, fighting to compose her voice as she extended her hand to him, "I am so glad we were able to rewrite that letter to your sisters. Have you passed it off to the mail boat?"

"I have, m'am."

"I hope you will soon see your family again."

"I hope so too. And don't worry," he said, his cheeks reddening, "I'll look out for Dr. Braden and Magpie for you."

"I will be forever grateful. And thank you ... thank you for pulling me from the sea—twice."

"It was my pleasure. You ... well ... you brightened up our simple lives," he stammered, quickly adding, "Mr. George ... sir."

Emily gave Morgan a warmhearted smile, then, proceeding down the line, gazed up at Fly Austen. Like Biscuit, he too had a gift for her.

"I received a packet of mail when your uncle's ships dropped anchor and was delighted to find amongst the letters a new offering from my sister, Jane. It's called *Pride and Prejudice.* As there is still a war to fight and I will soon be given another ship to command, I thought *you* might like to read it. I hope it will entertain you as well as her first novel did." He handed her the black, calf-leathered, gilt-banded volumes.

"Thank you, Mr. Austen. I doubt I shall like it as well as *Sense and Sensibility*," she said with a reflective smile, "but I can assure you I will look forward to reading it."

Fly nodded. "Good! And have you Captain Moreland's letter with you?"

"I do. Rest easy that I will guard it with my life, and that—once back in London—I will make certain it falls into the right hands."

"Godspeed, Emily."

"And you too, sir."

Emily took a deep breath and looked towards Magpie.

"I don't know if I kin stand it," said the little sail maker, struggling to withhold his tears. "Gus were the best friend I ever had."

Emily sank to her knees before him and took one of his hands in hers. "And he will want you to stay strong so that you can look after Dr. Braden for us. But cheer up! I will tell the Duke that you send your regards and remember well the kindness he and Mrs. Jordan once showed you long ago at Bushy House."

Magpie made an effort to return her smile. "I wish I could go too. I—I just can't bear bein' parted from ya, Em." His dark eye glistened like a star. "Why ... yer like a mum to me."

Emily squeezed his soot-stained fingers.

"Will ya promise me one thing, Em?"

"What is that, Magpie?"

"When ya come back to find Dr. Braden, you'll come lookin' fer me too."

"I promise," she said, planting a kiss below his eye patch, but so overcome with emotion she could barely stand again.

Leander was the last one waiting for her. He appeared agitated and embarrassed, like a young lad who has arrived at a birthday party without a present. He was dressed in an open-collared shirt and dusky-blue breeches that looked well on his tall, slim frame, and his complexion was suffused with high, healthy colour. Emily was barely aware that Fly, Morgan, and Biscuit had wandered away, taking Magpie with them.

"You *will* come back to me, Emily?" Leander asked, his eyes darting over the planks of the deck at his feet.

"I will, as soon as I can," she said brightly, hoping to gain his dear glance.

"You won't forget this poor doctor on the seas?"

She laughed. "How could I forget the man that introduced me to rum and laudanum? But you ... you may soon forget what I look like."

Leander shook his head. Assuming an air of mischief, he slowly pulled the miniature of Emeline Louisa from his coat pocket.

Emily gasped. "Ahh! How ... ?"

"On that last day ... just before your marriage ceremony ... I was summoned to Trevelyan's cabin to take a cup of tea with him and Mr. Humphreys. As Trevelyan's thoughts were naturally engaged elsewhere, I took the opportunity to take back what is rightfully yours." He held the miniature out to her, then—with a grin—snatched it back again. "However, unless you put up a monstrous protest, I have no intention of returning it to you ... not just yet."

"You will let Magpie know you have it."

"He already knows. We have agreed to share it."

They laughed and smiled at each other, but soon, knowing they had an audience, fell into an awkward silence. Above their heads, the sun blazed brighter, and around them, the world seemed to suddenly stir to life. Calls, commands, bells, and laughter drifted into their consciousness, like an unwelcome cue that their time together was drawing to a close. At last, Leander inhaled and said, "Good-bye, dear Emily."

"But, Doctor, this is *not* our last good-bye. My ship is set to sail at sunrise. Watch for me. I'll wave to you from the mizzen crosstrees."

"Not the crosstrees, Emily. I'll be sick with worry that you'll fall. Just to the platform, please? And make certain someone is standing ready to catch you, should you falter." Leander seized her hand and held it to his heart, the simple gesture raising a roar of approval from the onlookers, their applause and stomping feet shaking the ship's timbers beneath Emily's toes. Then, without warning, Leander pulled her to him and his lips found her mouth, lingering there until, in a choked whisper, he said, "I'll be waiting, watching every sail on the horizon, for your return."

Her eyes were so full of tears she could barely see him, but she nodded and gave him a fierce hug. "As will I, Doctor." Releasing him was the hardest thing she had ever done. With a final wave to everyone, and a last look at Leander, she turned away to face her next journey.

18

Saturday, July 3

6:00 a.m.
(Morning Watch, Four Bells)
Bermuda Harbour

SITTING CROSS-LEGGED on the mizzen platform of her uncle's ship, having successfully scrounged a pair of trousers for her climb, Emily narrowed her eyes in anticipation as they neared the anchored *Amethyst* in the Bermuda harbour. She scanned the aft decks, hoping Leander would remember, her heart drumming so loudly she was quite certain she could beat the men to quarters. The early morning winds whipped her untethered curls around her face, the rays of the rising sun highlighting their pale-gold colour. Above and around her the creamy yards of the mizzen sails rippled and snapped as if in secret communication with those on the main and fore masts. Far below her, the ship's bell rang four times, and the crew moved about swiftly, with purpose, as they always did when leaving port. For a second, Emily could not recall if she was on the *Amelia*, or the *Isabelle*, or the *Serendipity,* or her uncle's ship. From her lofty perch, the soaring masts, the sails, the weather decks, and the men all looked the same. It was her memories that were so different.

Another round of tears threatened to make their unwanted appearance. Emily squeezed her eyes shut to thwart them and dreamed she was back on the *Isabelle*. In her mind she could picture it: Mr. Crump was squawking like a squirrel over the inconvenience of his stump, and lambasting Osmund Brockley for slopping the fetid contents of the chamber pot upon his blanket; from his swinging hammock, Morgan was gazing shyly upon her, distracted only by the chirping Biscuit who was carrying on about the wonders of his sea biscuits; sunshine was pouring in through the open gunport beside her cot, and she was enjoying its warmth as Gus sat upon the three-legged stool, reading passages of *Sense and Sensibility* with careful diction; near the hospital entrance, little Magpie was stamping about like a spirited colt as he waited his turn to visit her; and Leander was writing in his medical journal, occasionally casting his blue eyes in her direction as if to make certain she was still there.

As the poignant images faded away, Emily opened her eyes. *He* was standing there now, alone at the taffrail, the beam of his smile evident across the distance, his right arm raised and waving frantically in farewell.

Afterword

Most of the characters in *Come Looking for Me* are fictional, but several require a word of explanation.

HENRY, DUKE OF WESSEX: George III had a large family. Six daughters and seven sons lived to adulthood, including his eldest son, George, the Prince Regent (later George IV), and his third son, William, the Duke of Clarence (later William IV), both mentioned in *Come Looking for Me*. The two youngest sons of George III, Octavius and Alfred, died when very young. The character of Henry and the title I bestowed upon him, "Duke of Wessex," are both fictitious. George III did not have a son named Henry, but even if he had, Henry would not have been given the title of Wessex. In creating the fictitious father of Emily, I initially considered an "if only he had lived" scenario with Prince Alfred, but as his date of birth would have made it impossible for him to have fathered Emily, I chose instead to take literary licence and imagine a son that never was. I gave him the name of Henry as it is a popular name among the royal family, and I borrowed Wessex from the present Earl of Wessex, Queen Elizabeth's son Edward. I imagined Henry to have been born between the Duke of Cumberland and the Duke of Sussex, as Queen Charlotte—who was pregnant most years of her early marriage—had a window of child-bearing opportunity between these two sons.

FLY AUSTEN: The novelist Jane Austen had two seafaring brothers, Francis and the younger Charles. Francis in particular had a most distinguished naval career. Many of the personal details I ascribed to the fictitious Fly are true to the real Francis Austen. For example, his nickname was "Fly," his eyes were described as being "alert," and he did—to his great disappointment—miss seeing action at Trafalgar. Still, I took literary licence with the character I ultimately created. Francis Austen did fight the Americans in the War of 1812, but not in the Atlantic, and not as the commander of a ship of seventy-four guns known as the *Isabelle*; in 1813, he had long since been promoted to captain. I do like to think, however, that the well-respected, intelligent, courageous, and humourous Fly Austen in *Come Looking for Me* is very similar to the man that once was.

WILLIAM, DUKE OF CLARENCE: William was appointed Admiral of the Fleet by his brother the Regent in December 1811, and maintained the post until 1821 when it passed to the Earl of St. Vincent. It was more of a titular position than an active role for him, although he was known to seek permission from the Regent and Parliament to go off on various missions now and again—thus lending credence to his mounting of an expedition to find his fictional niece, Emily. When at sea, he flew his own "Duke of Clarence" flag. William became the Lord High Admiral in 1827.

While researching over the course of writing my book, I found intriguing revelations in Philip Ziegler's biography *King William IV*. Although William was known as being hot-headed, impulsive, silly, and boorish, he also had a generous heart. It is well documented that he helped two penniless orphans—one in Newfoundland and one in Plymouth—by financing their clothing, schooling, and training as midshipmen. In time, one of these lads became a rear admiral, and William had the pleasure of signing his commission. I was delighted to discover that my fabricated storyline of Clarence's generosity towards young Magpie is in line with the man's true character.

SHIPS: Although there have been several ships known as HMS *Amelia*, HMS *Amethyst*, and the USS *Liberty*, the vessels and their crews in *Come Looking for Me* are fictional.

Credits

Come Looking for Me took years of research and writing. I could not have reached this point if it were not for the support of a group of individuals to whom I owe my deepest appreciation: My good friends and fellow writers Karen Hood-Caddy and Cathy Cahill-Kuntz—there is no one else with whom I would rather discuss the joys of similes and syntax; Dr. Walter Hannah, physician, retired midshipman of the Royal Canadian Navy, for reading my manuscript and answering my numerous nautical and medical questions; Canadian writer and journalist Roy MacGregor, for his support of the annual Muskoka Novel Marathon; Anne Millyard, co-founder and retired editor of Annick Press, who entered my world at the completion of the 2004 Marathon and has been my friend and mentor ever since; my sons, Evan and Brodie, who happily joined me in my dream of publication, and my husband, Randy, who has continually supported me in my desire to write; the Blue Butterfly team—Gary Long, for creating a cover design that captured the essence of my story; Sonia Holiad, for volunteering to do the final proofing, and Dominic Farrell, my meticulous editor, for his many excellent suggestions and his sense of humour throughout the substantive editing process. Heartfelt gratitude to publisher Patrick Boyer—how fortunate for me that our paths crossed while working on the documentary *Life on the Edge: Stories from Muskoka's Past*.

Finally, I would to like to acknowledge the excerpt from Jane Austen's *Sense and Sensibility*, and the lines and verses taken from the songs "While Up the Shrouds," "Can of Grog," "Spanish Ladies," "Heart of Oak," "Don't Forget Your Old Shipmates," and "The Coast of High Barbary" that appear in my book, all of which are in the public domain.

CHERYL COOPER *was born in Toronto and now lives in Muskoka. She holds degrees in English and education, and her articles and stories have appeared in numerous Canadian periodicals. Cheryl makes her book publishing debut with* Come Looking for Me. *She completed the first draft of this work of historical fiction in three days of non-stop writing to win first prize in the 2004 Huntsville Festival of the Arts "Novel Marathon." After several more years of research and writing, her greatly expanded and refined first novel is published by Blue Butterfly Books.* AUTHOR PHOTO BY RANDY COOPER

Interview with the Author

You portray life and death aboard ships of war in the early 1800s, offer readers details of real shipboard conditions, and describe the configuration of those vessels. How did you research these scenes from two centuries ago?

CHERYL COOPER: I avoided the temptation to read any contemporary novels; instead, I put myself on a steady diet of Patrick O'Brian, Captain Frederick Marryat, Jane Austen, and literature set or written before 1813. I read a number of works on the War of 1812, naval warfare, the history of surgery, and so on, and relied particularly on such books as Brian Lavery's *Nelson's Navy* with its clear illustrations of the various parts of the ships.

Anything else? Your images are so vivid.

COOPER: I studied hundreds of old drawings and paintings depicting scenes of a sailor's existence: working the sails, tossing the lead, raising the anchor, enjoying a meal or leisure time with his mates, being punished, or battling the enemy.

That must have been engrossing.

COOPER: Often, an afternoon of research would net nothing more than a few paragraphs of writing because the smallest of details might have taken me ages to research. But that was where so much of the enjoyment lay in writing this story—discovering the fascinating world of these old ships.

Emily, who is held hostage, is the centrepiece of this story. Did you set out to give readers a different perspective on war and the place of women in it?

COOPER: Yes, that is one perspective I wanted to offer. In researching, I discovered that, though there were restrictions on women being present aboard Royal Navy men-of-war, those rules were often not adhered to. Several ships carried women whose duties usually included helping with laundry, sewing, or cooking. When wives of the officers were on board, they often were assigned to assist the surgeon with the ill and injured. All these women would have been exposed to the same horrors and deprivations as the men. In a battle, they had to be prepared to wield a sword or a pistol, or risk perishing. There are several documented cases of women who joined the navy under the guise of a man. They learned the ropes and seamanship, just as the men did. How they kept their true identity a secret is beyond me. They must have been a brave lot. In imagining Emily, it was my hope to create a character who reflected the courage and spirit of these women.

In Come Looking for Me, *some characters live and others die, not always in predictable ways. Do you think survival is merely a matter of fate?*

COOPER: Sure, and a matter of luck. We're always asking why some of us are taken early while others enjoy long lives. The men and women on warships during this period faced the prospect of death daily. The ones spared the splinters and grapeshot of battle were fortunate, blessed by fate.

The War of 1812 is known to Canadians and Americans mostly for its land battles, yet these do not figure at all in your novel's action. Why did you take a different tack?

COOPER: When I was in school, the War of 1812 never seized my imagination. My teachers always breezed over its events and, perhaps naturally, concentrated on the Battle of Queenston Heights and the military victories of Sir Isaac Brock and Tecumseh. Had their history lessons also included the struggle at sea, I believe more students, including me, would have sat up straighter in our chairs. So my main intent is to shed much-deserved light on the men and women—old and young alike—who lived, dreamed, fought, and died in the crowded conditions upon those floating timbers.

As an author, you first came to public attention by winning a competition for writing a novel in seventy-two hours. How intense was that?

COOPER: Incredibly intense. It began at 8:00 p.m. on a Friday night and ran seventy-two hours straight. There were twenty-six of us, jammed into the old National Bank building on Main Street in Huntsville, pounding away on our laptop keys, completely high on caffeine and sugar. The camaraderie and energy around me was exhilarating. By Monday afternoon, my back was in knots—most likely from having slept two out of the three nights on the floor—and my brain was no longer functioning; but, in those hours, I had been able to complete seventy-five pages of my manuscript, and I had developed a clear idea of where I was going to take my story. It's amazing what can be accomplished when we leave our lives behind to focus exclusively on writing.

Writing Come Looking for Me *clearly took more than seventy-two hours.*

COOPER: Oh, I needed at least one or two further weekends to complete it! Actually, all told, it was three and a half years in the making.

How did your interest in historical fiction first arise?

COOPER: When I was eight years old, my parents took me to Washington, D.C., and Virginia. I was completely smitten by such places as Mount Vernon, the Custis-Lee mansion, and Williamsburg. The next year, our family went to Europe. Touring museums, castles, and cathedrals further intensified my interest in history. I've been a reader of historical fiction ever since.

Do you think a similar story could unfold in our present day, or is this tale of captivity and Emily's struggle to escape unique to the War of 1812?

COOPER: A story of captivity and escape could unfold in any century, in any country, but not one similar to *Come Looking for Me*. I like to think that my story goes beyond these themes, and is unique to the War of 1812, or at least to the period of the Napoleonic Wars. If you simply take into consideration the vast opportunities available to women in the western world today, and given our contemporary global communication networks, a character such as Emily would not have lived such a confined, unsatisfying life in England, nor been lost to her family, or to Trevelyan, for so long a time. Moreover, I cannot think of a present-day setting that has more scope for imagination than the sailing ships of yore.

Your decision to place virtually all the action at sea creates a closed universe. Did such a confined setting help you to dramatize the plights and possibilities more vividly?

COOPER: It did. I did not want the distractions of the outside world. I wanted to create a "closed universe" in order to heighten Emily's sense of captivity and the men's desperate realization that if they did not make the best of their circumstances, their only escape was death in battle or a watery grave. Making stops in various ports would have not only provided my characters with a potential means of escape, but also set before them pleasures and adventures that were not available on their ships.

While in captivity, Emily took comfort in reading Sense and Sensibility. *If you were held in captivity and had only one book to read, what would you choose?*

COOPER: *Wuthering Heights*. I've read a lot of good books—classics and contemporary novels—but there are soul-stirring passages in

Emily Brontë's book, and poignant images of isolation and graveyards and the windswept moors that have remained with me since I first read it at age fourteen.

If you were able to organize an afternoon of tea and literary conversation with any five novelists—dead or alive—whom would you invite?

COOPER: It would probably come as no surprise that I would invite Jane Austen and all three of the Brontë sisters. I would also invite my favourite Canadian author, Lucy Maud Montgomery. I adored Montgomery's novels as a child, but her personal journals—edited for publication in recent years by Mary Rubio and Elizabeth Waterston—reveal an astonishing woman whom I've placed on a pedestal and would love to have known personally. Now if you were to ask me with whom I would like to have dinner and drinks, I'd say Leon Uris. I always hoped I'd meet him one day. I've admired his heroic characters, his universal themes, and the way he was able to brilliantly convey human emotions in his writing.

More great reading from Blue Butterfly Books

If you enjoyed *Come Looking for Me*, you might also like the following Blue Butterfly historical fiction titles. Your local bookseller can order any of them for you if they are not in stock, or you can order direct by going to the Blue Butterfly Books web site:

www.bluebutterflybooks.ca

Three to a Loaf is the page-turning drama of Rory Ferrall, a young Anglo-German Canadian smuggled into Germany during the First World War to discover the Imperial General Staff's top-secret plan to break the deadlock on the Western Front.

Three to a Loaf: A Novel of the Great War
by Michael J. Goodspeed
Soft cover / 6 × 9 in. / 374 pages
ISBN 978-0-9781600-6-7 / $24.95 U.S./Cdn.
Features: author interview

Following the sudden end to her marriage, Meg Wilkinson, Canada's first woman veterinarian, leaves her practice in Halifax to seek the legendary working wolf-dogs of the Yukon. Arriving in Dawson City in 1897 just as the Klondike gold rush is beginning, she discovers a unique aboriginal connection.

City Wolves: Historical Fiction
by Dorris Heffron
Hard or soft cover / 6 × 9 in. / 449 pages
ISBN (h.c.) 978-0-9781600-7-4 / $36.95
ISBN (s.c.) 978-1-926577-01-2 / $24.95
Features: author interview, maps

On the rugged Muskoka frontier just after Confederation, simmering animosity between settler Richard Bell and local steamboat magnate A.P. Cockburn comes to a dramatic head during the 1872 Dominion election when Bell is appointed Returning Officer for the riding by John A. Macdonald's Conservative government, and Cockburn is a candidate for the Liberals.

No Return: A Novel of the Canadian Election that Vanished in Muskoka's Backwoods
by Gordon Aiken
Soft cover / 6 × 9 in. / 317 pages
ISBN 978-1-926577-04-3 / $24.95 U.S./Cdn.
Features: period photographs, maps, extended author biography

When Yaroslaw leaves his Canadian home to spend a short holiday in Ukraine searching for family heirlooms buried by his grandparents during the Second World War, he has no inkling his explorations will draw him into a dangerous quest for Europe's greatest treasure, or that he will be caught up in the swirling intrigues of Ukraine's "Orange Revolution."

Yaroslaw's Treasure: A Novel
by Myroslav Petriw
Soft cover / 6 × 9 in. / 293 pages
ISBN 978-0-9784982-7-6 / $24.95 U.S./Cdn.
Features: author interview, maps

About this Book

In *Come Looking for Me*, a mysterious young English woman named Emily risks a crossing of the Atlantic during the War of 1812 for the promise of a new adventure in Canada. But she never arrives.

Captured by Captain Trevelyan, a man as cold-blooded as his frigate is menacing, Emily is held prisoner aboard the USS *Serendipity*. Seeking to save herself, she makes a desperate escape overboard in the midst of a raging sea battle and is rescued by the British crew of HMS *Isabelle*. Yet Emily has only exchanged one form of captivity for another, and remains in peril as England escalates its fight against the United States on the Atlantic.

Aboard the *Isabelle*, Emily encounters a crew of fascinating seamen and strikes up unexpected friendships, but life on a man-of-war is full of deprivations and dangers to which she is unaccustomed. Amidst heartache and tragedy at sea, she struggles to find her place among the men until a turn of events reveals her true identity. And when Trevelyan's ship once again looms on the horizon, Emily fears losing the only man she has ever loved and falling into the hands of the only man she has ever loathed.

Come Looking for Me is a rich and compelling story of love and courage, friendship and treachery, triumph and loss. With humour and poignancy, author Cheryl Cooper captures all the colour, detail, and excitement of the great ships from the golden age of sail, while bringing to life those who fought upon them. She tells a story of the bravery of the men locked in the epic, brutal struggle that was the War of 1812, and the courage of a woman who, with extraordinary determination, labours to make her own way in life and in love.